The BEASTS of the BLACK LOCH

Also by Gay Marris

A Curtain Twitcher's Book of Murder

GAY MARRIS

The
BEASTS
of the
BLACK
LOCH

Publishers

First published in the UK in 2026 by Bedford Square Publishers Ltd,
London, UK

bedfordsquarepublishers.co.uk
@bedsqpublishers

© Gay Marris, 2026

The right of Gay Marris to be identified as the author of this work has been asserted in accordance with the Copyright, Designs and Patents Act 1988. All rights reserved. No part of this book may be reproduced, stored in or introduced into a retrieval system, or transmitted, in any form or by any means (electronic, mechanical, photocopying, recording or otherwise) without the written permission of the publishers.

Any person who does any unauthorised act in relation to this publication may be liable to criminal prosecution and civil claims for damages.
A CIP catalogue record for this book is available from the British Library.
This is a work of fiction. Names, characters, places, and incidents either are the product of the author's imagination or are used fictitiously, and any resemblance to actual persons, living or dead, businesses, companies, events or locales is entirely coincidental.

ISBN
978-1-83501-012-9 (Hardback)
978-1-83501-453-0 (Trade Paperback)
978-1-83501-013-6 (eBook)

2 4 6 8 10 9 7 5 3 1

Typeset in 11.5pt Garamond MT Pro
by Avocet Typeset, Bideford, Devon, EX39 2BP
Printed and bound in Great Britain by
CPI Group (UK) Ltd, Croydon CR0 4YY

The manufacturer's authorised representative in the EU for product safety is Easy Access System Europe, Mustamäe tee 50, 10621 Tallinn, Estonia
gpsr.requests@easproject.com

For S, F, & J.
The best people I know.

CONTENTS

Prologue – The High Road	9
Chapter 1 – The Low Road	11
Chapter 2 – Rest Ye Well	18
Chapter 3 – We Meet Again	26
Chapter 4 – Tolerable Hominids	37
Chapter 5 – Verdammte Mücken	48
Chapter 6 – First Impressions	58
Chapter 7 – An Eye-Opener	65
Chapter 8 – Party Pieces	73
Chapter 9 – Dead Drunk	88
Chapter 10 – So That's That?	93
Chapter 11 – An Irritating Itch	99
Chapter 12 – It Happens at The Hilton	106
Chapter 13 – Do You Mind if I Ask?	110
Chapter 14 – Anyone for Croquet?	115
Chapter 15 – Great Minds Think Alike	122
Chapter 16 – Window Shopping	135
Chapter 17 – Ruffled Feathers	145
Chapter 18 – Plain as My Nose	152

Contents

Chapter 19 – The Grass is Greener	160
Chapter 20 – Sacrilege	170
Chapter 21 – Hard to Shift	177
Chapter 22 – Eavesdroppings	185
Chapter 23 – Ta Dah!	196
Chapter 24 – Help Yourself	203
Chapter 25 – Any One of Us!	210
Chapter 26 – Whodunnit?	217
Chapter 27 – Mischief of Magpies	228
Chapter 28 – How Could You?	235
Chapter 29 – Barking up the Wrong Tree	245
Chapter 30 – What's Your Poison?	250
Chapter 31 – Period of Absence	263
Chapter 32 – Slap in the Face	271
Chapter 33 – So Long Sister!	280
Chapter 34 – The Missing M	288
Chapter 35 – Not a Child!	296
Chapter 36 – Out of His Shell	304
Chapter 37 – A Clever Thief	313
Chapter 38 – No Flies on Her	321
Chapter 39 – The Stuff of Nightmares	332
Chapter 40 – The Full Picture	338
Chapter 41 – You Cain't Help Who You Love	347
Epilogue – As it Ever Was	362

Prologue
The High Road

The car was speeding, true, but the driver knew the twisting single-track road through the forest like the back of his hand. Seldom another a vehicle, just blisters in the tarmac, hairpin bends, and the occasional rattle-tattle cattle grid to make him sit up straight. This January morning, though, there was a thick frost, he and his wife were bickering, and then, out of nowhere, there was a person... walking... not along the verge, but directly ahead of them. The walker didn't get out of the way. The driver hit the brakes... and hit them again, to no effect, because they'd been cut. And so it was that the car skidded full pelt into the trees and exploded into flames. Whoosh! The blazing vehicle sent a column of thick black smoke, tall and straight into the pristine, windless, sun-up sky. Acrid fumes mingled with the resinous scent of scorched pine needles and the stench of cooking flesh. These sounds and smells frightened the forest animals and made the deer scream.

1

The Low Road

The trip from the West Indies to Scotland is taking an eternity. That's what it feels like. Bloody forever. Dr Ava Wheatsheaf Dickens (BSc [Honours Zoology], PhD) hates aeroplanes, hates trains, and loathes sitting still. She left Trinidad yesterday afternoon, has barely slept since, and is utterly and completely travel sick. Not the puking up kind of sick, more's the pity. That would resolve itself with a few heaves. Ava's suffering from the insidious nausea she experiences every time she ends a lengthy spell in the jungle to re-enter 'civilisation'. She knows she'll acclimatise. Nevertheless, it's a shock to the system.

The flight was horrendous. The 1970s it may be, and Ava's generally fearless, but her gut feelings about modern air travel are basic. The thought of being catapulted into the sky to be kept aloft by the intangible forces of lift, thrust, and drag, always fills her with trepidation, which, she reminds herself, is why she'd requested a window seat. She hoped if she could see where she was going she'd feel less helpless. This was a mistake. No sooner was the gut-wrenching take-off complete than the lights of Port of Spain disappeared, swallowed up by the rapidly retreating landscape before she had time to watch them fade. And that had been that; all sight of earth or ocean concealed by a menacing carpet of cotton-wool clouds. Her only clues to progress, jaunty updates from the stewardesses. Underneath their inscrutable regulation-red lipstick and stiff little hats, surely they too were terrified?

Apparently not. 'We are currently cruising at thirty-five

thousand feet, one thousand miles from the coast of Africa and two thousand miles from the coast of America.'

Dangling smack bang over the bloody North Atlantic! Who needed to know that, for God's sake? Not that Ava believes in God, any more than she believes in the Devil. *The Origin of Species*, that's her bible. When it comes to the question of Creation, Charles Darwin answered it eloquently. Her own philosophy, derived from His, is simple: respect all life, keep an open mind, and leave flying to the birds.

'The air temperature outside is minus sixty degrees, my name is Penelope, and I'll be coming down the aisle with the cocktail trolley.'

All too soon, Ava had smoked her nervous way through her entire stash of rolling tobacco. Not till several long hours later, after three White Russians and a Harvey Wallbanger – 'don't bother with the cherry' – a tiresome headwind – according to the captain, 'just some mild turbulence' – and all the complimentary cigarettes Penny was prepared to dish out, did the plummet to London begin. And thanks again to her window seat, Ava had a perfect view of the urban sprawl hurtling up to meet her; a concrete vanguard of new tower blocks waiting, like a monolithic bed of nails, to rip out the plane's underbelly should the pilot misjudge its descent. Fixing her eyes on the antimacassar in front, hands locked onto her armrests, she'd forced her imaginings elsewhere.

The lush green ferns of the rainforest.

She'd felt the pop of the undercarriage as the landing gear lowered.

The iridescent feathers of a hummingbird.

How the fuselage had shaken as the wheels touched down!

The astonishing emerald wing cases of a jewel beetle.

Then the monstrous roar of the engines as the aircraft careered along the runway – memories of goat curry – until they finally juddered to a halt.

'On behalf of myself and the rest of the cabin crew, welcome to England. We trust you've had a pleasant flight.'

Darwin or no Darwin, Ava had murmured a private little prayer of thanks.

A bus took her to Victoria Coach Station, by which time the capital was already getting hot, and to Ava, who's no longer used to traffic fumes, the fuggy air tasted like burnt coal. She and her hefty rucksack made the sweaty trek to the underground where they fought their way onto a suffocating rush-hour tube. Gripping a ceiling strap, deafened by the squealing rails, she'd stood chest to chest with other passengers as everyone stoically jostled and jiggled and lurched around. Eying the younger commuters, she noted how summer fashions have changed since she was last 'home'. Then it was all miniskirts and cheesecloth; now, it seemed, denim jeans with flapping flares and shoes with breezeblocks for soles are the rage. Her own outfit – a crumpled linen trouser suit with plenty of pockets, belted at the waist – might not be 'hip', but at least she wouldn't fracture an ankle if she needed to break into a run. Relieved to reach Euston, she'd made a vital pitstop to restock with Embassy and Rizlas, and found a phone box. The call she made to Alastair, to give him her ETA, was succinct, with her feeding two-pence pieces into the slot as fast as she could talk – but still she only just boarded the morning train to Scotland in the nick of time… and she's been chugging due north ever since.

Ava peers at her travel-worn reflection in the grubby window. With features distorted by the thickness of the pane, she resembles one of her maiden aunts. Or her father? She touches her top lip, half expecting to feel his whiskery beard. She has his long nose and his high forehead. Lucky she has Mother's cheekbones, or she'd have been a lost cause. It's been a while since Ava made use of a mirror. She sees that her thick curls have gone haywire… and she's really quite grey around the temples. The first silvery strands appeared in her early forties, to be joined by bushels more in the ensuing decade. When did she last comb her hair? Before she got on the plane. She should probably drag a comb through it now, but she can't be bothered. Who cares what state she's in, anyway.

Suddenly, Ava realises she's being scrutinised. The man opposite, brown-skinned and very dapper, is observing her over the open review section of his *Sunday Telegraph*. She noticed him board at Stirling, several hours ago, caught a whiff of his cologne as he reached up to place his briefcase and neatly folded overcoat on the string luggage rack. He lowers his paper as if about to speak, but Ava looks away. She's in no mood for exchanging forced pleasantries with some passing stranger. Besides, as a means of communication, speech is overrated. Early humans expressed themselves with gestures; a lowered brow, a roll of the shoulders peppered with the occasional grunt, conveyed everything we needed to convey. But when a twist of evolutionary fate gave us a voice box that let us articulate sounds other creatures couldn't, we began to talk, and haven't shut up since. Of course, people never stopped giving off the nonverbal signals they relied on in the past, they've simply lost the habit of reading them. Which is, in Ava's learned opinion, a waste.

She steals a look at the chap opposite. It's obvious from the way he's shifted to face her directly, he's determined to catch her attention. His head-on positioning, ubiquitous throughout kingdom Animalia, means 'please take notice', though the way he keeps touching his nose betrays residual wariness, too. These involuntary little mannerisms are vestiges of self-checking gestures Ava's seen before. 'Olfactory investigation'. Not just in primates. Dogs, cats, and rats are forever sniffing themselves, especially in situations they're unsure of, seeking reassurances that their bodies smell right. So, without knowing he's doing it, this suave man's primal self is turning to his pretty much useless olfactory senses, asking them if he's ready to engage a weary looking woman in a banal chinwag about the weather.

Mind you, moments earlier she was checking her own appearance. Did he catch her doing it! Now he's stroking his immaculate moustache; a primitive act of preening, also ubiquitous. For *her* benefit? Surely not! Ava closes her eyes, shutting down any further attempts at conversation from him, or anyone else, and allows thoughts of her godson, Alastair, to swim to the fore. The only person on the planet for whom she'd make this trip. Not that they've been in regular touch. She hasn't seen him for a few years. How old *is* he now? Twenty-four? Twenty-*five*? But she was, at one time, fond of his father. 'Dashing Duncan Muirhead', as her mother used to call him. 'Why he married that Sheila Ferguson girl is *anyone's* guess!'

'*Love*, Mum. They fell in love. Couldn't help it.'

'Codswallop!'

Typical of Mother to take Duncan's whirlwind volte-face personally. *Her* daughter got cast aside in favour of the beautiful Sheila Ferguson. Ava smiles wryly. Even if Ava had felt bruised, she recovered quickly. She was well practiced at going it alone, and Duncan couldn't have found a kinder, more loyal partner than Sheila – who was also a far better candidate for domestication than Ava could ever have been. Sheila was the impeccable hostess of many a hunt ball. And it was Sheila, not Duncan, who kept in touch via letters throughout all the years Ava's been working overseas. Ava was honoured to become godmother to their only son. She grew to rank Sheila among her dearest friends, which greatly irritated Mother. Terrible to think both Sheila and Duncan are gone. Snuffed out, just like that. No wonder Alastair's struggling to cope.

Although raised as heir to the Loch Dorcha estate, he never expected to inherit so abruptly or so soon. One moment, a young man with a Master's in the History of Herbalism, no meaningful responsibilities, and a yearning to backpack across China; the next, laird of fifty thousand acres of remote Scottish mountains and moors, and the eponymous 'dark loch'. Not to mention Dorcha Hall. Now *there's* a crumbling ancestral pile, if ever there was one. Ava's most recent visit was ages ago and even then the place was going to seed. Duncan was aware of the amount of work it needed, but without the funds to start. His solution: angst-numbing quantities of whisky, self-administered, morning, noon, and night; enough to douse all embers of his 'dashingness', leaving behind an angry shell of a man Ava's mother would never have recognised. Sheila's strategy was denial. She focused not upon The Hall's rattling window frames, but the magnificent aspects beyond.

Poor Alastair. Clever and, at the same time, unworldly. Much more of his mother in him than his father. Whereas Duncan would stride through the heather, shotgun under one arm, fishing rod under the other, his son eschews all blood sports. When Ava saw Alastair graduate from The University of Edinburgh he was like a freshly moulted insect yet to harden its skin; full of youthful promise, yet easily squished. Is he still like that? The loss of his parents must've been devastating. 'A freak accident', that's what the police called it. Likely a deer jumped out, or a tyre blew… or Duncan simply skidded and lost control. Just one of those things. At least Alastair has his wife, Fiona, by his side, to console him. Ava missed the wedding, and the funerals, so she's curious to meet her. According to Sheila's final letter, 'The girl's a godsend', 'like the daughter I never had'. It's a blessing Sheila and Duncan saw their son married. But what now?

She knows the young couple hasn't a bean. Alastair's told her as much in the missives he's dutifully posted now that Sheila can't. Despite his circumstances, they're surprisingly heart-warming, full of appreciation for his new wife and his plans to keep the Loch Dorcha estate in the Muirhead line. In the last three months, he's thrown all they've got into turning Dorcha Hall into a hotel; a notion as impractical as it is romantic. 'My idea, but with Fee at my side, I can do anything.' When Ava first read of this venture, she assumed Fiona must have experience in that most modern of industries, 'hospitality', given Alastair has none. She also supposed Fiona to have completed a sandwich course in Business Studies or, at the very least, adding up. Turns out Ava was wrong on all counts. She's since learned that Fiona has a Master's in Earth Sciences, also from Edinburgh, and, Ava fears, an outlook as blindly optimistic as her new husband's. The fact 'The Hall' is failing is unsurprising, and also very sad.

Daft buggers, Ava sighs to herself. Perhaps she should have tried to dissuade them from such folly? Then again, who's she to crap on their dream? Hence her flying visit, to provide support, this being of the moral rather than financial variety. She's no better off than they are. Still, a few weeks' holiday as a paying guest will add something to their coffers. And she'll make the most of the northern latitude's long summer days, by getting in some good hikes.

2

Rest Ye Well

Twenty-four hours after Ava left her bunkroom at the Simla field centre, Ava's train scrapes to a halt at its terminus. Inverness. In their brief phone conversation Alastair said he'd 'send wheels' to meet her, but neglected to detail what form these 'wheels' would take. However, when she spots a mud-green Land Rover parked among a rank of taxis, she makes an educated guess. Sure enough, as she approaches, a familiar character slowly climbs out and opens the front passenger door. It's Angus Murdoch, Duncan's old ghillie. A heavy, hairy person with a full beard, huge hands, and *the* most expressive eyebrows, he greets her with a surly nod. Ava doesn't take this as unfriendly. Murdoch has always been a man of few words. She knows his character to be as solid as basalt, and his loyalty to the Muirheads, living or dead, is beyond reproach. That's why Alastair keeps him on at the estate, to hack back hedges and chauffeur godmothers, despite the fact that he has little use for Murdoch's skills.

Ava takes her seat and keeps quiet as Murdoch, with gear-crunching inefficiency, makes an eight-point turn to get out of the queue. While she's literally looking the other way, she notices another vehicle exit the station car park. A Bentley. Claret red. Lots of chrome. The driver is the man from the train. He must live locally; left his car here when he made his outbound trip to Stirling. Passing the taxi rank, he slows down as though looking for someone, but it seems he doesn't find them, for all at once he turns onto the main street and slides away.

'Dr Dickens, back again,' rumbles Murdoch when they eventually head out of town. 'You'll have had a lang ride.'

'Correct on both counts,' says Ava.

This will be the sum-total of their intercourse for the next sixty winding miles as they cross the Highlands from east to west, but Ava doesn't care. She's happy to sit in silence for a couple of hours and enjoy the scenery. In the blink of an eye Inverness is left behind and the towns they pass through become sequentially smaller, and fewer and farther between. Flat fields and undulating hills give way to less compromising vistas, as monumental outcrops, carved out by ancient glaciers, rise up all around. A' Ghàidhealtachd, 'home of the Gaels', is as imposing as it's wild. Above these crags and windswept plateaus, eagles may soar, and though it's July, Ava fancies she spies hints of snow atop the tips of the tallest Munros. The heather's in full bloom. Distant silver streams slice the imperial purple fells, and even inside the car, the air smells like honey. Eventually, Ava starts recognising landmarks; a croft here, a sheep fold there, and when they reach Knockinch, she knows the end of her journey is nigh. Until Alastair was dispatched to Gordonstoun, this is where he went to school, as did Duncan before him. Knockinch is big enough to warrant a bus stop with a shelter, a police substation with a blue lantern, and a pub that has a horse trough outside, but it's too out in the sticks and set in its ways for a supermarket. The Post Office doubles as a general store. By this time, however, all shops have long since shut for the day.

Murdoch's course now runs the length of a wide, green valley floor and, as the sun slips below the horizon, they finally reach the coast. Here, the moody, darkening mountains meet the ocean, palisading the vast tidal inlet that is Loch Dorcha. It's a sight Ava remembers well. Nevertheless, she catches her breath at the immensity, and the drama, of what's before her. To either side, terraces sweep upwards as if manifested by the sea itself, so high their jagged pinnacle crests threaten to sever the sky. Lower slopes are mantled by woodland and moors, but the upper fells are exposed, rocky and bare. Stretching before her broods the briny, untamed loch itself. Ten miles long, a mile across, and said to be five hundred feet deep, it looks endless. This evening, its lapping waters are calm.

At this juncture there are, unless one chooses to drive into the sea, only two ways to go. A right fork immediately leads to the tiny baile of Drumapple then onwards, upwards and round to the estate of Beinn Beithe. To the left, the road disappears into thick, forbidding, Caledonian forest. They turn left. Though they continue to follow the contour of the shoreline, the loch is obscured by trees. Occasional gaps afford split-second vistas, like flickering frames from a silent movie, of the shore, of the water, and the mountains looming ever large. They're on Muirhead turf now. And as another full mile rolls by, it strikes Ava that every larch and every pine she's seeing belongs to Alastair. And so does every hidden worm, woodlouse, beetle, ant or fly.

She's still contemplating the enormity of this responsibility when, out of the blue, Murdoch stops the car. He doesn't switch off the engine, but removes his deer stalker and bows his head. It takes Ava a moment to realise why. At the side of the road, part-lit by the Land Rover's headlights, is a clearing, like a bald patch in the undergrowth. In its centre, a mound of stones; a cairn. This is the crash site. Murdoch makes a curious noise, like a retch, or a cough, or a stifled sob. Ava blows her nose. She can think of many ways that sentient mammals express grief. To the trained ear, these all sound the same.

On they go, until a cluster of conical spires, made pink by the day's last rays, shows itself above the tops of the Scots pines. The Land Rover passes through double iron gates – one hanging off its hinges – and crawls up a leafy avenue of overgrown beeches. The drive itself is so pitted with potholes Ava has to brace herself as the car's chassis rocks from side to side. But such discomforts are short lived, for there, praise Darwin, it is! Dorcha Hall: a lofty sandstone lodge, with towers reminiscent of a fairy-tale castle, no more than a hundred yards from the banks of the deep, dark, enigmatic loch. Lights glow from within, smoke curls from its chimneys, and in the forgiving murk of the gloaming, it looks magical.

As Murdoch arrives at the front steps, Alastair tumbles out to meet them. 'Welcome, welcome,' he gushes. 'Welcome to The Hall Hotel. Murdoch, put away the motor and join us for a drink.'

'Thank ye, laddie, but I'm awa te ma bed.' Turning to Ava, Murdoch nods gravely and doffs his hat. 'Rest ye well, doctor.' With that, he leaves.

Without further ado, Alastair bends forward and kisses Ava on the cheek.

'Enough of that!' she blusters. 'Let me look at you!' She takes in his full six-foot-four-inch height, his mop of caramel hair just like Sheila's, and his candid smile. Though not handsome in the conventional sense – his slender build and fair complexion suggest 'misunderstood poet' rather than 'prize fighter' – since boyhood, Alastair has exuded a fey charm that transcends the need for more brutish physical traits. And now she's struck by what a compelling man he's become. Sheila commented, more than once, that women are drawn to her son like 'moths to a flame', Alastair's insensibility to his beauty only adding to this magnetism. Still, Ava notes the blue-black bags beneath his sad grey eyes.

'Will I do?' he asks, with a bashful grimace.

'Your mother would be proud.'

'Well, come on in!' says Alastair, bundling Ava over the threshold. 'I'll fetch Fiona!'

'Not if she's already hit the hay. It was very good of you to wait up—'

'Nonsense! I think she's in the office. We rarely make it to bed before midnight these days, and you're not the only guest to have arrived since dinner.'

Alastair disappears into a back room, leaving Ava in The Hall's capacious panelled lobby; not quite alone, but under the watchful gaze of four stuffed stags' heads, one of which has lost an antler, making it seem even deader than the rest. It's a dim, cold space. Last time she was here it was filled with damp dogs and Duncan's pipe smoke. Tonight, apart from a standoffish oak reception desk, a couple of leather armchairs, and a grandfather clock, it's empty. The tartan rug, which Sheila was once so pleased with, is well past its prime. So are the wall lamps, also made of antlers. Though mounted in pairs, no two shades match, and a bulb fizzes ominously, threatening to blow at any moment. Ava's contemplating rolling a cigarette when Alastair reappears with someone on his arm.

'Ava, this is Fiona Muirhead, my wife! Fee, this is Ava Dickens, my godmother.'

Fiona reaches forward to accept Ava's outstretched hand. 'So lovely of you to come, Ava.' Her grip is cool; her voice, measured.

Ava didn't know what she expected of Fiona, but it wasn't this. Compared to Alastair, his wife is tiny – she barely reaches Ava's shoulder; whereas he's ethereal, she's surprisingly... what...? *Tight.* For such a young person, her choice of dress is conservative: a maroon cardigan and sweater that exactly match her neat woollen skirt and, for that matter, the colours of that threadbare rug. Camouflage cryptic enough to satisfy a wattle bark moth. Her lack of makeup is striking. Not that Ava uses any herself, but it's likely Fiona's peers slap on the stuff in spades. Her mousy brown hair is swept back in a bun firmly fastened with a tortoiseshell comb. Is Fiona pretty? Ava's no judge, but it would be hard for anyone to tell since much of her face is obscured by a pair of tortoiseshell-rimmed specs. Hapless tortoises.

Alastair's beaming. 'My favourite women meet at last!' he says, wrapping an arm around Fiona's stick-thin waist.

'Has Murdoch put the car away, darling?' asks Fiona.

'Parking in the barn, then he's turning in. What about you Ava? Can I tempt you to a nightcap from the cellar, or a soothing nettle tea?'

'Alastair hand-picks his own botanicals,' interjects Fiona. 'You should try red clover.'

'Brilliant for rebalancing hormones,' chimes Alastair.

'Sounds delicious, but I think I'll follow Murdoch's example, and—'

'Has Alastair offered you something to eat?'

'God!' exclaims Alastair. 'Sorry, Fee. Totally forgot. Ava,' he asks duly, 'are you hungry?'

'No,' lies Ava.

'Perfect,' says Fiona. 'If you'd like to check in, then Alastair will show you to your room.'

Ava signs everything that needs signing, as directed by Fiona. Ava reminds herself that, only hours earlier, she was hoping Alastair's wife had a head for business, so it would be churlish to resent her being *quite* so business like now.

Fiona explains that breakfast is at 8 a.m., lunch is at 1 p.m., and dinner is at 7 p.m. 'I'm afraid there's only one sitting for each meal, otherwise things get too fraught in the kitchen.'

'More sociable, though,' says Alastair, 'everyone eating at the same time, but if you don't want a cooked lunch, just let us know the night before, and we'll do you a picnic. Some guests even take a packed breakfast if they want to stride out first thing.'

'I'm certainly looking forward to lots of long walks.'

'Let me write down those times for you,' says Fiona, 'so you have them to hand.'

'And I'll find the Magpie,' says Alastair.

Fiona throws her husband a sideways look. 'Please don't call her that, darling, and don't go anywhere either. Ring the bell, and Maggie will come to *us*.'

'Gosh, yes! Quite right. Without Fee at the helm, Ava, I'd be aground in no time.' He hits their brass concierge bell and, sure enough, a girl pops out from what looks like the cupboard under the stairs. Her sturdy frame is squeezed into an ill-fitting uniform: black stockings, white blouse, black skirt, white lace headband; monochrome plumage that quite accounts for her nickname. She has rosy cheeks, a willing grin, and marvellously bird-bright eyes.

'Hullo, Ali. What can I get ye?'

'That's "Mr Muirhead" in front of guests,' answers Fiona. 'Please take Dr Dickens's coat to the cloakroom.'

'And after that you may turn in,' adds Alastair. 'Use one of the empty guest rooms. We can't have you cycling all the way back to Drumapple in the dark.'

'Right ye are. A *doctor*, eh?' breathes Maggie, relieving Ava of her mackintosh. 'That sounds grand. *I'd* like te be a doctor, or a dentist. I think I'd be good at that. My sweetheart Jack says I'd make a bonnie nurse. I wouldnae mind the white shoes, nor one o' those pin watches for my apron, neither. I also think—'

'Thank you, Maggie,' interrupts Fiona. 'Alastair, Ava just needs her room key.'

'I don't have it.' He looks blank.

'You took it down from its hook a second ago.'

'Did I, Fee? Did I *really*?' Alastair starts to pat frantically at the many piles of paper littering the front desk; a feverish reaction which, Ava's suspects, betrays a molten seam of stress simmering just below his squamous epithelial layers.

'Try to stay calm, darling,' whispers Fiona.

'I *am* calm!' mutters Alastair.

There's an awkward pause. 'Well,' says Fiona, 'we won't worry about it now. I'll fetch the spare.'

'Dinnae fash yersel!' Maggie calls cheerily as she flies away. 'Ali put it in his pocket.'

'Blow me, so I did! Lucky the Magpie was watching.' Alastair heaves Ava's rucksack over his shoulder and, having bid Fiona goodnight, Ava follows him up the creaky staircase, across the galleried landing, and into the guest wing. Six rooms to the left of the corridor, six to the right. 'Fee's put you in the Belladonna suite.'

'Why?' Could this choice, like the tea, be for the benefit of her physiology?

'Because the plumbing works. Anyway, if you need anything, our room's downstairs next to the office.'

'I'll be fine,' says Ava, eying the shabby furnishings. 'Home from home.' She expects Alastair to leave, but for a moment he lingers.

'Thanks again, Ava, for coming,' he says quietly. 'Just having you here makes things a bit less... you know...'

The Beasts of the Black Loch

'I do.' Ava would hug him, if she were the hugging kind. 'And I hope *you* know how sorry I am about Mum and Dad.'

He nods. 'Good night, then,' he says staunchly, turning away. 'I look forward to talking in the morning.'

'Likewise, dear Alastair. Sleep well.'

Starving, and chilly, Ava dines on a slice of stale Dundee cake left on her dressing table, 'Compliments of the Management'. She washes it down with whisky supplied in a miniature bottle alongside the cake. Now that *is* a thoughtful touch! Too fagged out to roll up a smoke, she flops onto the bed and pulls a blanket over herself. Checking under her pillow for scorpions – old habits die hard – she switches out the light, and lulled towards sleep by rhythmic gurgling from The Hall's dodgy pipes, she closes her eyes and wonders what the morrow may bring.

3

We Meet Again

Ava dreams about two abandoned bear cubs left to fend for themselves in a large, draughty cave. They'd like to leave, but it's too late. Winter's set in and it's really, really, cold. They'll have to weather it out, living off their body fat and shrivelled berries, clinging together for warmth.

The following day dawns dry and bright. Drawn downstairs by the smell of coffee, Ava follows her nose to the library where, it transpires, breakfast is served. Aside from peeling paintwork, the room is as splendid as she remembers it. One wall is graced by a marble fireplace so cavernous it could house an entire society of troglofauna, as long as it stays unlit. Mahogany shelves line another. Ava's sad to see that apart from *The Illustrated World Atlas* and the works of Robert Burns, The Hall's antiquarian book collection is missing, replaced instead by a smattering of tomes about soil-types and plants. Must be Alastair's university reading list. Perusing their spines, she spots a bound copy of his Master's, and alongside it, what looks like another, fatter, thesis. Presumably Fiona's. His-n-Hers. Adorable. Neither looks well thumbed. A couple of paintings have gone AWOL too, judging by two bright rectangular islands in a sea of otherwise faded wallpaper. Sold to raise funds? Up above, the ornate plaster ceiling remains a lumpy homage to Victorian tastes. Straight ahead, however, is where the finest of all features can be found. Framed by a bay window as tall and wide as the room itself, lies the view. In the foreground, Loch Dorcha, sparkling in the morning sunshine, Drumapple's white-washed cottages just visible on its distant opposite margin. The backdrop, the timeless mountains, so still and mighty, their facets aglow, they seem unreal.

Outside, tranquil splendour; inside, hustle and bustle from all sides. A compact herd of diners is distributed around a group of tables – some square, some round, some oval – chewing the cud, while Maggie and Alastair, both sporting aprons, trot back and forth, ladling out porridge and dealing out toast. The air is filled with undulant chitter chatter and the dissonant scraping of cutlery on Spode. Seating comprises an eclectic array of chairs. Ava reckons the ones made of yellow pine, with ladder backs and sturdy legs, once belonged in The Hall's kitchen. Others are less substantial but more ornate, with upholstered seats and twirly, curled spindles. These would look more at home in a bedroom, which is likely from where they were conscripted. The crockery is equally mismatched. More than one floral-patterned tea set appears to be in play – all, Ava suspects, Sheila's... or possibly Duncan's mother's. The same could be true of the linen cloths, hand-embroidered in cross stitch. Whilst these things evidence Alastair and Fiona's sensible efforts to equip their hotel using what they had to hand, the electric coffee percolator, wheezing and *phutting* away on a sideboard, must be a recent purchase, along with the stainless-steel teapots, cruet sets and ashtrays. The overall effect of this meld of old and new is that of a charmingly eccentric tearoom, and Ava can't help smiling.

'Ava!' hails Alastair, crossing the room in three elastic strides. 'Come and meet people!' It occurs to Ava that not everyone likes to be interrupted while eating – a honey badger will rip off a lion's testicles for less – but this crowd turns out to be magnanimous enough to play ball.

Mr and Mrs Bernard and Barbara Addington, from Surrey, are more than happy to greet her. Bernard explains that they motor up to Scotland every year, bringing their boys with them. 'Been coming here myself since before I was in long trousers.' He also explains the exact routes they like to take, listing A-,

B- and C-roads, as well as his favourite humpback bridge. 'Just splashed out on a new OS Tourist map. Two and a half inches to the mile.'

Acne-struck adolescents Martin and Carl sit in uninterested silence as their mother downs her fork and elaborates upon just how much fun all four of them are having. 'The distilleries are a must-see, not that I touch more than the occasional drop. Bernard's the tippler in our house. The woollen mill is a treat—'

'*Barbara's* the knitter!' quips her husband.

Barbara chuckles fondly. 'Mind you, we've never had a family hols we've not enjoyed, have we, Bernard?'

Leaving Bernard to unpick his wife's double negative, Alastair manoeuvres Ava to the next table. Lauri Levi, 'our American guest', is an altogether different species.

'Well, how *do* you do? Dressed up for a safari and not an elephant in sight!' Loud, zipped into a psychedelic yellow-and-red jumpsuit, and reeking of hair spray, she's an assault to the senses. With warning colouration like hers, if Miss Levi was a tree frog, she'd be poisonous. Ava can only see her upper body, but it's an extraordinary shape. Her bosom is titanic and improbably pert... her face caked in powder and paint... and those eyelashes! Definitely false. Goodness knows how old she is. Twenty-something? Forty? Ava catches herself peering a tad too closely. Much to Ava's embarrassment, Lauri Levi catches her too, not that the woman minds one bit.

'Yes, it *is* me!' she hollers. Her voice is deep, almost masculine. 'Don't you worry, honey! I knew I'd get recognised sooner or later. Back home in Baton Rouge, it happens all the *goddam* time. Cain't set foot on the sidewalk without some Johnny wantin' my autograph... and the rest!' she adds, throwing a saucy wink at Alastair. 'That's why I chose this little ol' bolt hole in the back of beyond for my vacation, where a gal can just be herself.'

'Naturally,' says Ava, baffled.

'Say, Ali,' simpers Lauri, shoulders back, chest out, 'fancy a game of checkers later? I've been feelin' kinda lonesome in the afternoons.'

As Alastair grapples for an appropriate response, a spiky looking Fiona swoops to his rescue. 'Ava, I trust you slept well. Aren't Alastair and I lucky to have a star in our midst? We hope you'll sing for us one evening, Miss Levi.'

'Oh I'll sing all right, if you take away this godawful oatmeal.'

When it comes to the management, it seems only Fiona gets short shrift.

'The porridge isn't to your liking? Even with a pinch of salt?'

'Goddam baby food!'

'Sassenach!' growls Murdoch from his nearby seat.

'Good morning, Murdoch,' says Ava.

Murdoch reserves judgement, though he does manage a friendly scowl when Maggie slips him an extra slice of Lorne sausage to go with his tattie scones.

It becomes apparent that Fiona came into the breakfast room with the express purpose of speaking with Lauri Levi. The two women fall into conversation. Something to do with lost earrings and Fiona's efforts to find them. Alastair moves swiftly on.

'Nice to see that Murdoch eats with your guests,' Ava says to him quietly.

'To me, he's family,' replies Alastair. 'I'd have it no other way. You've missed our German visitor,' he continues brightly, stepping past a vacated setting. 'Mr Baumgarten. An interesting chap. Took off early for a day's birdwatching, but I'm sure your paths will cross one way or another. And so, without further ado…' he says, with a last-but-not-least flourish, 'I present scholar of The Arts and genius at card tricks, Professor Jayaweera Wickremesinghe, otherwise known as Uncle Wick.'

As they approach the bay window, a man who'd been sitting with his back to the door turns and rises to his feet. Ava gauges him to be about her age, perhaps a touch older, and more-or-less her height, but there ends the common ground. Ava is, as always, clad for the jungle, her gung-ho spirit pinned to her sleeve. The person standing before her, by contrast, oozes decorum. He wouldn't look out of place in a window display on Savile Row.

'Dr Dickens,' he says with a bow. 'An honour.'

Everything about him, from his clipped British accent to his two-tone brogues, is polished. Not one loose thread in his three-piece suit. Not a bell missing from the sprig of white heather in his buttonhole. His pomaded hair, as shiny as buffed jet, is styled with a tooled precision that sets off his equally dignified moustache. Though his features are chiselled, his face is kind. His irises are so inky they're practically black. He is also, unmistakably, and categorically, the man Ava so pointedly ignored on the train. She hopes he hasn't realised. Throwing caution to the wind, Ava does the thing she avoided doing yesterday: she meets his gaze. The intensity of his expression – enquiring and intelligent – disarms her. She's not used to being looked straight in the eye, and neither is she accustomed to blushing. Sod it!

It's a relief when introductions are interrupted by a raised voice. 'You're tellin' me you cain't find 'em!' shouts Lauri Levi. The whole room pivots to get a better look.

'I've had a thorough search, Miss Levi,' says Fiona. 'I'm afraid they haven't surfaced in the laundry. Neither have they been handed in at reception, so it's a bit of a mystery.'

'Jeez! What a *goddam* ball ache!'

Barbara Addington gasps, her boys snigger, and Murdoch's eyebrows rise. Watching from the sidelines is Maggie, and her eyes are alight with glee.

Fiona looks vexed. 'May I suggest that, just possibly, you dropped them somewhere? If you'd allow me to have another look in your room, after breakfast—'

'I'm *done* eatin', lady, so how's about we go look *now*?'

'Certainly,' says Fiona. 'Such small things could easily have been overlooked.'

'Small!' rails Lauri as the two women leave the room. 'Those are two-carat rocks you're yabbin' about!'

Drama over, the remaining guests' disappointment is palpable. Maggie stares longingly at the door as if willing them to return and the action reignite.

'Come along, Maggie,' rallies Alastair. 'Back to work.' Turning to Ava and the professor he continues cheerfully, 'Good old Miss Levi. Quite the handful, but underneath it all, a heart of gold. Anyway, if you two'll excuse me, I should get back behind the stove too. More toast, Uncle Wick? And Ava, how about a sorrel omelette, specialty of the house?'

'Yum!'

Wickremesinghe pulls out a chair. 'Please, join me! I insist.'

Ava accepts. He reaches for a clean cup from a neighbouring table and goes to fill it from the percolator jug. 'I'm not sure how stewed this is,' he says on his return, 'but still drinkable, I hope. Service here moves, shall we say, at its own pace.'

Ava takes a sip. 'It's good to meet you, Professor Wickremesinghe.'

'Strictly speaking, we meet *again*.'

'I don't count the train,' Ava says awkwardly.

'Neither do I. I'm referring to Alastair's christening. We are, if you recall, co-godparents... "Uncle" being an honorary title.'

'That was a quarter of a century ago! I'm astonished you recognised me!'

'It was twenty-three years, and alas I did not... any more than *you* recognised *me*. When I got here last week, our godson told me the date he expected your arrival, so, as I boarded the five-past-four back from Stirling – I had business there over the weekend – it occurred to me you might be on it. Then, I saw the magnifying lens round your neck... that rucksack "stained with the blood of a thousand squashed bugs", just as Alastair said it would be, and guessed the identity of its owner. Since my car was at the station – I chose not to motor all the way to Stirling and back when I could easily take the train from Inverness – it made sense to offer you a lift to The Hall, but I believe Murdoch beat me to it.'

'What else did Alastair tell you?' she laughs.

'That you're a scientist. What's your line of research?'

Experience has taught Ava that beyond the closed world of

academia, a brief answer to this question is all that's required. 'The behaviours of animals in their natural environments,' she answers succinctly, fully expecting the professor to veer onto another topic.

It seems this character isn't so easily satisfied. 'You're an ethologist, yes. I grasped as much from Alastair. I'm curious to know what that entails. Are you interested in the natural behaviours of a particular animal, or of wildlife in general?'

Though Ava suspects he's persisting out of politeness rather than real interest, nonetheless she risks a fuller reply. 'Professor, I'll make time for any multicellular organism that moves and respires, wherever in the world it lives, if it'll make time for me. I've spent my career observing the tiniest twitch or tic or curl of the lip in so many creatures, in so many places, I've lost count. Insects are, however, my forte.'

There's a pregnant pause. Is the professor expecting *more*? Ava chooses not to be drawn.

'You work alone, in the bush?' he eventually asks.

'Usually, but I'm never lone*ly*. After all, I have the glorious entirety of the local fauna for company.'

'Sounds like you don't much care for people.'

'No. I mean, I do. Well... some of them are tolerable. To tell the truth,' Ava says with a heavy sigh, 'humans are my least favourite hominid. Of the many millions of species on Earth, *Homo sapiens* is the only one that strives to separate itself so inimically from its natural environment. We live in fabricated dwellings, hide our bodies under clothes, have sex in the dark, and flush away our excrement. It's as if we're ashamed to be alive. Other creatures, our cohabitees on this planet, have no such hang ups. Apologies,' she adds, seeing Wickremesinghe has downed his cutlery. 'I've put you off your scrambled eggs.'

'I'd eaten sufficient anyway. You were saying...'

'Other creatures accept their evolutionary lot. They occupy their niches in the hierarchy of whatever habitat they've adapted to occupy, interacting with their allies, their enemies, and their food sources as they must. Their behaviours, basic or otherwise, are true to form and perfectly reflect their circumstances. I appreciate such transparency. It's why I prefer to read the world around me by watching what so-called "wild" animals get up to, rather than relying on the ambiguous actions of my own kind.'

'"Ambiguous", as in "two-faced"?'

'In some ways, yes. People give off mixed messages. On one level, our reflexes are reliable indicators of mood. If we're scared, we gulp... if we're nervous, we sweat; artless reactions we can't control. On the other, we invest immeasurable amounts of energy modifying how we come across to our fellow man, for *the* most abstract of ends.' Scanning the room, Ava spots a taxidermy fox collecting dust on a top shelf. 'Suppose I see a woman wearing a fur coat, I might surmise a dozen different things about her: She feels the cold. She's rich enough to afford a costly wardrobe. Maybe she's married to a wealthy man who likes to buy her expensive things to show off to her. Or to show *her* off. "See *my* mate! Aren't *I* the best?" Or, perhaps, it's a fake fur. The lady wants to *look* rich, successful... desirable and desired... so she herself made a strategic purchase from a stall in Camden Market. Who knows, professor.' She shrugs. 'I could be right or wrong on any of these counts. If, however, I see a *coyote* with the remains of a fox, I know that the coyote was hungry, but now he's not.'

Professor Wickremesinghe picks up his linen napkin, dabs the corners of his mouth twice on each side, then carefully folds it before replacing it on the table. He leans back in his chair. 'Intriguing,' he says, with a twinkle in his eye. 'I wonder what you were thinking, doctor, when you snubbed me on the train.'

Ava takes a glug of cold coffee. 'Something unfair. As I say, my understanding of hominids... man- and womankind... sometimes falls wide of the mark. Anyway, enough about me. You're a scholar of The Arts?'

'Technically, an art historian. And before you ask,' he continues, '*my* forte is the relationship between pigment and paper in eighteenth-century British landscapes, particularly in the context of plein-air works. I write, give lectures. I'm based in London but travel when I can; pastimes that aren't always rewarding in the monetary sense, but they deliver professional satisfaction. And I have other sidelines to keep the wolf, if not the coyote, from the door!' He chuckles. 'Precious bounty may come in modest guises, and when it comes to hidden gems, I have "a good eye".' He fixes Ava with another appraising stare, and Ava battles to suppress a second blush. 'We have divergent interests, Dr Dickens. You belong in remote places, whereas I need society. I dislike getting dirty or wet. I hazard, in your profession, mud and moisture come with the territory. Despite our differences, however, we've been drawn back to Dorcha by the same powerful force. Duty. In my case to Alastair's mother, Sheila.' He continues to stare.

'How did you know her?' asks Ava, blinking uncontrollably.

'I was at school with her brothers, and the Ferguson family took me under its wing, having me to stay every Christmas rather than letting me face a lonely time left in dorms. It wasn't practical for me to travel to and from home.'

'Home?'

'Ceylon. Sheila was a sweet girl. Innocent, funny, exquisite in every sense.' He sighs wistfully. 'I cared for her deeply. When we'd grown up a bit… or a lot… it was after the war, I hoped…' He falters. 'Suffice to say, she met her Duncan Muirhead, fresh and bloody from Burma, with his rack of medals and singularly disarming ways. But our friendship endured. She was generous enough to include me in her life at Loch Dorcha. More Christmases, some Easters, Alastair's wedding. As it happens, I was here the day she died.' He falters again. 'Fêtes and funerals; funerals and fêtes. Anyway, now that Sheila's gone, I intend to honour her memory by doing all I can for her son. And his wife.'

'You know about their cash problems?'

He nods. 'Dire. But I can't say I'm surprised by them. Alastair's hardly built for the cut-throat world of business. Do you have money, Dr Dickens?'

'No!' laughs Ava. 'Do you?'

'Never enough.' He, too, lets out a laugh, but it's hollow. 'Perhaps that's why the things I've desired most in my life have remained out of reach.' He picks up the silver sugar tongs and turns them over in his hand as if looking for a hallmark. Raising a judgemental eyebrow, he then helps himself to one, two, three, four lumps of sugar, and Ava watches as, with pinkie finger cocked, he slowly stirs them into his cup. Doubting that either his gold tooth – upper-left lateral incisor – or his car came cheap, she's pretty sure he's still referring to Sheila.

'Financially speaking,' he continues, 'I can't bail them out. Nevertheless, I *have* commissioned some expert assistance. A chum of mine, George Beckett, is a talented business accountant, till recently entirely London-based, but just made partner in Bloom and Beckett. And fortuitously for the Muirheads, B and B's head office is in Stirling. Not exactly round the corner, but a darned sight nearer than the Strand is. I gather the move north has been a bit of a culture shock.'

'You were in Stirling on Sunday.'

'Spent the weekend there. After some wining and dining, and much persuasion on my part, George has been through The Hall's books and, I'm relieved to report, agreed to meet Alastair and Fiona face-to-face on the Dorcha estate. They're lucky. If anyone can thrash out a rescue plan for those two, it's George. Such a tenacious character. Great head for figures.'

'I congratulate you, professor, on your practical approach,' says Ava. 'I can't offer half so much.'

'Apart from the benefit of your experience, doctor. No doubt a rich seam of wise counsel. Let each man play to his strengths! I've faith that, together, we'll save the day. George is vague on arrival dates – sometime in the next few days – but if you're around, why not sit in on meetings? I'd value your perspective. I'm sure the same goes for everyone else.'

'Glad to,' says Ava. 'Thank you.'

At this moment, perfectly composed, Fiona floats towards their table, bringing Ava's breakfast plate. Whatever unpleasantness just passed between her and Lauri Levi, it's evidently water off a duck's back. Or perhaps the earrings were found.

'Fiona,' says Wickremesinghe, 'Dr Dickens has agreed to join our pow-wows with George Beckett. What do you think?'

'The more the merrier, Uncle Wick.'

4

Tolerable Hominids

Despite the sword of Damocles dangling over The Hall's leaking rooftops, Ava uses the hiatus between her own arrival and the anticipated entrance of the fêted Mr Beckett to get acquainted with other residents. Thanks to the communal dining arrangements, she's soon on first-name terms with most; exceptions being Murdoch, and the professor. As for Herr Baumgarten, fully supplied with packed food, he's up and out before breakfast – and since he and Ava have yet to share a supper table, it's still nods-in-passing only. Barbara and Bernard talk a lot about nothing, but she gathers they've been to this area 'oodles of times', though, of course, never before stayed here. 'All very nice, in an olde-worlde way.' Bernard tinkers with his car engine – 'Something so *satisfying* about a socket wrench' – the boys climb trees, while Barbara tuts about snagged jumpers and grazed knees. Lauri is equally consistent, cheerfully finding fault with everything while at the same time sounding uninterested. Her only other subject matter is Lauri; hard-knock tales of life on stage which sound as exaggerated as her painted features look. Ava, however, prefers Lauri to the Addingtons. When it comes to making conversation, the woman's spikiness provides useful traction.

Though Alastair's busy, Ava snatches moments with him when she can. The more they talk, the more she's reminded what a genuine, clever, and thoughtful person he is. He shies away from the topic of money and his lack of it, and Ava doesn't push it – no harm in waiting till the expert's on scene to advise – but he's wonderfully conversant with natural remedies, botanicals, and all things green. Immersed in his happy headspace, the scales of anxiety clamped to his being seem to slough away.

'Your passion is infectious,' laughs Ava as he sings the praises of wu wei zi berries.

'Herbalism is my *second* love,' he says with a smile, 'my first being Fee. She's almost as into plants as I am, though she hides her light under a bushel. We may not have ginseng growing in our hedgerows, but we're *both* great believers in taking what the land around us provides naturally. I can harvest any amounts of wild dandelions, chickweed, burdock and so on in The Hall's grounds, all fresh *and* for free.'

'Laudable.'

Ava tries to engage Fiona in similar conversations – she'd like to get to know her – but the young woman forever has her hands full elsewhere. When it comes to running the business, for all Fiona's small size, she clearly shoulders the lioness's share of responsibility. Sometimes, Ava thinks this is by choice; that she prefers to do everything her way, martyring herself in the process, 'I'll do it, darling,' being her motto. But, other times, Ava views her actions in a more generous light. Fiona is, in fact, shielding Alastair from the pressures of their per diem grind. It's Fiona who informs Murdoch of 'the blocked drain in Room Four'. It's Fiona who instructs Maggie to 'stop lurking in the cloakroom and mop up the puddle in Room Seven.' 'Yes, Miss Levi, you *did* mention the smell.' It's Fiona who takes calls on the office telephone, checks in guests... and checks them out again. 'Do recommend us to your friends.'

Not that there's much of a turnover in guests. A party of cyclists comes and goes, as do a couple of hikers, but after spending several nights at The Hall, Ava notes that the residents she met on day one remain *in situ*, bending the Muirheads' ears with their gripes. It strikes Ava that whatever a hotelier's equivalent of a doctor's 'bedside manner' may be, Fiona doesn't have it. Her near-permanent air of being long-suffering, while understandable, is a chore to behold. Thankfully, this is where Alastair's good nature saves the day. Regardless of his worries, he has a ready smile. The Hall's quirks are many – cold bathwater, all meals served late – but Alastair's efforts to make light of them are beguiling. 'Sorry about the power cut, folks. Always happens when it's a full moon... Only joking! Generator's bust!' He looks wiped out, but he digs deep, humouring all guests' whims, just because he's nice. 'I'd *love* to drive you to Inverness, Lauri. I'm sure they sell bourbon there.' He really likes people, and people really like him. As his godmother, Ava finds this gratifying, and Professor Wickremesinghe is gratified too. Thus aligned, the pair fall into a comfortable routine.

Every morning, he and Ava breakfast together at 'their' table in the library's great bay window. Over racks of toast and a shared pat of butter, they talk, the loch's temperamental waters seeming to reflect their volatile discourse. As for challenging her viewpoint, he's bold; a compliment she returns. On the subject of The Elgin Marbles, they'll never see eye to eye. Ava contends that the Parthenon is the sculptures' natural habitat, *not* the British Museum. Wick counters that their removal from the Ottoman Empire was lawful. 'They belong in a global collection.' His scepticism regarding Darwin's evolutionary theory is heresy. Her dislike of Rubens, 'philistine'. But Ava relishes such verbal duelling, and there is one philosophical premise – 'All life is impermanent' – on which they do agree.

After a third cup of coffee, they part company. While the professor passes his time reading, or walking in The Hall's grounds, Ava strays further afield. Duncan always said Dorchan weather brings all seasons in a day, but rain or shine, Ava strides out, not returning till late afternoon. When it's dry, she climbs high, slogging on and up through twiggy, knee-high clumps of heather, kept company by eerie cries of curlew, and the boundless diorama of peaks and corries and islands out at sea. If the clouds should suddenly descend, rolling down the mountainsides like a soft, thick wave, Ava doesn't care. Blinking away the droplets that cling to her lashes, she relishes the sense of isolation... and shelter... her nebulous new world brings.

When she awakes to drizzle, she sticks to lower slopes, instead losing herself in the forest. With its canopy of ancient Scots pine, their trunks dead-straight like the soaring columns of a cathedral, it's a different feast for the senses. Whetted and wetted by rain, here Ava bathes in the earthy scents and euphony of dripping that come from all sides.

Each evening, after dinner, she and the professor regroup to sip whisky in The Hall's orangery. West-facing, with glass roof and walls, it affords unrivalled views of any Dorchan sunset, should there happen to be one. And thanks to its draughtiness – even in summer, Highland nights can be cold – they often have it to themselves. Here they sit, among Alastair's maze of house plants, blankets over their knees, comparing notes.

'This is my favourite time,' remarks Ava on her fifth evening, as the sky moves through its spectrum of collusions. Tonight, it began amber before melting into a curtain of purples and greens. 'It makes me less homesick for the rainforest.'

'I'm flattered,' says Wickremesinghe.

'Don't be. It's the parlour palms.'

Each swallows another mouthful of malt, savouring its peaty aroma as they exhale.

'How was today's trek?' he asks.

'Uncomfortable. I dressed for cool weather, but then we had that five-degree hike in temperature – Celsius, I should qualify, rather than Fahrenheit – and I ended up shedding layers.'

'You carry a thermometer?'

'That would hardly be very practical, would it! No. I merely observed the local population of *Omocestus viridulus*, or the male ones anyway, and drew my conclusions accordingly.'

'Not a species I'm au fait with.'

'Common green grasshopper. Granted, you're more likely to hear them than see them, though they don't stridulate until they're properly warmed up.'

'From the Latin, "stridulus"?'

'Meaning "shrill". It refers to the high-pitched vibroacoustic signals that certain arthropods, and a very few chordates, create when they rub together sclerotised body parts.'

'And, in English?'

'Some animals can scrape one crunchy bit of themselves against another crunchy bit to produce noises. In the green grasshopper's case, he's got a row of pegs on the inside of his hindleg which he drags over a modified vein in his forewing. Each peg-strike makes an audible *tick*, and because he rubs so fast, these *tick*s blur into a long, continuous chirrup: *ticker-ticker-ticker-ticker-ticker*. Bit like the sound of a free-wheeling bike.'

'I don't understand how any of this enabled you to tell how hot it was.'

'*Omocestus* needs conditions to be right before he can get going. If it's chilly and overcast… nothing doing; but on a fine day, out he comes to soak up the rays and wait, quietly, until the ambient temperature rises enough for him to hit the throttle. Like many orthopterans, he's picky about when that is. Thresholds vary, but on the whole, common green grasshoppers start sunning themselves when it's around fifteen degrees, and unbridled stridulation kicks in at twenty. When I set off this morning, I spotted plenty of silent basking males. By midday, I was treated to a full-blown symphony.'

'The wonders of modern science!'

'Amos Dolbear published his seminal work, "The Cricket as a Thermometer", in the 1890s. He postulated that if you simply count the number of times a snowy tree cricket chirps in one minute, subtract forty, divide by four, and then add fifty, that gives you the air temperature in Fahrenheit. For the sake of convenience, I prefer to work in SI units, so I'd reformulate by adding thirty to my counts per minute and dividing by seven.' Ava sighs. 'What a fascinating man he must have been. Sadly, there's no such formula for *Omocestus*, hence my relative imprecision.'

'Another research opportunity, ripe for the picking,' Wick says with a smile, stroking his moustache like he did on the train.

'D'you know, ounce for ounce, grasshoppers are among the loudest creatures on the planet? Bladder grasshoppers in particular. Darwin admired them, but the first time I heard one, I thought someone was being murdered. Sounded like shrieking. Guess how far their calls can travel.'

'A hundred yards.'

'Further.'

'One hundred and fifty yards.'

'You're being conservative. Imagine it's nighttime, when thermal conditions are most permissive. You can safely assume the layer of air closest to the ground will be cooler than the layers above, causing sound energy to be refracted downwards, reducing the rate of attenuation.'

'Thank you. Helpful. I'll say two hundred yards, then.'

'Way off! Two *thousand* and seventy-seven yards, which is over a mile.'

'I've never seen a bladder grasshopper.'

'Have you been to Africa?'

'No.'

'Then you won't have done.'

'It's nice to have something to look forward to.'

Ava narrows her eyes. 'Are you laughing at me?'

'Far from it. In my experience, people show their truest colours when they're talking about what excites them. Without aroused passions, there'd be no great art.' He turns to face her. 'The other day, when you said the behaviour of insects is your professional forte, I was interested in hearing more, but you chose not to elaborate. I've been wondering why not.'

'Because I'm a "boffin" aren't I? That much was established. To most people, a boffin of *what* hardly matters. You must find the same when you're asked what *you* do. One gamely begins to answer, only to be met with glazed eyes and stifled yawns.'

'True. But personally speaking, I love fine detail,' says Wickremesinghe, topping up their glasses. 'Therein lies God *and* the devil.'

'Tell me, professor, what did you read today?'

'Funnily enough, I dipped into Fiona's thesis. Heavy going, but important to make the effort. I thought if I showed an interest in *her* interests, she might relax a bit... be more forthcoming generally. I don't quite know what to make of her.'

'As hard reads go, Fiona's a tough one. Ethologically speaking, the behavioural dynamic between her and her husband is inconsistent, and the dominance hierarchy... it's very ambiguous...'

'In other words?'

'Can't tell who's boss. How did she and Alastair meet?'

'At university. I understood from Sheila that they were, for a while, simply "mates". Alastair had a local girlfriend, Peigi Hooley, a lass he'd been seeing on and off for years. A couple of summers ago, though, Alastair invited some buddies, including Fiona, to Dorcha. They camped in the grounds, went on hikes. Alastair and Peigi both hung out with them, then Fiona went abroad, to somewhere with even more mountains than here, to rack up relevant field experience for her Master's. Alastair and Fiona must have missed each other more than they expected, because she was barely back in Scotland before they were hot-footing it to the Registrar's.'

'I gathered it happened quickly.'

'So quickly, I felt bad for Peigi. Perhaps she and Alastair weren't that serious about each other, and the timing was certainly off for them – when Fiona reappeared at Dorcha, Peigi was in Glasgow, trying to get established – but even so, one minute a couple, the next...'

'Get established?'

'Peigi's a wonderful photographer – has a studio in Drumapple – and she did make a name for herself in "the big city", but her absence cost her Alastair. Our godson has many strengths, but till he married Fiona, he lacked direction. I think she's a tad older than he is, far more focused, and when she set her cap at him – which she did – he was smart enough to catch it. In the blink of an eye, his head was turned.'

'Fiona's not the archetypal siren.'

'It would be ungentlemanly of me to comment,' says the professor. 'But it helped that Sheila actively encouraged the match. Fiona was often here, another woman around the place... a shoulder for Sheila to cry on, I suppose, when Duncan was being... Duncan. I know Sheila felt Fiona was an asset to Dorcha and, more than that, she wanted Alastair to have a partner he could "rely on absolutely". Fiona fit the bill.'

'You say you attended the wedding.'

'Last August. In fact, a year ago next month,' says Wickremesinghe. 'Apart from myself, and Duncan and Sheila as witnesses, there was Angus Murdoch as best man. Maggie Kettleness, our waitress, was flower girl. None of Fiona's family made it. She has one sibling, I think. Not sure if it's a brother or sister. Either way, Alastair says they're not close. No idea what her parents do, but by all accounts they're delighted with the union too.'

'I wondered if it was a shotgun wedding.'

'Between you and me, Dr Dickens, everyone did. I think the bride and groom themselves had, shall we say, concerns that they should hurry up and make things official.'

'Must have been a false alarm, though,' says Ava. 'No baby.'

'More's the pity. If Fiona had been pregnant, Sheila would've at least known she'd be a grandmother.' The professor's voice drifts away.

'What a dreadful start to married life! Tied the knot, then less than six months later... such tragedy. Do you think they'll survive it?' Ava asks thoughtfully.

'Alastair worships the ground Fiona walks on!'

'I don't mean survive as a couple. I mean in business.'

'That I can't answer. With George's help, they have a chance. I know, when it comes to marriage, Alastair is committed to making a success of it.'

'Unlike his father! Duncan led Sheila on a merry dance. Reading between the lines of her letters, I'm sure there were other women, along with the grog. Only someone as conciliatory as Sheila would've put up with it.'

'She had her reasons,' Wickremesinghe says soberly. 'Sheila was Alastair's mother and decided, for better or worse, Loch

Dorcha was where she must stay. And in a way, she and Duncan did love each other. They had separate interests, and bedrooms for that matter, but when it came to looking after Alastair, they were of one mind. An extraordinary lady. I profoundly wish she had not got into that car.'

Ava lowers her tumbler and her voice. 'You think he was drunk behind the wheel?'

'He was drunk behind everything else.'

To Ava, Wickremesinghe's bitter reflection rings horribly true, but what he says next comes as a shock. 'You know, on the day they died, Sheila wasn't supposed to go with him to town. It was only at the last minute that she decided to join him instead of her.'

'I'm not following, professor. Instead of whom?'

'Fiona. Originally *Fiona* and Duncan were to have a day in Inverness. They'd set off at the crack of dawn; Duncan would visit the gunsmith; Fiona would run errands. Then, in a tragically banal twist of fate, Sheila remembered she had some stupid voucher to spend at the hairdresser's – a birthday present from Alastair and Fiona. Fiona, keen Sheila should treat herself to some pampering, stepped aside. Fifteen minutes later, lights out! The tire tracks suggested an animal jumped out into the road and Duncan hadn't time to react. Alastair chooses to believe it was an unavoidable accident. I, however, suspect alcohol played its part.'

'How awful!' breathes Ava. 'A chance change of plan and Alastair kept his wife but lost his mother.'

'Emotionally confusing for Fiona as well as Alastair,' concurs Wickremesinghe. 'I've often wondered how she feels about it. Not something one can easily ask, though.' He changes the subject. 'How long can you stay here, doctor, before the jungle insects get restless?'

'A few weeks, give or take. The peak of the leatherback turtle hatch is over by mid-August. Don't want to miss the excitement. Annual highlight. Yourself?'

'Open-ended. I've been here over a week now, bar my weekend jaunt to Stirling – arrived just after the German chap, couple of days before the Addingtons – but I won't leave until Alastair and Fiona are on an even footing.'

'You're confident they can turn things around?'

'One has to be.' He takes a big swig.

Ava's about to ask if Wickremesinghe's had an update on George Beckett's arrival date, when she's distracted by discordant voices coming from a nearby room. It's not possible to decipher what's being said, but the less-than-dulcet tones of Lauri Levi are clearly recognisable. It's equally clear she's complaining. Her antagonist is Fiona.

'Out of interest, professor, when did Lauri rock up?'

'Alastair and Fiona have had the pleasure of her company since the end of June, and her "vacation" is far from over yet. Miss Levi says she needs at least two months away from the footlights to "recover her sanity".'

'Two months!' Ava laughs. 'She's certainly helping to pay her poor hosts' bills…'

'Driving *them* mad while she's at it; just as she's doing now, by the sound of it. As far as I've seen, since I got here, she's left the surrounds of Dorcha Hall a handful of times. On each occasion, she'd run out of her favourite tipple, and/or cigarettes, and made Alastair take her all the way to Inverness to buy supplies. Four hours round trip.'

Ava pictures Alastair and Lauri, side by side in the front seats of the Land Rover, rattling along the winding country roads, slaloming potholes, and talking about… What…? The weather…? 'A *long* drive for him, I'll bet.'

'He's too good natured to refuse.'

'What about the newsagent in Knockinch? That's fifty miles nearer!'

'She insists on "Ali" chauffeuring her around.'

'Couldn't Murdoch take a turn?'

'He *could*. Getting Murdoch to do something he doesn't want to—'

'Is like pushing a boulder uphill.'

'Quite. And Lauri won't get into the car with "that Sasquatch" anyway.'

'Charming.'

They finish their Taliskers in companionable silence. Outside, the tide's peaked. The surface of the loch, at this moment as still as a millpond, perfectly mirrors the tangerine sky and the mountains. As if to accentuate the serenity of the scene, a pair of crested grebes glides across the water, leaving long and flawless chevrons in their wake. A charming sight, but Ava knows that this time next year they'll each have a new mate. Truth is, most animals aren't the marrying kind. Of the myriad warm-blooded organisms she's aware of, only a fraction partner for life, and even the ones who do are seldom faithful, especially not the males. After all, it makes biological sense to sow your seeds widely and, when you're young, often; notable ever-constant exceptions being some humans, the ironically named 'wandering' albatross, and European beavers... though the sex life of American beavers is a whole other story.

'Are you married, Professor Wickremesinghe?' she hears herself ask.

'Have been. Three times. Yourself?'

'Never.'

'Do call me Wick.'

'Then you must call me Ava.'

Ava has fretful dreams about a hairdresser who waits for a client who never comes, and a lake so populous with grebe chicks, you could traverse it on their backs.

5

Verdammte Mücken

The next day promises to be another hot one. Dry, with a benevolent breeze. Ava decides to walk to the other side of the loch, and since the tide's going out, she cuts across the newly exposed foreshore. Progress is slow. She must navigate streams of receding water that pour over treacherously slippery stones. Some she leaps; others, she fords. As she slithers and tromps through bedraggled brown carpets of seaweed, bladder wracks pop satisfyingly underfoot. Everywhere she looks, there are barnacles and worm casts and skedaddling crabs. The salty air sizzles with the sound of a million sets of crustacean pincers frantically picking through a fresh smörgåsbord of stranded jellyfish and upturned urchins before the sea washes back to reclaim them for itself. So much industry. When it comes to the littoral zone, invertebrates have life pegged. Nearing the far bank, Ava scrambles up the beach, past a trio of clinker-built fishing skiffs. High and dry, painted hulls tilted towards the sun, they wait patiently for the tide to turn.

The settlement of Drumapple, home to the boats' masters, is as picturesque as it is compact. Comprised of a handful of traditional, squat, stone-built dwellings, each with a slate roof and peat smoke curling from a chimney at either end, little can have changed here in centuries. Small children play among a scree of discarded mussel shells. Chickens scratch in the dirt. Ava could believe she's stepping into bygone times, but for the presence of an incongruous red phone box so close to the high-tide line, she wonders if callers ever get their feet wet.

The Beasts of the Black Loch

Outside the first cottage, an old man stacks creels. He nods in greeting, smiles a toothless smile, but continues with his work. The neighbouring house matches the dimensions of his, but appears to double as a gallery as well as someone's home. A sign in the window reads 'COME & TAKE A LOOK!' and Ava duly enters its tiny front room. No one's there to greet her, but she's bowled over by what's on display: not paintings, but photographs; portrait upon portrait of pine martens, otters, seals, each so perfectly capturing its subject, Ava feels she could stroke their whiskers. On a work surface to one side is a canvas portfolio, folded shut but tantalisingly untied. Ava goes to lift a corner...

'Please don't!' The instruction is firm, but not fierce, and the girl who issued it has the sunniest of grins. 'Sorry to startle you, but that's a private commission, for the client's eyes only. Peigi Hooley, by the way.'

It's a name that rings several bells!

Peigi Hooley offers her hand, quickly withdraws it and peels off a large rubber glove before offering it again.

Ava shakes it warmly. 'Ava Dickens.'

'Nice of you to take an interest, Ava. Forgive my appearance,' she continues, removing her goggles and tucking them somewhere in the folds of her overalls, 'I was in my darkroom. Don't always hear people come in... not that many people do come in... anyway, I'm rambling.'

'I love your work.' Ava smiles.

'I love my work too... that's to say being out here. There's something about Dorcha keeps calling me back. The quality of the light, I guess.'

'You don't live in Drumapple?'

'Not anymore. Based in Glasgow, but in summer I spend as much time here as I can. My brother puts me up, and I put up with him.' Peigi laughs.

'Well, it takes a true understanding of animal behaviour to take wildlife shots like these. You have a background in natural history?'

The answer is 'no', but Peigi seems thrilled by the question. She literally skips off to fetch her latest prints for Ava to see. As Peigi shares them, chatting away happily about shutter speeds and apertures, Ava makes her own quiet study of Alastair's erstwhile sweetheart. A petite brunette with small features, she's not unlike Fiona to look at, but whereas Fiona whiffs of reticence, Peigi smells of acetic acid with a touch of sulphur and she exudes an instant charm which, in Ava's opinion, her supplanter lacks. Still, it's Alastair's opinion that counts. Time to move on.

Outside the last cottage, a tall and weighty woman grapples with an unruly line of washing. There's something about the cut of her shoulders, her rod-straight back, that makes Ava look twice. *Maggie?* It can't be. When Ava set off on her walk, Maggie was with Murdoch. They were at the kitchen door, taking in a delivery of meat from a burly young man in plus fours whom Ava supposed to be Maggie's boyfriend; an assumption cemented by the pitch of the girl's giggles as he handed over a blood-soaked sack of dead rabbits, and the hard squeeze he gave her bottom as she trotted off 'te get these ready fer the pot.' To Ava's eye, that body contact had not looked affectionate, but presumptuous... even stolen... and the culprit's ever-shifting gaze made him seem shady rather than playful. Murdoch clearly thought the same.

'Helpin' yersel again, Jack Hooley?' he'd snarled, once Maggie was out of earshot.

'Jack' didn't answer – just handed Murdoch another sack – but the older man's words, summoned from the spleen, were sufficient to make him walk away. No love lost between those two! Still, Maggie hadn't seemed to mind the attention, and, Ava thinks, who touches what is nobody's business but hers.

All at once, the woman with the washing looks round, and her face lights up. 'Dr Dickens! That's who *ye'll* be. I'm Ollach. Ollach Kettleness.'

'Maggie's mother.'

'Och, nae! Mam and Daddy were taken when Maggs was a bairn, God rest their souls. I'm her big sister. Ten years older, twenty years wiser. Raised the wain mysel.' She drops her peg bag and wipes her red hands on her apron. Her features are softer than Maggie's, eyes further apart, but nevertheless the family resemblance is striking. 'Wee Maggs has been so excited te meet ye. "I've never seen anyone like her", that's what she said. Tells me yer kit bag's got more notebooks in it than clothes. And tobacco. In a *pouch*. Fancy! "Well, why *not* roll yer own?" That's what *I* said. *I* dinnae see that as masculine. Having a hotel on our doorstep, we're getting used te all sorts.'

It's plain that Maggie's gift for unfiltered monologue is carried in the genes. 'Good drying day?' asks Ava, noting that the billowing bedcovers match the one in her room.

'Aye, braw!'

'I see you take in The Hall's laundry.'

'Kettlenesses have always done fer Muirheads. Mam, then me, now Maggs too. But all this extra dirty linen! *What* a boon it's been,' Ollach says cheerily, selecting a shirt from her basket, inspecting its collar and cuffs... tutting when she spots that a button is missing. 'With Maggs bringin' home wages *and* tips and what-have-ye, we go te the pictures every month. And she gets te wear a uniform. Doin' for new people, tourists and the like, has brought her right out o' her shell. Not that she was ever in her shell, mind. It's me who's the quiet one! Maggs has *always* had an enquirin' nature. Loves the guests and what goes on with them. It's their wee dramas that colour her days. Before we had The Hall, she'd nae real company but the Hooleys, which wasnae company enough, though Peigi's a good lass, I'll grant ye.'

Ollach's very rhinal sniff suggests her opinion of ungentlemanly Jack is well-aligned with those of Ava and Murdoch. She pegs up two pillow slips and a tablecloth before continuing. 'Have ye met Miss Levi? Maggs says she's a card and a half. "Pure dead barry, Ollach!" Maggs is a great one for guessin' folks' habits, te boot. She said ye'd be out and about soon enough. And *I* said, "I expect a worldly lady like that'll have better things te do than prance about in muddy rock pools and peat bogs." But here ye are! Kitted out in the whole shebang. Boots, stick... but nae butterfly net,' she sighs, clearly disappointed. '*What* a shame.'

'An oversight. You're right. Perfect time of year to catch Lepidoptera on the wing.'

This silences Ollach... for a whole three seconds. 'Ye must feel naked without it. *The African Queen* is my favourite film. Or jungle film, anyway. Maggie prefers *Tarzan* on account o' the swinging vines and the trunks. Mind, I should say "swimmin' trunks", else ye'll be thinkin' I'm bletherin' on about elephants!' She breaks into a peel of hearty laughter.

'Or trees,' Ava adds over her shoulder, grabbing her chance to make a polite getaway.

'When ye next see Angus Murdoch,' Ollach calls after her, 'be sure te say halloo from me.'

Rather than take the metalled road that winds up the slopes behind Drumapple, Ava exits the village via a rutted cart track that hugs the shoreline. She passes a lichen-encrusted milestone. BEINN BEITHE 5 MILES, it reads, and a carved hand, index finger extended, points towards the Muirheads' opposite neighbour, the *'Birch Mountain'* estate. Not a well-beaten path. Undeterred, with the loch to her left, the mountains to her right, and the expectation of sweet solitude ahead, Ava presses on. She feels herself relax, and after an hour's walking, she's confident she's the only *Homo sapiens* around. It's thus a surprise when she spies an unmistakeably human figure coming towards her. It's a small, round, cleanshaven male, wearing a Tyrolean green felt hat.

'Guten Tag!' the man hails. 'What a good afternoon we are having!' His German accent is as broad as his grin. 'We meet in my favourite of places. Here I come to see birds.' As if to clarify, he raises the binoculars that hang around his neck. A camera hangs there too.

'I guessed as much from your hat band,' says Ava. 'I see a tail feather from the turquoise-browed motmot—'

'*Eumomota*!' he cries. 'Gnädige Frau, we are the same species. We are both ornithologists!'

'And guests at The Hall, too. I'm so pleased our paths have crossed, Herr Baumgarten. I've been hoping for a proper chat for days but you're always, as the saying goes, "up with the lark".'

'And in the evenings, we have roosted with separate flocks.'

Ava proceeds to introduce herself and they converse for a while; exchanging tales about the birds they've seen, the birds they'd like to see, and their quests to locate the rarer varieties. '*Picoides tridactylus*, in Swedish Lapland! Outstanding! I've not seen a three-toed woodpecker outside of North America.'

Baumgarten talks so animatedly, he becomes quite breathless. 'Forgive my English. It is broken, and I speak too much. My obsession carries me away.'

'Not at all. You put my linguistic abilities to shame.' Ava's impressed by how knowledgeable he is, and how well travelled.

'In these last eighteen months I have made the journeys from Sweden to Sudan, Kiruna to Khartoum. After this time again in Scotland, I will have to be tightening my belt. Isn't that what you say?'

'Yes,' concurs Ava. 'I know such pursuits don't come cheap.'

'I must hope the book of my bird stories is soon becoming ein bestseller! Then I can be rich. It has very good pictures,' he adds, tapping the top of his camera case, 'which I am taking myself. You have been to Fräulein Hooley's gallery? Fantastisch!'

'I have, and it is. Tell me more about your book! What's it called? I'll buy a copy.'

'I will write the title for you, then you will have it without remembering German words.'

After a fumble in her jacket, Ava produces a pencil, but nothing to write on. Baumgarten improvises, fishing out a sheet of paper from the top of his knapsack and tearing off a strip. On it, in a firm, neat hand he writes: *tausend schöne vögel*.

Ava tucks the memo away for safe keeping. '"A Thousand Lovely Birds". I look forward to reading it.'

'Scheiße!' In the very next instant, the remaining, larger fragment of paper slips from Baumgarten's fingers. Both make a grab for it, but off it flies, merrily pirouetting over the tops of the heather, across the shore, towards the loch. There it lands on the water, flat on its face on the wet, wet waves.

'Nothing important, I hope,' says Ava.

'No. Alles ist in Ordnung. Tell me more of the voyages *you* are making. Have you ever seen a kakapo? What about the emerald rondonia or the dacnis blue?'

'On my birding life list.'

They talk a little longer, and Ava would have gladly extended their discourse, but after a while the air falls still, the clouds descend, and so do the midges.

Baumgarten looks uncomfortable. 'Verdammte Mücken! These insects are a trial to me.'

'I know what you mean,' says Ava, wafting a hand through the gathering swarms. 'They'd crawl inside one's ears if one let them.'

'I suffer badly. Worse than other Menschen. Just a few bites, ten minutes later, I am swelling like the overripe tomato.'

'Let's walk together, then. At a brisk pace we'll leave them behind.'

'Nein. I have done my walking today. I shall rely on my special protection, a gift from Herr Muirhead.' Again, he fishes in his knapsack, this time retrieving a glass medicine bottle. 'This repellent,' he says proudly, 'he is making just for me. Mein Apotheker.'

'*Alastair* made that for you?' Ava wonders if she's misunderstood.

'Ja! Just so. He is clever with plants and their juices. I am *never* going outside without it on my body. Now, we shall return to the hotel together?'

'Thank you, but I choose to go on a little further.'

'Then you are in for a treat. Around the next bend you will find flycatchers. So much prettiness, I know you will appreciate them.'

They part company. Ava would like to spot a flycatcher, one of her favourite passerines, so she's grateful for the tip. In anticipation, her step quickens as much as the rutted track will allow. After an uneven half mile, she's yet to have any luck, but she does come across a meadow of pink flowers with the wee-est of wee stone houses in the centre. It has a single window, a single door, and one or two dusty memories lurking within. It's been a *long* time since she last saw that, on a walk with Duncan, when he was still 'dashing'. One minute the sun was shining, the next, the heavens opened, and he'd dragged her here; the only cover at hand. She remembers his insistence... his muscular arms.

She'd been afraid they were bursting into someone's home. How Duncan laughed! 'This is a *bothy*, Ava! Built to provide shelter for travellers, whatever their journey, be they strangers or friends.' Such a laudable tradition. For old time's sake, Ava risks a look inside. Same hearth, chair, and bare wooden bed. Had Duncan kissed her? That, she cannot recall. Nope. He never was the man for her.

Ava presses onwards until she comes to a dry-stone wall which, she surmises, marks the boundary between the Loch Dorcha estate and the lands of its neighbour, Beinn Beithe. Sure enough, she can make out in the distance a mansion even loftier than Dorcha Hall. Beithe Towers. The wall does have a wide, metal gate, but it's padlocked. As she weighs up whether to climb over and take a nosy, the distinctive crack of shotgun fire echoes through the air, reminding her that, in these parts, it's always open season for some poor bastard. On cue, a roe deer buck leaps the wall and ploughs past her, barking in terror. Clearly, when it comes to venery, the laird of Beinn Beithe doesn't share Alastair's sensibilities. Once again, there's a stirring in the bracken. Ava steps aside, expecting a fast-moving doe to follow her mate's suit. None comes. But, turning to leave, Ava does catch sight of something... or someone... retreating into the distance.

'Halloo!' she calls. 'Murdoch!'

No answer. No flycatchers. No grasshoppers. Just the bubbling of curlews and caws of hooded crows. But suddenly, these bucolic songs are drowned out by an altogether different sound. *Chop-chop-chop-chop-chop-chop-chop-chop.* A helicopter is sweeping down the glen. Military? Searching for a lost hiker? Ava thinks not; too small, too shiny, its bright-white livery suggests private aircraft rather than RN or RAF. Nearer and nearer it comes. Louder and louder it gets, the noise of its rotor blades amplified by the natural amphitheatre of the mountains. Lower and lower it descends, and for a mad moment, Ava imagines it's heading for her. Instinctively she ducks, covering her ears. It passes right overhead, the downdraft pancaking the surrounding scrub and making a bird's nest of her hair, before coming to rest out of sight somewhere in the grounds of Beithe Towers. Good grief! The last thing she expected to see, and not an encounter she enjoyed. Any chance of spotting a flycatcher has been well and truly blown away. She dusts herself off. It's mid-afternoon. Aware of the distance she's covered and how long it'll take her to walk back, Ava abandons her search and retraces her footsteps to safer ground.

When, at last she returns to her room, Ava's disconcerted to find the door ajar and Maggie busy within. Not turning down the bed pane or emptying the ashtray, but standing at Ava's dressing table, slice of cake held mid-air.

'I've just met your sister.'

The girl looks taken aback and, for a fleeting second, decidedly shifty, but she recovers well. 'Ollach'll have enjoyed that,' she says, placing the cake on a saucer. 'I came te replenish yer complimentary pastry, and yer wee whisky,' she adds, taking a miniature from her apron pocket. 'Expect ye're ready fer a wee bite o' somethin' after yer walk.'

'Thank you. I am indeed. Are you fond of Dundee cake, Maggie?'

'Aye!' This knee-jerk response is followed by an ill-disguised blush, then some adept backpedalling. 'That's te say it's all *right*, I spose. Better than shortbread. Though, te my mind, it can be a wee bit claggy. Ollach's cake… which is what ye guests get here… *that's* a different matter. She bakes a super one, with sour cherries. It's them that saves it. *Everybiddy* loves a dried cherry, don't they? Ali… that's Mr Muirhead te the likes o' me… he picks them from all around wherever he can get them, which is off o' cherry trees… obviously, and then he desecrates them.'

'You mean "desiccates".'

'Aye, that's what I said. So they'll keep. Though exactly what else he does te them te make them as good as they are, I couldnae say... and those are what Ollach puts in her recipe. I could eat Ali's special cherries till the coos come home, just as they are, ne'er mind in a cake. Cannae resist, cos they are pure, dead, *barry*!'

'I'll have to ask Alastair how he does it,' Ava says wearily. She was tired when she came in; after two minutes with Maggie, she's whacked. She opens the door wide in the hope she'll take the hint and go. 'So, if you'll exc—'

'Och, he'll *nae* tell ye,' says Maggie. '*Everybiddy's* asked him, but his lips are sealed.' With thumb and forefinger, she zips up her mouth and, pockets rattling, she scuttles out.

Ava contemplates giving the cake a second chance, till she notices a magpie has pecked all the almonds off its top.

6

First Impressions

That night, Ava dreams she's Katharine Hepburn. She lives on the banks of the Congo River, where she makes ends meet by taking in laundry. It's a nightmare. Next morning, she awakes out of sorts. Nothing a hearty Scottish fry-up won't fix! As she pads downstairs in search of black pudding and tattie scones, she wonders whether Wick is much of filmgoer.

The tables in the library are set out and populated as usual. Same waterhole, same grazing omnivores… plus one new addition. Tall, red-haired, smart… and very obviously female… the incomer is sitting with Wick. Perched at his elbow, leaning in as he talks, she looks predatory.

Spotting Ava's arrival, Wick jumps up. 'Ava! Look who's here!'

'This *is* a surprise,' says Ava, positive she's never met the woman before.

'Typical of George to get ahead of the game,' Wick says proudly. 'Drove up from Stirling at cock's crow.'

'*You're* George?' The old-school, balding, caricature of an accountant Ava had expected to meet packs his briefcase and scampers back into his fusty office on the second floor of Ava's imagination.

'Georgina Beckett,' the woman says with a smile. She has very straight teeth. 'Wick has been telling me *all* about you, and you are *exactly* as I imagined. Oh dear,' George continues, half rising to her feet. 'I've taken your seat.'

'Don't worry,' says Wick, 'we can make room.'

'Absolutely,' says George, moving her coffee cup an inch closer to his.

Alastair appears with an extra chair. 'Morning, Ava. Sleep well?'

'Like a log.'

'Great. Has Uncle Wick told you our plans?'

'I was just getting to it. Ava,' says Wick, 'Alastair and Fiona have offered to give the three of us a tour of the grounds, so George can see how the land lies before she presents her ideas.'

'The Hall's *interiors* speak for themselves,' says George.

'Straight after breakfast,' adds Alastair. 'If that suits?'

'Terrific,' says Ava.

'Terrific,' agrees Alastair, before he drifts away.

Conscious she needs to eat up, Ava sets about buttering a piece of Alastair's homemade Bannock bread while Wick and George fall into conversation about 'old times'.

'I can't believe I was ever that young,' laughs George, throwing back her head, showing off her canines *and* her molars.

'Still are, surely,' says Wick.

Ava reckons George is in her thirties. Not born yesterday, but compared to a sturgeon, or Wick, no age at all.

'Enough of the smooth talk!' George does not direct her grin at Wick, but at Ava. Some ethologists believe the human gesture of smiling evolved from apes, who display their teeth in a gesture of friendliness and submission. Ava, however, knows that in many other mammals, bared gnashers are a warning of imminent attack.

Maintaining a steady chomping rate, Ava looks out at the loch. The two crested grebes have been joined by a black-throated diver. Quite the mixed flotilla.

At 10 o'clock prompt, Ava, Wick and George congregate on the front steps where Alastair and Fiona are waiting, hand-in-hand. Last night, after what'd been a dry spell, it rained, and the couple's smiles this morning are as upbeat as the grateful grass smells. Murdoch is with them. He's clutching the handle of a ram's-horn crook, and his eyebrows suggest he'd rather be elsewhere. George has a clipboard and fountain pen; the latter looks platinum, and its ink is red. The tour kicks off with a guided amble down the beech avenue gracing The Hall's drive. Planted in the 1840s, when the house was built, its trees are colossal in stature and utterly unmanaged. Stopping under the largest, Alastair encourages all to 'stand, look up, and take in the theatre of foliage!'

There's a breath of wind. Branches creak. Murdoch steps out from under its boughs. Everyone moves on. Carried forwards on a tender cloud of pie-in-the-sky thinking, the newlyweds escort their party to the erstwhile barn, currently serving as a large garage. Not a cow or sheep in sight, but the smell of damp straw and over a century of dung still lingers in its fabric. Ava quite likes it, but she can tell George and Wick are less sure.

'Just ripe for conversion, don't you think?' effuses Alastair.

'Ripe indeed,' sniffs George.

'Are those mouse droppings on the bonnet of my Bentley?' asks Wick.

'Bat guano,' offers Ava.

'Well, *that's* a relief!'

Ava picks up one of the twisted little sausages and rolls it between her thumb and forefinger. 'If you pushed me to name the species, I'd go with brown long-eared. Pipistrelle's faeces are less knobbly, Daubentons's tend to be more rounded. Sorry, Alastair, I'm interrupting your flow.'

'Fiona and I have a ton of plans for this space. We want to create a yoga centre.' Alastair plucks a cobweb from Fiona's hair. 'Always good to have one's chakras aligned.'

'Anything to reduce anxiety.' Fiona squeezes her husband's hand.

'Sounds expensive,' says Wick, brushing flakes of lime mortar from his sleeve.

'I'm sure it will be,' says Fiona, 'but it's important for Alastair, for *us*, to have something to work towards.'

The Beasts of the Black Loch

'What man needs yoga when he has the mountains?' grumbles Murdoch, poking his stick into an abandoned bird's nest in the rafters above.

Ava considers this a good question, but it goes unanswered.

The adjacent building is the old stables; no horses, more lingering pongs, and there's a sapling mountain ash growing through its roof. Another 'super' conversion opportunity. George writes that down. The former pig parlour, and a pile of bricks that was once a dovecote, are similarly showcased. When they arrive at the empty kennels where Duncan kept his hunting hounds, Murdoch excuses himself. He cuts a despondent figure as he tramps off. As Fiona carelessly explains how the dogs were given away as pets, Ava pictures them dozing, fat and wasted, in front of other men's fireplaces, twitching in their sleep.

Ava, too, is disheartened. Alastair's forefathers cleared this land, fabricated these structures, and expected them to stand forever while Mother Nature looked the other way. But once their backs were turned, Mother Nature did what she always does. Armed with tendrils of ivy, beetles' jaws, and the pendulum swings of the seasons, she began to claw back what was, by rights, hers. Ava's usually on Nature's side, but given Duncan's lack of care and Alastair and Fiona's naivety, the young couple don't seem to have a sporting chance in their battle to save the estate.

Unbowed, still hand in hand, Alastair and Fiona forge ahead. Whilst out of their earshot, Wick turns to Ava and George. 'What's that expression? "Everything tends to chaos"?'

Ava smiles. 'Second Law of Thermodynamics: "All closed systems tend to entropy unless there's an energy input to maintain order", or something like that anyway. Officially credited to Thomson and Clausius, but long known to be true by anyone who's kept meerkats in captivity. William Thomson developed the theory when he was living in Scotland, you know.'

'Perhaps The Hall was his inspiration,' gibes George.

As they skirt alongside a high wall, Alastair calls to them. 'Hurry up you lot! I need to start lunch prep, and you *have* to see this first.' He's waiting at a ramshackle wooden gate which he shoves wide as they approach.

'After you, ladies,' says Wick, with a playful bow.

'Coward,' whispers Ava, as she passes through. Having exhausted her repertoire of realistic-yet-not-too-discouraging adjectives at the dovecote, she's afraid of what'll come out of her mouth next. And as soon as she sets eyes on the kitchen garden, her tongue does indeed run away with her. 'Holy *shit*!'

It's immaculate! Divided into four quarters by herringbone-bricked walkways, with a central lawn and a well in the middle of that, the plot is a model of symmetry. On all sides are deep borders stocked in regimented rows. To the front, salad leaves, onions, carrots, fists of cabbage and bushy heads of purple chard; at the back, canes of raspberries, runner beans and peas. The branches of lovingly cordoned fruit trees – apples, pears and plums – are laden with their ripening crops. Built into the north-facing wall is a large potting shed; rooftiles and windowpanes all intact. Against the south facing wall is a vine. Next to this, raised beds, every inch filled with herbs. Some Ava recognises as culinary: parsley, sage, rosemary, and thyme. Others are unfamiliar. Sheltered from the wind, in this haven of order, bees flit undisturbed from bloom to bloom, absorbed in their work.

'My acre of paradise,' Alastair says proudly.

Wick pats him heartily on the back. 'An aesthetic triumph.'

'Alastair grows all The Hall's green produce himself,' says Fiona. 'Completely self-sufficient, veg-wise, aren't we, darling?'

'Not counting the bits and bobs I forage. Berries, fungi and so forth.'

'*Really* impressive,' says Ava.

'Wait till you see my lab!' says Alastair.

Fiona lets go of his hand. 'There isn't time.'

'There is if we're quick. Come on!' He bounds off to the potting shed and everyone follows, then waits while he scrabbles to unlock its door. As they step inside, Alastair flicks a switch and a fluorescent tube flickers into life, bathing the space in harsh white light.

'*This*,' he says, with a twirl of his hand, 'is the laboratory where I create my extracts. The essences I use in cooking and for my herbal remedies… or "lotions and potions", as Fee calls them.'

Where Ava had expected to see utilitarian wooden benches and sacks of compost, she instead finds spotless Formica-topped counters and a white ceramic sink. There's a box of surgical gloves, a large canister of sterilising alcohol, and a pervading smell that reminds her of the dentist's. Pestle and mortar, test tubes, a Bunsen burner… 'Quite a setup,' she says with a whistle. Glass shelves support jar after labelled jar of dried plant tissues, methodically arranged in alphabetical order: angelica stems, carraway seeds, fennel pollen, pine nuts. 'You make herbal remedies! Like the insect repellent you prepared for Herr Baumgarten.'

Alastair nods excitedly. 'A bespoke formula, whipped up just for him. Seems to be doing the trick, too.'

'I know he's pleased with it.'

'What's this for?' asks Wick, picking up a small, steel, double-headed hammer: one facet flat and square, the other, pointed.

'It's a rock pick,' says Alastair, taking it from him. 'Not mine, but Fee's.'

'Part of my old geology kit, repurposed for splitting echinacea roots!' Fiona scolds her husband with a playful nudge.

Alastair opens a metal wall unit reminiscent of a medicine cabinet and carefully places the pick on a shelf inside. Ava catches sight of more jars and various vials arranged within, some marked with warning skulls and crossbones, black and yellow like a wasp's abdomen.

'Crikey! Hardly your average cook's ingredients.'

'More clobber from our uni days,' Alastair says idly. 'All out of date.'

'Lord *knows* what's in there,' tuts Fiona. 'We really must have a spring clean.'

Alastair closes the cabinet's door. 'We should be getting back. Maggie'll have started the spuds without me.'

'You've certainly given us plenty to digest,' jests Wick.

'Yes,' George agrees crisply. 'We'll reconvene as soon as lunch is cleared.'

7

An Eye-Opener

Chairwoman Georgina Beckett sits in the orangery. The upward tilt of her nose suggests this indoor jungle isn't her idea of Eden. Nevertheless, with the quicksilver loch and its stockade of majestic mountains behind her, sunlight streaming through her red-gold halo, she looks heaven-sent. Ava suspects that when George positioned herself as she did, this was the effect she was going for.

'A gem of a location,' comments Ava.

'Isn't it,' says George without a glance over her shoulder to catch the transcendent view beyond.

Ava, Wick, Alastair and Fiona arrange themselves in four of the five vacant rattan chairs.

'For whom are we waiting?' asks Wick.

'Murdoch,' says Alastair. 'If we're discussing the future of The Hall, I need him here.'

After fifteen minutes of watch-checking – 'Can't think what's keeping him' – George will wait no more. She hands out her agenda, pre-typed on crisp headed paper from her Stirling office. 'To make sure we're all on the same page.'

Item one, 'Introductions', is all about George: her business credentials, which are many and varied; her wish to 'explore all reasonable options to shore up Alastair and Fiona's financial future'; and her excitement at 'being somewhere that oozes as much *history* as this old pile.'

Item two, 'Where are we now?', is all about the Muirheads. 'Alastair... Fiona... thank you for this morning's tour. A real eye-opener. Alastair, you say your family has lived here a long time?'

'My great-grandfather's great-grandfather built this place himself, using stone quarried from the estate.'

'You're from gritty stock, then.'

'Yes,' says Alastair, looking thinner and paler than ever. 'Tell everyone about the rocks, Fee. You'll do it better than me.'

Fiona dutifully launches into a spiel, and the more she talks, the more she comes alive. As she speaks of 'gneiss outcrops of the ancient Lewisian complex', her eyes sparkle; at the mention of 'Cambrian quartzite peaks', her cheeks colour; when she comes to the 'Torridonian strata of sandstones, mud deposits and conglomerates', Ava almost expects her to break into song. 'It's these sedimentary layers that give our hillsides their distinctive stripes and The Hall's turrets their reddish tinge.'

While Fiona reels off her potted lecture, George looks mystified, observing her as if she were speaking in tongues. Alastair, on the other hand, gazes adoringly at his wife, transported. Smiling inwardly, Ava wonders if this is a glimpse of the young couple's pillow talk, but she quickly upbraids herself. She should not mock! As Wick remarked, people show their truest colours when sharing what excites them. It's clear that, in marrying Alastair, this young woman put aside academic interests which were important to her; a real sacrifice, which deserves respect.

'And this is relevant *because*...?' asks George when Fiona eventually stops for breath.

'Dorcha Hall is, quite literally, part of the landscape,' answers Alastair. 'It belongs here and, as its custodians, so do Fee and I.'

'You don't keep sheep or cows.'

'Farming's not my thing, and it wasn't really Dad's. Previous generations had herds of Scottish Blackface... some Cheviot, and when Dorcha Hall was new, the only way to get around was on horseback, hence the outbuildings. At one time, Dad kept up a family tradition, running a few head of Highland cattle, but those were more for show than anything else. The terrain's steep and the soil's too thin and acidic for profitable grazing. Fee's looked into all of the what'll-grow-where. Technically speaking, she's a phytoremediator.'

Fiona squirms in her seat. 'People aren't interested in *that* much detail, Alastair.'

Ava steals a look at Wick, and he winks back at her.

George changes the subject. 'What about wildlife?'

'Thriving!' Alastair says proudly. 'Dorcha's birdlife has already attracted an overseas visitor.'

'So I understand. All the way from Munich, Wick tells me. He's happy with his stay?'

'Seems so.'

'I shall have to ask him.'

'He's spotted siskins, crossbills... as well as ptarmigan, even a capercaillie. Partridge galore.'

'Ah! *Game*! That brings us nicely to agenda item three; the *bedrock* of my rescue plan.' George pauses to chuckle at her own pun. 'I've done some homework, and it turns out that shoots are *in*. Either Prince Philip's just bagged himself another tiger, or Roger Moore's been spotted wearing tweed – who knows – at any event, it's good news for you. The City's full of people with cash in their pockets and the itch to kill. If you were to host bespoke parties for them... small groups, up from London... provide them with hospitality and a "ghillie" – isn't your man Murdoch good at stalking, gutting, etcetera? – with his help, you could clear hundreds of pounds a pop—'

'No!' The vehemence of Alastair's objection takes the room by surprise. 'No blood sports on Dorchan soil. That's something Fiona and I feel very strongly about, and Murdoch knows my views.'

'You two don't shoot?'

'I'm not sure Fee's ever held a firearm, have you darling?'

Fiona shakes her head meekly.

'As for myself, I'm a good shot,' says Alastair. 'I'd hardly be Duncan Muirhead's son if I weren't, but I'm guessing you haven't seen what happens on a grouse shoot. Lines of "beaters" marching across the moors, clapping and shouting, whacking the heather with sticks to flush out birds, while oh-so-sporting men with guns hide in dug-outs to wing them as they fly over. Dozens of them. Just for fun. And the noise! The men wear ear protection, so they can't hear their own din, or the whirring shrieks of wounded birds as they thud to the ground. There's a world of difference between killing for sustenance, Georgina, and literally a *party* of hipflask-swigging Hooray Henries killing for recreation. As for deer stalking, I wouldn't let crowds like that near our herds.'

'Where does The Hall get its meat from, then?' George asks tetchily.

'We use a local supplier, Jack Hooley in Drumapple. Hooley supplies fresh game, humanely dispatched, and butchered especially for our kitchens. No more than what we need when we need it.'

'What about angling?'

'I feel the same about fly fishing as I do shooting. Hooley keeps us stocked with salmon and trout.'

George scores out several lines of text from her notebook, pushing down with such force, her pen's platinum nib scratches audibly. 'All right,' she says scathingly, 'talk us through *your* vision!'

Alastair looks confused. 'Isn't it obvious? We run The Hall as a hotel, as we're doing now. A retreat where discerning holiday-makers can spend time away from it all. As Fee made clear, we'll develop the outbuildings—'

George raises a hand to silence him. 'You simply don't have the funds to tackle projects like that. If you're determined to offer any kind of accommodation to paying guests – and the odds of that working out are *heavily* stacked against you – invest in what's still standing. Fix the plumbing. Put a TV in the guests' lounge; a colour one. Redecorate the bedrooms. You could have an "executive suite". People love a trouser press. Think *pizzazz*. I'm sure your wife gets what I mean.' George looks searchingly at Fiona, today a study in beige, and changes tack. 'You need to come up with a gimmick to set The Hall apart from other country house hotels. Alastair, your garden laboratory is unique. Capitalise on it. Create merchandise to sell as souvenirs. You could even offer behind-the-scenes demonstrations. Show off where the magic happens.'

'Alastair could certainly do that, couldn't you?' says Fiona. 'You've had some real successes desiccating berries...'

'And I'm experimenting with a natural insect repellent—'

'No.' George is having none of it. 'Too mundane. You need to manifest the mists of Brigadoon! Handmade soaps, homegrown lavender in tartan bags; items to remind guests of Dorcha and make them want to come again. Bottle your Celtic atmosphere, then hawk it. I've a paperweight in the shape of a cheese – a memento from a weekend in The Cheddar Gorge – which I treasure.'

Is Ava imagining things, or did Wick just shift in his seat?

'Okay.' George cracks her knuckles as she changes tack. 'Let's talk staff. Who's your cook?'

'I am,' says Alastair.

George frowns. 'Just you?'

'Mostly, but I enjoy it. Fee mucks in when things get busy. We come up with the menus together. Maggie Kettleness from the village preps veg, plucks chickens, trusses grouse. As it happens, the butcher Hooley is her beau. She also helps with breakfast porridge and toast. Maggie's mother was housekeeper here for years and years—'

'*Breakfast*,' George interrupts again. 'All stodge, zero flare. Nowhere did I see a stuffed mushroom or a melon ball. And you can't go wrong with half a grapefruit, cherry on top. There are children staying. Stock up on Nesquik. Offer diners their food prewrapped and let them choose for themselves: pots of yoghurt, individual cereal packs... those come in all *sorts* of varieties. People are here on holiday. Meals should be fun! And the girl, Marjorie, is it...?'

'Maggie.'

'She's whipping teaspoons. A thieving staff member will steal a hotel's reputation faster than they can pocket guests' loose change. I'd sack her, pronto. Now, remind me what old Murdoch does.'

'More than I could ever ask of him,' says Alastair. 'He helps in the grounds, brings supplies from Inverness. He's a brilliant mechanic. Since I lost my parents, I've come to rely—'

'When I arrived, he was in the lobby, scowling away, sharpening a *dagger*.'

'His sgian-dubh. A ceremonial dress knife.'

'I'm not a Scotswoman, Alastair. Whatever the thing's called, it was an unwelcoming start. Next time you see Mr Murdoch, ask him to keep his weapons to himself. He could do with a wash and brush up, too. Why not rope *him* into kitchen duties, seeing as he's not doing what he's actually meant for.' If George notices Alastair wince, she doesn't show it. 'And who does the laundry?'

'Maggie's sister. As I tried to say, the Kettlenesses and the Muirheads—'

'You may as well invest in a commercial grade washing machine. Fewer heads on your payroll equals cash to spend on essential changes. The whole mood of this place needs updating. So much oppressive wood panelling! Paint over it. Add notes of warmth wherever you can. Cushions, throws... a bowl of sweets at the front desk, or some of those dried berries you mentioned, Fiona. Use your imagination. Create a first impression that says, "Make yourself at home", rather than, "I'll slit your throat while you're sleeping", if you get my drift. And while we're on the subject, lose the shrine.'

The smile that's been stuck to Wick's face since George started speaking, falls. 'Shrine?' he asks quickly.

'That heap of stones by the side of the road.'

'It's a memorial cairn, marking the site of Sheila and Duncan Muirhead's passing.'

'Precisely. It's morbid.'

Alastair turns beetroot. 'Really!' For a moment, Ava thinks he may finally lose his cool but, somehow he checks himself. Ava's reminded that he's his mother's son. Duncan might not have tolerated such summary treatment, but Sheila, gracious at all times, would've risen above. 'I'd prefer the cairn to stay put.'

'All right, all right,' says George, throwing up her hands. 'If you don't want to sweep it away altogether, get Murdoch to tuck it away in the undergrowth where it's less obvious to visitors.'

Ava guesses that it was Wick's aggrieved expression, rather than Alastair's tame dissent, that led to this compromise.

'Talking of undergrowth,' continues George, snapping a frond from a nearby tree fern, 'this lot has to go. The orangery is valuable floor space. It needs to start paying its way. Ditch the pots and bring in tables, then you could offer cooked lunches to passing ramblers.' She clicks the lid back onto her pen and folds her arms across her chest. 'Any questions?'

'I don't like to put tender specimens outdoors.'

Ava reflects that the air *inside* the orangery already feels distinctly nippy.

'Risk it,' George says uninterestedly. 'Plants are trivial. More table settings mean less of a scrum at mealtimes. It was frankly *hideous* the way guests were crammed together at this morning's breakfast.' She looks pointedly at Ava. 'When there was no need for them to share at all.'

'My husband and I *do* have ideas, Miss Beckett,' volunteers Fiona. 'Guest activities we'd like to trial.'

'Such as?' George taps the spiny top of a large cactus with the tip of her pointy forefinger, then inspects her skin for punctures.

'Star gazing.'

'Sounds about right,' mutters George.

'Fungal forays,' chips in Alastair, 'led by me. Wood-whittling afternoons with Murdoch. He's not totally on board yet, but he will be. The Addington lads seem keen. And photography workshops. There's a woman in the village—'

'Or dinner parties,' counters Fiona, 'hosted in the grand dining room rather than the library. Formal attire. Every Saturday, with entertainment thrown in.'

George releases the cactus from her attentions. 'Dinner parties? Now *that* sounds more like it. When you say "entertainment"?'

Alastair and Fiona exchange nervous looks. 'We want that to be a surprise,' says Alastair.

'*Today* is Saturday,' points out Wick.

'We know.'

'Well, congratulations Mr and Mrs Muirhead,' says George, with a slow handclap. 'You've piqued my curiosity. I look forward to tonight. Let's hope no one's disappointed.'

8

Party Pieces

At the bunkhouse in the Research Station in Trinidad, Ava's suppers comprise a one pot dish of meat and rice, maybe a helping of callaloo on the side, eaten off a tray, with a fork. Alone. Since leaving there a week ago, she's got used to company at evening meals, and hearty helpings of Alastair's lovingly cooked fare, served by Maggie and Fiona from a row of chafing dishes lined up along the library's sideboard. It's an unceremonious set up that's reminded her of feeding times in her old school's refectory, with scoops of mashed potato, and plenty of custard poured over the spotted dick. This Saturday, however, promises to be an entirely different experience and, for some reason she can't fathom, Ava's nervous.

Lit by a host of dancing candle flames and the blaze of a roaring fire, the grand dining room is a sight to behold. No doubt its plaster work is as mouldy as in the rest of the house, and its floorboards as riddled with woodworm, but tonight such earthly failings are exiled to the shadows by a pervading celestial glow. Centre stage is just one stately round table. It seems everyone will eat together, as if at a dinner party in someone's home, which, Ava reminds herself, this is. There are thirteen settings – is that bad joss? – already laid. But when Ava does a mental head count, she's puzzled. She arrives at only a dozen, including Alastair, Fiona, and Murdoch.

Above the mantlepiece stand Duncan and Sheila Muirhead, life sized, immortalised in oils. Duncan's right foot rests upon the carcass of a red deer. From his left hand hangs a brace of pheasants dripping blood from their beaks. Creative licence allowed the artist to paint his jaundiced eyeballs zinc white and soften the rosaceous shades of his swollen souse's nose. Sheila, her lovely hair loose and flowing as if lifted by a breeze, is holding a thistle flower upon which sits a bee. Ava reminds herself this is not a whimsical reference to pollination, but a nod to the clan Ferguson crest. Given Sheila's stoicism in the face of Duncan's infidelities and his drinking, the clan's motto is sadly apt: *'Dulcius ex Asperis'* – 'Sweeter after Difficulties.'

There's a festive smell of wax, wood smoke and booze, and the air's filled with chitchat. Scanning the scene, Ava realises she's the last to come down, yet she must appear to have made the least effort to get ready. She doesn't own such a thing as a frock, and neither could she find the one vanity tool she owns apart from tweezers: her comb. All the other women have tidy hair. Fiona's dress is brown velvet and unadorned. Barbara Addington has opted for a floral number, its shape and fabric not unlike the lampshade in Ava's bedroom. Lauri Levi's floor-length gold lamé creation is so figure-hugging that her nipples – perched atop her rock-hard breasts like a pair of limpets caught inter-tide – are clearly visible. Although she has little flesh on show, these two details are more confronting than any depth of cleavage. As Lauri's strident laughter ricochets off the walls, she is, in every sense, the loudest person there. George Beckett is wearing a gown of emerald satin that perfectly complements her fair skin and green eyes. She's chosen not to accessorise with jewels, instead enhancing her elegance by standing very close to the immaculate Wick, upon whose arm she's leaning. Ava concedes this stance may, in part, be necessary due to the height of George's stiletto heels. But only in part.

Scotsmen Alastair and Murdoch are sporting kilts. They're not the only ones with long socks and bare knees. Herr Baumgarten, too, is in national attire: Bavarian Lederhosen. Wick is in black tie. No surprise. Ava doubts he travels anywhere without one. The Addington males have brushed up as best they can. Bernard's blazer is smart. Martin and Carl are wearing matching knitted tank tops with zigzag stripes, coordinated with apathetic scowls.

Fiona and Alastair have pulled out all the stops. The silverware sparkles, as do the gilded plates and the cut-glass decanters, almost as brightly as Lauri Levi's cyclonic arrangement of baubles and beads.

'This is jolly,' says Ava when Alastair approaches her with a tray of drinks.

'All Fiona's handiwork.' Glancing towards his wife, who's passing round canapés, his eyes shine with pride. 'Champagne or whisky?'

'What's the whisky?'

'A single malt from Dad's cellar.'

Ava helps herself.

'Mingle, Ava! Please!' instructs Alastair as he resumes circulating.

'Will do.' Ava hates mingling. Mingling is for braver species, like penguins. She takes a large swig of Dutch courage, then raises her tumbler to make a private toast. 'Duncan, slàinte mhath! Sheila, I'm underdressed!'

Sheila continues to stare politely into the middle distance. Duncan looks down upon the assembled company with an air of bemusement. *Don't blame you!* thinks Ava. *We're certainly an eclectic bunch.*

Before Ava can attempt conversation, she's saved by a disturbance coming from the direction of the dining room door. 'Listen up everyone! A moment's hush!' calls Alastair, clapping his hands. 'Hasty introductions are in order. This is our neighbour, Sinclair Stewart. Sinclair, these beautiful people are our guests. Please, join the party!'

The crowd parts, and the Muirheads' latecomer cruises through. A similar height to Alastair, he moves with an easy grace. His hair is dark and wavy; his features, clean-cut and extraordinarily symmetrical; his smile, as dazzling as it is assured. Sporting a tux more dapper than Wick's, and a chest as broad as any incarnation of Tarzan's, his film-star good looks elicit excited giggles from Maggie and a spontaneous curtsy from Barbara Addington. Other present males adjust their ties. George twists her focus onto him so abruptly, it's a wonder she doesn't dislocate her cervical vertebrae. Jettisoning Wick's arm as if it were contaminated meat, killer heels forgotten, she glides over to greet the new arrival.

George may have got to Stewart first, but Lauri Levi comes in a close second. While the women monitor each other through narrowed eyes, he nods graciously, then pays his respects to everyone else who wishes to make themselves known. An orderly queue forms. When Ava gets to the front, she finds his manners affable and his handshake firm.

'Pleased to meet you, Mr Stewart. Ava Dickens.'

'Likewise. I prefer to be called Sinclair.'

'You are my godson Alastair's neighbour?'

'I own the Beinn Beithe estate. Bought it last year.'

'What an undertaking! No regrets?'

'I've had to plough money into the place, but in terms of quality of life, it's one of my better investments. I already spend more time up here, in Beithe Towers, than in any of my other homes, though I'm not managing the land as well as I am the house. Not *yet* anyway. Compared to the Muirhead family, I'm a tenderfoot.'

'Am I right in thinking you have a helicopter?'

'You are! In this terrain, it's a boon, and the bird's-eye views are spectacular. I'll gladly take you up some time.'

'What a generous suggestion.' Ava's stomach flips at the thought.

'Have you ever visited Beinn Beithe, Ava?'

'Never been further than your boundary wall.'

'Well, consider yourself invited to breach the border.'

'Thank you, Sinclair.'

With that, Ava steps aside, and the progression of pleasantries rolls on, but when Stewart reaches out to greet Murdoch, Ava registers a tiny hesitation before the older man accepts the younger's hand.

'Good to see you again, sir,' says Stewart.

'Aye, well...' harrumphs Murdoch without repaying the compliment. Even by Murdoch's truculent standards, it's a standoffish response. No eye contact, no attempt to engage, and no time for Ava to dwell upon why, for once again Alastair summons order.

Armed with gong and mallet, with a reverberating *bong* he announces, 'Ladies and gentlemen, Dorcha Hall's Saturday dinner is served!'

Though each setting is marked with a hand-written name card, there's a brief skirmish as people find their places. Ava ends up between Lauri and Murdoch; a location she's content with, especially because it isn't immediately next to the less-than-scintillating senior Addingtons. She'd have liked to be nearer Herr Baumgarten to get clarification about where to spot flycatchers, but no doubt she'll get another chance. George and Lauri slot themselves either side of Sinclair Stewart.

'A thorn between two roses,' he says gallantly.

'Cain't *wait* to see who gets pricked,' says Lauri, with a million-dollar smirk.

George's smile transmutes into a snarl; a reaction no doubt as gratifying to Lauri Levi as it was easy for her to elicit. For all her sexual swaggering, though, to Ava it's obvious she's not particularly interested in Stewart. Her pupils aren't dilated, her lips are neither inflated nor wet... in fact, she's giving off none of the signals you'd expect to see when a female is genuinely willing to mate. Not when she looks at *him*, at least. Miss Levi, it seems, is engaged on another chase: Alastair-watching. How intriguing. Ava notes how the woman's eyes follow him wherever he goes. He does not, however, return her glances.

Alastair, and Fiona too, have seats at the table, but he spends most of the meal flitting in and out of the kitchen. When each course is ready to be presented, by Maggie, with another resounding gong beat he proclaims accordingly:

Bong! 'We start with mussels, harvested locally, bathed in a seaweed broth.'

Bong! 'We follow with venison cutlets and haggis, both courtesy of our friends, Hooley's Meats.'

The mention of this evokes a titter from Maggie, but a disgruntled harrumph from Murdoch. *Poor man*, thinks Ava. This time last year, it was he who put meat on the Muirheads' table. Understandable to feel usurped.

'Haggis?' queries Baumgarten. 'What is this?'

'A pudding containing lamb's heart, liver, lungs—'

'The pluck!' interjects Murdoch. 'Seein' as it's plucked oot their chest, wi' a good, firm *tug*.'

'Tremendously rich in iron,' adds Ava.

'Thank you, Murdoch and Ava,' says Alastair. 'Yes, the lamb's "pluck", mixed with oats, onions, spices—'

'Stuffed intae the beast's stomach then steamed.'

'Thank you again, Murdoch. I shall be serving it with baby neeps, and veg various from The Hall's kitchen garden. Mr Baumgarten, if you'd prefer an entirely vegetarian option…?'

This last suggestion elicits another disparaging huff from Murdoch, but it seems such derision is unfounded. Baumgarten is more than game. 'Bratwurst!' he exclaims, rubbing his hands together. 'Sausage! That is what you describe. Sausage I eat with pleasure.'

Bong! 'Elderflower mousse with a rosehip sauce. Enjoy!'

All of everything is washed down with whisky and wine. By the time Maggie's pouring the homegrown chicory coffee, Ava's ready to call it a night. Alastair, however, bongs-in a final surprise.

'Dear guests, I trust you've eaten well and are replete.'

'Hear, hear!'

'Jawohl!'

'Scrumptious!'

'As good as any Gumbo I've tasted!'

Alastair bows in acknowledgement. 'Then it's time for some distractions!'

Wick chuckles into his napkin. 'Brace yourself for the bagpipes!'

'Not to be supplied by Fiona or me,' continues Alastair, 'but *yourselves*. In recompense for your supper, each of you must present a "party piece". It can be anything you like – a poem, song, riddle – and it needn't be lengthy. Just one rule: it must be diverting!'

A murmur of trepidation, in Lauri's case obviously false, passes between guests. Fiona stands. 'I suggest, since we have a star in our midst, we invite Miss Levi to kick things off, then we move clockwise round the table.'

Ava's relieved that, being second in line, she has a few minutes to think up something to offer. Lauri Levi, by contrast, needs no pause for thought. Jumping up, she grabs a pepper grinder as a makeshift microphone. Holding it suggestively to her lips, eyelids lowered and bust raised, she launches into a breathy rendition of 'Big Spender'. Her voice is, in Ava's opinion, average, her performance, world class. As she postures and pouts her way around the room, all eight males stare unashamedly. Baumgarten, in particular, seems mesmerised. She blows kisses at the open-mouthed Addington boys and their father. Ava catches sight of Maggie, star struck, watching from the wings, trying to mimic her every move. Lauri tousles Murdoch's hair; a half-teasing, half-mocking gesture that makes him recoil. She ends her act by dropping into Baumgarten's unsuspecting lap. Everyone, apart from Murdoch and Baumgarten, claps... the latter appearing too stunned to react.

Sinclair Stewart, evidently the butt of her song choice, seems in no way offended. 'Miss Levi, let me help you up!'

'Why thank you,' she drawls. 'I have always depended on the kindness of strangers.'

As he pulls her to her feet, Ava sees that the woman's focus is locked on Alastair. It remains locked on Alastair when she plants a peck on Stewart's cheek, and as she wipes away a trace of face powder from Stewart's collar – 'Silly ol' me' – her searching eyes look sad.

All too soon, the clapping stops, and to Ava's horror, all eyes are on her. 'Next,' Fiona says crisply, 'it's over to Dr Dickens!'

Shit! Distracted by Lauri's shenanigans, Ava's failed to come up with a 'diversion' of her own. She's about to make a plea for extra thinking time, when she feels her hearty helping of haggis shift within, and an idea finds her. 'I have a conundrum. What, pray tell, do the following things have in common: pet dogs, a number plate, a rubber tyre, tinned food, and a porcupine?'

She's asked to repeat the list a couple of times and then her fellow diners fall silent as they inwardly digest.

'Which breed of mutt are you talking about?' Lauri Levi asks eventually.

'Potentially any you care to name. One would be a bulldog, and another is a pint-sized lapdog. Let me see...' Ava struggles to recall the details. 'That's right... a Pomeranian... answering to the name "Lucky". And, before you ask, the porcupine is of the African crested species, *Hystrix cristata*.'

'And the number plate?' asks Bernard Addington. 'Where's that from?'

'America. I'm not good on which US state has which plate, but let's say this one comes from somewhere coastal. The plate that comes to mind has a bird on it.'

Baumgarten latches on like a leech. 'Bird?'

'A pelican.'

'A pelican?' he slurs. 'A *pelican*?'

'Yes. I'm not sure that gets you any warmer.'

Clearly displeased, Baumgarten folds his arms across his chest.

The room falls quiet before Bernard Addington comes back with, predictably, another motoring-related query. 'Is the tyre from the same car as the number plate?'

'Not necessarily. In fact, I fear I've misled you, since the plate could just as well come from a truck, as could the tyres.'

This leaves Addington scratching his head.

'What's in the tins?' asks Alastair.

'That I don't know. All their labels have come off. Does it help if I add a snorkel and mask to my list?'

'I've got it!' Wick laughs. 'It's the stuff my ex-wives kept in their handbags!'

The Beasts of the Black Loch

'You may jest, but you're getting closer. Everything mentioned has, in a manner of speaking, been stowed for transit.'

'I'm sorry to rush you, Ava,' says Fiona, 'but time's nearly up and we're thoroughly stumped. So...'

Tapping her fingers on the table to simulate a drumroll, Ava makes her big reveal. 'They are *all* things which have been found in the guts of sharks!'

There's a collective gasp.

'Gee-whiz!' yelps Lauri Levi. '*Poor* Lucky! How the hell did you know his name?'

'Recovered still wearing his collar... though his back legs were missing.'

Lauri Levi starts to gag.

'Frau Muirhead,' Baumgarten sounds very drunk, '*I* am ready to speak.'

'Not yet,' Fiona says decisively. 'Next, my husband and I are delighted to present our resident seanchaidh, storyteller of the finest Gaelic tradition, Angus Murdoch.'

Alastair tops up Baumgarten's drink, and the man defers.

Murdoch rises slowly. His rheumy knees squeak. 'Ye'll have seen the baile beag o' Drumapple. A wee, cowrin' village wi' muckle history. Fer, once upon a time, lang, *lang* ago, two sisters from that place, one a bonnie redhead' – George tucks a stray curl behind one ear – 'the other a sleekit grey làbh-allan—'

'That's a water shrew,' says Alastair.

'Nae interruptions! These two lasses, they fell fer a young laird. The laird, *he* only had eyes fer the prettier o' the pair. He and she would meet on the banks o' Loch Dorcha, te copulate in the auld stane bothy.'

Barbara Addington coughs pointedly.

Murdoch ploughs on unabated. 'Writhin' and roarin' like ruttin' *miscreants*!'

Carl and Martin are agog.

'So loud were their cries o' passion, the shrew heard them. Discoverin' the couple – limbs wrapped aboot each other, lips locked – a jealous rage surged inside her. All at once, she tore the naked lovers apart. The tim'rous boy slunk awa, cuppin' his peely-wally parts in his hands, leavin' his lass te the mercy o' her sister. The shrew, rabid... *crazed*... wasted nae a second. She dragged her ootside, pinned her rival te the ground, and bit her. Wi' all her might. In the neck.' Murdoch leans towards the Addington boys, pointing at his own pulsating jugular. 'See, boys? It would ha' been *this* vein, right *here*, and just one bite caused the luckless lass's lifeblood te gush awa. The bleedin's nae what killed her, mind. As that lass still fought fer breath, the shrew rolled her into the loch. She drowned! The cruel shrew watched from the shore, nae a drop o' sorrow troublin' her breast, till the last bubble broke the water's surface. A dark tale.' He sighs and shakes his head. 'Dark indeed. Because so much blood was spilled, nae again in that *tainted* place... Raon Murt... has grass grown te fill the bellies o' hungry cattle, only useless pink flowers.'

'Raon Murt?' queries Ava, as Murdoch breaks off to wet his whistle.

'The Murder Field,' clarifies Alastair.

Ava realises Murdoch's talking about the spot where she'd looked for flycatchers. Wondering if Baumgarten has made the connection, she tries to catch his eye, but he's too preoccupied with pouring another large whisky to notice. He downs it in one.

Murdoch carries on with his story. 'Legend has it, on the five-hundredth anniversary o' that slayin', on the stroke o' six o'clock, the ghost o' the lass wi' the auburn hair'll rise up from the waters te haunt the house o' the lily-livered laird. Where Dorcha Hall now stands! It is to *here* that she'll crawl, spewin' the black waters of the loch, droolin' like a banshee, and rantin' wi' vengeful rage. The anniversary bein' a week on Tuesday. Be warned!' He plants his fist on the table so hard it makes everyone jump. 'Be warned!'

The Addington boys burst into a round of applause even more fervent than the one they gave Lauri Levi. Others join in. Murdoch's unmoved.

'Well, roll on Tuesday week!' Lauri says pettishly. She clearly didn't appreciate being so soundly upstaged.

'Uncle Wick!' directs Fiona. 'The floor is entirely yours.'

Alas, the inebriated Baumgarten is having none of it. 'Genug!' he cries. 'Enough of these stories. It is my turn now.' Despite Fiona's civil protestations, in he dives. Wick, ever the gent, lets him.

'I have travelled the world and seen many sights that would amaze you all if I had time to tell them. I have met many interesting people... very interesting... noted many interesting birds in my ledger.' He reaches up to tap the side of his bulbous nose, and misses. 'But tonight, I am wanting to share with you a sight that excites me the most. The sight of a sea hawk, your "osprey", as you say it, hunting. Soaring overhead, it sees its prey, the young sea trout... darting this way and that. But the sea hawk, he can see them from so very high, even when they hide... and down he swoops. He grabs. He locks his talons, snatches the young sea trout up. It is easy for him. This I photographed on my expedition to Scandinavia, and I shall not forget it.'

While Baumgarten rambles on about watching the magnificent creatures stoop and dive over frozen land-locked lakes, all through Nordic winters, their cry so shrill it can be heard for 'miles and miles', Ava notices Murdoch's shaggy eyebrows raise in bemusement. Baumgarten is so obviously worse for wear, it's a relief when he draws to an unexpectedly abrupt close. 'That is it. Alles!'

He inspects his empty glass. Alastair moves to replenish it, but Fiona throws him an I-think-he's-had-*more*-than-enough look. 'Thank you, Mr Baumgarten, most evocative. *Please*, Uncle Wick, do share your party piece now.' She sounds almost imploring.

Wick requests a pack of cards, which Alastair provides, and he proceeds to perform a trick. His sleight of hand is remarkable, making the queen of diamonds vanish, only to find it behind Lauri Levi's left ear.

'Very clever, buddy,' she drawls, adding acerbically, 'If you're so smart at magic, perhaps you can make my missin' earrings reappear too. God knows, no one else has.' She slides a barbed look at Fiona. 'If y'all will excuse me, I must powder my nose.'

Ava sees Fiona's jaw tense. 'Miss Levi, if we might have a

quiet word?' She trots after her, and the two women withdraw into a shadowy corner. If Fiona was hoping to placate Lauri, she must be disappointed. Ava can't hear what they're saying, but judging by their body language, the conversation goes badly. Sure enough, without so much as a curtsy, Lauri flounces away.

Fiona re-joins the throng. She puts on a brave face. 'Remind me, Alastair, who's turn is it next? The Addingtons, surely?'

The Addingtons, however, decline to take part. Thanks to Lauri's carryings-on, the atmosphere has taken a nosedive.

'Time these two were in their beds,' says Bernard.

Martin and Carl look crushed.

'What a pleasant sojourn this has been,' says Barbara. 'I've loved every minute.'

Baumgarten is next to retire. '*Straight* to bed for me too. Schönen Abend. Gute Nacht. And, dear Mr Muirhead, I will be wanting my usual pack-up in the morning.' Whistling to himself, he sways out of the room.

Lauri soon follows, then Murdoch and Wick. In an opportune reminder of the lateness of the hour, the grandfather clock strikes twelve.

'Sinclair, George, a nightcap?' offers Alastair.

'Not for me,' sighs Stewart. 'High time I hit the road.'

'Nonsense. Stay. Spend the night! Fee and I won't take no for an answer.'

'In which case, thank you both,' says Sinclair. 'I'm more than ready to hit the sack.'

'Oh, me too,' yawns George.

'Maggie,' instructs Fiona, 'show Mr Stewart to one of our empty rooms—'

'And dig out some clean pyjamas from Dad's closet.'

'Will do, Ali,' says Maggie, as she and George escort Stewart away.

Alastair sighs wearily. 'Guess it's back into the kitchen for me, though I can't think Baumgarten'll be in any state for birdwatching in the morning.'

'Let me do his picnic, darling,' says Fiona, 'and then I'll lock up. If you'll give me the keys...'

'I thought *you* had them, Fee.' Alastair pats his pockets... before breaking into a mischievous smile. 'Just kidding. Here they are!'

'Very funny,' says Fiona though she doesn't actually laugh.

'When you catch Maggie,' he adds, 'let her know she can stay over again. In fact, tell her she can turn in now. And I want you to go to bed too.'

'Don't be silly! What about clearing up? You've been on your feet half the night, darling. Ava, doesn't he look *bushed*?'

'Alastair and I will do it together,' says Ava.

'Well... all right... Don't forget to put out the candles.' Fiona gives her husband a peck on the cheek and hastens away.

'That was kind of you, letting Maggie off the hook,' reflects Ava, pleased to be left alone with her godson.

'Not really,' says Alastair. 'Truth is, she can't be trusted with the silver. Fee tells me I'm imagining things, but that's Fee all over, turning a blind eye to the girl's failings. *I'm* sure George is right, Maggie pockets things when we're not looking.'

'Ah!' says Ava. 'Hence "Magpie"?'

'Bingo!' Alastair flops into the chair beside hers, his long lean legs stretched out in front of him, a forearm covering his brow. 'Jesus, Ava! I'm knackered. Another night like that, I swear it'll be the death of me.'

'Don't say that. Your food was a triumph, and the party pieces were... extraordinary. Who knew Murdoch had it in him? Give him a couple of drams, and it's he, not Loudmouth Levi, who should be treading the boards.'

'Ava, you're wicked, and I love you.'

She pats his bony knee.

'You know I'm scared, don't you? Scared that we... *I*... can't save this place?'

Ava nods.

'When Fee and I got married, she thought we already had a baby on the way – as it happened, turned out not – but there's no way we could start a family at the moment, is there? Because I've dragged Fee into this *mess*. The hotel business was all my idea, I talked her into it, and now *she's* suffering for it, much more than she ever lets on. She struggles to sleep. Don't tell her I told you, but the doctor's written her a script for NarcoVal. Refuses to take it, the brave thing. Still, shows how stressed she is.'

In the remains of the flickering firelight, Alastair's cheeks seem hollow, and he looks far older than his years. 'Remember, your Uncle Wick is here to help, so is his friend Georgina, and I'll do all I can too. Let's hope for the best.'

'The best?' he repeats ruefully. 'Fee deserves nothing less.'

After what's been a long day, Ava lies awake and runs through her own debrief. Alastair and Fiona are on their knees. If their 'special evening' was anything to go by, their business may be beyond salvation. Lauri Levi is a piece of work. Credit where credit's due, though, the woman can hold a crowd. As for the other party pieces, those were food for thought. Tonight, she heard Murdoch string more sentences together in one go than she's ever heard him do before. The prize for the oddest turn, though, must go to Baumgarten. It was riddled with mistakes. Ospreys are rarely found in northern climes in winter. By that time of year, they've migrated to the warmth of West Africa... Southern Europe at the very least. It's strange that Baumgarten, seasoned ornithologist, got his facts wrong. He was on shaky ground with the sea trout, too. Strictly speaking if the osprey in question was sighted over an inland lake, the prey would have been a freshwater-resident brown trout, *Salmo trutta lacustris*, rather than the anadromous form, *Salmo trutta trutta*. Hopefully such inaccuracies aren't illustrative of his book's content.

Ava knows she wasn't the only diner who noticed Baumgarten's slip-ups. Man-of-the-mountains Murdoch cottoned on too. He hadn't looked one bit impressed, although he didn't call Baumgarten out. He probably felt, as she did, that the drunken guest had embarrassed himself enough without anyone else laying in. Still, being half cut is no excuse for sloppy natural history. Ava wonders if he's actually watched a hunting osprey at all.

9
Dead Drunk

Ava dreams she's swimming with sharks. Hammerheads. They're circling her, her every move reflected in their glassy retinas. She's not afraid – *Sphyrna mokarran* rarely attacks unless startled – but she *is* confused. Somehow, she can breathe underwater. Also, she's wearing a long, beaded ball gown that keeps snagging on the coral. As she tries to tug it free, a loud cry makes the sharks scatter.

'Dr Dickens!'

Ava sits up in bed and rubs her eyes. Still groggy, she untangles herself from her sheets. Glancing at her wristwatch, she sees it's barely 5 o'clock.

'Rouse yersel!'

'Murdoch!' She hastens to open the door.

'Yer needed at once!' Ava can tell by the man's eyebrows this is no time to ask questions. Without another word, he bustles her along the corridor and into another bedroom… where she's confronted by a shocking tableau.

In the crepuscular dawn light, she sees Herr Baumgarten stretched out on his bed, and even from ten feet away, it's obvious he's dead. Clad only in vest and pants, his body looks stiff; his face and, strangely, also his knees are red and puffy, but his lips are blue. Congealing vomit is all over the pillows. He's not alone. Fiona, ashen faced, in her nightclothes, is pacing nervously back and forth. When she sees Ava, she stops in her tracks.

'Ava! What are *you* doing here?'

'Quite honestly,' says Ava, 'I've no idea.'

'Ye said te summon a doctor,' Murdoch says flatly.

'A *proper* doctor, not a zookeeper!'

Murdoch looks unapologetic and Ava chooses not to put Fiona right regarding her exact qualifications, though she knows Wick would have done. 'What on earth's happened?'

'I don't know,' Fiona answers, wringing her hands. 'Murdoch came to rally Mr Baumgarten for a birdwatching foray. It was all planned. An early start. Baumgarten should've been ready and waiting, but Murdoch couldn't get him to come to the door.'

'I fetched Mrs Muirhead te come wi' her keys—'

'And this is what we found! Jesus! This is like a bad dream.'

'Where's Alastair?' asks Ava.

'Asleep,' says Fiona. 'Oh God! This is going to be too much for him. What will we tell him, Murdoch?'

'It's reekin' in here,' is his only reply. He walks to the tall sash window, but try as he might to open it, it won't budge.

Woken by the commotion, other bleary-eyed guests arrive from their rooms. Wick, Lauri Levi, Georgina Beckett, Sinclair Stewart, and then Bernard Addington. Lauri – brow, cheeks and chin coated in a face pack, curlers in her hair – is no sooner over the threshold than she proceeds to faint. Wick and Stewart catch her and lower her into an armchair. As she comes to, she whimpers and moans, fluttering her lashes and threatening to be sick. Ava's irritated. Someone's died, yet Miss Levi must still have all eyes on her.

'Will I slap her te her senses?' asks Murdoch, as if reading Ava's thoughts.

'No thank you,' says Fiona.

'I think she needs some air,' says George.

'Yes! Air…!' stammers Lauri.

'I'll tek her,' says Murdoch, making a move to get Lauri upright.

'Keep your hairy paws *off*!' snaps Lauri.

'I'll take her downstairs myself,' says Fiona, 'where I can telephone for help. Murdoch, you wake Alastair and… oh *God*… explain!' She looks towards the door. The hubbub in the corridor outside is mounting. 'Georgina, Mr Addington, Sinclair, I need you to return to your rooms and stay there. Uncle Wick, Ava, would you mind sitting with the... er... that's to say... Mr Baumgarten?'

As Fiona half-lifts-half-drags Lauri Levi away, and the others retreat as directed, Ava and Wick draw up two chairs and duly take their places at the foot of the dead man's bed.

'Tsk, tsk,' tuts Wick. 'This won't help The Hall's reputation one iota, will it? A fresh corpse, I mean.'

'*Poor* Baumgarten,' Ava replies pointedly.

'Of course, "poor" Baumgarten. Goes without saying. I can be as mawkish as the next person, Ava, but I hardly knew him. Alastair and his wife are *my* first concern.'

'No mawkishness required, thank you,' Ava says with a sniff, without admitting her own first thoughts ran on similar lines.

They sit in silence, Ava fighting her cravings for a cigarette, Wick picking at the silk tassels of his dressing gown cord. Spotting a stack of books on Baumgarten's nightstand, all titles about birds, Ava feels a twinge of sadness. What a crap end to a twitching holiday. Next to the books is his complimentary whisky, unopened. The nightcap he never got to drink. She wonders what killed him. A heart attack? Stroke? Must have been sudden.

While Ava continues to cogitate, her eyes are drawn to Baumgarten's livid crimson face... and livid crimson knees... as 'red and shiny as overripe tomatoes'; the words he used to describe his allergic reaction to midges. The mere sight of him makes her want to scratch. She looks up at the ceiling light. There's a moth, flapping at the bulb. Could be a Hebrew Character, or more likely, a Silver Y – Lepidoptera have such uncommonly lovely common names, it's always a delight to recall them – but there's not one specimen of *Culicoides impunctatus*, or any other biting insect for that matter, to be seen. Baumgarten's skin didn't look like this at dinner, so he must've been bitten later, somewhere out of doors. So, when he staggered out of the room, claiming he would immediately hit the sack, somehow or another, this ended up not being the case. And *that* strikes her as decidedly off whack!

After what seems like a long wait, they hear voices approaching. It's Fiona and Alastair, accompanied by a beakish, elderly man carting a Gladstone bag, and a uniformed policeman. As Alastair, already a shade of pale green, silently processes the state of Baumgarten, Fiona makes the introductions.

'This is Dr Carson Sween, our GP.'

'Practitioner to all souls between Knockinch and Inverewe, for my sins,' adds the doctor, peering at Baumgarten over the tops of his thick-lensed spectacles.

'And this is Sergeant Hamish Pratt.'

'Good mornin',' says the officer, removing his peaked cap. 'We've quite the crowd in here, haven't we, so if ye'll all step back...'

The two men unhurriedly appraise the scene. Ava, Wick, Murdoch, and the Muirheads – lined up shoulder to shoulder, backs to the wall – look on. Dr Sween goes through the medical formalities, checking Baumgarten's pulse, inspecting the man's chilblains. While he asks after Murdoch's rheumatism – 'Ye'll nae catch me gurnin', Carson,' – Sergeant Pratt questions the others:

'The door was locked?', 'Who found the body?', 'What time was that?', 'Was it already cold?'

He listens, nods some more, and makes notes. 'And how did the chap seem when he took te his bed?'

'Terribly drunk,' says Alastair.

'Seriously sloshed,' adds Wick.

'Blootered,' confirms Murdoch.

Ava feels a nudge in her arm. Fiona, who's standing next to her, whispers, 'What's that?' She's pointing towards Baumgarten's clenched fists.

'What have ye spotted, Mrs Muirhead?' asks the sergeant.

'Look! He's holding something.'

With the help of the doctor, Pratt prises open Baumgarten's right hand to reveal a small bottle; empty, made of glass, it's the kind that might contain medicine. Its label, handwritten, is clearly legible: *For Baumgarten.*

As Sween lifts it up to the light to get a better look, both Alastair and Fiona gasp. Ava knows why.

'It can't be!' cries Alastair. Fiona grabs his arm as if to silence him, but he pulls back. 'That's the repellent I made for him, to ward off midges. Roots and herbs, it's mostly just roots and herbs... my own recipe.' He's starting to garble his words.

'Nae for drinkin', I tek it?'

'It's for rubbing on, but there's nothing poisonous in it, I assure you. You don't think my recipe *killed* someone?'

'Steady on, son,' says the doctor. 'This is how I see it. The German gentleman came upstairs, three sheets te the wind. He started te get undressed, then lay down. Fancyin' a hair o' the dog, in his intoxicated state, he reached fer whisky – see the wee dram still there by his bed – but instead gulped down yer concoction, Alastair, which didnae agree wi' him. Flat on his back as he was, he choked on his own vomit. I cannae think yer brew helped matters, but if he hadnae been as drunk as ye good folk say he was, he'd at least o' turned over in bed, if nae made it te the bathroom. He coulda saved himself.'

Sergeant Pratt puts his cap back on his balding head. 'An accident, Sween? We're agreed on that?'

'Aye, Hamish, we are.'

'Are you *sure*, doctor?' asks Ava.

'I suppose ye *could* call it misadventure, at a push.'

'Suffice te say, if Mr Baumgarten had been able te handle his whisky' – Sween shakes his head mournfully – 'this wouldnae o' happened.'

Murdoch tuts censoriously. Fiona and Wick let out audible sighs of relief. Alastair stands frozen to the spot.

'Come on now,' says Fiona, tucking an arm under her husband's. 'Let's get everyone some coffee, and Maggie can come and mop up.'

Ava takes a last glance at Baumgarten's knees before she follows the others out of the room.

10

So That's That?

With considerable difficulty, two policemen manhandle a stretcher down The Hall's staircase. From her vantage point in reception, Ava can tell by the shape of the zip-up body bag strapped on top of it, Baumgarten's leaving head first. Dr Sween barks instructions from the landing above; Sergeant Pratt does likewise from below.

'Backs straight, elbows in!'

Progress isn't aided by a marked discrepancy between the officers' heights. The taller man being at the feet end causes the angle of the stretcher to be precariously obtuse. Until five minutes ago, the Muirheads were also on deck, but when the shorter man threatened to lose his grip they withdrew into the office. Ava doesn't blame them. To her, everything about this situation feels wrong. Not just the undignified way the deceased is being removed; the lack of circumspection around how he came to be dead in the first place seems decidedly offhand too. An accident; at a push, 'misadventure'. A tricky word, that. Makes it sound as though the person who died was enjoying something daring, or fun – like riding a zebra – when they stupidly slipped off the saddle and broke their neck. Baumgarten merely swigged what he thought was a whisky nightcap, and the fact he lost his life doing it may not, in Ava's view, have been caused by a misstep on his part.

'Ewan! Robbie! Mind the walls!' shouts Sween as the bearers negotiate a narrow turn.

It occurs to Ava that the state of The Hall's paintwork, like the condition of Baumgarten, can hardly be made worse than it already is. 'May I help?'

'Nae, nae,' says Pratt. 'This isnae women's work. A few more ticks, they'll be done and dusted.'

Sure enough, with a heave and a shove, and some very colourful language, in sixty ligament-twisting seconds they make touch down. On Sween's count of, 'One, two, three, and... lowerin'... from... the... *hips*!' they rest their load on the lobby floor. 'Nip out and see if the undertaker's ready fer us, lads, then ye can come back te fetch our friend here.'

The duo duly disappears, leaving Ava and Baumgarten with Pratt and Sween. The air is still. A single, lonely-looking bluebottle zigzags overhead. Pratt's collie dog Bess gnaws diligently between the toes of her hind paw.

'What an unfortunate business,' says Pratt.

'Regrettable indeed,' says Sween, checking his watch.

'I'd go with "disturbing",' says Ava.

Neither man rises to this remark. Sween whistles to Bess to come over for a 'wee tickle like a good lass.' Bess lifts one ear, wags her tail, *thud, thud* on the flagstones, but remains otherwise intent on her gnawing. Pratt rocks back and forth on his heels.

'Where will Herr Baumgarten go now?' asks Ava.

'The mortuary in Inverness,' says Pratt.

'What about further inquiries?'

Pratt and Sween look bewildered. 'Further inquiries?' repeats Pratt. Bess's ears prick up.

'The police, and you too Dr Sween, may think he died by some sort of fluky mishap—'

'Accident,' the men riposte in unison.

'But doesn't Her Majesty's Coroner need to check?'

'The *Procurator Fiscal*,' corrects Pratt, 'will be informed o' events, and he can ask all the question he likes, if he sees fit. But Mr Baumgarten's death, while unexpected – that much I *will* grant ye – isnae unexplained. Law officers have attended.' He puffs out his chest. 'A doctor is satisfied as te the cause and can sign a certificate te that effect.'

'Will do,' says Sween.

'Capital, Carson. Capital. Mr Baumgarten's passed accidentally, by his own hand, because he was cockeyed. The PF will likely determine… *very* likely determine,' revises Pratt, 'no other action is needed. His team'll do the necessaries regardin' release o' the body for repatriation and so on. I doubt there'll be any delays.'

'You're absolutely certain about that?' queries Ava.

'Our crown officers ken their business, madam.'

'That's not what I'm getting at. I'm asking whether either of you has a sense that Baumgarten's death was, in any way, suspicious. To be specific, has the condition of his knees given you pause for thought?'

Pratt stops rocking.

Ava's on a roll. 'The colour of them, sergeant. Bright red. And that puffiness… as though he'd been attacked by midges, and then flared up. His face was the same. If we were to unzip the—'

'Naebiddy's unzippin' anythin'!' Sween says stoutly, positioning himself between Ava and the stretcher. 'I did notice the man had experienced some insect bites around the time o' death, yes, but nothin' that woulda proved fatal. The notion—'

'I'm not suggesting midges killed him!' blusters Ava, conscious she's not being as coherent as she might. 'But having any bites at all doesn't fit with what he said he was going to do. If he'd gone up to bed when—'

'Dr Dickens,' Pratt says firmly, 'are you sayin' somethin' *unlawful* happened te Mr Baumgarten?'

'No, not exactly, just that I'm open to that possibility.'

'You knew Baumgarten well?'

'We spoke once.'

'On that *single* occasion, did he give ye cause te believe he was in danger?' Pratt's scepticism is undisguised.

'No.'

'Did ye hear any person make untoward comments about the man or express a desire te harm him?'

'No.'

'And when he left the dinin' room, after dinner, was he not *extremely* intoxicated?'

'He was, sergeant.'

'And his body was found in a locked room.'

'Yes, but the keys hang here, at the front desk. Anyone could—'

'All things considered, Dr Dickens,' says Pratt, with a cautionary wag of the forefinger, 'unless ye produce evidence te the contrary, I'm stickin' wi' ma first conclusion.'

'As am I,' adds Sween.

Ava's attempts at protest go unheard. The stretcher bearers return and, on Sween's count of, 'One, two, three, and... liftin'... from... the... *hips*!' they raise Baumgarten up and cart him outside. Ava and Bess watch as they slot him into the back of a waiting hearse. They're not the only onlookers. Visibly upset, Ollach Kettleness hovers in the background, straddled by laundry bags, wiping her eyes with the hem of her pinafore. The Addington boys, by contrast, stand as close as they can to the action, whispering excitedly as Sween and Pratt shake the undertaker's hand. All five men look skywards, exchange a few words – perhaps Sween's roses could do with a drop more rain – before going their separate ways. As the hearse disappears from view it fails to take Ava's sense of unease with it.

She wanders back indoors. The atmosphere in the sitting room, where others have gathered to marvel at the morning's tragedy from the semblance of a respectful distance, is buoyant. The kitchen was shut during breakfast, so Maggie's in the throes of serving alternative refreshments. Appetites and curiosity equally whetted, a queue has formed at her tea urn. Revelling in this windfall step up in responsibility, she's delivering cups of lukewarm blueberry infusion and red-hot hearsay in generous measures. Guests lap it up as fast as she can pour.

'Stiff as a board, he was, when they scooped him onto that stretcher... help yersels te sugar, finger rolls on the side.'

Choosing not to partake, Ava heads for the office, where she finds an altogether gloomier ensemble. Alastair is sitting with his face in his hands, as Fiona, Murdoch and Wick rally around.

While she'd expected her godson to be upset by Baumgarten's death, he looks devastated — far more so than anyone else in the room — and the contrast between his demeanour last night as he sounded his dinner gong and the sight of him now is sobering.

'The police, and Baumgarten, they've just left,' reports Ava.

'How did I let this happen?' he groans.

'We've been over and over this,' says Fiona. 'It's *not* your fault.'

'Of course it is! My repellent, my hotel—'

'Duncan's whisky,' interjects Wick.

'If you say the repellent wasn't poisonous, darling, then it wasn't. No one doubts you.' Unfortunately, Fiona doesn't sound like she believes her own pep talk.

'I'm sorry,' says Alastair, jumping to his feet. 'I need some space!' He opens a desk drawer, grabs, of all things, a trowel, and dives out of the back door.

'Don't leave, darling! It solves nothing.' Fiona makes a move to follow him, but Murdoch intervenes.

'Let the man be, missus! Diggin' soothes him. Has done since he was a bairn.'

'Where's he going?' Ava asks.

'The kitchen garden,' sighs Fiona. 'This is a disaster! First that wretched Levi person says she's been robbed on our premises, then a guest wakes up dead. I need Alastair beside me in reception. Where I can see him...' Her voice trails away.

'"See him"?' Ava probes.

'Oh, *please*! You must have noticed how fragile Alastair is. The loss of his parents, worries about money, the hotel, it's all making him ill. I'm at my wits' end. He's permanently exhausted, he's been making all *kinds* of silly mistakes at work; mislaid keys, forgotten appointments, and...' Fiona wavers.

'And what?' asks Wick.

'Well, if you must know,' Fiona blurts, 'Alastair's been having "absences"; blank periods, like he's here-but-not-here. He denies they're happening, has no recollection after the event, but they're getting more frequent... lasting longer. Really, he's stressed to breaking point. So, in answer to your question, Uncle Wick, I like to know what he's up to at all times. In case.' For a moment, Ava thinks Fiona's going to cry, but the young woman's eyes remain resolutely dry. 'Still, someone has to run this ship, and that someone is me. So, if you'll excuse me, I must get on.'

11
An Irritating Itch

Ava and Wick head outside. 'Shall we stroll?' Wick's tone is casual, but he looks tense. 'It wouldn't hurt to check on the carrots.'

'Nor the spuds,' agrees Ava.

Wick sets off briskly, Ava in tow, his pace picking up as they enter the kitchen garden. There's no sign of a digging Alastair, just a pair of blackbirds methodically pulling up a row of lettuce seedlings.

'Should we look for him?' asks Wick.

'He wanted time to himself. Let's wait and see if he shows up.'

They settle on a bench. Ava roots out her tobacco pouch. Wick slips a little brass box with mother of pearl lid – a portable ashtray – from his top pocket, places it between them, then unwraps a cigar. Both light up, drag, and exhale. Their smoke does a fair job of keeping the midges at bay. Even so, Ava's aware of them teeming in the air above her head, making her brain itch.

'Penny for your thoughts, Ava.'

'I'm troubled.'

'You and I both. Fiona saying "in case" like she did. Suggesting Alastair might harm himself—'

'*Alastair*? He's far more sensible than he looks *and* he's like his mother. Loyal. He'd never bail on his spouse.'

'So, why the furrowed brow?'

'It's the verdammte Mücken. The "damned midges". When we were on sentry duty with Baumgarten's body, did you notice his knees?'

'I did my best not to look at any part of him!'

'Scientists aren't squeamish people, Wick. *I* had a good old gander, and those knees were seriously swollen, so was his face, like he'd been bitten by midges. Baumgarten told me he was particularly susceptible, but something about that *pattern* of inflammation got me thinking. Anyone who's been to this neck of the woods knows the miseries *Culicoides impunctatus* can inflict. Queen Victoria herself was "terribly plagued". Enterprising as the blighters are, though, they can't get at those bits of us which are covered by clothes. The concentration of bites on Baumgarten's knees tells me these were exposed when his thighs and calves were not, i.e. when he was wearing his evening attire, Lederhosen... which is odd, because *that* means he must have gone outside after dinner, even though, when he left the table, he said he was going straight to bed.'

'Not necessarily,' says Wick. 'He could have got bitten when he was all dressed up before dinner, then nipped out for a breath of air.'

'When it was still light? I don't think so. It's true *Culicoides* females will attack at any time of day, but they're far more lively during the hours of darkness. The trigger for biting activity is an ambient irradiance of twenty-four watts per square foot, give or take a watt, and when light levels fall to around ten watts per square foot, they really get stuck in. To have been as badly bitten as Baumgarten was, it's far more likely he was out after sunset. Besides which, if he'd been bitten in the early evening, he'd have had a red face and knees when he did his party piece... and he'd neither.'

Wick sucks on his cigar. 'Okay. Suppose the midges *did* attack him after dinner. Why not in his room before he got undressed?'

'There wasn't a way for them to get indoors. His bedroom window was jammed closed when he died. Even Murdoch couldn't budge it.' Ava pauses to observe a blackbird play tug-of-war with a resolute earthworm. 'I wonder why Baumgarten went outdoors?'

'Spur of the moment thing? Had second thoughts about

turning in and decided to go for a sobering stroll. God knows he needed it.'

'It would have to have been a brisk one; no slower than five-and-a-half miles per hour, to make sure of leaving the midges behind.'

'Who "strolls" that quickly?'

'You!' Ava chuckles. 'Just now! Kitchen door to garden gate in under sixty seconds, and *you* weren't trying to outpace your six-legged nemesis. Anyway, I don't reckon Baumgarten walked or jogged anywhere. Given his number of bites, I reckon he stayed still. As for his reasoning,' she ponders, 'I accept his exit was unplanned. Otherwise, pie-eyed or not, he'd have slathered himself with repellent first. Bearing in mind the severity of his allergy, it must've been something pretty pressing that made him venture out unprotected. Do you know how many sensory receptors a female midge has on her antennae, professor?'

'Surprisingly, no, doctor.'

'Have a guess.'

'Ten.'

'More.'

'A million.'

'Don't be ridiculous! The answer is approximately two hundred and forty-one, a whole gamut of them adapted to detect the gasses in her hosts' exhaled breath and the heat of her hosts' lovely warm body fluids. I've often speculated how our world would smell to us if *we* had sensillae ampullacea.'

'Do you know how many bristles there are on a fine-art sable paint brush?'

'You digress. My point is, the second Baumgarten set foot al fresco, the midges would've been onto him, cutting into him with their serrated mouthparts, sucking up his blood a millionth of a fluid ounce at a time. The average man has a good ten pints of blood coursing through his veins, but even so, it hurts to part with it. Within a jiff of his skin being pierced, Baumgarten's immune system would've caught on to what was happening and released a surge of histamines to mop up the midges' saliva.

A brave frontline, but not without collateral damage. Itching and swelling. Baumgarten had a nasty flare up, but *he* was hypersensitive. For him, the interval between bite and reaction was short; ten minutes, he told me.'

'And the significance of all this?'

'Baumgarten wouldn't have to have been outside for long to get badly bitten, and for the exaggerated effects of those bites to be obvious. Furthermore, he probably died only shortly after he returned to his room.'

'How ever did the midges tell you that?'

'They didn't. He was in his underwear when he was found. Probably still getting ready for bed when he downed the repellent.'

'Poor fellow,' sighs Wick. 'It's hard to picture him loitering alone in the gloom, at the mercy of a horde of hungry blood suckers.'

'I don't picture him alone. I imagine he was with someone. It's interesting no one's mentioned being with Baumgarten after he left the dining room, especially since that person was the last to see him alive. It was much more likely to have been their idea to hazard a midge-mingle than his. I wonder how they persuaded him to join them, what they talked about, and why they're holding their tongues now.'

'How, if this shy and nameless stranger does exist, could they have anything to do with his death?'

'Don't know. Could be utterly irrelevant.'

As Ava and Wick continue to ruminate, the garden gate scrapes on its hinges and Fiona steps through.

'Have you seen him?' She sounds anxious.

They shake their heads.

Without another word, she makes a beeline for Alastair's laboratory.

'So much for giving him space,' sighs Ava. 'Tell me, what do *you* think about Baumgarten's bitten knees?'

'You present a neat hypothesis.' He puffs out a row of smoke rings and watches as they dissipate. 'I enjoyed hearing it, but it doesn't stack up. I left the dining room within minutes of

Baumgarten, and when I got to my room he was already next door. I heard him through the wall, knocking about, getting washed.'

'Are you *sure*?' Ava's thrown by his answer.

'Positive. Thanks to a quirk in The Hall's plumbing, whenever he turned on the taps in his sink, the water from mine reduced to a dribble. Same thing happened last night when I was mid sluice. I suppose he *could* have completed his ablutions and gone out later.'

'Fiona locked up. If he somehow slipped out, he'd have had to ring or knock at the front door to be let back in again. He'd have been seen and heard.' Ava falls silent as she grapples to reconfigure her timeline. If he left the table at eleven forty-five, went straight outside... back in again fifteen minutes later, just before lock-up... had a wash, lay down—'

'Another thing, doctor. If, one *does* suppose Baumgarten had an assignation – though I really don't see how you can know he did – surely his companion would've been bitten too.'

'True. But they may not have been as sensitive to the bites, or were wearing repellent. Though you make a fair point.' Ava smiles. 'I shall be on the lookout for surreptitious scratchers.'

'Have you run any of this past the police?'

'Tried to. Not interested.'

'Whatever the case,' Wick says with a sigh, as if drawing a line under the whole subject, 'Baumgarten ended up accidentally swigging Alastair's botanical potion and choking on his half-digested haggis. Nothing sinister. Just a mess.'

All of a sudden, a chorus of screeching erupts from every corner of the garden. Avian alarm calls, but for one blackbird the warnings come too late. Like a bolt from a crossbow, in an explosion of feathers, a sparrow hawk slams down on an unsuspecting male, nailing him to the ground. Crouching over its prey, it squeezes with its talons till the shrieking and flailing cease. Unconcerned by the proximity of Ava, Wick, or the blackbird's mate, the hawk coolly dines on its victim's pluck.

'Brutal,' mutters Wick, looking away.

'Food chain,' says Ava. She notes, however, that in its death throes the blackbird did in fact let go of his worm.

Ava's mind flies to another bird of prey – the osprey – and Baumgarten's curiously inaccurate account. 'Do you remember Baumgarten's party piece, Wick?'

Before he can formulate a reply, they're interrupted by another cry of distress. Loud, shrill, and this time, human. It's coming from Fiona, and she sounds desperate. 'Please! *Darling*! Don't!'

Ava and Wick spring to their feet, dash across the garden, and burst into Alastair's laboratory... where they find man and wife locked in a tussle. In his right hand, Alastair holds a glass vial high above his head. His long, fully extended left arm is keeping the diminutive Fiona at bay as she frantically tries to reach up and snatch the vial away. To Ava's horror, she sees the poison cabinet's door is ajar.

'Fee, let me do this.' Alastair sounds perfectly lucid and terrifyingly resigned. 'It's the simplest way.'

'Thank God you've come!' wails Fiona, swinging round to face Ava and Wick. 'Make him stop this madness! He's going to kill himself!'

'Alastair!' Ava commands. 'Don't you bloody well dare!' She lunges for his right arm. Too late. Alastair throws back his head and quaffs the vial's contents in one decisive draught.

'Cheers.' He wipes his mouth with the back of his hand.

For the longest minute Ava's ever experienced, all four persons present remain transfixed, eyes wide, mouths closed, waiting. She hears only Wick's panicked breathing and her own heartbeat thumping in her ears.

It's Alastair who finally breaks the spell. With a burp. 'Well, I can't say that tasted nice, but I *am* a hundred per cent still alive. Phew!'

'What the *devil* were you playing at?' Wick asks angrily.

'I wanted to satisfy myself that the repellent I gave Baumgarten was safe to drink. I had some of the same batch left over, and the quickest way to find out was to use myself as a guinea pig. I thought you knew that, Fee. And it turns out it's fine.' For all his bravado, Alastair looks decidedly shaky. 'As I say, I'm very relieved.'

'Or very lucky!' Ava's furious. 'You scared the pants off the bloody lot of us.'

'You mean you weren't trying to commit suicide?' whispers Fiona.

'Oh, Fee!' Alastair folds her into his arms. 'How could you ever think I was?'

'No reason, my love,' she says quietly. 'No reason at all.'

12

It Happens at The Hilton

George calls an emergency meeting; a sub-assembly, no Murdoch, no Muirheads. 'Honestly,' she sighs, holding court from her rattan throne in the orangery. 'How *disappointing*. Just when things were looking promising. Saturday night's food was really okay. Five out of ten for presentation, but full marks to our hosts for delivering such a sense of plucked-from-hedgerow-piled-on-plate. Unsophisticated yet *sophisticated*, if you know what I mean, and quite trendy. I paid a *lot* of money for something similar in Soho, and the fact Fanny Cradock wouldn't serve anything like it is, on the whole, positive, though a Black Forest gâteau for dessert would've been nice. And Mr Murdoch's gothic yarn, oh *my*! Bursting with that Scotch ambiance I was hoping to see. The crowd lapped it up. But then, *whoops*, someone dies in their bed, and Alastair's catapulted into... what did you call it, Wick? "A personal crisis"?'

'Please lower your voice,' requests Ava, flinching at the thought of Alastair or Fiona overhearing.

'I stand corrected,' continues George without adjusting her tone. 'A *secret* personal crisis. Whatever it was, I'm glad I missed it. If Alastair's nerves aren't up to this, he's in the wrong line of work. Hotel guests drop dead all the time. Global chains like Hilton expect to lose one a week. More, in a heat wave. People go on holiday, let their hair down, and have the same heart attack or aneurysm or fit of the heebie-jeebies they would've had at home, only sooner, because they've been overindulging in rich food and, in Mr Baumgarten's case, bucket loads of booze.'

'Still, it's an unwelcome shock,' hazards Wick.

'Obviously not an ideal situation when it comes to The Hall's customer-facing image. Foul timing, I grant you, but *not* foul play. It's a pity the doctor didn't sign off the death himself without inviting the police on scene. Police are never a good look, PR wise. Still, we are where we are. How *is* your godson today? Back in the saddle, or rocking in a corner with his head between his knees?'

'He's fine,' Ava says solidly. 'He cooked today's lunch. Oyster soup.'

'That's what it was? Tasted more of soil than sea.'

'He made it with oyster *mushrooms* rather than shellfish,' says Wick. 'Foraged them himself. And I agree with Ava. I believe Alastair's quite sound.'

'Well, I hope you're right, because in the long run, a nervy manager can be far more damaging to a business than the odd incidental death. Frankly, I recommend the Muirheads abandon this enterprise now.'

'Quit while they're ahead?'

'Hardly "ahead", Wick!' scoffs George. 'It'd be a case of cutting their losses. Alastair and Fiona need to sell up.'

'What, the whole place?' gasps Ava.

Before George can answer, Fiona bursts into the room. 'No *way*!' she cries. 'I can't believe you're chatting away about liquidating my husband's and my livelihood without inviting *us* to the discussion.'

George remains nonchalant. 'You and Alastair have a lot of land, Fiona.'

'Fifty thousand acres,' Fiona says defiantly, plonking a loaded tray onto a tabletop so firmly, hot tea slops out of the teapot's spout.

'As much as that?' George continues evenly. 'Lying around all wayward and windswept, not earning a penny. You've vetoed livestock farming. You've poo-pooed shoots *and* fishing. Given your husband's sensitive disposition, running any kind of hotel business is, in my view, also a no-go. Financially speaking, flogging a few hundred acres of Dorchan sprawl from around your margins is by far your best option.'

'Not one. Square. Inch!'

'If you'd take a look at my figures—'

'I said no! This is Alastair's heritage. We'll part with it over his dead body. Promise none of you will even *suggest* such a thing in his earshot!' Fiona knots her fingers together in a pleading gesture so tight, her knuckles turn white. 'He's beside himself as it is.'

'We promise,' say Ava and Wick.

George leans back in her seat, surveying Fiona through squinched up eyes. 'Very well. *I* shan't mention it to him either.'

'Thank you. That's all right then.' Fiona smooths down her woollen skirt and pushes the bridge of her huge glasses back onto the bridge of her afterthought-of-a-nose. 'Sorry for that outburst, but the integrity of the estate is paramount to this family. Enjoy the tea. Alastair's peppermint blend. I'll fetch some lavender and chickweed shortbread.'

'Wow!' George breathes as soon as she's left. '*That* was an eye-opener.'

'I'm sure her apology was genuine.'

'I'm not offended, Wick, I'm pleasantly surprised. Turns out one of the Muirheads has a backbone after all.' George stands up and starts to gather her papers.

'You're leaving us?' asks Ava.

'Leaving!' George snickers. 'Why would I do that?'

'Because you've hit too many "no-goes".'

'Oh, don't worry, Ava. I'm known for my tenacity. The Hall needs a rescue plan and it's still *my* call to come up with the goods... unless either of you has an idea you're not sharing?'

Silence.

'Thought not.' George snaps her attaché case shut. 'Now, I must concentrate on my spreadsheets.'

No sooner has she departed, Ava turns to Wick, keen to share her less-than-positive opinions. 'Talk about hard-nosed! I've met more empathic water buffalo—'

To her disappointment, however, he too rises. 'Forgive me, Ava.'

'Where are you going?'

'Um...' Caught on the spot, it's clear Wick would rather not answer her question, and Ava regrets asking it. Georgina Beckett is his friend. He invited her to Dorcha Hall. Stands to reason he doesn't want to listen to Ava griping behind the woman's back. More's the pity.

'Please. No excuses needed.'

'I've my own business to attend to, that's all. No doubt you have plans?'

'Someone should wait for the shortbread.'

'Then ciao it is.'

With that, he's gone, leaving Ava smarting. She feels reprimanded, like a naughty child who's been caught gossiping in class. Blasted man.

13
Do You Mind if I Ask?

Ava pours herself a cup of pee-coloured tea and, as she sips, she mulls. She really wanted to talk to Wick. Never mind bitching about George – cathartic as that would be – as co-godparents they've yet to discuss Alastair's antics in the potting shed, which have left her decidedly rattled. Closing her eyes, she can see him now, potion in hand, his frantic wife clawing at his breast. What an incredibly *stupid* experiment. *'Guinea pig', my backside!* Alastair clearly has no notion of how many laboratory rodents lose their lives in the name of research; though Ava must admit, he had a hypothesis *and* the balls to test it out, albeit in a reckless way. 'Or,' she ponders further, 'was it more serious than reckless? Was it *unhinged*?' When it comes to Alastair's disintegrating judgement, perhaps his wife has a point. Still, as a scientist, Ava herself likes to rule a theory out just as much as she likes to be proved right. If she can. And, if she can't? Goodness! Ava's not sure *how* she'd feel. As per hurricanes in Hertford, Hereford, and Hampshire, that's hardly ever happened.

She pictures Wick as he was yesterday in the kitchen garden, blowing smoke rings, flicking his cigar into his preposterous portable ashtray. He's rattled her too, or at least his flippant summation of Baumgarten's death has. 'Nothing sinister, just a mess.' Damn him! She's *sure* there's something amiss. Wick may not believe Baumgarten had a late-night rendezvous, but she cannot understand why the man would've faced that onslaught of midges unless it was to meet someone. If this character is connected to Dorcha Hall, as a guest or staff member, why haven't they come forward? 'By the way everyone, after dinner, I chatted with Mr B outside. Can't *believe* a blink of an eye later he kicked the bucket!' or words to that effect. And if the person isn't connected to the hotel, who the hell are they? What did they want with Baumgarten? Wick might be able to brush aside such awkward questions, but to Ava, that's anathema.

Ava replays the conversation she had with Baumgarten, when they met on the track beyond Drumapple. Was that really only three days ago? He revealed little about himself. They'd mostly talked about birds... his book... the joy of exploring new habitats... the expense of travel; something about tightening his belt after his 'time in Scotland'. Then it comes to her. He actually said, 'time *again* in Scotland', like he'd been here before, perhaps to Loch Dorcha itself. He was certainly familiar with the lie of the land. She encountered him in an out-of-the-way spot, yet he wasn't lost. She wonders how he chose The Hall. It's barely been in business, and Ava highly doubts Alastair and Fiona have done much advertising.

At this moment, as if on cue, both Fiona and Alastair show up in the orangery. Alastair's bearing a plate of the promised shortbread; Fiona, a rueful expression. 'Oh dear, where's everyone gone?'

'Needed elsewhere. Why don't you two join me? I'm sure The Hall can look after itself for five minutes, and it's a shame to waste the nice pot of tea you made, Fiona.'

'Maggie made it.' As Fiona perches on the edge of George's vacated seat, Ava's struck by the dissimilar ways in which the two women hold themselves. No fiery sparks spitting from this one; more a miasma of weariness, like she's sick of lugging around some bulky unseen load. Or perhaps Fiona's given in and popped some NarcoVal after all.

'Did Georgina Beckett's meeting go as she hoped?' asks Alastair, drawing a chair next to his wife's.

'Absolutely. Cooking up new ideas left right and centre.'

'Fee and I couldn't be more grateful to her, could we?'

Fiona manages one of the thinnest-lipped smiles Ava's ever seen.

'While I have you both here,' Ava ventures, 'I've a question.'

'Fire away!' says Alastair.

'How well did you know Herr Baumgarten?'

Alastair swallows audibly. Fiona's body stiffens; a flash of musculoskeletal tension that betrays apprehension. Neither reaction surprises Ava. When it comes to discussing a dead guest, Ava expected the pair to shut down like startled goats.

'Not well,' is Fiona's answer.

'Not well at all,' agrees Alastair. 'Why?'

'Oh, I'm probably just picking for nits, but something doesn't sit right about his death. If I could understand who he was, then perhaps it'd all make better sense. For example, Alastair, you and Baumgarten must've discussed his midge allergy, since you mixed a repellent for him.'

'It was the one real chat we had, and even then it was only about ingredients, quantities he'd need: literally, "clinical". He was touchingly grateful... offered to pay me for the stuff, but I refused.'

'You never told me that,' says Fiona.

'Seemed wrong to take his money. I think he was quite hard up,' says Alastair, 'and we know what that feels like.'

'Baumgarten? Hard up? Surely not, darling! Ava, may I refresh your cup?'

'No, thank you.'

'Remember what happened with *Knockinch Motors*, Fee?' Alastair continues.

'That was a silly mix-up.' Fiona turns to Ava. 'Mr Baumgarten arrived here in a hire car. Not long after, two men from the rental company came and took it away, because the cheque he gave them bounced. But Mr Baumgarten explained the whole thing to us. It was some nuisance or other to do with having a foreign bank account and the Deutsche Mark going down, or the pound going up... Nothing to worry about. When Alastair asked him to settle his bar tab, he paid in full, in cash, no problem at all. Do try the shortbread.'

Alastair looks forlorn. 'The best opportunity Baumgarten and I had to get to know each other was a few days ago, when I ferried him to and from Inverness – seeing as he was without his own transport – along with Miss Levi, but Lauri hogged the small talk. She sat up front, next to me. He was alone in the back. Barely exchanged a sentence.'

'What was the purpose of the trip?'

'Lauri wanted to go shopping, and Baumgarten... I'm not sure. When we got to town, I parked at the station, and we all walked to the high street. We agreed a time to gather for the drive back, then she went one way, he the other. I went to the ironmonger's, and I *think* Baumgarten headed off in the direction of the chemist's.'

'Was he unwell?'

'Seemed fit as a flea... till he died.' Alastair looks to Fiona.

'For all we know,' Fiona says briskly, 'he'd run out of toothpaste, or shaving cream, or corn plasters... which would make sense, given all the walking he did.'

'In short,' sighs Alastair, 'he never volunteered why he might need a pharmacist, and I didn't ask.'

'Quite right too, darling.' Fiona looks pointedly at Ava. 'None of *anyone's* business. Why are you asking these things, Ava?'

Sensing Alastair's growing despondency, Ava directs her next questions at Fiona. 'Did Herr Baumgarten ever mention why he chose the Dorcha estate for his holiday?'

'No. He wrote asking if we had vacancies for mid-July. He'd heard we'd recently opened as a hotel.'

'Heard how?'

'Didn't say.'

'And, when he arrived, twelve days ago...?'

'Two weeks,' corrects Fiona. 'Would've checked out today.'

'That was the first time you set eyes on him?'

'Yup.' Fiona's answers are becoming more succinct by the second.

'Actually,' Alastair says slowly, 'he did say something about walking around Loch Dorcha before. I commented how funny it was that we'd never bumped into each other. I remember his reply, too: "And you British say it's a small world!" Do *you* remember, Fee?'

'I'm afraid not.'

'Maybe he had local friends, then. People he met on previous trips?'

Alastair shrugs. 'Couldn't tell you.'

'And neither of you spoke to him after Saturday's meal?'

'Unfortunately, no,' says Alastair. 'I wish he and I *had* talked more. I should have seen him upstairs to bed…'

'That's the thing with running this place,' nips Fiona. 'Too busy keeping the show on the road to spend time gossiping.'

'Perhaps Baumgarten chatted with his fellow guests, shared things with them?'

'You know he was an early riser,' says Alastair. 'Rarely sat down to breakfast. Tended to retire early too, so his daily routine didn't usually overlap with Miss Levi's. Nor would their interests have overlapped, I'd imagine. They didn't talk on that trip to Inverness, anyway. He and Georgina Beckett can hardly have seen each other, apart from… you know… at his last supper. He died less than twenty-four hours after she got here.'

'True.'

'Same goes for Sinclair Stewart,' continues Alastair. 'Not sure about Murdoch. Ever since the Addingtons arrived, Baumgarten ate his evening meals with them. Maybe they shot the breeze together—'

'Or maybe they didn't,' Fiona cuts in brusquely.

'I'll ask them,' says Ava.

'I'd rather you didn't go bothering people, especially not guests. Better for all concerned to let matters lie.'

'Really, Ava,' Alastair adds wearily as Fiona takes his hand. 'I couldn't agree with Fee more.'

14

Anyone for Croquet?

When it comes to 'bothering people', Ava gets where her young hosts are coming from. The death of a guest, under any circumstances, *is* bad for business. In their eyes, drawing attention to it, especially since the police moved on so quickly, is stirring up unnecessary interest. More importantly, there are Fiona's wifely concerns about Alastair's state of mind, and it's clear he's taken Baumgarten's death personally. Ava doesn't want to make either of them feel worse than they already do. Any plans to curb her curiosity are, however, short lived. Minutes after parting company with the Muirheads, she encounters Maggie in the library, and like a garter snake caught in a barrel of frogs, she senses her natural instincts kicking in.

The girl's standing tiptoe on a dining chair, cleaning the bookshelves. With each flick of her cloth she rouses another cloud of dust motes, sending them to dance in the shafts of sunlight that breach the gaps in the curtains. She's singing to herself; a wistful reprise of Lauri Levi's showstopper. 'Good looking, so refined... Wouldn't you like to know what's going on in my mind.' Ava's entrance makes her jump.

'Sorry to disturb, Maggie.'

'Och, dinnae be mindin' *me*,' she says, hopping down from her perch. 'Dustin' is my worst job. Well, *nearly* my worst, seein' as how I really dinnae like hooverin', scrubbin' steps, nor emptyin' bins. But who would, eh? Got te be done though. Like the lavvies. The sights I've seen! Dinnae be askin' me what I mean, Doctor D,' she chortles, 'otherwise I'll have te tell ye!' She takes down Alastair's thesis and gives it a cursory rub with her grubby rag. 'Still, I love workin' here. My favourite thing is servin' at tables. Isn't Miss Levi dreamy? A proper star. Such lovely clothes. *Ever* such a bonnie singin' voice. I'd like te be a star someday. When I told *her* that, d'ye know what she said te me? She said, "Ye never know what can happen in this life, *baby*." Wasnae that just pure dead *barry*!'

'Absolutely.'

'She's beautiful inside and outside, even wi'out makeup. I told her that too. And Mrs Muirhead. "Mrs Muirhead," I said, "ye'd look just like her if ye made a wee bit o' effort." Didnae go down so well, though!' Maggie chuckles. 'Fee says all personal remarks are bad manners, but that cannae be true if they're compliments. Miss Levi likes te be complimented, I like te be complimented, and I'll bet ye'd like te be complimented on *yer* looks one day...'

'You enjoy the visitors?'

'They're the reasons I come te work.'

'And Herr Baumgarten—'

'What about him?' The girl tucks her cloth into her belt.

'Well, the fact he's *dead*, Maggie, has prompted me to ask a few questions.'

'Och, *that*!' Maggie flushes. 'Dearie dear, such a shame.'

'Did you get to know him while he was staying at The Hall?'

There's a pause; very short, but detectable, nonetheless. 'I didnae, doctor,' she says firmly, 'and I'd be lyin' if I said otherwise. But this is somethin' I shouldnae be speakin' about. Angus Murdoch thinks I talk too much as it is. So does Ollach. "Least said, soonest mended" is what she cautions, *and* I gave my word te Fee and Ali. *Mrs* Muirhead calls Mr B's passing "a fiasco". "Rakin' over that *wretched* fiasco won't help anyone, least of all my husband" is what she said te me yesterday after I had a wee chat wi' Mrs Addington. And Mr Addington. And Miss Levi.' Maggie sighs. 'Mind, Fee's right enough. Ali... Mr Muirhead... *has* been frettin' himself good and proper. Ever since the accident he's been rollin' on three wheels. Still, he's always been grand te me... though in *my* opinion...' In an uncharacteristic moment of self-restraint, Maggie stops mid flow.

'You've something to add?'

'In my opinion,' continues Maggie, 'it's awful sad Mr Baumgarten's gone. At the end o' the day, that's all needs sayin' about *anybiddy* who's passed on and' – she adds an afterthought – 'he did appreciate Big Sis's bakin'. She's grateful fer that.'

Now Ollach's tears when Baumgarten was carted away make sense. It seems doubly sad they're the only ones anybody seems to have shed for him.

A bell rings. Maggie shoves the book back on its shelf. 'Fee's wantin' me in reception, doctor, so I'll say cheerie-bye just now.'

'Cheerie-bye, Maggie.'

Bernard and Barbara Addington are ensconced in the sitting room; he, poring over OS maps; she, working on a jigsaw. The latter is a scene of a Scottish loch, which seems either a very apt or very ironic choice since she could simply look out of the window and see much the same view. After some probing, it's clear that while both of them spent time in Baumgarten's company, *they* did all the talking. They hadn't even gleaned the fact he was a birdwatcher. Barbara did pick up on his midge allergy; a crumb of personal information dropped by Baumgarten which, by her own account, she'd swiftly crushed with a loaf-sized list of her own. 'I can't look at a crab without breaking out in hives! As for strawberries, you're safe as long as they're cooked. And blue cheeses give me a run for my money.'

'I found him insufferably dull,' says Bernard. 'Nothing else to add.'

'On Saturday night, you didn't happen to bump into him after he left the table? In the gardens, perhaps?' asks Ava, wrangling the conversation back on track.

'Gracious, no. We didn't venture out after supper. To be frank,' she leans in conspiratorially, 'towards the end of the party Mr Baumgarten rather let himself down. Too tipsy to be worth talking to. He was in the dining room when I went up with the boys. Bernard was two minutes behind us, weren't you, Bernard?'

'Correct. What is the purpose of your question, doctor?'

Before Ava can answer, a voice pipes up from the corner of the room. 'In case you're interested, honey,' drawls Lauri Levi, '*I* scarcely looked at the man.' Swathed in a slithery nylon kaftan, chewing on a lump of pink gum, she's reclined upon a moth-eaten chaise longue, painting her nails. 'And,' she continues without looking up from her task, 'what I *did* see hardly popped any corks, if you catch *mah* drift.' She blows on her fingertips then holds her hands out at arms' length to admire her work. 'Never got acquainted. Too late now.'

The Addington boys are outside on the large unkempt lawn that stretches between Dorcha Hall's west face and the loch's shore, playing croquet; or, rather, playing with a croquet set.

'Watch this!' calls Martin as she approaches. Standing, legs astride, he clasps a wooden mallet by its handle and proceeds to swing it round his head one... two... three times. On the fourth swing, with a primal roar, he pivots on his toes and releases his grip, sending the mallet flying over his shoulder to land some distance away in the long grass. *Thwump*. Carl attempts a suitably gladiatorial cry of his own; an octave higher than his older brother's since his voice is yet to break. Martin then sets off towards the site of impact, walking in a straight line, solemnly counting his paces.

'Impressive!' Ava claps. 'Your very own Highland fling. Mr Murdoch's been giving you lessons in hammer throwing!'

'Couldn't find him, so we worked it out ourselves,' Carl says proudly, picking the scab off a midge bite. 'When we're done with this, we're going to toss the caber.'

'Good for you.' Necessity may be the master of invention, but Boredom is its mistress.

'Twenty yards,' Martin says proudly, returning with the mallet. 'Would you like a turn, Dr Dickens?'

'In a moment. If you wouldn't mind, I was hoping to pick your brains about my friend Herr Baumgarten.'

'The man who died?' asks Carl. 'We didn't think he had any friends. He was *so* dull, always going on about birds.'

'Birds can be fascinating, if you make an effort to learn about them.'

'Is that why you're asking about *him*?' asks Martin. 'In case he turns out to be interesting after all.'

'Very perceptive!' Ava laughs. '*Apart* from the birdwatching, did he give any other reasons why he chose Loch Dorcha for his visit?'

'He said he liked coming here for the weather, which is nicer than the last place he went.' Carl raises his mallet in preparation for his throw.

'Where was that?'

Martin shrugs. 'Somewhere really cold. He said when you stay there in winter you *have* to wear gloves, otherwise your fingers turn black and drop off.'

'Did you see him talking to other guests, or people who live here?'

'He definitely spoke to Mum and Dad,' says Carl.

'Though he didn't have much to say to the "American singer". That's what Mum calls her,' says Martin, giving Carl a nudge, 'but we think someone told him it wasn't allowed!'

Carl snorts.

'Private joke?' asks Ava.

The boys exchange looks. 'We're banned from talking to Miss Levi as Mum doesn't approve of that much makeup,' says Martin.

'Or bosom!' blurts Carl. Unable to contain themselves, the brothers give in to a fit of salacious sniggering.

'Dad's supposed to be banned too,' says Martin, 'but he says he can't completely ignore her as that would be rude, so he still asks her to "pass the salt", that sort of thing.'

'He likes a lot of salt on his food,' chimes Carl, with the most angelic of grins.

'So, other than an occasional word with you two, and some conversations with your parents, Mr Baumgarten wasn't chatty with anyone else?'

'Well...' reflects Carl, 'he and the professor, the one who likes reading the writing on the bottom of vases...'

'Wickremesinghe,' Ava clarifies, with a smile. The boy's comment is both fair and well observed.

'... they didn't seem to get along. Mr Baumgarten called him a "Schweinhund".'

'And we know what that means,' peals Carl. '"Pig dog", which is an insult, isn't it?'

Ava nods. 'I wonder what made him say that.'

'Dunno. When our family came down for the big dinner, that pair were already in the dining room. Just them. Mr Baumgarten had a fancy stick in his hand, and he must've told a joke or something, because the professor suddenly laughed, and that's when Mr Baumgarten swore. He also said "Leck mich im Arsch". They stopped talking after that. Do *you* understand German, Dr Dickens?'

'Enough to get by,' she mutters. She's pretty sure the same would be true for oh-so-erudite Wick.

'After that, the lady with the red hair and a boy's name...'

'George Beckett.'

'She showed up, and the professor went and stood with her instead.'

'That's all you remember?'

The boys pick at a few more scabs and make a couple of preparatory mallet swings while they have a think. 'Yup.'

'Well thank you both for your time,' says Ava. 'I must let you finish your games.'

'Dr Dickens,' Martin says quickly. 'Before you go, I want to ask something. Carl and I have been talking about the legend of the naked woman who ended up in the loch. We'd like to see the place where she got murdered, but Mr Murdoch's never around to show us. Do *you* know how to get there?'

'I do know the way to Raon Murt, yes, but I'm afraid I can't take you. Not now, anyway. Try asking your dad.'

'Already did. No dice.'

'All right, then. Tomorrow any good?'

'Brilliant!' Martin's clearly pleased. Carl's *so* excited by the prospect he jumps up and down on the spot.

'Meantime, if anything "interesting" about Herr Baumgarten, or anyone else, does occur to either of you, will you tell me?'

With a flurry of vigorous nodding and boy-scout salutes, each gives his zealous assurance that she can 'count on me'. Although Ava declines to spit and shake on it, she does take her turn at throwing – thirty yards clear – before she gives her apologies and moves on.

15
Great Minds Think Alike

Ava paces the kitchen garden counting slug species – she identifies twelve – before settling on the bench. She rolls a fat cigarette which she smokes in a state of grouchy contemplation. What a cagey sod Wick is! He and Baumgarten had a barney, mere hours before the man died, yet Wick's never breathed a word about it. Turns out he's not such a tolerable hominid after all. As for the rest of her fact-finding mission, little of what she learned seems significant. Sounds like Baumgarten may have been short of money, but Fiona thinks otherwise, and he may have gone to the chemist's in Inverness, though he hadn't complained of being ill. It's interesting Baumgarten visited this area before, but where he stayed is unknown. Strange, and sad, to think, that whenever it was, it's likely Duncan and Sheila were then still alive. Apparently, his previous holiday, which wasn't here, was 'somewhere cold'; likely a reference to his bird-spotting hols in Sweden. No one claims to know him in any personal capacity. No one admits to meeting him outside.

What else? Fiona and Alastair don't want Baumgarten's death 'raked over' – surprise, surprise! – and Baumgarten liked to eat Ollach's homemade cake. This last gem of intelligence she does believe, but none of her findings amounts to what the police would call a 'lead'. Of course, Ava's groundwork is incomplete. She still needs to speak to the rest of the Saturday night diners, especially the disingenuous professor! For now, though, these loose-end characters will have to wait. Wick hasn't reappeared since this morning when he skulked off to 'attend to his business'.

Sinclair Stewart has returned to Beinn Beithe. Murdoch keeps disappearing. And George? *She's* no doubt kicking around somewhere with her clipboard and pen, but Ava's had enough of her for one day.

Stuff her! she thinks, marching doggedly back to The Hall. When it comes to tenacity, Georgina Beckett does *not* have a monopoly. Ava tugs on a pair of washing-up gloves requisitioned from Maggie's understairs cupboard, pockets her hand lens, and heads for Baumgarten's room. She's not sure what she expects to unearth. Ideally, a key piece of evidence to establish his death was suspicious, or some hint as to why he went out after dinner, but any titbit she could wave under Sergeant Pratt's nose to make him sit up and take notice would be good. Nearing her destination, a thought strikes her. What if the room's locked? She can't ask Alastair or Fiona for a key. Then again, she could just help herself from the hooks in reception. Turns out, though, she won't have to. The door's ajar and somebody's already in there. Back turned, arms raised, they're holding something... a picture... up to the light.

'Ava!' Wick's so startled he nearly drops the little watercolour he has in his hands. 'Christ, you made me jump!' He too is wearing gloves. His aren't yellow rubber, but crocodile skin, by the look of it cut from the belly of an adult *Crocodylus*; the species being *niloticus*, rather than *porosus*, given the large rectangular scales and lack of discernible integumentary sensory stomata. Costly items, especially for the crocodile.

'What *are* you doing?' asks Ava, guessing at least half the answer. Judging by the rifled-through drawers, open bedside cabinet and general disarray, Wick's mounted a hunt of his own. From such a neat man, she'd have expected a more systematic approach.

'Our conversation yesterday got me thinking,' he says lightly. 'I pride myself on attention to detail, yet, in retrospect, I realise I glossed over your concerns about a man's death with less than due regard. I remain doubtful anything amiss happened in this room, but I fancied a quick "delve", just to set my mind at rest. Yourself?'

'Likewise.' Ava notes how his thumbs rub at the painting's gilded edges. 'Looking for anything in particular?'

'Nope. Came here on a whim. Then I got side-tracked by this. It's a view of Dorcha Hall. Exquisite colours. Such luminosity. Lovely condition. Can't make out the signature, though. Might I trouble you for your magnifier?'

'Didn't bring it.' Ava's in no mood to share.

'Pity.' He carefully repositions the picture on its hook above the fireplace. 'A charming piece.'

'Bit washed out for my taste.'

'I've always been fond of it. I get why Alastair and Fiona moved it into here. The light's better than it was in Sheila's bedroom.'

'If you say so.'

Wick clears his throat. 'Now we're both here,' he says, prising his attention away from the landscape, 'shall we search together?'

'May as well,' Ava says with a sniff.

They move about the room, picking things up, putting them down again, trying not to step on one another's toes. Apparently happy in his work, Wick hums to himself, which Ava finds incredibly peeving. Given his supposed detachment regarding Baumgarten's demise, and that hushed-up tiff, him being here at all has got her back up. She asks herself what's worse: the fact he took it upon himself to have a 'delve' without telling her, or the fact he started his delving before she started hers?

She examines Baumgarten's toiletries, arranged on the shelf above his sink. No unopened medications, pills, or ointments; stuff he might have got from a pharmacy in the last few days. There's a crumpled tube of toothpaste, a flannel, a razor... all well-used.

Wick takes a can of shaving foam and squirts a dollop of white lather onto the back of his hand. 'Sandalwood,' he grimaces, taking a whiff. 'Smells cheap.'

'It's supposed to smell like human steroid hormones. Appealing to women and, some say, healthy cobras and dying dogs. Draws in all sorts once they catch the scent.'

'The cons would seem to outweigh any pros. I'll stick to

cologne.' Wick returns the can to the shelf and resumes humming.

Having rummaged through Baumgarten's clothing, Ava picks over the contents of his wastepaper basket. There's not much in it. A couple of sweet wrappers... some used paper hankies. She tips it upside down. With a metallic *ping*, something small and silver – the screw-top of a miniature whisky bottle – drops to the floor and trundles under the bed. It's when she kneels down to retrieve it that she notices a suitcase tucked away at the back. She drags it out to get a better look.

Small, leather, and much weathered, it's covered in a blizzard of luggage stickers. Predictably, Baumgarten favoured those depicting national birds. An emu for Australia, a red-billed streamer tail for Jamaica, a blackbird for Sweden. Some she recognises. Others are worn and faded, and more difficult to decipher. Nevertheless, all are testament to the global adventures of the case's owner.

'He certainly got about,' says Wick. 'Best not open it though. Probably private.'

'Really!' exclaims Ava. 'Sixty seconds ago, you were sniffing his sundries... passing judgement,' she adds under her breath. In two swift movements, she pops the catches and flips back the lid, to reveal... absolutely nothing. 'Bugger!'

'Must've unpacked everything.'

Ava sits down on the stripped bed, hands tucked under her buttocks, legs swinging. The brass bedframe is so high, her feet don't reach the floor. Wick sits next to her, a bit too close for comfort. Ava shuffles awkwardly.

'I share your unease, you know,' he says. 'It's a peculiar sensation, finding oneself in the exact spot where a man took his last breath.'

For a minute or two, each remains quiet. Wick's gaze softly re-alights on the painting. Ava's thoughts ricochet freely this way and that before landing heavily upon his 'old pal' George. When Wick speaks again, it's as if he's reading her mind. 'It's very blatant, your dislike of Georgina Beckett.'

'Is it? Well, she dislikes me. In some ways, I respect her for that. In the natural world, mutual antipathy maintains order. There are predators and there's prey. If people didn't view each other with a peck of instinctive chariness, there'd be carnage. Murdoch doesn't like Jack Hooley or Lauri. Fiona doesn't like Lauri either, and I imagine there's no love lost between Peigi and Fiona. I could go on.'

Wick chuckles. 'Where do I stand in your pecking order?'

'Depends on the wind direction.'

'Ouch!' Wick clasps his chest as if struck by an imaginary bullet.

'What do you expect? You were dismissive about Baumgarten's death, then had the hypocrisy to check out his room without even inviting me to join you, which was rude. If we're supposed to be proxy co-parents, I've grounds for a proxy divorce. On top of which…' Ava wavers.

'On top of what?'

'Given what an undiplomatic pain in the backside Georgina Beckett can be, I've concerns about the *deficit* in antipathy that exists between you and her. It's one thing to wheel her in and listen to what she has to say about the Muirheads' business, quite another to stand back while she rides rough shod over Alastair and Fiona's values… everything they're trying to do to help themselves. Your silence speaks volumes. It's *obvious* you were involved with each other in the past, the only thing I'm not sure of is whether that's water under the bridge.'

'Ha!' cries Wick. 'You truly are the most direct person I've ever met.'

'Chuffed to hear it.'

Wick laughs. 'What gave us away? In fact,' he says, tapping his chin, 'let me guess. A specimen of the lesser loose-tongued butterfly dished the dirt while you were measuring its wings.'

'Not quite. It was the cheese-shaped paperweight. George's "treasured" souvenir from her lovely weekend in Cheddar. You horripilated at the very mention of it.'

Wick looks blank.

'The hairs on your forearms stood on end. A reflex dating

back to when our more hirsute ancestors would puff up, making themselves look bigger to scare off would-be attackers. If you ever saw a startled porcupine, Wick, you'd know how it works. Anyway, humans may be as good as bald these days, but horripilation is still a helpful pointer to someone's emotional state. Passion, a sense of peril… feelings of acute embarrassment… can be equally triggering. When George brought up Cheddar, I'd say you were a man grappling with all three.'

'Cheese has always excited me.'

'Ha, ha, *ha*!'

'Okay, okay,' Wick says with a smile, holding up his hands in surrender, 'you're right! George and I did have a fling. It was a while ago and fun while it lasted, which wasn't very long. I moved on, she has too, but I do still admire her, Ava. George is good at what she does and it's generous of her to devote her energies to The Hall's future. Don't dismiss her skills when they're so sorely needed.'

'Fair enough,' concedes Ava, though she thinks Wick's a mug to believe George is done with him, and George is easily smart enough to know he's not quite done with her. 'I'll try harder to be nice. Do you know how many quills there are on a porcupine's back?'

'No.'

'Guess.'

'I don't feel like playing.'

'Thirty thousand, each with its very own arrector pili muscle, just in case. That's over a hundred per square inch. Not a single one on their ventral surface, though.'

'The epitome of a soft underbelly, then.'

'True. May I ask you something else?'

'You're considering holding back?'

'Did you have an affair with Sheila?'

The room temperature plummets ten degrees. Wick's gloves creak. 'Why would you think that?'

'The very first conversation we had, Wick, you said you were in love with her, you go dewy eyed at the mention of her name, and just now, thanks to the way you were handling that watercolour, the one that used to hang in Sheila's *bedroom*, I'd say I've got circumstantial evidence too.'

'Sheila and I were never lovers, Ava,' Wick says heavily. 'Our relationship went far deeper than sex. We were *friends*. It's no secret I adored her, but her heart belonged to another man. On that she was immoveable. She and I did spend many hours together, though... yes, in her bedroom... talking... sharing things I doubt we shared with another living soul. And I made promises to her which, by being here, I'm endeavouring to keep.' Suddenly Wick doesn't seem suave and self-assured. He looks caved in, and the sigh he heaves is so desolate, Ava shudders. 'You can't help who you fall in love with, can you?'

'No.'

'Still, "it is what it is", as the saying goes.' He straightens up. 'Tell me, has this exercise proved useful for you?'

'Not really.'

'I meant searching Baumgarten's things.'

'So did I.' Ava scans the room, with its fraying upholstery, outdated furniture, and Baumgarten's few belongings laid bare. She can't shake the feeling there's *something* to be found here, maybe even staring her in the face, only she's just not seeing it.

'What were you hoping to discover, Ava, when you came searching?'

'Oh, I don't know. Nothing as sensational as a smoking gun—'

'Since Baumgarten wasn't shot!'

'I suppose I want a morsel pithy enough to nudge the police into action, like you'd get in a crime novel. Initials scratched into the wall with his fingernails as he took his dying breath, a suspicious note slipped under his door: "Meet me in the garden", or "Tonight you will die!"'

'Frankly, I'm glad there's nothing incriminating here, Ava. Makes it even easier to take what happened in this room at face value, and for Alastair, Fiona, and everyone else to move on. Tell me,' he continues robustly in a clear attempt to change the subject, 'how's the rest of your afternoon been?'

'I went round asking people if they knew Baumgarten, or had got to know him during their stay, but no one's owning up to anything. How about you?'

'Well, I went to my room, then I—'

'No. I mean did *you* ever speak with him?' Ava takes care to watch how Wick reacts. There's a microsecond's hesitation, and another nanosqueak of tanned reptile hide before he gives his very dissatisfactory reply.

'Not beyond passing pleasantries.'

'Really? Perhaps you'd like time to consider your answer, because I've heard that you two had a less-than-friendly chat on the very evening he died.'

'I'd forgotten.'

'Well, that makes you a Schweinhund with a short memory!'

A flash of irritation whips across Wick's face. 'Ava, if you already knew he and I spoke, why dance around with facile questions?'

'I wanted to see if you'd confess without having to be asked.'

'*Confess*! What kind of a word is that?'

'Apt. It describes what someone does when they come clean about something they've been trying to hide. Why be underhand, Wick? Why not confide in me earlier?'

'Because I saw no need and, frankly, what passed between me and Baumgarten doesn't show him in the best of lights. However, for the sake of transparency, I now acknowledge he and I did have one, short, uncomfortable interaction. I made an admiring remark about his walking stick. His reaction was not what I expected. Rather than accept the compliment for what it was – a polite aside before we sat down to dinner – he offered to sell it to me, for no less than a hundred pounds! I thought he was joking. I mean, it had an attractive carved handle... bone rather than ivory... a nice-enough blackthorn shank... but it wasn't worth a quarter of that amount. Besides which, do I look like some shifty dealer on the watch for a quick steal?' Wick gives each of his crisp white cuffs a reassuring tug.

'Hmm,' mutters Ava. 'I see.' This account does ring true.

Baumgarten failed to pay for his hire car... he himself told Ava that he needed to 'tighten his belt'. Wick's words add another layer of colour to the picture of a man on his uppers. 'What happened next?'

'I laughed it off, said I wasn't interested, but instead of letting it drop, he simply knocked a fiver off the price. On he went till it became so excruciating, I walked away. He threw a few ripe words after me. Baumgarten was neither gentlemanly nor dignified. Now he's dead, though, I chose not to tarnish your good opinion of him, so bringing this up seemed unmerited. And that's the truth. Go ahead and check my arm hairs!' He makes a move to unfasten his cufflinks.

'No need,' says Ava. 'I've decided to believe you.'

'Thank you.' Wick says scratchily.

'It's a shame the only time you and Baumgarten spoke was soured. If he had his time again, I reckon you two would've hit it off, you so well read, him being an author.'

'Author?'

'He published a book of birding anecdotes; I imagine along the lines of his fanciful story about that hunting osprey. I've got the title somewhere. Just a sec.' She retrieves Baumgarten's scrap of paper from a pocket and hands it to Wick. 'It's in German.'

Wick unfurls it, glances at it, and throws a puzzled look at Ava before reading out loud: 'Things have changed. You cannot stay here. Okay.'

'Very funny!' Ava says sourly.

'See for yourself!'

Ava snatches it from him. Just as she remembered, there's the book title, but then she turns it over to see two more lines of writing on the flipside. She whips out her hand lens. 'Would you look at that! Those big bold, letters are Baumgarten's; he wrote in capitals, with a pencil. But these spidery words are much fainter, and they're in cursive script. Somebody else penned them.'

'Interesting. Lucky you found your magnifier! I take it you didn't notice this before.'

'No,' breathes Ava, 'I bloody well didn't! When Baumgarten

jotted down the title, he tore this slip from a larger piece of paper he had on him at the time. I just stuffed it in my pocket without another thought. I could *kick* myself! Searching high and low, and all the *buggering* while I had this. A message to Baumgarten, warning him to leave The Hall!'

'You read that as a warning?'

'From his killer, yes, which Baumgarten ignored, and *that* was his undoing. What other way could one interpret it?'

There's a pause. 'I don't know, Ava, but it lacks the "or else" element I'd expect to see in a traditional poison-pen letter. Besides which, why would anyone want to hurt Baumgarten? Where's the *gain*? He seemed so run of the mill.'

'Give me strength, Wick! You were open-minded enough to poke around looking for clues. Now we've found one, you're not prepared to see it for what it is!'

'I'm just not convinced—'

'You sound like Pratt.'

'That's an insult, I take it?'

'It is.'

'What I'm struggling with is Baumgarten's choice of makeshift note pad. If he was carrying around a menacing letter from some mortal enemy, why in heaven's name would he pass on any part of it to anybody else?'

'Because he forgot what it was,' is the *absurd* answer that flies out of Ava's mouth before she has time to clip its wings.

Wick chuckles. '*I* think, chances are, your fragment came from something perfectly mundane. Let's focus on finding the rest of it, then we can get some context before leaping to conclusions.'

'Ah. Well. We *do* have a teensy problem there. "The rest of it" has either dissolved into pulp, been swept out to The Minch, or passed through the gizzard of a gannet – the least environmentally damaging of these scenarios being the first.'

'You're saying it's lost?'

'I am.'

'So you'll hand over that detached scrap, just as it is, to the police?'

'Too right!' Ava says defiantly. 'Because it's a "detached" threat from a murderer-in-waiting, and the police are lucky *I* found it! I'll phone the station tonight. Meantime, I think we should keep this between ourselves.'

Lauri Levi reels into the room so abruptly, both Ava and Wick jerk to attention. 'Oh *my*!' she crows, hand over her open mouth in mock surprise. 'Catch a load of you fellas, getting cosy and acquainted!'

'Hardly,' blusters Ava.

'Miss Levi is joking.' Wick laughs.

'If you say so, honey.' Lauri smirks. 'The walls of this joint ain't as thick as they look, and neither am I. It sure sounded like someone was havin' a good time. *Jeez*, it's a tip in here!' She whistles. 'Missy Maggie needs to up her game.'

'Apologies if we disturbed you. As you can see,' says Ava, kicking the suitcase shut, 'we've been packing up Herr Baumgarten's things... to send on to... er... Germany.' She hastily rights the upturned wastepaper basket and drops into it the bottle cap, sweet wrappers, and tissues. Wick nervously realigns the toiletries. He, like her, clearly doubts Lauri is buying a word of what Ava's saying. Ava sure as hell wouldn't if the shoe was on the other goddam foot.

Lauri, however, seems uninterested in making further mischief. 'You can keep your shirts on, sunshines! It ain't nothin' to me what other folks get up to in their spare time. If you don't rattle my cage, I ain't gonna break *mah* nails rattlin' yours. Fact is, I'm on the lookout myself. Don't s'pose *you* know where the Muirheads' dee-*vine* next door neighbour is hidin' himself?'

'Mr Stewart went home this morning,' says Wick.

'Shucks, that's *too* bad! Still,' says Lauri, 'he ain't with that redhead. Talk about easy meat!' The laugh she allows herself is coarse and long.

Ava uses the time to frame a question of her own. 'What you just said, Lauri, about walls being thin... did you hear anything on the night Herr Baumgarten died?'

'Such as?' The fissures that form on the woman's brow crackle her face paint.

'Voices… Noises to suggest he was in distress…'

'Didn't catch wind of a dickybird till you and Mrs-Bug-Up-Her-Backside started crashin' around in here like the place was on fire. That's when I came in for a looksee and I do *not* care to be reminded of what I saw.' She changes the subject with an indolent waft. 'What about Ali? Where is *he* now?'

A head appears round the door. 'Mr Muirhead?' asks Maggie. 'He's busy. Golly! There's quite the wee gang in here!'

'We were just leaving,' says Ava.

'*I'm* come te fetch Mr Baumgarten's belongin's and drag the mattress down. Murdoch's on his way up te help. Needs burnin', the mattress. Apparently. Mrs Muirhead doesnae want anybiddy else sleepin' on it. "I simply can't bear the thought," that's what she said. On account o' the "leakage".'

Wick starts to inspect his trousers.

Maggie isn't done. 'But *I* said, "Fiona, just let me try one more time wi' the bicarbonate o' soda." Bicarb'll shift anythin', given time. Then *she* said—' Maggie's needle-sharp gaze hones-in on Ava's rubber-gloved hands. Her lips purse. 'What's that paper ye're tuckin' away in yer pocket, doctor? Somethin' o' Mr Baumgarten's?'

'Nothing.'

'Looks like a note te me. Oh! My! *God*! I'll bet it's a *suicide* note!' she says excitedly. 'Wait till I tell—'

'We don't know what kind of note it is, Maggie,' volunteers Wick. 'That's for Sergeant Pratt to decide.'

'That ain't what your lady friend was sayin' when I rocked up.' Lauri nods towards Ava. '*She* was sayin' a murderer wrote it.'

'A murderer!' Maggie gasps. 'But he wasnae murdered, was he? Made himself sick wi' the drink. Besides which, the handwritin' looks so *friendly*. Let me tek a proper gander, doctor.'

Ava zips her pocket shut.

'Och, shame,' sighs Maggie, 'Ye can tell a lot by a person's writin'. The way they dot their I's and cross their T's. *Ye'll* have stylish writin' Miss Levi, fer doin' autographs.'

'Got that right, kiddo,' Lauri says lazily. She sticks out her lower lip. 'Well this *sucks*! It's cocktail hour. No handsome stranger, no *darling* Alastair, and I *hate* to drink alone.'

'We'll join you,' says Wick. 'Won't we, Ava? I know I'm parched.'

'Guess I'll just have to pang-wangle, then,' Lauri says, clamping one arm around Wick's, the other, around Ava's. 'What *is* that smell, by the way?' she asks, nose up, nostrils splayed.

'Sandalwood.'

'*Dee*-vine!'

'Pure dead barry,' says Maggie.

16

Window Shopping

Ava has the strangest dream she's had since she came to Scotland. Wick's in it. At her behest, he bends down to stroke a passing porcupine and, while thus distracted, he's knocked over and killed by a runaway wheel of Emmental. She awakes thirsty and sweaty, regretting that she drank so much the night before. She couldn't help herself. At the risk of being disrespectful, she'd felt like celebrating. She suspected Baumgarten's death was 'off', and she was bloody well right! She literally has it in writing that he was warned to keep away from The Hall. That's got to mean something... no matter what Wick thinks. Ava does wish he hadn't made that qualifying statement to Maggie, about what 'kind of a note' they'd found. He could've just brushed it off as none of the girl's business. Maggie's no doubt used to people asking her to keep her nose, and her thoughts, to herself. Then again, what difference did it make? Lauri Levi had already heard enough to let the cat well and truly out of the bag.

Inspecting herself in the mirror, Ava sticks out her tongue. It's the texture of a toad. *How* many cocktails did she put away? Too many. Lauri turned out to be surprisingly easy company, in a crass no-holds-barred sort of way. Ava had fully expected to be dodging questions about murderous memos, not to mention being caught 'casing the joint', but Lauri was breathtakingly self-absorbed. She belted out a couple of songs, then knocked back half a gallon of Alabama Slammers – or their Dorchan equivalent – while basking in the attention her extraordinary mammary glands were attracting from any nearby males. By

Lauri's standards, a subdued soirée, and since Alastair was mostly busy in the kitchen, for her the stakes must have felt low. Wick was good company too, considering. Thinking back to their search of Baumgarten's room, and how barbed things got, she's glad they parted for their beds on merry terms. The fact George didn't join the party was, in Ava's opinion, no loss. 'Having dinner with Sinclair Stewart,' according to Wick. If Wick minded, he hid it well.

Ava throws open her curtains and her window, and takes in a deep, refreshing lungful of air. The mountains look like they've been up for hours. The sun's already dismissed any low clouds and there is no mist, so their burly faces are exposed in all their perfect glory. It appears the dry spell's set to continue for another day. Rather than sit about twiddling her thumbs, she should make the most of it. After washing and dressing in haste, and giving a last salute to her own reflection, she exits her room, and – 'Jesus *Christ*!' – walks smack into Wick.

Each jumps back in surprise. There's a very awkward intermission while both fumble to release the lanyard of her magnifying lens, which has snagged on Wick's tie pin.

'Perhaps if you were to step forward a bit, to release the tension...'

'Or... maybe... If you lift it over your head...'

'What are you doing here?' asks Ava when she's at last set free.

'I was going to knock,' says Wick, dusting himself off. 'Clearly picked the wrong moment. I was merely wondering if you'd like to join me on an excursion, unless you've other plans...'

'I said I'd take Carl and Martin to The Murder Field, and then Sergeant Pratt's coming to see me.'

'He's interested in your cryptic message?'

'Naturally. I telephoned him yesterday evening. He's grateful for my vigilance and is looking forward to reading it for himself.' She decides not to mention Pratt's remarks surrounding the whereabouts of the rest of the letter and any presumptions vis-à-vis the ill will of its content.

'In that case, another time.'

As Wick turns to leave, a pang of disappointment needles at Ava's chest. She'd be glad to put some proper distance between herself and The Hall, and a jaunt with Wick would be a better distraction than another trek all the way to Raon Murt. 'As it happens,' she says quickly, 'Pratt and I aren't meeting till later, and I'm sure the Addington boys will accept a rain check. What do you have in mind?'

Wick's answer, 'Your choice,' is music to Ava's ears.

'I'd like to go to Inverness, please.'

At Ava's request, they leave the Bentley in the station car park, where Alastair parked when he took Lauri Levi and Baumgarten on their excursion, and make the short walk to the high street. Almost immediately, they find themselves outside a chemist's; not just a dispensary, but a large branch, stretching over several floors. There's a steady flow of customers going in and out. Its windows display all sorts, from toiletries and towels to books and bath toys.

'Why've we stopped here?' asks Wick.

'Alastair thinks this is where Baumgarten headed when he came to town.'

'Ah! *Now* I get it. We've come to follow in his footsteps.' Wick chuckles. 'Should've guessed! What did he buy here?'

'Don't know. Maybe nothing. Alastair didn't actually see him go in. At any rate, he was in town for a while. He can't have spent the whole time in Boots. Let's have a wander... try to see the place through Baumgarten's eyes.'

The strip is bustling. Though the pavement's broad, it's crowded, and there's a lot of traffic. Buses, coaches, cars. The tall storefronts are an eclectic mix of old and new. Modernised establishments sporting flat, concrete facelifts and metal-framed swing doors stand cheek by jowl with premises lucky enough to retain their original, yellow-grey stone façades. Some have chimneys, some have turrets topped with finials and conical slate-tiled roofs, many have both, but none matches the architectural grandeur of the city bank. Graced with Corinthian columns two-stories high, a pediment of sculpted goddesses, *and* a pair of huge Grecian urns, this building alone is enough to remind anyone where they are. The capital of The Highlands.

Ava and Wick pass three shoe shops, an optician, several tailors, and a kiltmaker. They agree that neither he nor she saw Baumgarten wearing new shoes, new glasses or any obviously new clothes, tartan or otherwise. There's a seed merchant's, a dry cleaner's, 'But not one dealer in fine arts,' rues Wick. The only business he looks at twice is a jeweller's. Ava has to drag him away. 'Who's to say he went shopping at all?' he eventually asks. 'Could've just popped into a tea room.'

'He could,' says Ava. She buys postcards for her nephews then nips into Woolworths for two bags of pick 'n' mix; one, a compensatory gift for Martin and Carl; one to share with Wick as they progress to the river Ness. Above them, on a rocky outcrop, is the castle. Thickset and proud, it's made of the same red sandstone as Dorcha Hall. The blue and white saltire of St Andrew flutters above its castellated towers while seagulls and crows bicker for position along the tops of its bastioned walls.

'Tides going out,' Wick says morosely, peering over the railings into the fast-flowing water.

'I'm sensing your heart isn't in this.'

'Sorry, but I'm not sure what you hoped to learn about Baumgarten by spending two hours window shopping.'

'Nor I, but thanks for humouring me. It's nice of you to take me out.'

'Pleasure. Truth be told, I wanted to make amends. On reflection, I was unfairly facetious about Baumgarten's note. If you let me take another look—'

'I don't have it on me.' Ava laughs. 'Given what happened to the other half, I left it safe and dry, under my pillow.'

'Aren't you afraid the scorpions will get it?'

'They wouldn't dare. Care for a sherbet lemon?'

'Not really.'

'How about a Black Jack?'

'You've twisted my arm.'

The Beasts of the Black Loch

They take a different route back to the car, wending their way through quieter side streets. 'Do you know,' says Ava, rolling a pear drop from one side of her mouth to the other, 'crested auklets smell like tangerines, honey bees smell like bananas, and hooded sea slugs smell like watermelons. Guess what Jervis Bay tree frogs smell like!'

Receiving no answer, she finds Wick is no longer at her side. He's peering intently into a frontage twenty yards behind her, and it doesn't look like an antique shop. She trots back to join him.

'Seem familiar?' he asks, pointing at a resin mannequin. Painted pinkish grey, with a yellow-brown coating of nicotine, it's shaped like a woman... sort of. The limbs are twisted at such unlifelike angles, to Ava it's clear whoever posed it doesn't understand the pliancy limits of the human musculoskeletal system.

'If you're thinking of Lauri Levi, you're being unkind!'

'Try again.'

'Not George!'

'Now *you're* being unkind. Look carefully, at what she's wearing.'

'Men's ski boots. Fur coat... mink, I'd say. She's got four wristwatches on each arm! A wig of white, nylon hair. 'Oh my God! That Tyrolean felt *hat*! It's Baumgarten's. I recognise the *Eumomota superciliosa* feather stuck in its band.'

'Or, rather, pinned there with a solid silver hatpin, which probably explains why it's here.' Wick looks up, and Ava follows his gaze to see a trio of golden orbs hanging from a bar above their heads.

'He pawned his hat! Or I'm assuming *he* did, rather than anyone else.'

'Should we check?'

Ava doesn't need to be asked twice. She pushes open the door, a shrill *ding-a-ling-a-ling* announcing their entrance. The dimly lit interior, being filled with wall-to-wall cabinets, these in turn being stuffed with all kinds of hocked trinkets, gewgaws, and knickknacks, is immediately oppressive. It's as if the weight of so much borrowing has appropriated the very air in the room.

'Afternoon.' The little man behind the counter hails them with a gap-toothed grin. 'How can I help?'

'We're interested in that,' says Wick, gesturing towards the hat. 'Or rather the person who left it here.'

'I dinnae discuss customers wi' other customers. In my line o' work, it's all about discretion wi' a capital D. Is the German fella who pledged it last week a friend o' yers?'

'An acquaintance, yes.'

'In which case ye need te be talkin' te *him* about what he chooses te do wi' his things. I gev him a pound fer it, on account o' the fancy plumage. Best I could do. It's nae fer sale... yet. I just popped it on Flora MacDonald's heed, there, meantime... te make her look bonnie. He seemed te think he'd be back fer it soon enough. Now, is there anythin' else caught yer eye, or are ye wanting a loan yersels? Those are very nice cufflinks, sir—'

'Nothing at the moment, thank you,' says Wick, stuffing his hands in his coat pockets. 'I think we'll be on our way.'

Ava splashes out forty pence on a fried feast of white pudding which they eat outdoors, from newspaper, using little plastic forks. Ava knows Wick would have preferred a more formal dining arrangement, but once again he upholds his promise, 'your choice.' 'So now you know,' he says. 'Baumgarten came here to raise funds. Must've been his hatpin money he used to settle his bar tab. No way would that have covered the rest of his bill, though.'

'True. I wonder how he planned to square that.'

'Sadly, another hole in Alastair and Fiona's pocket now,' sighs Wick.

The drive back to Dorcha is pleasant. They talk little, and Ava's content to sit back and enjoy the scenery along with her sense of satisfaction that she understands the purpose of Baumgarten's trip to Inverness. One mystery solved. She just needs to put that note into the hands of the authorities and, all in all, it'll have been a very good day.

*

On arrival at The Hall, Ava's taken aback to see there's already a panda car outside. 'Blast! Pratt's early. I'd planned to beat him here.'

'Go straight in,' says Wick. 'I'll put away the Bentley.'

On entering the lobby, however, the person awaiting her at the front desk isn't the man she anticipated, but Alastair. Arms folded across his chest he's not smiling. 'You have a surprise visitor,' he says without preamble. 'Sergeant Pratt.'

'Thank you, yes. I was expecting him.'

'I realise *you* knew he was coming. *I*, however, did not. I wish you'd said something, Ava; warned me, so I could have steered him clear of Fiona. He's been sitting at our kitchen table for the past half hour, spinning her some yarn about Baumgarten receiving a message to stay away from The Hall. A message that's now in *your* possession. How did you find it? *When?*'

'Baumgarten gave it to me himself a few days ago, by accident, but it was only yesterday that I understood it's significance.'

'Why didn't you tell Fee and me about it straight away?'

'Wick and I—'

'Uncle Wick's seen it?' Alastair sounds hurt. And angry. 'The man died in my house! Haven't *I* the right to be kept informed? Fee specifically asked you to let matters lie.'

'I thought telling you about it would cause extra anxiety, and judging by your reaction now, my concerns were founded.'

'It doesn't matter about me. It's Fee I'm worried about. Just when she thought guests had stopped talking about Baumgarten and things were getting back to normal, look what's parked on our doorstep!'

'Well, I'm sorry if I've upset you both, but I had to inform the police, Alastair. The suggestion Baumgarten was threatened—'

'Is very concerning,' says Fiona, who's appeared at Alastair's elbow. She seems perfectly calm. 'Of course the police should be involved, Ava. And, *darling*,' she continues, giving her husband's hand one of her earth-rod squeezes, 'I'm fine. It *was* rather embarrassing, not knowing what brought Pratt here, but we soon got past that. So there's no need to get tetchy, is there? Especially not with Ava. She always has your best interests at heart.'

'Absolutely. God! I'm *so* sorry, Ava,' he says, shaking his head as if in disbelief at his own actions. 'I don't know what came over me.'

'Stress,' says Fiona, before Ava can answer, 'and exhaustion. I'm sure Ava understands.'

'Where's Pratt now?' asks Ava.

'I left him with Maggie, a pot of tea and a plate of Alastair's best iced biscuits. I'll fetch him for you.'

'Now, what was it ye're wantin' to show me, Dr Dickens? I've jotted down here that you've found a wee "note"?'

'Evidence, sergeant,' Ava says stoutly. '*Hard* evidence. It's in my room.'

'Alastair will lead the way,' says Fiona.

As the foursome heads upstairs, Ava's excitement mounts. 'Less of a note, more a written warning. A game-changer. As soon as you see it, sergeant, you'll get what I mean.'

The moment Alastair unlocks the door, Ava marches straight to the bed, thrusts her hand under her pillow, and feels around for the torn scrap. She feels around some more.

'Anything we can help with?' asks Fiona.

'No!' Ava tosses the pillow to the floor and throws back the covers to expose… nothing, but a taut, white, freshly laundered sheet! Stepping back, to her horror, she realises that since this morning, the bed's been made up with clean linen. 'Shit!'

'I tek it the "evidence" isnae where ye left it,' says Pratt.

Just then, from the corridor outside, there comes a distinctive *squeak, squeak, squeak*; the stiff old wheels of The Hall's laundry wagon trundling by. 'Ollach!'

The woman's head pops round the door. 'Afternoon, doctor. Everythin' all right? Ye're looking a wee bit wabbit. And Hamish Pratt! How's the family?'

'Where's my bedding?' Ava asks frantically. 'The set from last night?'

'Boiled and bleached and hangin' in my yard.' Ollach turns to Fiona. 'I've done the towels too. Cannae waste these fine dryin' days, can we? That's why Maggs and I did this week's change overs early. Hasn't the weather been grand? No rain fer *four* days.'

'Ye're nae wrong there. Mrs Pratt has just seen te our winter drapes.'

'Has she, Hamish? Well, be sure te give Aileen my—'

'But what did you do with the note, Ollach?' Ava's struggling to keep her temper. 'The paper that was under my pillow?'

'Och, I'm everso sorry, doctor. Never saw it. And it'll be long gone now. Anythin' that goes into my washin' copper gets good and proper cooked.'

'Pity,' says Alastair. But he doesn't look or sound one bit sorry; just relieved, as does his wife. 'Oh dear, sergeant. Looks like you've had a wasted trip.'

Ava understands this reaction. From their point of view, no note equals no police interest equals 'let's move swiftly on'. She, however, cannot.

'Somethin' important, was it?' Ollach asks.

'Yes, it *bloody* well was!'

'Please, Ava!' chastises Fiona. 'Ollach has done *nothing* wrong.'

Seeing Ollach's cheerful expression crumple, Ava immediately regrets her sharp tongue. 'Forgive me. I let disappointment get the better of me. This was an idiotic cock-up entirely of my own making.'

It's humbling how quick Ollach is to forgive. 'Och, nae bother, doctor. "Da gabh dragh", as we say in these parts.'

And shocking how fast Alastair wants to forget. 'Whatever that note was,' he reflects, 'guess we'll never know. So, apologies sergeant, I must crack on with supper.'

'If ye'll excuse me...' Ollach also heads for the door.

'Let me come with you,' says Fiona. 'Help turn down the bed in room nine.'

Squeak, squeak, squeak.

'Well, well, well,' sighs Pratt. 'I'll be on my way too.'

'No, wait! You came specially.'

'Not at all, not at all. There was a report of a stolen creel in Drumapple, but turns out Fraser McKenzie cannae count, so I thought I might as well roll by The Hall too, seein' as I was in these parts. And Maggie Kettlenesss makes a braw brew.'

'At least let me give you a detailed description of the message. In fact, I'll have a bash at writing it out—'

'No need, doctor. Ye say it was torn from a longer letter?'

'Correct.'

'How do ye ken it was addressed to Baumgarten?'

'I don't. But—'

'What does the rest o' the letter say?'

'We've no way of knowing. It's lost.'

'So, doctor, it coulda said *anythin*'.'

'I'm assuming it was malicious, sergeant.'

'Yet Mr Baumgarten handed it te ye himself, happy as Larry.' The policeman puts on his cap. 'Dr Dickens, Dorcha Hall is a faraway place. Beautiful, I'll nae deny, but very quiet. Ye're an energetic woman with an enquirin' mind – I dinnae doubt yer heart's in the right place, te boot – but ye're whippin' up stories where there's nae stories te be told. Take my advice. Stick te the birdwatchin', and enjoy the rest o' yer holidays.' Pratt closes the door behind him.

Ava buries her face into her pillow – it smells like seaweed and heather – and screams.

17

Ruffled Feathers

A week after Baumgarten's demise it's as though he never existed at The Hall. Murdoch burns the mattress on which he died. His room is reallocated to the next guests who arrive… and leave again. Maggie repacks his suitcase and inters it in the office, under a pile of box files, to 'await instruction from Pratt.' And when Ava mentions his name in earshot of the Muirheads, they look at her as if to ask, 'Herr *who*?' The faster they can erase all traces of Baumgarten from their visitors' book, the better. Wick appears to be on the same page as them.

As far as Ava's concerned, though, questions remain. And that lost note! Bloody infuriating. But the painful fact is, now it's gone, she's forced to let things lie. It'd be different if she had any other evidence that his death was suspicious. More importantly, it'd be different if the Muirheads weren't so shot to pieces. Alastair's all over the place; one minute his usual self, the next, an irritable neurotic. There's an edge to his voice when he's talking to Maggie, similar to the biting tone he used toward Ava the day Pratt turned up unannounced. It also reminds Ava of the clumsy way *she* spoke to Ollach. Though Ollach's friendly enough when their paths cross, the woman seems subdued, like she's still smarting. 'Darling Fee' is keeping it together better than her spouse, but Ava does overhear a hushed call between her and Dr Sween, in which both 'nerves' and 'tablets' are mentioned. All things considered, Ava accepts that the meniscus between laying her own doubts to rest, and shit-stirring, is paper thin. It'd be selfish to tear it.

Thus the ebbs and flows of life at Dorcha return to some sort of normal, and Ava falls into some sort of line. Daily dramas default to the mundane. The last pair of sugar tongs vanishes from the cutlery service; Wick dislikes having to make do with his fingers. Barbara Addington can't finish her jigsaw, because a piece is missing; she redirects her focus into knitting Bernard a sweater. Their testosterone-fuelled boys pester Ava about that promised visit to The Murder Field. Her conscience pricked by letting them down, but keen to keep up her regime of hikes, Ava renegotiates. 'Let me bag just one more Munro, then it's Raon Murt, here we come.' Only somewhat mollified, Carl and Martin have a stop-gap bash at archery. Luckily, no stitches needed, despite a couple of close calls. Apart from showing the lads how to whittle hazel-wood arrows, Murdoch continues to make himself scarce. Lauri Levi picks up her complaining where she left off. If anything, she's worse and, by Ava's reckoning, more fixated on Alastair than ever. Everyone's treated to a tour of Alastair's laboratory and given a free bar of soap. Chemistry teacher Bernard says it's the highlight of his holiday. Others are less-than floored.

As for George, she makes phone calls and rolls her eyes; more often than not, simultaneously. She issues Alastair and Fiona with a 'Must Do' list, written in red ink, which she pins to a board in their office. Some tasks – *Scatter-Cushions In ALL Reception Spaces*, and *Scented Candles In Downstairs WC* – are ticked off quickly. Others – *Empty Orangery*, *Fill Potholes*, and *Shift Shrine* – await the attention they deserve. *Sack Maggie*, while unregistered, is inferred from George's rigorous haranguing: 'Put that back! Put that down! *I've* got my eyes on *you*!' Given the woman's obvious frustrations, and how long she's been away from a desk that she's no doubt handsomely paid to sit at, Ava thought it odd she hadn't by now buzzed off back to Stirling. But when Ava totted up the number of times George has dined at Beithe Towers, all confusion evaporated.

On Ava's second Saturday at Dorcha, and George's too, she encounters her outside. Wick is holding her clipboard while she takes photographs of The Hall's soaring moss-covered north face.

'Holiday snaps?' asks Ava. 'Say "cheese", professor!'

Wick doesn't find this funny. 'George is compiling an inventory of essential repairs. "A picture speaks a thousand words".'

George yanks a wet print from the front slot of her Polaroid camera and flaps it around impatiently. 'This place must have a hundred windows, every sill rotten. There are six turrets, all of which need reroofing. As Alastair's bank balance stands, he can't afford to replace a single tile.' She aims her lens at a leaning chimney stack. Wreathes of light blue smoke fly from its pots, and seep through the cracks in its masonry. 'I'm confident my little album will make him see sense.'

'Good luck with that.' Ava wasn't aiming for sarcasm, but judging by the expression on Wick's face, she achieves it.

Ava leaves them to it. As she laces her boots in preparation for a long, solitary walk, she notices Baumgarten's binoculars hanging from a hook in the cloakroom, faithfully waiting for their owner to return. She sees this poignant discovery as a sign. Ever since his death, she's felt she owes it to him to spot a flycatcher, but without her folding field glasses – Ava's buggered if she remembers where she put them – this hasn't been possible. Today, however, could be the day! Certain that, for such a worthy cause, Baumgarten wouldn't mind her borrowing his gear, she drapes the binocular's weathered leather strap around her neck. The sun's shining, Diptera will be out in force and, on this matter at least, she won't let a fellow twitcher down.

First stop, reception. It's unattended, so she helps herself to what she came for: a generous handful of dried berries, 'home-desiccated' by Alastair, which she grabs from a dish labelled 'You Are Welcome' on the front desk. This is another of George's tweaks to boost The Hall's ambience. One of her better ideas. Ideal snacking-fodder for later use. Ava's about to head off when she hears Fiona's voice coming from the office. As Ava steps inside to say hello, Lauri Levi – brash and bright as ever – steps out.

'Stupid *cow*!' Fiona mutters without looking up. 'Look for your *goddam* self!'

'Don't let Lauri get to you,' says Ava. 'It's not worth it.'

'Jesus! Ava! How long have you been standing there?' Fiona's cheeks turn beetroot. 'Sorry to sound unprofessional, but that woman has *no* sense of proportion!'

'Which woman?' asks Alastair, meandering in through the back door. Looking tired and distracted, he opens a desk drawer and roots through its contents.

'Miss Levi, whinging as usual. Honestly! It's only a pair of earrings.'

'Trouble is, Fee,' Alastair says irritably, 'it isn't *only* earrings. Every day we're down another teaspoon from Mum's set with the jade handles, Dad's decanter is missing its crystal stopper, and now I can't find the ruddy keys to the lab; the ones attached to that nice, eye-catching, polished-agate keyring, so no prizes for guessing who's got them. Georgina Beckett thinks Maggie's a liability, and I agree with her.'

'Are you *sure* you haven't miscounted the teaspoons? And the decanter stopper could easily have got broken. Okay, Maggie should own up if she's the one who broke it, but *stealing*? As for your keys, darling, if they're not hanging in reception, try the console table in the lobby. That's where I last saw them. You shouldn't leave them lying around—'

'Well, *I* didn't see them!' He bangs the drawer shut. 'Maggie's nicking things, and she needs disciplining!'

Fiona remains calm. 'What do you propose we do? Dismiss her? You've no proof she's done anything wrong. Darling, you're sounding a little…' she slides a sideways look at Ava, 'paranoid.'

'Well, *you're* sounding a lot too trusting!'

'Let's just think about this, shall we,' Fiona's voice is soft, her tone, fatigued. 'How would we manage without Maggie? Or replace her? There wasn't an employment agency in Drumapple last time I looked. What do *you* think, Ava?'

Ava remembers the cake that lost its almonds, and her misplaced field glasses. She also recalls a pair of squabbling mongooses and her attempts to arbitrate. Still bears the scars. When it comes to skirmishes between opposite sexes, it's never wise to take sides. Ava declines to comment.

Alastair isn't backing down. 'We'll just *have* to manage. Only a minute ago, Fee, you were having your ear chewed off by a disgruntled guest, all because of Miss Stickyfingers. Lauri Levi has every right to complain till she's blue in the face if her property has been stolen while she's under our roof. What Georgina Beckett says is true. Maggie *is* damaging our reputation and, frankly, getting on my nerves!'

'Okay,' says Fiona, 'if you say she must go, then she must. I'll fire her myself.' Ava wonders if she's calling Alastair's bluff. Seems not. 'Right now.' Fiona smacks the concierge bell to summon Maggie to her fate.

Unable to watch, Ava leaves, but she's barely halfway down the avenue when she comes across Murdoch. He's standing at the foot of a tree, staring at the ground.

'Morning, Murdoch. Long time, no see. What've you found?'

'Pits.'

Sure enough, there's a cluster of five holes, several inches deep, among the trampled grass. They look fresh. 'Who's the culprit?'

'Squirrels.'

'Grey or red?'

'Red.'

'I don't think it was either. Squirrels leave shallow craters a couple of inches in diameter, and without the discard-piles we're seeing here.'

Murdoch scratches his head.

'And it's the wrong season for *Sciurus* to be looking for stores they buried last autumn. There's enough fresh food around without resorting to stale nuts. Besides,' Ava continues, 'judging by the undisturbed dew, this lot appeared in the middle of last night, not this morning. Squirrels are diurnal, working in daylight. We need to consider nocturnal species.' She omits to add, 'As you very well know.'

'Badgers,' offers Murdoch, kicking at the dirt.

'*Meles meles*! Hmm. These *are* about the right size for a badger's latrine.' Ava picks up a twig, pokes it around in the disturbed earth, then sniffs its tip. No droppings. No musky smell. 'How far are we from a sett?'

'A tidy mile.'

'If a badger made these, I'd expect them to be nearer to his home.'

'Let's say it was a fox, doctor.'

'You may say it was a fox, Murdoch. I'll say it wasn't. *Vulpes* doesn't expend energy scratching for invertebrates unless they're near the surface, and there's not so much as a springtail's furca in sight here, let alone an earthworm. No surprise, given how dry it is under this tree. Hasn't rained in over a week.' Ava scoops up a handful of soil and lets it fall through her fingers. 'Don't quote me, but I'd say we're looking at a volumetric water content of less than ten per cent. Anything worth eating will have retreated deeper than this.'

'Nae foxes?'

'Definitely nae foxes, though if you'd said, "ground hog" and we were in North America, I might have believed you.'

'Rabbits?' Murdoch's trigger finger twitches.

'Hardly! Look at the length of the grass round here. Not so much as a nibbled blade. Anyway, Duncan personally shot all Dorcha's resident *Oryctolagus* years ago.'

'Allreet. *Mice*.'

Why, wonders Ava, is Murdoch the veteran ghillie, who could deliver a lecture tour on the fossorial species of Highland Scotland, acting this dumb? Nevertheless, recognising there's no mileage in pressing any subject Murdoch doesn't want pressed, she backs off, turning instead to a question she's been wanting to ask for days. 'Murdoch, you took Mr Baumgarten out and about, didn't you? Showed him the right places to spot birds? So you spent a bit of time together.'

'Aye.'

'Did you talk much?' As soon as these four words quit Ava's

lips, she realises how laughably inevitable Murdoch's answer will be.

'We didnae.' He replaces his deer stalker and slogs off.

Ava takes a closer look at the holes. They aren't the work of a four-legged mammal. Not a single pawprint, claw mark, or any other kind of spoor to suggest a wild animal is responsible at all. The depth and regularity of these earthworks tell her they're *man*made, with a tool. And for all Murdoch's stolid refusal to play ball, Ava could tell they're as anomalous to him as they are to her. Who dug them? Why the secrecy, shovelling away in the dead of night to avoid being seen? And what's the phantom prospector looking for? Perhaps several things; there are, after all, several holes. Then again, could he or she have been looking for just one thing, but they didn't find it straight away. Maybe they *never* found it.

Ava's ruminations are sent packing by an approaching ruckus, in the form of Maggie. Without acknowledging Ava's presence, and spitting expletives, the girl wobbles past on her bicycle, the craterous driveway making a dignified departure unfeasible. She's still wearing her black and white livery. It occurs to Ava that when pickings are plentiful, Magpies are known to bury their loot.

18

Plain as My Nose

Ava resumes her mission. If she's to see flycatchers, she must find the right habitat; an open space that will allow free flight, but with a perch – a stump or fence post – from which a little bird can make aerial sorties to catch insects on the wing. Luckily, she doesn't have to look far. Having scrambled up a steep and thickly wooded embankment at the back of The Hall, she comes upon a clearing with a convenient telegraph pole in the middle. Perfect. She takes up position. Flat on her stomach, propped up on her elbows, she adjusts her focus and waits.

For a midge-riddled hour, she observes titmice, pipits, and a pleasingly bold wren, but sees nothing resembling a flycatcher. She eats her dried fruit, carefully picking out and discarding the cherries. They'll be a nice surprise for passing pine martens… or squirrels. She thinks about those holes in the ground. For the next sixty minutes, she listens for a piping *tseet* or give-away descending *djeer*, to no avail. Perhaps she's on a wild-goose chase. Maybe Baumgarten was mistaken about seeing flycatchers, same as he was wrong about ospreys hunting in midwinter. Mindful that the longer she lies in the grass, the greater the chances she'll pick up a wood tick – devils to remove – Ava rises stiffly to her feet. Dusting herself off, she trains her sights on other things.

In the distance she spies three boats on the loch. Brightly coloured hulls, red, green, and blue, all in a row. Bernard Addington was planning to take his boys kayaking. It's probably them. Closer at hand, Ava has a partial view of Dorcha Hall a couple of hundred feet below. She immediately spots someone, a woman, teetering down the avenue. Not George and her clipboard, but Lauri, a whole ten yards from the front door. Quite an excursion by Miss Levi's standards, her ankles repeatedly buckling as she slaloms the potholes in her high heels. She's dressed in a custard shade of yellow attractive to fungus gnats. Ava doubts the woman will stay out long... and she's right... Lauri soon totters back indoors.

Alastair is next to appear, with his trusty trowel. He stops in the drive, peering around as if working out what to do. Ava calls his name. No reaction. He can't have heard. A vehicle arrives; the butcher's van, judging by the insignia, 'Hooley's Mobile Meats', painted on its flanks. Jack Hooley himself climbs down from the front passenger seat, opens his van's rear doors, and hops inside. Ava spies racks of carcasses within; deer hanging by their hind legs, geese by their necks. Hooley hops out, a brace of mallard ducks in each hand, blood-stained sawdust on his boots. He kicks the van doors shut before heading towards the back of the house. Who, wonders Ava, was his driver? As Alastair approaches the van, the answer to Ava's question steps into the sunshine: Peigi. It's clear Alastair's pleased to see her, and she, him. They fall into conversation, but although they're smiling and laughing, there's something mutinous about their over-the-shoulder glances and bowed heads. Whatever their discourse, it's short. The ever-vigilant Fiona emerges onto the front step. She has the air of a mother calling her child in from play, and Alastair duly skips home. Reaching his wife's side, he turns and waves towards Peigi, but Ava doesn't get to see if Peigi waves back. She's disappeared beneath the trees.

More action on the drive. Not a van this time, or a car. A man on horseback comes trotting up with a dog jogging on ahead. It's Sinclair Stewart, and he and his animals cut quite a dash! His scout is a smart pointer with a smooth, loose gait, and such a sheen on its white coat, it almost glows. His horse is a large grey. Around sixteen hands, Ava reckons. Taller than an eland, but shy of the height of a moose. Athletic, by the look of it. Good shoulder angle, well-set neck, and a strong top-line.

Built for jumping, rather than a gentle hack to a country hotel. Ava guesses it's a hunter. Readjusting Baumgarten's binoculars – which are far superior to the ones she's lost – she takes in its long, well-defined face and bright, bold eyes. She can even make out the whiskers on its pink velvet muzzle.

Stewart draws to a halt at the front door. As he dismounts, Murdoch emerges from within. The dog bows and stretches, then lies on its back at Murdoch's feet. Ava sees it's a bitch. The horse, a gelding, champs unconcernedly on its bit.

The two men talk for a minute or two but then George turns up, and their conversation abruptly ends. Stewart steps forward... so does George... and they plant kisses in the air to either side of each other's beautiful cheeks. Stewart passes Murdoch his crop and the horse's reins. Murdoch leads the animal off in the direction of the stables, the dog mooching along after him, tongue lolling, tail a-wag. George escorts Stewart inside Dorcha Hall.

Ava lowers the binoculars. No joy with the flycatchers. Not here, anyway. She could trek to the other side of the loch, to The Murder Field, where Baumgarten first directed her. But that's a fair walk away, and it would be unfair to go without Carl and Martin. Besides, it *is* lunchtime. Best pop back to The Hall first, see what's cooking.

George and Stewart are in the sitting room. At first, Ava thinks they're stuck in a game of Snap, but as she gets closer, she realises George is dealing out photographs rather than playing cards. George tries to conceal her hand, but not quickly enough. Ava sees it's a flush of images of the Dorcha estate. Pictures of fences and fells, though. Not bricks and mortar. Ava settles herself in a nearby armchair. 'I recommend the fennel sandwiches,' she says cheerily, balancing a plate on one knee, mug of coffee in hand.

Stewart rises to his feet. 'Dr Dickens.' He nods cordially, clicking the heels of his riding boots. 'We meet again.' Ava notes the spray of pink flowers in his buttonhole, and knows where they were picked.

'You too,' says Ava, trying not to spit crumbs. 'I'd shake hands, only I've just applied tick-bane.'

'I trust we aren't in your way?'

George dives straight in. 'Without wishing to shoo you away, Ava, Sinclair and I—'

'Don't mind me. Once I've stuffed this lot down, I'll be out of your hair. Though I must say, Sinclair, you have a magnificent mount.'

'You've seen Pegasus?'

'Admired him from afar. I observed your arrival through these.' She dips her chin at the binoculars still hanging from her neck.

George mutters something under her breath.

'I wasn't spying,' Ava continues breezily, 'just trying to track down a bird that's proving flighty.'

George has another try. 'I'd *hate* to keep you from—'

'Not at all. I've been hoping to run into you, Sinclair. I'd love a proper natter. We never got a chance at dinner, and then, with events unfolding as they did...'

'Terrible business.'

'Terrible,' says George.

'Anyway, you're here now.'

'At Georgina's kind invitation. Rode over rather than motored. One of my favourite hacks.'

'Aah! That explains why you and Angus Murdoch have become good friends.'

'*Friends?*' For a second, Stewart's creaseless brow wrinkles and his dazzling smile dims. His forearms are covered but Ava bets that, right now, his arrector pili muscles are fully contracted. A robust reaction. She wonders what it means. But by the time she's finished her mouthful, she's made up her mind not to explore it; not for now. Which is just as well because any opportunity to follow through is summarily swept away.

'Sinclair has made a proposition,' George says tartly. 'A *business* proposition, which I'm toying with.'

'Really?' Ava waits for either George or Stewart to expand on this statement, but it seems further elaboration is to be as elusive as flycatchers.

George uncrosses then recrosses her legs. Stewart clears his throat. 'If you're interested in birds, Dr Dickens, then do visit Beinn Beithe. I'd love to show you my collection of exotic fowl. In fact, you and your binoculars must come for lunch, any day that suits. We can have our "natter", too.'

'May I bring Professor Wickremesinghe? I'm sure he'd appreciate the change of scene.'

'If you feel you need a chaperone, by all means! The Muirheads have my number, so drop me a bell. This is the second invitation I've offered, doctor, I'll be offended if you don't take me up on it.'

'Then I'm delighted to accept. Would you like the rest of this, George?' Ava asks, proffering her half-eaten sandwich. 'It's more doughy than I expected.'

'No.' George's legs rearrange themselves again, more successfully than her face does.

'In which case, I'll see if Murdoch fancies it. I'll bet he's still in the stables.'

'Goodbye,' says George.

'Thank the man for watering Pegasus,' says Stewart.

'Will do,' says Ava.

Murdoch's glad of the food. However, when Ava passes on 'your friend Sinclair's best regards', he explodes.

'*Buddies*, is it!' he bellows. 'I hardly *ken* the man, and dinnae go bletherin' otherwise!'

Both Pegasus and Ava are shocked. Even by Murdoch's stellar standards of irascibility, he's scarily irate. By now, he's probably found out about Maggie's dismissal. Perhaps that's coloured his mood? Deciding it's best not to enquire, Ava makes a U-turn. 'Have you ever seen a flycatcher at Raon Murt, Murdoch?'

'Ne'er!'

This rings true. The stuff about not knowing the neighbourly Mr Stewart, though, *that's* bollocks.

*

'George out for dins again?' asks Ava, as she and Wick watch the sun go down on the day.

'Believe so. Saturday night it may be, but it'll be a long time before the Muirheads host any more parties here.'

'She and Stewart seem to have hit it off. Funnily enough, I fancy a trip to Beinn Beithe myself, if you wouldn't mind taking me?'

'What, *now*?'

'Don't be daft! In the morning. I need you to drive me there.'

'Why?'

'Because I've been invited, for once I don't feel like walking, and I'm curious to know why Murdoch, life-long stalwart of telling-it-like-it-is, has started spouting porkies.'

'Murdoch's a liar? What makes you say that?'

'Body language.'

Wick looks surprised. 'Can't imagine unbending old Angus gives much away in that department.'

'He doesn't. I'm talking about a horse and a dog. It's all in the nostrils and nipples.'

'*Please* explain!'

'Murdoch told me that he and Stewart barely know each other, yet the way Stewart's animals behave around him suggests otherwise. Horses, Wick, are obligate nasal breathers. They can only inhale through their noses… unlike us, who can use our mouths as well. If you're that reliant on your nose for getting oxygen into your body, you *have* to be able to adjust your nostrils, especially if you're a beast built to run at speed. Literally, a matter of life or death. And the horse's facial musculature is exquisitely fit for purpose. Off the top of my head, it's the contraction of the lateralis nasi that dilates the nostril, rotating the conchal cartilages laterally and expanding the nasal vestibule. Of course the caninus, dilator naris apicales, and levator nasolabialis all play their parts. Guess how many facial expressions—'

'You're meandering.'

'Sorry. Quite right. If ever there was an autonomic motor pathway crying out to be abbreviated! Though one has to be careful. So many biological acronyms end up spelling ARSE. Still, long story short, thanks to complexities in their anatomy necessary to allow breathing while galloping at forty miles per hour, horses happen to have sublimely eloquent nostrils. When *Equus caballus* encounters someone he's not met before, he tends to flare them out, trying to take in their smell, work out who he's dealing with. By contrast, if he's around someone he knows well, is comfortable with, then he won't bother.

'No way are Murdoch, and the gorgeous grey which Sinclair Stewart rode in on this morning strangers. I deduce this because, when they met at the steps of The Hall, his nostrils... the grey's I mean... barely deviated from their relaxed oval shape. No elongation or narrowing. Nothing. There were postural indications, too. The way Stewart's horse stood with one hind leg resting, mouth closed, erect ears... extra clues that he was, as Alastair might say, "chilled out" in Murdoch's company. But for me, it was the nostrils that clinched it.'

'Obvious now you've explained it. You mentioned nipples...?'

'Ah, yes! Cherries on the cake!' Ava laughs. 'Like many animals, dogs instinctively protect their vital organs, so they're wary about being touched on their underside. When Stewart's pointer bitch greeted Murdoch, she flipped on her back and exposed her belly, nipples and all, signalling she felt safe. She trusts him to bend down and give her a tickle and not rip out her spleen, and she *respects* him, too. Low-ranking timber wolves rollover in subservience to a dominant pack member... lionesses do the same in deference to their alpha queen...'

'I can flare my nostrils, y'know,' says Wick. 'Taught myself as a boy.'

'To what end?'

'Impressing girls.' He smiles as he demonstrates. 'Is it working?'

'You've got nothing on huacaya alpacas, and *they* can spit ten feet in all directions too. Anyway. Murdoch is on very matey terms with Sinclair Stewart's menagerie, and I can't see how that would be unless he's at least somewhat matey with the man himself. I want to know why Murdoch's cagey about admitting as much, but since he's in no mood for sharing, I'll have to try Sinclair instead. Hence a visit to Beinn Beithe for a heart-to-heart. Which brings me back to my original request for a lift.'

Wick strokes his moustache.

'I'll bet the hospitality at the other end will be top notch.'

'All right. Yes. From the little I know of Stewart he comes across as a man of good taste. If I'm honest, I'm intrigued to see his home.'

'Have a "nose around", you mean?'

'Careful, or you'll end up hitchhiking!'

That night, Ava dreams about a little tenrec called Pinocchio. Pinocchio looks like a hedgehog, lives in Madagascar, and has made a nest at the foot of a banyan tree. She has thirty babies. And three dozen nipples, which Ava asks to count. Pinocchio objects. She and Ava haven't been formally introduced, so she's coy about the supernumerary six.

19

The Grass is Greener

Breakfast is a protracted affair. With Maggie off the payroll, what was already a slow process takes twice as long. Alastair and Fiona's efforts to manage without her are painful to watch, never mind experience, but Ava's offers of help are refused. Guests sit and wait, only to be served burnt toast and congealed fry-ups by their frazzled hosts. Lauri Levi nit-picks throughout. George mutters about grapefruits and croissants, while rolling her forever-spinning eyes. Murdoch glares at her. 'Ye wished the lass awa, and now ye're mumpin'!'

When the Bentley finally heads down the avenue, to Wick's obvious irritation, he and Ava are running late. Still, Ava asks him to slow down. 'Intriguing,' she ponders, as they turn out of the gates and into the sylvan shade of the forest. 'Yesterday morning, I counted five holes under one of those beeches. Now there are three more.'

'When's Stewart expecting us?' Wick asks uninterestedly.

'"For sherry", whatever time anyone drinks that.'

'I could use one now.'

They haven't gone far when they meet Carl and Martin walking purposefully, single file along the side of the road. Each boy has a stick with which he cheerfully whips the undergrowth as he trudges along. Martin waves as the car purrs past. Carl sticks out his tongue.

'Cheeky so-and-so,' says Wick.

'My fault he's cheesed off,' says Ava. 'Since I'm not up a mountain, they'd have expected me to take them to The Murder

Field. It's the second time I've let them down. Wonder where they're off to now?'

'Headfirst into mischief, by the look of it,' says Wick, eying them in his rear-view mirror.

'I feel sorry for them. The Hall can hardly be their idea of fun. They keep nagging me to take them to Raon Murt, and I keep disappointing them.

Next, they pass the crash site. 'Cuiridh mi clach air do chàrn!' says Ava.

'Meaning?'

'It's a Gaelic blessing: "I'll put a rock on your cairn". Duncan once told me. Clan warriors would add stones to existing piles to honour their dead. Do you reckon this one's grown?'

Intent on the road ahead, Wick neither answers nor slows down. Ava, however, notices that the warrior who's added to Duncan and Sheila's memorial, whoever he or she is, also left flowers. Thistles. A prickly offering, but a symbol of devotion, nonetheless.

Minutes later they're at Drumapple, where Wick stops to let a flock of chattering chickens scratch and peck its way to safety. It's betwixt tide, the fishing boats are out, and other than the witless fowl, the place seems deserted. But then Ava realises they're being watched by a young woman. Grim-faced she stands, her back against the telephone box, arms folded, chewing on the end of blade of grass.

Ava does a double take. Lowering her window, she calls out and waves. 'Maggie! Didn't recognise you without your uniform.'

Maggie neglects to wave back. Or smile. The chickens move on, and so does Wick. Ava needs a moment, though, to recover from her own lack of tact. Avoiding the cart track through the village – Wick would never put his car's suspension through ruts like that – they take the long way round, following the metalled road on its up-hill-down-dale route to the official frontiers of Sinclair Stewart's domain. The vegetation changes quickly. No heather. No bracken. Instead, an army of deciduous trees with slender white trunks covers the surrounding slopes, blocking all sight of the water. The Beinn Beithe, 'Birch Mountain', estate is living up to its name. Leaves shimmer. Dappled sunlight dances on the green and mossy woodland floor. It's a serene, almost mystical landscape which feels a world away from the straits of Dorcha. Ava fears she's disloyal to find it as beautiful as she does. Upon reaching the perimeter of the residence itself, as if by magic, tall electric gates hum apart, and what lies before them truly does resemble a foreign country.

Unlike The Hall, lurking as it does at the end of its avenue of ancient beeches, Beithe Towers stands proud in open parkland. No one can creep up on Stewart's castle. You must advance in plain sight, along a drive that bisects ten closely mown acres of fairway, under the stony gaze of heraldic statues. Unless, of course, you arrive by air. His glossy helicopter – windows tinted, blades drooping like the petals of a thirsty flower – kips in the foreground. Waiting at ease till next cleared for take-off.

Wick progresses unhurriedly. Gravel, so clean it could have been washed, chomps under the wheels of the Bentley and *ping, pang, pings* like hailstones off its undercarriage. Guinea fowl scatter before them as they crunch along, and ornamental pheasants, with golden crests, scarlet breasts, and chevron tails, dart under the skirts of rhododendron bushes the size of small houses.

'Whatever next!' chuckles Ava.

A peacock struts across their path. A white one.

Stewart greets them at Beithe Towers's enormous front door. 'Great to see you,' he says, stepping forward to shake hands. 'Sorry about the chopper. Bit of an eyesore. Doesn't matter where you live, eh? Never enough parking. Anyway, come on in.'

The first thing that strikes Ava, as she wriggles out of her mackintosh, is the quiet. No creaking and sighing from the fabric of the building, no echoes; such sounds of austerity being absorbed by the opulence of the soft furnishings. Dorcha Hall may have ceilings just as high and fireplaces just as wide as Stewart's, but the depth of his wall-to-wall shag pile carpet is a luxury unknown to his neighbours. Ditto, his properly lined curtains… not to mention functioning central heating. She bets all his roofs are watertight, none of his windows rattle, and the clock on his campanile keeps perfect time. When Ava first met Stewart, he said he'd invested in this place. Well, she's barely over his threshold, and it's obvious no expense has been spared. Beithe Towers screams comfort. And money.

Ava's not keen on the décor, big budget or not – too many paintings of nude women; a woeful lack of spiders' webs. However, she does admit to herself, begrudgingly, that it *is* nice not to be cold indoors. Wick's clearly pleased with what he sees, cooing over this and that, if not actually drooling. 'Don't tell me that's an *original* So-and-So!', 'May I *touch* it?', 'I've never seen one of *those* outside of the Royal Academy.'

Ava doesn't recognise any of the names he drops, but the two men evidently speak the same language. 'How wonderful to welcome a fellow connoisseur,' Stewart says appreciatively. 'Would you and Ava be interested in seeing my bronze doohickie hoojamaflip? A fine example of baroque lost-wax casting, from the studios of Thingamajig.'

'You're spoiling us!'

He leads them to his well-appointed, draught-free sitting room. Each settles at either end of a vast, cream-coloured, L-shaped sofa, and Stewart duly produces the lauded lump of metal, over which Wick salivates some more. George wouldn't fail to be impressed by the number of velour-covered cushions, or the fibreglass floor lamps shaped like space rockets.

At last, they're given sherry, then lunch. Ava dislikes being able to see everyone's thighs through the top of the glass-topped dining table, but the food is superb. Wick is effusive in his praise.

'Thank you, Wickremesinghe. I fly Sébastien up with me whenever I visit the Highlands. I consider him an essential. Other than Sébastien, I make do with a skeleton staff: Sébastien's sous chef… a housekeeper, a few groundsmen. I muddle through without my man, Jarvis. He remains in London to look after my home there.'

'How wonderfully uncomplicated you make it sound.'

'This *is* only my holiday residence, remember. I prefer to live simply while in Scotland.'

'What about Pegasus?' asks Ava, helping herself to more caviar. 'Who takes care of him?'

'I do,' says Stewart.

'Your horse may have a winged god for his namesake, but given he can't actually take to the skies, I'm guessing he's stabled here on a permanent basis. So he must have a groom, someone who mucks out, exercises him… when you're not around.'

'Ah… yes… I have a local chap to do that.'

'Gosh! Well done *you*. I know Alastair and Fiona find it difficult to recruit. From Drumapple, is he? Or as far afield as Knockinch?'

'Not exactly. I thought you came here for the birdwatching, Ava, but I'm sensing another agenda.'

'To tell the truth, I spotted enough interesting specimens on my way in. But I do have a couple of questions about Mr Murdoch. I believe he's a pal of yours.' Ava scrutinises Stewart's face, assessing his reaction. As far as she can tell, he's quite calm. No sweaty top lip. No clamping of the jaw. If anything, Wick looks more uncomfortable at her directness than their host does. The only hint at any reserve on Stewart's part is the long pause he allows himself before he decides to respond.

'Did Murdoch tell you that?' he asks carefully.

'Angus Murdoch hasn't said anything. It was your four-legged friends: Pegasus, and your pointer… I'm afraid I don't know what she's called…'

'Pax.'

'Well Pegasus and Pax spilled the beans.' Ava proceeds to give Stewart a precis of the account she gave Wick, which he receives with wide-eyed surprise. 'Suffice to say,' she concludes, 'your horse and your dog are on first name terms with Murdoch, so I surmise you and he must be well acquainted too. Yet when I suggest such a thing to either of you, you retract your heads like long-necked turtles. I'm wondering why that is.'

Sinclair Stewart leans back in his seat and breaks into a slow round of applause. 'Astounding, Ava! Ten out of ten for your powers of deduction. Isn't she spectacular, professor? It's quite true that I know Murdoch, and if it was up to me, I'd make no secret of it. It's Murdoch who's... *diffident*. I won't insult either of you with further rebuffs, but if you permit, I'd like to explain my position.'

'Go ahead,' says Ava, adding a fourth quail's egg to the clutch on her plate.

'I'm a very wealthy man. That's not something I hide. I'm good at making money, and when it comes to real estate, I have the Midas touch. Since I was a boy, I've dreamt of owning my own wilderness, and I'm always on the lookout for my next acquisition. As soon as I saw this place, I had to have it. Not for its turrets and battlements. I've enough grand city-houses, and the resources to enjoy all the sophistications of grand-city life. From Beinn Beithe, I ask for more. The opportunity to experience those primal privileges which only the wilds can offer.' He swills his wine. 'And what could be more primal, and at the same time, more *noble*, than tracking down and killing animals for sport? Nothing!' he continues. 'I seek the adrenaline rush, and the kudos, of hunting on *my* land.'

'Sounds like a plan,' says Ava. She can see perfectly how Sinclair Stewart ticks all of Georgina Beckett's 'Must Do' boxes.

'Trouble is, I lack the expertise to realise it. I mean, I can point a gun at something and pull the trigger... goes without saying... but where's the art, or prestige, in that? I want the thrill of the chase, to know what to look for, how to stalk it, when to fire. When I entertain my friends here, they'll expect a shot at the biggest stags, the fastest hares, the feistiest salmon. Providing anything less would be crass. In short, I need—'

'Murdoch?'

'Bullseye, Wickremesinghe! Angus Murdoch. The finest ghillie this side of Lairg. I'm lucky enough to have seen him in action, only once, but it left a very deep impression. Not long after the renovations here were complete, Duncan Muirhead invited me to shoot on the Dorcha estate. I'd no idea what to expect, how to conduct myself, but thanks to Murdoch, I felled a stag. Four feet at the shoulder and five hundred pounds in weight; brought him down with a single shot between the eyes! I still remember the sound it made when it hit the ground. Murdoch made sure every man there felled one too. An extraordinary day. God, I envied Duncan! Aside from the sheer amount of land he possessed – I'd double, even triple, my hectares if I could. Told him as much, but couldn't persuade him to sell me any – I coveted his lifestyle and admired his attitude; the way he *owned* his terrain, in every sense of the word, and Murdoch's mastery in facilitating that.' He sighs wistfully. 'Duncan invited me back to bag a few brace of grouse, but it wasn't to be. He and his wife lost their lives in a car accident. Just like that!' he adds with a snap of his fingers. 'Not a mile from their home.'

'We know,' says Ava.

'Ghastly. But now their son's taken the reins, and Alastair's aspirations for the family domain couldn't be further from his father's. Murdoch's skills are being squandered and that, in my opinion, is an unnecessary waste. So, a few weeks ago, I offered him a job. I'd have done it when Duncan was alive, but it seemed bad form to poach a man's gamekeeper. There's a joke in there somewhere!' Stewart laughs. 'Anyway, I put everything on the table: free use of Beithe lodge, spanking new four-by-four, his pick of horses and dogs, not to mention guns, no expense spared, just come and work for me. The man's not interested! Refuses to speak about it anymore.'

'"Anymore"?' queries Wick.

'Murdoch's been here several times. We've walked the land together, talking terms. At one point, I thought I might have turned his head. But no. His mind's made up. He simply will not leave the Muirheads, which is stretching loyalty too far, if you ask me. He doesn't even want them to find out he entertained the idea. Hence his standoffishness with me when they're around.'

'And his disappearing acts...' muses Ava.

'Those being the times he slipped away to meet you,' says Wick.

'I imagine so, yes. Bottom line is, old Murdoch made a pledge to Sheila Muirhead. Something along the lines of "I'll always keep an eye on the bairn", "the bairn" meaning Alastair. Murdoch takes it very seriously. Abandoning The Hall would be abandoning his duty.'

Ava's struck by how similar this promise is to the one Sheila elicited from Wick. It seems Sheila was good at getting people… men… to protect her offspring. A top survival trait in the animal world. Especially if you somehow anticipated you wouldn't be around to do it yourself.

Stewart clicks his fingers again, this time signalling for one of his skeleton team to bring dessert. 'I get the impression Alastair's unwell.'

'From Murdoch?' asks Wick.

'Fiona Muirhead. Nothing specific, just a general defensiveness. None of my business, of course, but I wouldn't want to be the one to push her husband over the edge. So I've respected Murdoch's wishes and been discreet. Anyway!' Stewart says decisively. 'Are we done with the third degree?'

'We are,' says Ava. 'Thank you for being so frank.'

'It's a relief to talk about it. I've found the need for secrecy awkward. Now let us do justice to Sébastien's lemon posset, then I'll introduce you to Nirvana, my peacock.'

'Bit of a fish out of water in these parts,' comments Ava.

'But quite a sight when he struts his stuff.'

Ava appreciates the rest of her afternoon at Beithe Towers. Wick clearly enjoys himself too. Although Nirvana fails to perform, Stewart is amusing and attentive. When it's time for them to head back to The Hall, Ava feels comfortable enough to ask a favour. 'Might I take a rock from somewhere in your grounds, Sinclair? Something the size of a coconut would suffice. I'd like to add it to Sheila and Duncan's memorial.'

'By all means. Take three! One for each of yourselves, and another from me.'

And so, as the Bentley *ping, pang, pings* its way back down the driveway, and the trio of stones rattle in Ava's lap, Ava decides that as neighbours go, the laird of Beinn Beithe is decent enough. She got to pose her questions. She's satisfied with the answers he gave. Poor Murdoch. 'Did you know that the peacock is the national bird of India?'

'No. But Baumgarten must've been there. He had a peacock sticker on his suitcase.'

'Well remembered! Did you *also* know that the sight of a peacock feather made Charles Darwin feel sick?' asks Ava once the gates hum shut behind them.

'No!' laughs Wick.

'It's because of how the males look. It seemed to blast a hole in his "survival of the fittest" theory. All those iridescent eyespots, a train of feathers five feet long, and a body chockful of delicious, nutritious meat; impossible to miss and, if you're a predator, easy to catch. They shouldn't even exist. In evolutionary terms, what payoff could make such gaudy, cumbersome plumage worthwhile?'

'His answer...?'

'Pea*hens* like it. The larger and fancier a male's fan, the more interest he gets from suitable mates, and the greater the chances of passing on his genes to the next generation.'

'You're saying that, at the end of the day, it matters less about the practicalities of a thing, as long as women are impressed? I could have told Darwin that myself.'

'Do you wish you had a helicopter, Wick?'

'Sometimes. Sinclair put on a good spread, didn't he. I wonder what peacock tastes like.'

'Cross between wild turkey and budgerigar. Needs a fruity sauce, though.'

Nicely full, lulled by the winding road home, Ava could almost nod off. Within twenty short minutes, however, her state of comfy complacency is rudely dislodged by one of jarring confusion.

'What the?!' exclaims Wick. The car judders to a standstill.

They've arrived at the crash site, but the cairn is gone! Both leap out to inspect the scene. Wick storms to and fro, muttering expletives under his breath. 'Did a vehicle hit it?' Ava asks hopefully, afraid she's already guessed the answer. The lack of debris, the way the vegetation has been trampled and the stones spread near and far…

'It's been *dismantled*!'

20

Sacrilege

When Wick pulls up outside The Hall, it seems Murdoch's arrived just ahead of them. He's in the process of hustling the Addington boys from the back seats of the Land Rover. His face is the colour of a peat bog, his fury, flagrant. He doesn't acknowledge Ava or Wick. Gripping each lad by the upper arm, he unceremoniously frogmarches them towards the front door. They squirm in vain to free themselves – Martin lands a left hook onto Murdoch's shoulder, Carl is crying – but Murdoch's unmoved. As he hauls them up the steps, Carl trips and falls. Murdoch simply drags him inside on his knees.

Dumbfounded, Ava and Wick hasten after them, and in the space of a minute the lobby's full of people. Alerted by the ruckus, Fiona and Alastair dart out of their office. George, Barbara, and Bernard materialise from the sitting room. Murdoch releases his hold. Carl runs straight to his mother. Martin makes a weak attempt at squaring up to his aggressor, but a withering snarl from Murdoch sends him scuttling to his father's side.

'Goodness! Whatever has happened?' asks Barbara, clutching her knitting to her chest.

'Ye need te teach yer bairns respect. Nae son o' mine—'

'It's not your place to discipline our children, sir!' Bernard pulls himself up to his full five-foot nine-and-half-inch height.

'It *is* when they're left te run amok... mess wi' things they shouldnae!' Murdoch's fists and forearms constrict into lump hammers.

Bernard turns to the Muirheads. 'Is this how you allow your staff to treat guests?'

'There's clearly been a misunderstanding,' Fiona says earnestly. 'Nothing that can't be ironed out—'

'Nae misunderstandin'!' blasts Murdoch. He turns to address Alastair, and Alastair alone. 'These two *bawbags* ha' been at àite màthar agus athar… yer mother and father's cairn. They've *destroyed* it!'

Alastair and Wick gasp in unison. Ava senses Wick flex beside her.

'Are you referring to that little tower of rocks down the lane?' asks Barbara.

'It marked a place of special significance to my husband's family, Mrs Addington,' says Fiona. 'And to Mr Murdoch.'

'Carl and Martin didn't know that. Otherwise,' continues Barbara, looking to her sons, 'you'd never have interfered with it, would you?' The boys shake their heads gravely. 'Though I can't for the life of me comprehend what made you take it to bits.'

'Is it altogether demolished, Mr Murdoch?' asks Bernard.

Murdoch's throbbing jugular says it all.

'How *annoying*,' George says airily. 'I only asked them to move it. They've completely overstepped the mark. I've a mind not to pay them.'

'That's not fair!' Martin cries indignantly. 'We shook on it.'

'*Pay* them, Georgina?' Wick asks flatly.

George rolls her eyes. 'The lads were at a loose end, the job needed doing, and no one else round here has lifted a finger, so we struck a deal. One Scottish pound. Half to take the thing down, and half to rebuild it, twenty feet back from the road. Remittance on completion. I was very clear—'

'*Ye* did this!' roars Murdoch. 'It should ne'er o' been touched! Nae one stane!' He lurches towards George at such speed, Ava fears he's going to fell her with a punch.

Alastair, however, positions himself in between. 'Enough!' he shouts. 'This is *unacceptable*!'

'*Totally* unacceptable,' echoes George, without batting an eyelid.

Ava feels like decking the woman herself.

Murdoch looks ready to explode. 'Awa an boil yer heed, ye *fuc*—'

'*Murdoch*, get a grip!' Alastair stands his ground. 'Think of Mum. Would she want us to make a scene?'

There's an antsy pause. Murdoch takes a deep breath, then slowly shakes his head. Lowering his fists, he exhales, expelling the same sound he did two weeks ago, when he and Ava first stopped at the shrine: a throttled, broken-hearted choke. A similar noise comes out of Wick.

'Good man,' says Alastair. 'Good man.' He pats him on the shoulder, then ushers him to one side.

Ava can't make out what passes between them next, though she does try. Alastair seems to be telling Murdoch something, or issuing some kind of instruction. Murdoch doesn't speak, but listens and nods. Meanwhile, Fiona makes suitably placatory peals to the Addingtons, and Barabara and Bernard offer suitably no-harm-done noises in return. 'Boys will be boys.' Their sons seem happy enough with the promise of extra ice cream at dinner – 'Say thank you to Mrs Muirhead' – though Martin mutters something petulant about still being 'owed fifty p', for which Bernard gives him a clip round the ear.

Murdoch leaves. Without looking right or left, or uttering a word, he sweeps through the lobby. Everyone steps back to let him pass. As he stomps down the front steps, he pushes past Lauri Levi, who's on her way in.

'Jeez!' she tuts, rolling her shoulders to realign her bust. 'Wouldn't want to get on the wrong side of *him*.'

After an angry crunching of gears, Ava hears the Land Rover rumble away.

'Miss Beckett,' says Alastair, 'may I suggest we go into the office? Ava, Wick… do join us.'

'Why not,' George says wryly. 'I love a chat.'

They're barely through the door when Wick turns on her, and Ava's taken aback by his tone. 'What were you *thinking*?'

'At our brainstorming session, we talked about relocating the—'

The Beasts of the Black Loch

'It was an idea you floated, true, but no one in this room agreed to it. I'm very disappointed.'

'You're disappointed! *You* are!' George sounds incensed. 'For crying out loud, Jayaweera! If I spent my life waiting for people to realise what's best for them, I'd never get anything done. Sometimes, one just has to forge ahead. Okay, so you *really* didn't want the thing moved. I realise that now, and I'm sorry – more fool me, I didn't have you down as a sentimental man – but I came here, at *your* invitation, as a favour, to suggest changes that could save this place—'

'For which we're very grateful,' says Alastair.

'Let! Me! *Finish*! Pretty much all of my suggestions have been snubbed. Never mind the bloody rockery, what about the rest of my Must Dos?' George tosses her curls at the list on the cork board. 'Anyone looked at those lately?'

'I have,' says Fiona.

George ignores her. 'And I'll tell you another thing too. I take back what I said about the paperweight.' This, Ava realises, is not a round-table confab; it's a one-on-one, get-it-off-your-chest, row. She also realises that, while George and Wick continue their spat, a patch of something red, runny, and wet is seeping through the front of George's blouse... and the patch is growing... fast.

Fiona sees it too. 'Miss Beckett! *George*! You're bleeding!'

'What?'

'Fee's right!' exclaims Alastair.

In a move to offer assistance, Wick takes George's arm, but she brushes him aside. She places a hand on the carmine blotch spreading across her bust, studies her palm, rubs the tips of her thumb and forefinger together... and swears. 'Damn, damn, damn!' Reaching into her top pocket, she whips out her fountain pen, the lid of which is plainly missing. 'The *bloody* thing's leaked everywhere.'

'Ink!' laughs Fiona. 'It's only *ink*.'

'Don't give me "only"!' mutters George, dabbing herself with a tissue, making the mark worse. 'This is raw silk. *Aagh*! I could *scream*!'

The ringing of the telephone is a fortuitously timed interruption. Alastair answers it. 'Good afternoon. The Hall Hotel. Oh, Hello! How are you? Are you wanting to speak to Georgina Beckett?'

George reaches for the receiver, but Alastair shakes his head. 'It's for me,' he mouths, before continuing into the mouthpiece, 'Sorry… Didn't catch that… *Jesus*!' Visibly shaken, he sits down heavily in the nearest chair. 'Well… Yes… I really don't know what to say. May we talk later? Now's not a good moment… No. I'm fine. I think I'm fine. I'll let you know.'

'Who was that?' asks Wick, as Alastair hangs up.

'Sinclair Stewart,' breathes Alastair. 'He wants to buy The Murder Field, Raon Murt.'

George stops dabbing.

'*What?*' Fiona looks and sounds appalled. 'How dare he! Where did he even get an idea like that?' Her eyes fly from Ava, to Wick, and then to George. 'I asked… no… *begged* you not to consider selling my husband's land. And you each *promised* you'd never suggest such a thing—'

'To *Alastair*,' George interjects sharply. 'And I didn't. Though I've had detailed discussions with Mr Stewart.'

Wick appears as stunned by this revelation as Fiona is. Ava, though, is merely surprised by their surprise. From the moment she caught George and Stewart in their clandestine game of Snap, she'd suspected something along these lines was afoot, along with a let's-make-it-interesting suggestion of casual sex on the side.

'Did you make George promise that, Fee?' Alastair asks quietly.

'She's twisting words, darling!' cries Fiona. She kneels down next to him, and takes *both* his hands in hers. 'You don't have to go through with it. Forget it was mentioned.'

'I take it the offer he's made is generous,' says George.

'Very.' Alastair nods. 'And I'm all right, Fee. Just shocked. I understand why Sinclair wants those particular acres. They're directly on his border with us. I know we don't have to sell, but it's okay for him to ask.'

'The Dorcha estate is not up for grabs.'

'In my opinion,' says George, 'you'd be crazy to refuse. I did some tough negotiating on your behalf, and it's paid off. The money—'

'Thank you, Georgina!' For a split second, Alastair's cool grey eyes burn with anger. 'We appreciate all you're doing, but your scheming...' He checks himself. '... comes as another surprise. Please don't challenge my wife. She and I need to confer between ourselves.'

'But darling—'

'At the very least, we need to sleep on it, Fee.'

'I wouldn't sleep for too long,' says George. 'Mr Stewart has deep pockets, but, like me, limited patience. If you don't start making changes, fast, you'll go bankrupt. You won't just lose a couple of crappy acres, you'll lose the whole damned lot. For God's *sake*!' she curses, scrubbing at herself harder than ever. 'This is a Chanel, and the pen is Swiss... Useless incomplete.' She shoots a spiteful look at Wick and her green eyes flash. 'It's a souvenir from a *very* lovely sojourn in Geneva.'

'When did you last use it?' asks Ava.

'I don't know! I had it in the orangery. The lid must be in there. The sooner that blasted space is cleared, the better! I'm going upstairs to get changed.'

Wick and Ava leave the office too. 'What are the chances that stain'll come out?' asks Wick, as George's angry mutterings fade from earshot.

'Vanishingly slight. *Bombyx mori* caterpillar silk weakens when it's wet.' Ava sighs. 'Spider silk, on the other hand, may be a faff to harvest, but in the long run it's far more durable. Lightweight, bullet proof... the tensile strength of steel. Guess the diameter of the golden orb weaver's web!'

'I dislike guessing games, Ava,' Wick answers testily. 'Especially yours.'

'Sorry. I'm guessing you've not been to Geneva.'

'No.'

*

Gay Marris

That night, Ava dreams George gets shot clean through the heart. The injury isn't serious. There was a queue of masked assailants, each armed and ready to take aim, so it's unclear who fired the winning bullet. It's a white peacock, however, that pecks it out.

21

Hard to Shift

The following morning Ava finds a dozen holes, all in the same small area where they first began to appear. Someone's had another busy night. Perplexed, Ava strolls up and down the avenue examining the ground to the left and right, checking. There's no sign of digging anywhere other than under one particular tree, which begs the question, 'Why prospect *here*?' She steps back and stares at it. It's a mighty specimen of beech. Deep splits in its gnarly old bark provide purchase for clusters of fungi that stick out, like overlapping shells, from the shady side of its trunk. *Thock*, she snaps off a piece of velvety, greyish-white flesh, and inspects its underside. The gills are yellow, and pristine. No teeth marks from a passing rodent. No stab wounds from hungry birds' beaks. No silvery slug trails. Ava holds it up to her nose. There's a faint smell of the seaside, and a tentative bite confirms her hunch. It's an oyster mushroom; an inviting food resource for all sorts of species, and a soup-ingredient used by Alastair. This, however, is a fresh crop which the creatures of the wood, and Alastair, have yet to plunder.

She's polishing off the rest of her sample when Alastair himself approaches. She can tell by the bounce in his step and easy wave that he's in good spirits. 'Greetings, godson. Are these anything to do with you?'

'No. Hadn't noticed them,' he says casually, kicking the ground. 'Started popping up a couple of days ago.'

Alastair shrugs. 'Probably just squirrels. Anyway, I've a favour to ask. I was hoping you'd give me a hand shifting plants from the orangery, if I'm not interrupting anything.'

'Be delighted.' Ava jumps at the chance to muck in, and as she and Alastair set to, the depth of his gratitude is touching.

'Honestly Ava, your support means the world to me and Fee. Till you and Uncle Wick got here, we'd been feeling pretty lost.'

'Understandably,' says Ava. She gives a mental nod to the two timorous bear cubs that pop up to pitapat across the icy tundra of her imagination. She also makes a private promise that she'll stay up tonight to mount a covert watch. With any luck, she'll catch the nocturnal digger in the act.

'And I know we're not out of the woods yet,' continues Alastair, 'but we've got real direction now. Georgina Beckett's got enough mettle to keep us all on track, hasn't she!'

'Where shall I begin?' asks Ava. 'Small pots for starters, or kick off with the big buggers and get them out of the way first?'

'Big buggers it is!' Alastair points towards a luxuriant shrub, several feet tall, with a purple stem and large, glossy leaves. 'Do y'know what that is?'

'A Triffid!' jokes Ava.

'Castor oil plant.'

'Castor oil, eh,' says Ava as they place themselves either side of its container. 'Mother swore by the stuff. Dosed up my brother and me on a daily basis so we'd get "biceps like Popeye".'

'Dad told *me* it'd put hairs on my chest!'

'Well, let's see if our parents were right.' On the count of 'one, two, three… and… lifting… from… the… hips,' they heave it out through the French windows and onto a handcart. This, in turn, they drag to the kitchen garden where they unload before returning to the orangery to repeat the process. It takes them a dozen trips to get the job done. Alastair pays as much attention to their first cargo as he does to their last, arranging each specimen against a south-facing wall, whispering reassurances that, 'you'll be fine here… face in the sun… out of the wind.'

'It's nice to see you relax,' says Ava. 'I've been worried about you.'

'You mean the set-to over the cairn? I've let that go. Georgina did the wrong thing, granted, but for the right reasons. Murdoch's much more pissed off than I am. And Wick comes in a close second.' Alastair picks up a yard broom and starts to sweep.

'Whatever you said to Murdoch, it certainly diffused things.'

'I asked him to go to Drumapple and tell Maggie she could have her job back. I felt terrible about sacking her.'

'*You* didn't sack her. It was Fiona.'

'Because *I* goaded her into it, which I've regretted ever since. Murdoch knew it was wrong, of course, but instead of blaming me, he's been holding Georgina Beckett responsible. "We'd nae trouble at Dorcha till that bana-bhuidseach blew in." I'm not sure he's being entirely fair. Anyway, I thought it would pour oil on troubled water if I reinstated Maggie and let Murdoch be the one to give her the good news. And it seemed to work. I shouldn't have been so accusatory about my missing keys in the first place.'

'You don't think Maggie's a thief? Because a *lot* of stuff has gone missing—'

Alastair stops sweeping and leans on his broom. 'I've got my "stolen" keys back, Ava. Martin and Carl found them over there,' he says, nodding in the direction of his lab, 'still stuck in the door, where *I* must have left them. Not that I remember doing it,' he adds ruefully. 'Fee worries I'm losing it.'

'Don't be too hard on yourself,' says Ava.

He manages a slight smile, and Ava decides to change the subject. 'What about Sinclair Stewart's offer? You looked like you'd been hit by a ton of bricks when you came off the phone.'

'And I felt like it! God, I was angry with Georgina. Not over the land sale, so much as her disingenuous dealings.' Alastair's voice starts to rise. 'Technically, she may not have lied to Fee, but Fee feels like she did, and that's not on.'

'You're still angry?'

'Perhaps, but as I said, "right reasons". Fee and I stayed up late, talking it through. At first, she was anti the whole thing; partly out of sentiment, but mostly because she cares about me. She believes my stability... as a person... is interwoven with the integrity of the estate; sell any part, and I'll somehow feel, or be, less too. She thinks I literally won't be able to "hold it together".' He smiles. 'Don't look so worried, Ava. Fee's wrong. My priority is to realise our dream, which is to make The Hall work for *us*; her and me. With Stewart's money, we could fix the roof and have enough spare change to tackle some of the outbuildings. The parcel of land he's talking about, Raon Murt, it's less than a hectare and no good to us anyway.'

'You mentioned it has sentimental value?'

'Oh, that!' Alastair blushes. 'It's where Fee and I got engaged.'

'No wonder she's attached to it, if that's where you got down on one knee.'

'Actually, she proposed to me, and I count my blessings for it every day. That woman, Ava, knows me better than I know myself.'

'What does Stewart want the plot for?'

'A helipad!' Alastair laughs. 'Anyway, Fee's coming round to the idea now. She's keen we discuss things with our bank manager, and the solicitor, before we finally decide, though I'd like to snatch Stewart's hand off before he changes his mind.' He takes up his sweeping with renewed vigour. 'Shame George's pen lid hasn't turned up. We've emptied the orangery and there's no trace.'

'Yes. Shame. At least she's got her extra dining space, and look who's coming to see us, now the heavy lifting's done!'

'So this is where the action is,' calls Wick, making his way over to join them.

'What do you think?' asks Ava, as she and Alastair stand back, arms akimbo, to admire their work.

Wick, strolls up and down the rows of pots like a colonel inspecting his troops. 'Looking fine. But what is *that*?' he asks, nudging a toe at a large, winged insect busying itself on a sunny patch of flowerbed.

Black, thin-waisted, with an orange-banded abdomen and long, slender legs, it has a manifest sense of purpose, and Ava recognises it at once. 'A female sand wasp, digging away like there's no tomorrow! Rare this far north.'

The trio crouches, elbow to elbow, watching as the wasp disappears into her ever-deepening tunnel then re-emerges with scoops of earth. Eventually, satisfied with her excavations, she takes off, wavering here and there for a moment, before departing in the direction of Alastair's vegetable plot.

Wick straightens up. 'All that effort, only to throw in the towel!'

'She hasn't given up. She's fetching provisions.'

And, just like that, the wasp is back, clutching a big green caterpillar. She vanishes into her tunnel, dragging her prey down with her.

'What's she doing? Why doesn't the caterpillar put up a fight?'

'She's stung it with venom – to paralyse it rather than kill it – so it stays nice and fresh. And now she's got it underground, it won't see the light of day again. She'll lay an egg on it, the egg'll hatch into a grub, the grub'll eat the caterpillar alive. I wonder how that feels, being unable to escape or defend yourself while, bit by bit, you're consumed.'

'Like a living larder,' reflects Alastair. 'Still, one less pest on my cabbages.'

'She's not done yet!' says Ava. 'She'll want to make sure her baby has plenty to eat.' And Ava's right. The wasp repeats the process three times, returning with a selection of doomed caterpillars which she entombs with clockwork efficiency.

'It's impressive how she always comes back to the right place,' says Wick. 'Almost as if she has a map.'

'In a way, she does,' says Ava. 'Remember when she'd finished digging, just before she set off foraging for the first time, she hovered at her tunnel's entrance? She was taking stock of its surroundings, noting natural landmarks to guide her home.'

'"X marks the spot"?' says Alastair.

'Or,' says Ava, 'the pebble and two shrivelled rose hips that happen to be outside her own front door. Let me demonstrate!' When the wasp next flies away, Ava quickly picks up these bits and pieces and moves them one foot further down the flowerbed, taking great care to arrange them in their original configuration. No sooner has she done so, the industrious little creature is back... and misses her target! She comes to rest not beside her hole in the ground, but in the midst of the relocated items.

'My word!' exclaims Wick, as the wasp walks in circles, tapping the soil with her antennae till she finally feels her way home. 'She actually *looks* confused!'

'And no wonder. She followed her trusty visual cues, so as far as she's concerned, she must have landed in the right place: an inch below a pair of rosehips, one and a half inches to the right of a pebble. *She* can't be lost, yet where is her painstakingly stocked pantry? And her baby? They seem to have disappeared.'

'It brings to mind those silent-movie car chases,' says Alastair, 'when the escaping bank robbers turn around a street sign to fool pursuing cops into taking a wrong turn.'

'Good analogy!' laughs Ava.

'And an enlightening experiment,' says Wick.

'Thank you,' sighs Ava. 'I stole it from Nikolaas Tinbergen. Shall we leave her in peace, now?'

'Yes,' says Alastair. 'We've interrupted her business long enough, and she ours.'

While Wick fetches a watering can, Alastair fills a trug with runner beans. Meanwhile, with measured precision Ava replaces the pebble and the rosehips where she found them. And, order restored, straight as a die, down into her burrow the wasp dives. Tinbergen may have won a Nobel prize, but as far as Ava's concerned, it's the *aculeate Hymenoptera*, subfamily *Ammophilinae*, who are the true geniuses.

That night, George checks out. Ava's heading for bed when she encounters her at the front desk, biro poised over open chequebook, a small crowd in attendance.

'I'll fetch yer bags,' says Murdoch.

'I'll help!' chimes Maggie brightly, evidently pleased to be back.

'Not necessary,' George says tersely. 'If you'd let me know what I owe you, Alastair, I'll settle up now. I'm pushing off first thing in the morning and don't want to be messing about with paperwork when I could be on my way.'

'Really,' protests Fiona, 'Alastair and I have no intention of charging you for your stay, have we darling?'

'Lord, no. You've been here as our guest.'

Wick cuts in. 'Georgina is *my* guest, so *I* insist on settling her account, and you two must accept payment. This is a business, remember.'

Ava looks on from a safe distance as the polite protestations fly. In the end, George wins. Ava knew she would. Still, it's decent of the woman to stump up.

Lauri Levi saunters in, stage left, chest held full and high. Through narrowed eyes, she makes her own, brief, assessment of the situation, and smiles. 'Well, knock me down with a pretzel, look who's bailin'! The Sasquatch shouts you down, no dice with the handsome stranger, so you're quittin' town.'

Murdoch's eyebrows knit into one. Maggie giggles freely.

George smirks. 'This isn't goodbye, Miss Levi, but à bientôt. I've urgent matters to attend to in my Stirling office. I shall be back at Dorcha Hall long before I'm missed.'

'You ain't wrong there,' mutters Lauri.

'*What* did you say?'

'I said drive carefully. Roads get awful twisty in these parts.'

'Thanks for the warning.' George's voice is steeped in derision. 'I suggest you watch *your* step too.'

As the exchange threatens to escalate into a full-blown verbal spat, Fiona shifts topic. 'Georgina, let me thank you in advance for giving Alastair a lift as far as Inverness. It's a huge help.'

'No problem.'

'But what about you, Fee?' asks Alastair. 'You're *sure* you won't feel abandoned?'

'Quite sure! Tomorrow's by far the best day for you to meet our bank manager, darling. We agreed. Murdoch can fetch you back, but what with him using the Land Rover in the morning, and if you take my car… The thing is, Georgina, the appointment's important, but Alastair doesn't want me to be left without wheels—'

'As far as I'm concerned,' says George, 'no explanation required, though it *is* good to know you'll be talking finances. You know my feelings regarding Sinclair's offer, so I shan't go on.'

'Excellent!' says Fiona. 'Sounds like everyone's sorted.'

'Don't it just,' says Lauri.

'Then good night it is!' Wick says decisively. 'Miss Levi,' he continues, offering her his arm. 'May I escort you to your room?'

'And here was little ol' me thinkin' you'd never ask! Catch you later, Ali.'

Ava observes as the duo disappears upstairs, Lauri blabbering away while Wick nods decorously, never letting his smile slip. Ava's grateful to him. His ruse – to remove Lauri before her attempts to detonate George proved explosive – was selfless. Now he's having to field a storm of breathy innuendos and, no doubt, a very sticky parting when they reach her bedroom door. Still, of all people, Wick'll be able to navigate that. She gives them a generous head start before she too makes tracks.

Ava dreams she's stuck down a mineshaft. There are loads of scorpions hiding from the heat of the day, but they're not the problem. Glued to her ankles is a large, pearlescent, soft-shelled egg. There's something moving inside it; a huge, creamy maggot, writhing around, chewing its way out. She can see its mouthparts. She tries to kick it off, but her legs don't work. Neither do her arms. She rolls her eyes upwards, towards the light. There are two faces peering down at her. Wick and Alastair. They're discussing how to rescue her, who should fetch a trowel and dig her out, when George calls them away.

22

Eavesdroppings

Ava awakes with a start. Momentarily disorientated, she realises she's stretched out, fully clothed, on top of her bedcovers, just as she was when she lay down to rest her eyes. She also realises that must've been many hours ago. The flaking plasterwork on the ceiling and the washed-out prints on the walls are bathed in the pale light of dawn. *Bugger*! No chance of any dead-of-night vigil under any beech trees now. Tired out by yesterday's heavy lifting, she's slept through. Ava rolls a cigarette. While she lies there, smoking, contemplating the gloom, she hears a car drive away. The grandfather clock chimes five times. George meant it about making an early start! As Ava listens, though, she hears more sounds. The gurgling of The Hall's plumbing tells her that, in the room next door, George herself is running a tap, flushing the bog, pulling herself to order before hitting the road. Curiosity piqued, Ava heads out into the dew-kissed break of day.

First stop, the avenue. More holes – as many as twenty – and more trampled grass, as Ava had fully expected there to be. This time the newly dug ones look deeper and wider, as if their maker has become more determined, or perhaps more frantic, in their efforts. So *bloody* annoying to have missed the action! Ava resolves to lay off the after-dinner whisky, drink a gallon of black coffee instead, then try again tonight.

Next stop, the barn, double doors open wide. George's nippy green MG is indeed still here, adjacent to Fiona's mustard-coloured Hillman; Wick's Bentley is alongside the Addingtons'

Ford Cortina. Then there's a gap. The estate's Land Rover is missing... and Ava remembers! Fiona said Murdoch needed it this morning. No mystery here. She's about to wander elsewhere when something small, fast-moving, and brown zips across the periphery of her vision. There it is again! A bat, flitting to and fro, before disappearing among the beams above her head. A straggler, home after a night's hunting. At last, a chance to make a positive ID.

Ava sizes up the rickety wooden hayloft ladder. Taking care not to frighten her quarry... or break her neck... she ascends cautiously, one shaky rung at a time, and peers into the fusty shadows. The bleachy smell of ammonia makes her eyes water. How exciting! Must be a well-established roost. Pulling herself into the cramped roof space, she crouches under the eaves as her pupils adjust to the half-light. If she stays still and quiet, perhaps another bat'll show itself. Fingers crossed, a Daubenton's.

Ava's been waiting less than five minutes when the Land Rover swings back into the barn. Murdoch steps out of the driver's side and begins to unload bags of clean linen from the back, muttering through his whiskers. She's about to announce her presence when Ollach slowly emerges from the front passenger seat, in floods of tears. The woman makes no move to help Murdoch, instead resting her ample frame on the bonnet of George's car, causing the MG's suspension to groan in protest. Luckily for George, Murdoch remains standing.

'There, there, woman. Calm yersel,' he says. 'Ye're weepin' o'er what cannae be undone.'

'But it's *my* fault,' Ollach wails, burying her face in a handkerchief. 'I cannae keep it in any longer. I'm fit te explode.'

'Dinnae talk daft!' Murdoch reaches forwards as if to deliver a comforting pat, but seems to think better of it.

'Poor Heinrich. He was always so good te me. And Maggs. If only I'd left things as they were, he'd ne'er have come here.'

'Hush, Ollach! Words like that'll get ye in trouble.'

'Och, if you'd seen the state o' his beddin'.'

Murdoch shakes his head. 'I found him.'

'Why d'ye stay here, Angus? Come bide wi' me and Maggs on our side o' the water, where the likes o' us belong.'

'I ken my place.'

'Ye *used* te. If Duncan Muirhead were still alive, it'd be different. *He* knew how te be a laird. But he's gone, Sheila alang wi'im. Ye've nae debt te their son.'

'I've bin wi' Alastair since he was a bairn.'

'So have I, Angus! He's nae cut out fer the life he's tryin' te live, *and* he's puttin' himsel in the way o' ye livin' yours. As fer his skinny-bit o' a wife, sackin' Maggs fer nae good cause!'

'Nae good cause?' Murdoch lets out a dry laugh. 'Awa wi' ye Ollach!'

'Aye. Well,' Ollach says with a huff, 'another reason te come te us. I cannae get Maggs te quit her wee games, but *ye* she listens te. Ne'er mind Alastair Muirhead, ye've known her... her and me both... since *we* were bairns.'

'It was that Beckett piece who wanted her gone. Alastair's tekken her back.'

Ollach stands up. George's MG groans with relief. 'Aye. But fer how long? Typical o' the Muirheads! Pickin' people up, puttin' them down again, playing wi' their livelihoods. They've got yersel tinkerin' around wi' loose washers and blown lightbulbs like an odd job man, when ye should be out on the *land*. Mr Stewart sees that, and he's prepared te give ye plenty of his fancy London money te prove it. What keeps ye here, Angus? Answer me that!' Ollach steps closer to Murdoch. Murdoch holds his ground.

Ava has a cramp in her leg. She's also struggling to hear what's being said. It's no good. She'll have to move. As she repositions herself, a bat flits out from behind a beam and a shower of twigs and straw rains down on the pair below. 'Shit!'

Ollach and Murdoch spring apart.

'Who's there?' shouts Murdoch, his huge hands clenching into huge fists, much as they did when George was explaining about the cairn. 'Show yersel or I'll drag ye doon feet first.'

Ava considers keeping schtum. Touch wood, he'll think she's a rat. But, then again, of all people likely to follow through on a threat, that'd be Murdoch. She decides to hand herself in. 'Don't worry. It's only me,' she calls. 'Stalking bats.' As she descends the ladder, she keeps talking, talking, talking; hoping a battery of words will diffuse the tension in the air. 'I just wanted to satisfy myself vis-à-vis species. *Plecotus auritus* or *Myotis daubentonii*? Based on droppings alone, I'm leaning towards the former, but faeces are a *notoriously* subjective diagnostic tool. Ideally, I'd keep a portable reference collection on me, so's not to be caught on the hop.'

The talking plan seems to work. Though Murdoch's eyebrows remain knotted, his fists unfurl. Ollach blows her nose. Both stare at Ava blankly.

'Really,' sighs Ava when she reaches the floor, 'it doesn't matter *what* I was looking for. Point is, I didn't come here to snoop on you two. *I* was in here first, and couldn't leave because interrupting your conversation felt awkward.'

'Reekin' lang-nebbit,' mumbles Murdoch.

'How much did ye hear, doctor?' Ollach asks nervously.

'Um, let me see,' Ava says lightly. 'You, Ollach, blamed yourself for Herr Baumgarten's death. *You*, Murdoch, warned her to keep quiet about it. Then discussions turned to the Muirheads, specifically Alastair and Fiona's failings, both as custodians of the Dorcha estate and as employers.'

Ollach erupts into a renewed fit of wailing.

'Ach! Ye've set her off again,' harrumphs Murdoch. 'This isnae how it sounds!'

'Ollach,' Ava asks gently, once the woman has regained her composure, 'am I right in thinking you and Herr Baumgarten were friends?'

Ollach nods. 'Aye,' she replies with a doleful sniff. 'We were. Nae secret in that… nor nothin' smutty neither if that's where that brain of yer's is taking ye. I'm naebiddy's floozy.'

'Of course not, and I'm sorry for your loss.'

'Thank ye, I appreciate that.'

'May I ask how you knew him?'

'It's a plain enough story. Before the Muirheads turned their home into a hotel, I ran a wee business o' my own. There's always been a steady trail o' visitors te these parts, wantin' te see birds and whatnot, lookin' fer somewhere te stay. So I let out my backroom. It's nae fancy, mind, but clean towels twice a week and nae extra charge fer hot water. The birds are what first brought Heinrich to Drumapple a couple o' years back. Mad fer them, he was, and not just the eagles, like some o' those other spotters are. *All* Scottish birds. So I had him fer bed and breakfast. Two summers, one winter.'

'So he *did* know the area,' Ava mutters to herself. 'Thought so.'

'I'd rustle him up a bit o' dinner too, if he was wantin' it. And off he'd go wi' his binoculars, out for the day while I got the cookin' done. Very partial te a bowl o' my Cullen skink, wasn't he, Angus? Such a seemly person, ever so grateful.'

Murdoch licks his lips. 'Ye did him proud, Ollach. Ye did him proud.'

'Murdoch!' exclaims Ava. '*You* knew Herr Baumgarten too, yet you said nothing to me?'

'I'd met him, aye, but I didnae *ken* the man.'

'But I asked you—'

'—if we'd talked,' he shrugs. 'I answered we hadnae.'

'But—'

Deaf to Ava's frustration, Ollach heaves a reflective sigh. 'Heinrich and I had *lovely* chats, bletherin' fer hours. He wanted te stay wi' me and Maggs again this year, but I couldnae accommodate on account o' havin' my hands full wi' hotel laundry. So I wrote him nae te come, and he booked himself in at The Hall instead which I feel terrible about, because if I'd said te him te come te me anyways, like last time, he wouldnae have drunk so much… I run a dry house, doctor… and he wouldnae have ended up dead.'

'I told ye before, lass, ye're nae te blame.'

'*You* wrote to Herr Baumgarten?' Ava asks thickly as the penny drops. Hard.

'Aye. Nae a proper letter like ye'd have come up wi', doctor. I'm nae much of a writer… just a few sentences explainin' things, saying he'd be better elsewhere. But why am I tellin' *ye* this? Ye've seen what I wrote, or the last part o' it, anyways. "Things have changed. Ye cannae stay here",' recites Ollach.

'"Here" being your cottage in Drumapple, *not* The Hall?'

'Aye. Then I signed it wi' my initials.'

'"O" and "K"? An abbreviation of "Ollach Kettleness", rather than slang shorthand for "All Correct"?'

'Aye. Who'd have thought a couple o' lines from a letter could cause so much bother.' Ollach shakes her head in sad disbelief.

'Who indeed,' mutters Ava, deeply regretting that she hadn't let Maggie get a 'proper gander' when the girl asked. Maggie would've recognised her sister's handwriting, and Ava wouldn't be standing here now, egg on her face.

'As soon as Maggs told me ye'd ended up wi' that scrap o' paper, and that ye'd put two and two together and made five, thinkin' it was a warnin', tellin' him te stay away or else he'd be *murdered*... when all the time it was just a friendly wee message from me... I panicked! I didnae want the police te see it, and I knew ye'd plans te show Hamish Pratt and tell him all yer wild ideas the next second that ye got the chance. So... I'm nae proud o' what I did next... I stole it from yer room.'

'*Stole* it?'

'It wasnae an accident the note was lost, doctor. When I changed yer beddin', it wasnae a laundry day. I came on purpose te take the note, and destroy it. Which I did. I threw it on the fire.'

'How did you know where to find it?'

'Maggs suggested it... said how guests are ferever tuckin' things they value under their pillows. I shouldnae have needed remindin' o' that, should I, the number o' beds I've changed in my time.'

'But *why*, Ollach? What would it matter if Sergeant Pratt *had* seen it? You could simply have told him what you're telling me now. Any misunderstandings would have been nipped in the bud.'

Ollach throws a glance at Murdoch. Murdoch mutters something Ava doesn't quite catch.

'Thing is,' Ollach continues sheepishly, 'I wouldnae have minded if the police talked te *me* about Heinrich or anythin' else. Happy te blether away till kingdom come. But I wasnae keen on them talkin' te *Maggs* on account o'...' She hesitates. 'Well, things have a habit o' goin' missin' at The Hall – absolutely nae fault o' Maggs's, ye understand – and the maid's always the first te get the blame. And what wi' Miss Levi in such a stushie about her earrings, I was afraid Maggs might be tricked into sayin' somethin' daft and lose her job.' Ollach sighs. 'I didnae know she'd end up sacked anyway. Anyways, I reckoned if the note was te disappear before Hamish Pratt had his beady eyes on it, then naebiddy would have te explain anythin', and it would be nae harm done. Because nae harm *was* done te Heinrich, in my opinion. Though I'm awful sorry he's gone.' Ollach gives her nose another resolute blow. 'As Mam used to say, "better oot than in", and I apologise te ye, doctor, and hope ye can put what I did past ye.'

Ava's thoughts reel as she runs through the crushing upshots of Ollach's confession: The fragmentary note, despite *all* the significance Ava attached it, had nothing to do with Baumgarten's death. A stinking red herring. The evidence that he was murdered is as slim now as it ever was, if not non-existent. And – bugger, bugger, *bugger* – Wick was right! 'No,' she says slowly. 'No harm done, Ollach. Very little harm at all.'

'Mind you, Heinrich wasnae happy about stayin' at The Hall,' sniffs Ollach. 'Very uncomfortable. If it wasnae fer the birds, he'd ne'er have come at all, and after what happened, I can see why.'

'*Happened?*' Ava notes that Murdoch looks as puzzled as she feels.

Ollach looks from one to the other, her gaze lingering a little longer on Murdoch before she decides to continue. 'While I have ye here, there's somethin' else I'd like te get off my chest, about Heinrich and the Muirheads.'

'Don't tell me Herr Baumgarten knew Alastair and Fiona too, because they looked me in the eye—'

'Nae, nae! I'm speakin' about Duncan and Sheila.' Ollach's voice lowers to a whisper. 'Their accident, he saw it.'

Murdoch straightens up, growing several inches in height as he does so. 'What are ye sayin', Ollach?'

'He saw the crash,' she repeats. 'At New Year's, he was out and about early, doin' his spottin', and he was walkin' along the road lookin' fer one o' his birds, and a car... their car... he told me it came out o' nowhere. Heinrich thought it would hit him... he froze te the spot... but it skidded off the road and into the woods. Duncan Muirhead didnae even slow down.'

'There wasnae a deer?' Murdoch asks slowly.

Ollach shakes her head.

'Duncan swerved to avoid *Baumgarten*!' breathes Ava.

'Aye, and hit a tree.'

Murdoch looks incredulous. 'He didnae try and help them? He couldnae drag her oot? I'da dragged her oot. I'da saved her.' As he speaks, he moves his brawny arms as if wrenching open an imaginary door, dragging out an imaginary Sheila, hauling her to safety.

'The flames were too great. Heinrich said there wasnae anythin' te be done, Angus.'

'Nothin'?'

'Nothin'. But it wasnae Heinrich's fault. The way Duncan Muirhead was drivin'. He never braked, or if he did, he was too late.'

Murdoch's shoulders drop. As fast as he rose up, he wilts before Ava's eyes. There's no roar of rage, he just whimpers; like a dog that's been whipped, or a baby elephant crying for its mother, or a man who's been told that a loved one's death was avoidable.

'He didnae tell the police because he was worried he'd get in trouble, doctor.'

'Why would he fear that, Ollach, unless he felt a degree of responsibility? And who else knows about this?' asks Ava, immediately thinking of another person more than likely in the loop. When she asked Maggie if she'd got to know Baumgarten while he was staying at The Hall, the girl said no, which was true, but Ava bets they got very well acquainted during those holidays he spent in Drumapple.

Before Ollach can answer either question, they're interrupted by a harsh clatter from somewhere nearby. Not, it turns out, the sound of Ava's faith in human nature crumbling around her ears, but approaching footsteps. A quickening *click, clack, click, clack* of high heels on cobbles that herald the arrival of George. Alastair's with her, carrying a small suitcase in one hand and a large vanity case in the other.

'What do you mean "changed your mind", Alastair?' she snaps.

'It's not right to leave Fee on her own, and I'm inconveniencing you. I can reschedule—'

'For the tenth time, I don't mind going out of my way, just as long as we get on the road soon. Goodness, what's all this?' she asks spikily as they enter the barn. 'A farewell committee? If I could just find my car keys...' She starts rooting around in her pockets.

'Morning!' Alastair says brightly. 'Look at all us early birds!'

Murdoch and Ollach mumble their hellos.

'Shit!' mutters George. 'Hold this!' She shoves her briefcase into Ava's hands. Ava stands there while George pops it open and hoiks out her clipboard and a calculator... 'Where the *hell* are they? I know I had them last night. They were in my jacket pocket when I hung it in the cloakroom. Why didn't that local girl stay sacked? What did I say about thieving staff, Alastair?'

Ollach exits so hastily, she almost slips over in her rush to get away.

Murdoch lets out a series of muffled snorts; utterances which, Ava presumes, reflect an internal battle between shock and rage. But then she realises he is, in fact, sniffing, as though catching a scent. Is he picking up on the bat droppings? Ava spots something, a puddle of oily liquid, trickling out from underneath George's car. Ollach must have stepped in it as she ran off. Ava bends down, dips in a forefinger and holds it up to her nose. 'Smells like fish.'

'Nae fish,' says Murdoch. 'Brake fluid!'

George looks like she might actually explode. 'Brake fluid! From *my* car! I don't believe this. Those bloody potholes. How many times have I said they should be filled in?' She stuffs her things back in her case and slams it shut. Alastair opens his mouth as if to speak, but George is far from done. 'Don't bother to answer, Mr Muirhead, because I've lost count. You know what this means? I'll tell you. Even if I hadn't had my keys filched, I'd still be unable to leave. So ridiculous, you couldn't make it up! I'm going to my room to lie down. Do not disturb me until my keys are found and my car is roadworthy.' With that, she flounces away as fast as her high heels will allow.

'Oh dear,' says Alastair. 'I've rather let her down. What do you think Murdoch? Likely to be a quick fix?'

Murdoch looks dumbfounded.

'The car, I mean...'

'I'll tek a gander and let ye know.'

Alastair picks up a laundry bag. 'Okay, but first, let's get this lot to The Hall, and I'll bring Fee up to speed, too. She's *not* going to be happy.'

Sadly, he's right. When she claps eyes on Ava, Alastair, and Murdoch, her face falls. 'How come you're still here?'

As her husband explains why he is not, as planned, en route to meet their bank manager, and how his and Georgina Beckett's departure came to be thwarted, her initial annoyance is swept away by an apparent tidal wave of exasperation. Even when Alastair gives her a hug, she looks decidedly prickly.

'I was in two minds about going anyway, Fee. And aren't you a *little* grateful we didn't set off, given the dodgy brakes?'

'Of course I am,' she says pettishly. 'Now put that trowel to good use, and see to the driveway before anyone else's car comes a cropper. Murdoch, get the laundry out of reception. It's cluttering the place up.'

There's something in the way Fiona issues this second order that makes Ava smart. Murdoch says nothing, but allows Ava to help with lugging the hefty bags upstairs. 'Murdoch,' she says quietly, when they reach the top landing, 'I agree with what

Ollach said earlier, in the barn. You needn't feel tied to Dorcha Hall. You've been a wonderful friend to the Muirheads... to Alastair... but you don't owe them more than you've already given. For what it's worth,' she continues, 'I think you should take up Mr Stewart's offer and start again at Beinn Beithe.'

Murdoch doesn't meet her gaze. 'Will ye be repeatin' what else Ollach had te say fer hersel, doctor? Will ye be tellin' Hamish Pratt about the German man and the crash?'

'I don't know. I have to think about it. It's not really my tale to tell. Will *you*?'

Murdoch lifts up Ava's laundry load and swings it over his shoulder. 'Thank ye, doctor,' he says, as though her question went unheard. 'I'll tek it from here.' Thus burdened, he lumbers away.

23
Ta Dah!

That evening, Ava watches from the sitting room as dark clouds gather. Against the blue-black sky, the tree tops look unnaturally green. The mountains glow red. As Ollach said, 'the fine dryin' spell cannae last forever', and when the storm breaks, the weather seems to be making up for lost time. Stair rods of water pelt down with such fury, the loch's surface seethes. They lash at the window. Chutes cascade from blocked gutters while insidious rivulets find their way under the cracked roof tiles of the bay canopy. Ava becomes aware of a tinny *ptang, ptang, ptang* coming from a metal bucket strategically placed beneath, to catch drips; reminders of The Hall's decrepitude, which the Muirheads could no doubt do without.

Despite the surrounding disorder, Ava feels on an even keel. Thanks to Sinclair Stewart and, to be fair, George, Alastair's been thrown a lifeline which he intends to accept. Her worries regarding his future are easing. Ava's suspicions about Baumgarten's death may not have been put to rest, and during the arid interval since it happened, she's certainly questioned the behaviours of those around her: Murdoch's secrecy, Baumgarten's seemingly random trip to Inverness, that teasingly ambiguous note. But, through luck as much as design, each of these anomalies has been explained. She wishes she could forget the excruciating phone call she had to make to Pratt, giving a suitably edited version of how she learned the note was, indeed, as banal as he'd guessed it was. Was she wrong not to tell him about Baumgarten and the crash? Should she have told Wick? Both questions require thought. Although the rain can't flush away her embarrassment, or indecision.... or what those bitten knees continue to tell her... just for now, she intends to hold her tongue and park her sense of unfinished business. She'll have a nice, quiet evening, and an early night.

Fiona's lit the fire, and guests are gathered in a loose preprandial drove. The Addingtons' game of Monopoly has reached a fractious conclusion. Martin, the winner, gloats shamelessly while his sulky sibling refuses to help pack away. 'You cheated,' whines Carl.

'Did *not*! I won fair and square because you landed on Mayfair, twice, and I had a hotel on it.'

'*I'd* have won if I had my lucky top-hat playing piece, which *you've* hidden... because you're mean.'

'Have not!' Martin thumps Carl on the arm.

'Have so!' Carl thumps Martin on the thigh.

'Suck it up, sonny!' snaps Lauri Levi without looking up from her magazine. 'Whinging gets on my tits.'

Barbara Addington's lips purse.

Bernard Addington's ears turn mauve.

Sinclair and George, seated either side of the hearth, pay no attention to the fracas. They're too immersed in their own conversation. George looks happy, almost glowing, in his presence, this morning's vexations apparently forgotten. Clever Fiona. The last-minute dinner invitation she extended to Stewart is proving a strategic success. Wick, legs outstretched, a weighty book resting open on his chest, is dozing. And the riveting read that's put him out for the count? Ava guesses he's had another bash at Fiona's thesis. She considers having a flick through herself, but doesn't want to disturb him. Neither is she that interested. She's contemplating elbowing in on George and Sinclair's one-to-one and the irritation that would cause, when she spots a new arrival standing in a corner. Peigi! Ava didn't see her come in. She's watching the spat between Carl and Martin, nodding along awkwardly, trying not to look as alone as she does.

Ava suspects the young woman's dress is her best, making the satchel that's hanging from her shoulder seem incongruous. Ava greets her warmly, and Peigi reciprocates.

'Are you joining us for dins too?'

'Alastair asked me to pop over, and I was pleased at the time, but now I'm here, I've got butterflies. Stupid, isn't it? It's not like I haven't eaten at Dorcha Hall a thousand times before. I'm not sure Fiona knows I'm here. I'm part of Alastair's surprise.'

Ava feels her eyebrows raise. Last time the Muirheads sprang a surprise on their guests, Baumgarten's night ended very badly. Ava's since assumed that impromptu diversions of any kind would be off the table.

'He hasn't told you about it?' Peigi lets out a quick, uncertain laugh.

'Not breathed a word.'

'I'll say no more, then. Honestly' – Peigi shifts from foot to foot – 'I don't know where to put myself. He cooked up the whole thing, so I'm hoping he'll provide stage directions when the time comes.'

Right on cue, in wanders Alastair. Peigi gives him a nervous little wave, but he doesn't seem to see her. Clearly on a mission, he crosses the room, unknots a long, tasselled cord from around one of the heavy brocade curtains and, without any explanation, takes it away. Ava and Peigi follow him to the lobby where Murdoch's dragging dining chairs out of the library as Fiona supervises.

'I want a semicircle so everyone's facing the staircase, backs to the door. Ava, if you'd move to one side, then Alastair can put up the barrier rope.'

'That should do it,' he says, duly securing the curtain tie across the bottom two stair spindles.

'So much industry!' declares Ava. 'I'm intrigued.'

'Getting ready for tonight's entertainment,' Alastair says excitedly. 'It's a—'

'Wait and see!' Fiona cuts in, giving him a teasing poke in the rib. But then she spots Peigi, and the smiling stops. 'What are *you* doing here?'

'Peigi!' says Alastair. 'You made it!'

At that moment there's a flash of lightning and a crack of thunder so close, the chandeliers shudder; from somewhere above comes a dull *thud*.

'She's reet overhead,' says Murdoch, rolling his eyes to the heavens.

Fiona, too, looks up at the ceiling, then at the face of the grandfather clock. 'It's a bit early, but the storm brings so much extra atmosphere.' There's another *thud*. Fiona and Alastair exchange glances and Fiona smiles. 'If "you know who" is ready for us, why not seize the moment?'

'Let's go for it,' he agrees.

'Murdoch, get dressed! Alastair darling, the gong! Ava, could you nip into the sitting room and encourage folk to come out here? Then the fun can begin.'

Murdoch withdraws.

Alastair *bongs*.

Ava corrals her fellow guests, and all assemble, variously nonplussed, at the bottom of the stairs. Fiona does a head count. 'Great! Full house. If you'd like to sit down wherever you're comfortable and please don't interfere with the barrier.'

'Gee whiz!' carps Lauri, swinging the curtain-tie rope. 'Trapped! No sneakin' to our rooms to catch a few zees.'

'Bear with us, Miss Levi,' Fiona says crisply. 'I'm sure you'll find it worth the wait.'

Barbara and Bernard position themselves centre front. Lauri plants herself squarely at Sinclair Stewart's left flank, George having placed herself at his right. Wick and Ava land the other side of the Addingtons, Peigi choosing the end of the row. Alastair and Fiona remain standing, hovering in the background, while the Addington boys, still squabbling, arrange themselves cross-legged on the floor at their parents' feet; elbowing and pinching each other till Bernard deals each son a swift cuff to the back of his scruffy head. Once again, lightning flashes, thunder claps, and everyone shuffles in their seats.

'Ladies and gentlemen,' says Alastair. 'Welcome to this

evening's mystery show. Fee and I ask you to hold tight, suspend disbelief, and prepare to be amazed!'

'Take it away, Murdoch!' calls Fiona and, as she dims the lights, from the direction of the office rise the distinctive reedy drones of bagpipes inflating. At first, Murdoch himself remains out of sight while his music fills the air. But when he finally emerges in resplendent Highland dress, a swathe of plaid draped from his shoulder, dirk on his hip, it's an arresting display. His deliberate, broken gait – pausing, feet together between steps – evokes a wedding march. Father of the bride. Or chief mourner at a funeral. He's playing a lament; a poignant, legato dirge so intense, Ava feels her teeth chatter. With unexpected exactitude, Murdoch's sausage fingers move up and down on the chanter and, as he squeezes and blows, his red cheeks swell like the taut, shiny throat of a tomato frog. Ava blinks away the image of Baumgarten's florid face as it reels through her brain.

Murdoch comes to a stop at the foot of the stairs, and with a seemingly infinite breath, ends on a note so long and pure, even Lauri Levi dabs her eyes.

But such sappiness is, on her part at least, transient. 'Is that *it*?' she asks, after the briefest of pauses.

Murdoch fixes her with a scorching glower. She sends daggers right back.

Then, for what seems like a very long minute, nothing happens.

Ava looks at Peigi, but it's clear from her expression, Peigi doesn't know what's going on either.

Sinclair Stewart checks his Rolex.

'Should we remain seated, Mrs Muirhead?' asks Barbara Addington.

Fiona and Alastair are not, however, focused on their guests. They're staring expectantly towards the top of the stairs, watching, and listening... 'Should I ring the bell?' whispers Fiona.

Alastair shakes his head.

Thud. Wallop. Thud.

Now *everyone* looks up, craning their necks, eager to get a better view of the commotion on the unlit landing. There, part-hidden in shadow, lies a figure. Curled in the foetal position, chest heaving, long red hair in straggles, it appears drenched in mud. Other than these delicious details, it's hard to make out much else. But in the unforgiving split-second glare of a lightning flash, all is laid bare. To the mob's excruciating delight, a scene worthy of the hammiest B-movie comes alive before their eyes.

First, very gradually, the figure unfurls. As it does so, it starts to make sounds. Dreadful, guttural howls. Then, to a collective gasp of glee, it suddenly flips onto its belly. On all fours it half crawls, half slithers, to the banisters. It's here that it drags itself upright, and reveals its identity to a gobsmacked audience.

'Maggie!' breathe the Addington boys.

'She's naked!' cries their mother.

'Apart from those earrings!' says George. 'What an extraordinary sight!'

Ava sees Fiona mouth something to Alastair. 'Where's her costume?'

'Search me,' Alastair mouths back.

Maggie, arms outstretched, begins to stagger and sway around. Drool pours from her slack, open mouth. Her huge, dilated pupils give the impression of wide-eyed surprise, yet she snatches blindly at the air.

Fiona looks studiously at Murdoch, as if she expects him to say something, but he averts his gaze.

'She should cover hersel',' he mumbles.

Alastair shrugs his shoulders. Clearly irritated, Fiona takes a deep breath. In stilted tones, she addresses her guests. 'In celebration of Dorcha's rich history, on the quincentenary of her legendary death, we give you The Lass of The Loch!'

Right on cue, Maggie speaks. 'God help me!' she rattles, clawing madly at her own neck. 'I'm drownin'! Drownin'!'

'*Awesome*!' sighs Martin.

'So, *so* cool,' agrees Carl.

George clutches Wick's arm, and leans in. 'This,' she whispers excitedly, 'is *exactly* what I was talking about. Authentic atmosphere in spades! Seems people *were* listening after all.'

Again, Fiona glares at Murdoch. 'Narrator!' she prompts under her breath. *'Please!'*

Murdoch, a picture of abject resignation, slowly turns to face the expectant crowd. 'And so,' he mumbles through his beard, pointing up at Maggie, 'the sleekit làbh-allan's bonnie sister has kept her promise. She has risen up te haunt this cursed place, home o' the gutless laird... spewin' black waters, droolin' like a banshee... ranting wi' vengeful rage...'

Maggie lets out a deep moan. The saliva pouring from her lips turns crimson. 'Assassin!' she rattles. 'Assassin! I willnae be the last!' Her entire body shakes. As she rotates in a clumsy pirouette, dollops of reddish-brown sludge run down the backs of her legs and the insides of her thighs, slopping like fresh cowpats onto the floor beneath her bare feet. A stench of faeces fills the air.

As the grandfather clock begins to toll the sixth hour, it's Murdoch who acts first. 'This isnae right!' he cries, wrenching down the barrier rope with such force, a stair spindle snaps. Wick smacks on the ceiling lights. Ava and Peigi scramble up the stairs. But for all their speed, realisation has come too late to save Maggie. Still grasping her neck, the girl drops to her knees and falls, facedown, into a lake of her own bloody excrement.

24

Help Yourself

Dr Sween and Sergeant Pratt's inspection of the scene is observed by the same congregation who, two hours and forty minutes earlier, saw Maggie Kettleness die horribly before their very eyes; the latest Act in a hideous melodrama for which the hotel residents have front row seats. Glued to their chairs by a tacky mixture of repulsion, fascination, and shock, they watch from below as the two men pocket the hankies they've had pressed against their noses and gingerly peel off the carrier bags protecting their boots.

Dr Sween unhooks his stethoscope from around his neck and stows it in his battered Gladstone bag. 'Tragic,' he tuts, stepping over what's left of the barrier rope.

'Aye,' concurs Pratt, dabbing beads of sweat from his forehead. He turns to Alastair. 'And ye're *all* witnesses?'

'Every one of us,' answers Fiona.

'I couldn't bear to look!' volunteers Barbara Addington.

'Quite right too,' says her husband, patting her knee.

'I missed some as well,' says Martin.

'I saw everything,' says Peigi. Her red and swollen eyes brimming with tears. Ava wonders what the 'surprise' she referred to earlier was supposed to be. Surely not the one she got.

'I may not be one o' yer modern TV doctors, ladies and gentlemen,' says Sween, 'but te say the girl ate somethin' that disagreed with her would be the understatement o' my career. Does anybiddy else feel unwell?'

The crowd, every one of its members as white as a sheet and

half of them no doubt ready to vomit, shakes its head. Lauri Levi appears the worst of the bunch. She sits apart from the rest. Shivering. Hugging herself as if to keep warm. Ava's surprised at quite how traumatised the woman seems. Then again, Lauri did buckle at the aftermath of Baumgarten's comparatively tidy demise; perhaps it's no wonder she's so undone by the intensity of what occurred tonight.

'What was on the supper menu?' asks Pratt, notebook at the ready.

'We haven't served supper yet,' whispers Alastair, sounding as devastated as he looks. 'Maggie and I were going to dish up after the... performance. I've known her all her life...'

'*All* her life!' Peigi says hotly. 'This is terrible. You sacked her, didn't you? If only she'd never come back! God knows, I wish I hadn't!'

'Why *are* you here?' Fiona asks. '*I* didn't invite you.'

'Alastair did, and if he needs me to do something, I'll always try to help.'

'How could you possibly help? Alastair was just being kind because you're alone. There's nothing here for you anymore. And *don't* give me that line about the West Coast light being better, because it doesn't wash.'

Alastair tries to speak, but Pratt cuts in. 'I'm aware Maggie was yer friend, Peigi, and I ken yersel and Alastair have, shall I say, "a history". But what brought ye te The Hall today?'

'I've got a present for Fiona. Not from me, from her husband,' Peigi answers without looking at Alastair. 'He asked me to take a photograph... all in secret... and he wanted her to have it tonight.' Reaching into her satchel, she takes out a flat parcel. This, Ava realises, must be the private commission Peigi referred to the day Ava visited her studio. Peigi hands it to Fiona. 'Open it, why don't you!'

Fiona rips off the wrapping paper, and stares. It's a picture taken at The Murder Field, but the perspective is unusual. Peigi must've lain on her stomach to take it. The pink flowers, up close and in perfect focus, now look like a forest of trees, golden rays of light filtering through their tops, like sunbeams through branches. To Ava's mind, it's a beetle's eye view, and she thinks it's wonderful. Fiona, however, doesn't.

'Alastair, I don't understand.'

'It's an anniversary gift.' He answers sadly.

'That's not till Sunday.'

'Not *our* anniversary, Fee, The Lass of The Loch's. I wanted you to have the picture tonight because it's a special date and' – he hesitates – 'because The Murder Field will always be a special place to us, even if we sell it.'

'*Darling*! That's so sweet! I wasn't thinking.'

Pratt utters an enquiring cough.

'It's where my wife and I got engaged, sergeant.'

'I see. Touchin'. Tell me about tonight's show.'

'It was a last-minute thing. Something George… Miss Beckett… put into our heads.'

'No way has what just happened got *anything* to do with me!' George's indignation is so explosive, Alastair recoils as if physically punched.

Fiona intervenes. 'My husband merely means we took on board Miss Beckett's suggestion, about injecting local colour into The Hall's entertainment programme. We decided to spice things up with an impromptu re-enactment of The Lass's story. It's about—'

'I'm aware o' the legend,' says Pratt. 'I've lived in these parts a deal longer than ye have, Mrs Muirhead.'

'Sorry. Of course you have.' She turns to Alastair. 'Are you okay to continue?'

'Maggie agreed to play the part of The Lass's ghost. Fee sorted out a costume… a wig… a long black gown with lots of seaweedy lace.'

'My mother-in-law's,' adds Fiona.

'Maggie was excited about the whole thing. Said she couldn't wait to "be the star of the show".'

Peigi mutters under her breath.

Lauri whimpers.

Alastair falters.

Fiona squeezes his hand.

Alastair rallies. 'We left her to get dressed in one of the spare bedrooms. The plan was she'd "manifest" on the dot of six o'clock, in character, and Murdoch would recite the legend… or at least the more sensational lines from it. But when the storm broke, and we heard Maggie moving around upstairs, banging… This beggars belief. I can't get my head round it…'

Once again, Fiona takes over. 'We assumed that enthusiasm overcame her, and she was ready early. So Alastair, Murdoch and I simply went ahead with things, not realising what state she was in.'

Sween addresses the assembly. 'Did anybiddy see what young Maggie ate, or drank, today?'

'She had porridge for breakfast, a plate of Alastair's borage quiche for lunch,' says Fiona.

'Nae a mouthful others didnae swallow too,' mutters Murdoch.

Just then, like eager pupils trying to catch the eye of their schoolteacher, each Addington boy shoots his right arm up in the air. 'Please, sir,' says Martin, 'my brother and I saw Maggie eating something.'

'She was stuffing herself with sweets,' says Carl. 'Wouldn't let us have any. She'd a box of 'em tucked up under her jumper. Kept sneaking one when she thought we couldn't see.'

'What sweeties were they?'

'Dunno,' shrugs Martin. 'Not the type from a shop. More like the dried fruits Mr Muirhead puts on the front desk for everyone to help themselves.'

All eyes spin towards Alastair. Ava swallows hard.

It is not he, however, who speaks next. 'They were sour cherries. Chocolate-dipped.' The voice from the back of the room is immediately recognisable, but its usual razor edge is missing. '*I* gave them to her.' Once again, eyes wheel, to land upon Lauri Levi. 'Easy, folks! Reel in your peepers, it ain't how it sounds.' Fighting talk, yet Lauri, wan and cowering, looks like a woman on the ropes.

'Please, Miss Levi, explain,' says Pratt.

'This morning, after breakfast, I go to lay down on my bed, and someone rocks up at my door. Maggie. She knocks... *That* made a change!... But before I get to say a word, in she bounds. Poor dumb kid. Never did wait for an invite. Right off the bat, she shoves a box into my hand, all done up with a bow. I ask her who it's from, and she says, "Read the message!" and I sees there's an envelope tucked under the ribbon, with a note inside.' Lauri stops short.

'What did it say?'

Lauri throws a sideways look across the room. At whom? The Muirheads? Or only *Alastair*? Thanks to the thickness of Lauri's false lashes, Ava can't tell.

'Lauri!' George says brusquely. 'The sergeant needs an answer!'

Roused by this verbal slap, Lauri fishes around in the sleeve of her kaftan and retrieves a folded white card. 'See for yourself.'

Dr Sween opens it, holds it up to the light, then peers at it through his spectacles, squinting to decipher what Ava sees is handwritten scrawl. He passes it to Pratt. Pratt carefully inspects it front and back, clears his throat, and adjusts his tie before reading aloud: '"Te Lovely Miss L. Sorry." Hmm. So, the chocolates were intended fer you, Miss Levi?'

'Sure looks that way,' she mumbles. 'Don't it.'

'Can ye think of anybiddy who wishes ye harm?'

'Oh, everyone loves *me*, officer!' Ava notes that, as blasé as Lauri sounds, her hands haven't stopped trembling since she began speaking.

'The message is unsigned. Who did'ye think the gift was from?'

Again, Lauri appears to look at Alastair. He shows no reaction, but she holds him in her sights while constructing a reply. 'I'd rather not say.' She folds her arms across her chest like a recalcitrant child.

'Och, awa wi' ye!' protests Murdoch. 'Five weeks o' tongue flappin', *this* is when ye haud yer wheesht?'

'That's right, shout at me!' mutters Lauri. 'Bet you wish I'd eaten them.'

'Ye're nae wrong there!' Murdoch snarls back.

Rancorous words from Murdoch, but Ava's as puzzled as he is. Why is Lauri, a person so in love with the limelight, suddenly reluctant to speak?

'This is no time for reticence, Miss Levi,' says Sween.

'The doctor's right.' Alastair's tone is encouraging and kind. 'Anything you can say would be helpful.'

'All right, all right,' she sighs, arms still folded. 'I thought the gift was from the girl herself, Maggie. She said it wasn't, but I figured that was a lie.'

'Why did you think she was lying?' asks Ava.

'*I* am speakin', Dr Dickens!' Pratt rebukes irritably. 'Miss Levi,' he repeats, 'why didnae ye believe Maggie?'

'Because of my earrings. They were in the envelope too. I reckon she filched them when I first arrived. But later, as the days went by... well... she kinda took a shine to me and I guess she felt bad about stealin'. The candies, the note, perhaps they were her way of returnin' the earrings without losin' face. Anyways, *I* didn't want no souped-up cherries. I'm watchin' my figure. And there she was, standin' right in front of me, hoppin' from foot to foot and fit to bust, gushin' how they're her absolute favourite thing in the whole goddam world; so I says she can have 'em and keep the earrings too.'

'You gave her your earrings!' Fiona's aghast. '*Gave* them to her? After all that fuss!'

'Guess I didn't want them as much as I thought.'

'Let it go, Fee,' Alastair says gently, putting an arm around his wife's rigid shoulders. 'It hardly matters now.'

'Exactly,' says Lauri. 'They're paste, anyhows.'

Fiona glowers at her. Lauri Levi glowers back.

'What did Maggie do next?' asks Pratt, trying to regain the reigns.

'Took off,' Lauri shrugs, 'like she'd won a million bucks. I took a nap. Turns out she ate the candy. The rest is, as they say, history.' Another show of verbal indifference so quaky, Ava doubts anyone's fooled.

'You two lads, do ye know where the chocolates ended up?' asks the doctor.

'She had them in the lobby,' says Martin, 'then the library...'

'The last place was in the sitting room, before lunch,' says Carl. 'The box was empty, so she stuffed it into the fireplace.'

'Oh no!' cries Fiona. 'I lit it!'

Pratt dashes off, returning moments later, cursing under his breath. 'Grate's full o' ashes.'

'Well ain't that a bummer!' Lauri says mockingly, swaying to her feet. 'Don't know about the rest of you schmucks, but *I'm* gonna pack my suitcase—'

'Miss Levi,' Pratt interjects, 'there's been a suspicious death. Highly suspicious. Evidence suggests *ye* were the intended victim. Ye need te remain here till the police get te the bottom o' things. That goes for everybiddy else too. Mrs Muirhead, Alastair, make yer guests comfortable in the library and keep the door closed. I caution ye not te speculate amongst yersels. Dr Sween, stay with the body. Detective Inspector Clowdy left Inverness an hour ago. Ye can expect him soon. I must get te Drumapple—'

'Steady yersel, Hamish!' commands Murdoch. He removes his piper's bonnet and jams it under his left arm, crushing its gay ribbons and the pom-pom on its top. '*I'll* tell the sister.' Without waiting for sanction, or the torrential rain to stop, he evanesces into the bleak, black, pitiless night.

25

Any One of Us!

Clowdy does not, it seems, work alone. A fleet of cars pulls up, higgledy-piggledy, blue lights flashing, and out spills a swarm of uniformed officers. Despite the rain, they don't immediately come indoors, but mill about among the puddles and potholes, walkie-talkies crackling, while a sleek unmarked Jaguar parks parallel to The Hall's front entrance. A tall man in a smart suit carefully decants himself, and as he marches up the steps, only then does the rest of the crowd follow suit. Quite the turnout. As there should be. Ava's pleased for Maggie – 'pleased' seems an ill-fitting word – but what about Baumgarten? Surely, with a second death such as this, even the Hilton's general manager would be experiencing qualms.

Once inside, the policemen fan out like army ants on a raid. Some go straight upstairs; others head for the kitchen, dining room, library. One by one, each of their shell-shocked spectators has his or her fingerprints taken, 'for the record', along with a mug shot. The photographer, a jolly and nimble young man, 'call me Paul', chats away as if working a wedding, complimenting George and Lauri on their outfits, rueing the weather. The Muirheads are permitted to provide soup, which no one eats.

It's long past midnight when Maggie leaves her workplace for the last time and everyone is dismissed to bed. Alastair and Fiona retire to their room, while the exhausted guests, Peigi and Stewart included, are escorted past the crime scene as they trail upstairs. 'Nae talkin'! Ye'll be questioned in the mornin'.'

The Beasts of the Black Loch

'Are you okay?' Wick mouths to Ava before they go their separate ways.

Giving him a chipper thumbs up, she wishes she felt so valiant inside. Outside, the storm continues to lash at The Hall's leaky roofs and windows, and the wind wails long and low; at least, it's most likely the wind and not the keenings of Ollach Kettleness from the other side of the loch.

When day finally breaks, it brings clear skies, and stark reality. A scratched-together breakfast is served in near silence, under the watchful gaze of Pratt. Neither of the Muirheads look as though they've slept. Residents chew on stale bread, swallow stewed tea, and observe each another with distrustful stares. Meanwhile, a crew clad in boiler suits methodically scrubs the landing carpet, and the landing skirtings, and the landing walls. Murdoch mends the broken stair spindle; sawing, and hammering, and cursing under his breath. Grating sounds of industry. For all her foibles, Maggie was part of this place. Ava doubts there's enough elbow grease in Scotland to shift her traces from the very many surfaces the slapdash girl failed to dust.

The police commandeer the Muirheads' office as an interview room. Clowdy wants to speak to everyone separately with the exceptions of Carl and Martin, who are accompanied by their father. This family trio is seen first. All others sit in the lobby, like patients lined up in a doctor's waiting room, till he or she is called. Ava appraises the group. George and Sinclair, heads bowed, are locked in another of their private tête-à-tetes. The former is doing most of the talking. Peigi looks like she's cried all night.

Wick, who's next to Ava, nods towards Barbara Addington. 'How *can* she be knitting at a time like this?'

'"Displacement activity". Classic example. When an animal experiences intense, conflicting urges it can't resolve, it may resort to seemingly inappropriate behaviours to deflect its negative energies elsewhere. Barbara wants to be with her sons, yet she doesn't want to be *here* at all. She has no say in either matter. Barbara can't run away, or hide, so she'll knit-one-purl-one till she regains control. A cornered parrot will pull out its feathers. A cat caught in a threatening situation from which it can't escape may simply fall asleep.'

'And ostriches stick their heads in the sand,' adds Wick.

'They do, but that's to regulate the temperate of their eggs. Underground nests, etcetera, etcetera...'

'Silly old me,' Wick says pettishly. 'Arguably, giving an off-the-cuff tutorial in ethology could be seen as "deflective". *I* was merely trying to join in.'

Alastair and Fiona sit side by side, still as statues. He stares at the ceiling; she, at the floor. Barbara Addington's needles click furiously. Lauri Levi picks at her painted nails. Murdoch, slumped in a corner, chin on his chest, emits a rumbling snore.

'Poor devil,' rues Wick. 'Heaven knows what time he got to bed if he got to bed at all. I wonder what he's dreaming about.'

Ava's pretty sure it won't be anything nice; car crashes, birdwatchers, dying girls and broken hearts. As she rolls another cigarette, she considers what displacement activity a murderer, stuck waiting to talk to the police, might get up to, just to kill time?

The office door opens, and the Addington males are 'free to go'. Murdoch rouses. Everyone looks up expectantly, hoping... dreading... that they'll be the next to be called. It's Wick who gets the longest of the short straws.

'Professor Wickremesinghe!' announces a woman constable. 'DI Clowdy will see ye now.'

'Are we gonna be sittin' around all day?' Lauri drums her fingertips on the arm of her chair. Her legs are crossed but her feet tap uncontrollably.

'Everything okay?' asks Ava.

'Jeez, lady! Just when I thought your questions couldn't get any dumber! No, Doctor I'll-Be-Darned Dickens, I *ain't* all right. You saw what happened, same as I freakin' did. I'll never *un*see it. Poor kid. She didn't deserve to die like that. When I came to this place, I never expected it could get so... so... goddam *cruel.*'

'No one could have expected a scene like that,' Alastair says dully.

'Except the person who poisoned the cherries,' mutters Ava. Not a soul seems to hear.

'Miss Levi,' sighs Fiona. '*Please* pull yourself together. I'll fetch you some water—'

'Water!' Lauri chuckles dryly. 'You can stick *that* where the sun don't shine. Make mine a whisky with an arsenic chaser, speciality of the house. Or how's about plain ol' strychnine on the goddam rocks.'

Fiona's cheeks colour. 'I'm sorry, but we all need to remain calm and, frankly, your "humour" is not helping.'

'Sister, *I* stopped laughin' at the first stiff!'

'Blast!' curses Barbara. 'Dropped a stitch.'

Lauri leans forward in her seat. 'Tell you what, Fifi,' she whispers meanly, '*you* can go boil your head. Ali, fetch the car! This shitshow's over and we're leavin'.'

'I don't understand.' Alastair sounds bewildered, but to Ava, Lauri's meaning is transparently clear, and rational. She was given a box of poison-laced chocolates, literally with her name on it, likely by someone in this room. No wonder the woman wants to hightail it to the hills.

As far as Fiona's concerned, however, it seems such reasoning is beside the point. '*You* are not going anywhere with my husband.' She's practically hissing.

'No one's allowed to leave,' says Alastair. 'The police were adamant.'

Lauri addresses Alastair as if Fiona wasn't there. 'I'm outta here, kiddo. If you want to hang around like some turkey waitin' for Thanksgivin', that's on you. But don't forget, when you're lookin' death in the face, *I* offered you a choice.' Lauri's eyes bore into his, and for a brief moment, her façade cracks. She looks exactly like who she is: a woman in love. 'So, what's it gonna be?'

Alastair stares back at her. Fiona's grip on his hand is so tight, his fingertips are turning red. 'We should all stay here, Lauri,' he says evenly, 'like we've been told.'

Lauri rises to her feet. Her painted lips slowly part as if she's about to speak, but the moment's swept away. The office door reopens, Wick reappears, and so does the policewoman. 'Miss Levi! Nae runnin' awa, I hope?'

As quickly as Lauri's mask slipped, it clamps back in place, as tight as it ever was. 'Keep your hair on, lady. Just stretchin' my legs.'

'If ye'd like te come through, please, the insepctor's ready fer ye now.'

Ava's turn comes last. She's placed directly facing Clowdy. The policewoman sits in a corner, while Pratt remains standing. Without preamble, the interview begins, and she supposes she's getting asked much the same as other guests:

'What brought you to Dorcha Hall?'
'How well do you know the Muirheads?'
'Did you see what happened last night?'
'What is your relationship with Miss Levi?'
'What was your relationship with Margaret Kettleness?'

A predictable list of questions to which she gives straightforward replies. But then comes the nitty gritty. 'Take a look at this note,' continues Clowdy. 'Do you recognise the writing, or have an idea about who its author was?'

'No, and I won't speculate. Recent experience has taught me that messages, even short ones, can be very misleading.'

Pratt coughs.

'What can you tell us about dried cherries?'

'Nothing, other than the fact I don't like them.' Ava's response comes easily, but she's seriously worried about what Alastair's answer may have been. When he was ushered into the interview room, he resembled an injured antelope stumbling towards a clan of hyenas, afraid of being eaten alive; when he re-emerged, an hour later, he seemed thoroughly chewed. Now, as Pratt takes notes and the DI refills his pipe, Ava imagines how the police must have drilled down:

'Do you have cherry trees on your land, Alastair?' Or

perhaps they're calling him 'Mr Muirhead' now.

'When you say "foraging", *Mr Muirhead*?' 'And you preserve them yourself? Correct?' 'Explain how.' 'An involved process, then?' 'Did you make the chocolates that Margaret Kettleness ate?' 'Really? How *did* she come by them, then?'

Ava pictures her godson, squirming in his seat. Did he sweat? *Horripilate*? Of course he did! Especially without Fiona at his side, clutching his hand in hers, ratcheting up her vice-like hold each time the going got tougher. Ava doesn't believe he killed Maggie, or tried to kill Lauri Levi, not for a moment; but someone did...

'Well, thank you for your time, Dr Dickens,' says the inspector.

'Is that it?' asks Ava.

'Unless there's anything you wish to add.'

'I've a query. After what's happened to Maggie, I assume you will be viewing Herr Baumgarten's death through a different lens?'

Clowdy draws on his pipe. Realising it's extinguished, he tamps it down with his thumb before slipping it into his top pocket; a small act that underlines his air of finality. 'Dr Dickens, the police maintain an open mind. Our investigations regarding yesterday's death are my priority, but should you have any evidence pertinent to other recent events, you are urged to bring it to our attention.'

Ava takes a breath. She's about to mention Ollach's account of Duncan and Sheila's crash, but something makes her hesitate, and the inspector ploughs on. 'Until otherwise informed, you're not to check out of the hotel without my authorisation. Remain in the immediate bounds of the estate. I've instructed other guests, and those visiting The Hall on the night of Miss Kettleness's death, to do likewise. Being persons of interest, *everyone* in this building is to make themselves available to the police at all times, and be prepared to travel to headquarters for further questioning. Between the hours of 6 p.m. and 6 a.m. is curfew. Stay indoors. Failure to comply will be taken very seriously. Arrests will be made. Until we have more clarity, and our perpetrator is apprehended, one of Pratt's officers will reside at The Hall where, I trust, he'll be a reassuring and accessible presence.'

'Most helpful,' says Ava.

26

Whodunnit?

PC Rory Cargill from Knockinch is duly installed to, in George's bitter words, 'mind the inmates', and is given Baumgarten's old room to use as his own. He's a fat man, similar in age to Sergeant Pratt, with a weather-beaten complexion and such heavy-lidded eyes, they look half shut. Nevertheless, he proves a punctilious watchman, and despite his size, is adept at appearing as if from nowhere to ensure 'ye're ne'er alone'. Over the next twenty-four hours, more police steadily come and go, The Hall's office remaining at their disposal. If their investigation is making any headway, they don't share what that is. Meanwhile, they've a captive audience, each member presenting a different front.

Bernard Addington is indignant at being kept here 'when some of us have homes to go to. At this rate the Cortina's engine'll seize up'. Barbara's regretful that she 'didn't pack for longer. The boys are running out of clean clothes.' The frenetic click-clacking of her needles suggest she's planning to knit them a fresh wardrobe.

For the most part, Carl and Martin act unfazed, but at times they're uncharacteristically subdued; choosing to sit with their father as he talks them through the key to his two-and-a-half-inches-to-the-mile OS map. He tests them on the symbols, and they answer up amenably: 'Disused windmill, church with spire, footbridge, ford and ferry.'

Sinclair Stewart is insouciant. 'I'm happy. Would've felt like quitting to slope back to Beinn Beithe when no one else can leave.' Righteous words. Ava supposes that being at The Hall for two deaths could forge some sense of camaraderie, though not, it appears, in George's case. She's permanently furious. Part of her rage is directed at Wick, the rest at herself. 'How I was persuaded to come to this place is beyond me, though kind-heartedness has *always* been my weakness!' Ava's comment that Dorcha Hall is, at least, an 'open prison', is not well received.

Peigi keeps a low profile, wedging herself into a sitting-room armchair, playing solitaire. She looks up only if an officer should pass by, and her plea is always the same. 'Please, please, let me go.' Ava feels for her. Fiona does nothing to make her welcome, and neither does Alastair. Either he daren't try, or, more likely, hasn't the energy. He seems destroyed. 'Maggie was under my roof. She was in my employ.' This is his mantra, and he'll be neither silenced nor soothed. He remains under the near-constant watch of his wife, and that of Lauri Levi. Darling Fee barely bothers to mask her antipathy towards Lauri. Lauri's feelings for Alastair are equally unguarded. In not-so-hidden corners, the women gibe at one another in lowered tones. Though their words go unheard, their body language says it all. The claws are out. Alastair, apparently oblivious, is entirely passive, as if his light's gone out.

Such a mix of sentiments makes for a febrile atmosphere. Ava, however, knows they all belie a single, shared truth. Everyone's scared shitless. Not just the innocent parties who realise they're cooped up with an as-yet-unidentified killer; the murderer, too, must be fearful of being found out. Who is the monster among them, and when will he or she strike again? Residents speculate, both privately and in furtive pairings, alliances shifting as fast as suspicions. Ava's bemused by people's abilities to simultaneously hold two conflicting beliefs. On the one hand, they're certain that the killer is a fellow inmate; on the other, they're equally sure that whoever they happen to be talking to at the time cannot possibly be the person in question.

'Farcical! Keeping us here like common crooks,' snaps George. 'Do *we* look like murderers?' Her laser-beam gaze is directed at Murdoch's pointedly turned back.

'Hardly,' says Barbara, scrutinising Lauri Levi over the top of a complicated Aran stitch. 'You stick with us Addingtons, Georgina. Safety in numbers.'

'You reckon?' says the fox to the chicken.

'Absolutely,' says the lone wolf to the fox.

'It's bad enough the girl lost her life,' Wick says to Ava when they're next alone, 'but the notion she was killed by accident – not that I wish Lauri Levi dead, of course – somehow makes it so much worse.'

'Thing is, Wick, how can one be certain *who* was supposed to die?'

'The chocolates were meant for Lauri Levi. The note said so. *Maggie* said so. They only fell into Maggie's hands when Lauri rejected them.'

'To quote Miss Levi herself, "It sure looks that way". Thanks to Ollach, though, I'm acutely aware of how misleading a few scrawled words can be. Still, as an object of antipathy, Lauri *is* a prime candidate. Do you like her? George doesn't. Murdoch *loathes* her and makes no secret of it. The way Lauri belittles him! She's so loud and sassy. Neither is she flavour of the month with Barbara Addington. A ribald influence on her impressionable boys. As for Fiona, Lauri's had *her* running pillar to post since she got here, complaining about the food, the plumbing, stolen jewels… and *then*, to add insult to injury or, let's say, "rub salt in the wound", Lauri's fallen hook line and sinker for her husband.'

'Lauri Levi has designs on Alastair?' Wick looks confused.

'Didn't I mention that earlier? Thought I had. What did you think those theatricals were about the other day? "Whisk me away from all this, Ali!"'

Wick shakes his head. 'The woman's an outrageous flirt, granted, but it's a game. I've never taken her seriously.'

'Why would you? To her, you're a toy. Alastair's *way* more than that.'

'Charming!'

'Don't pretend to be offended,' chuckles Ava. 'She's not your type, any more than you're hers!'

'Lauri may be interested in Alastair, but surely that's unreciprocated?'

'Of course! Even so, Fiona's cheesed off. Despite her cool exterior, she's capable of a passionate reaction when roused. Remember how misty-eyed she got on the subject of Torridonian conglomerates, and the way she blew her top over a mooted land sale.'

Wick strokes his moustache. 'I don't buy it. Bumping off Miss Levi, a guest in Fiona's own hotel, would seem an insane act of self-sabotage.'

'Agreed. So, aside from the fact that Lauri's brash and annoying, can you see any of those petty gripes *other* people have with her being credible motives for murder?'

'Not really, no.'

'Exactly!' says Ava. 'Which is one reason why I believe the person who ended up eating the chocolates was indeed the person who was meant to die. I liked Maggie, but she had her shortcomings; listening at doors, searching through coat pockets, she neither minded her own business, nor held her tongue. Dicey traits, especially to a killer who's got away with it and wants it to stay that way. If ever there was a someone who found out a something they shouldn't have, and was likely to let the cat out of the bag, that was Maggie.'

'She caught wind of who killed Baumgarten?'

'If she did, it would be a great motive for dispatching her.'

Wick nods. 'It really would.'

'Another telling thing is the killer's choice of bait: candied cherries. Maggie's favourite. Told me she couldn't resist them. I'll bet plenty of other people knew as much too.' Ava falls silent as she cogitates.

'All right,' challenges Wick. 'Talk me through your scenario. You obviously have one.'

'For reasons we're still guessing at, person or persons unknown wanted to get rid of Maggie. They laced her very favourite treats with substance X, put them in a gift-wrapped box and placed it somewhere she was bound to come across it. In the cloakroom, for example. She was always hanging around down there.'

'Or maybe in her ad hoc bedroom?'

'Maybe. I wouldn't mind taking a look in there,' Ava adds as an aside. 'But anyway, true to form, Maggie found it. At this point, it wasn't labelled, not that a label would have interfered with their plan. Maggie-The-Magpie Kettleness wouldn't give a second thought to *who* those cherries were for, she'd simply help herself. What the killer couldn't have predicted, though, was the effect Maggie's particular fascination with Lauri Levi would have on her decision making. When she found those chocolates, so prettily presented, she thought of her idol... her crush... and wanted to give them to her. An innocent act of devotion. She'd pop over to Miss Levi's room right then and there and surprise her.'

'And the earrings?'

'I was coming to that. Chocolate box in hand, Maggie hesitated. She thought of those earrings, burning a hole in her pocket, and she felt bad. As Lauri reasoned, Maggie wanted an excuse to return them without losing face. Now she had an opportunity. She wrote that little message, her apology, and took the chocs *and* the earrings to Lauri where the scene played out exactly as Lauri described.'

'No doubt about it,' sighs Wick. 'Lauri Levi dodged a bullet. No wonder she was such a mess the day Maggie died.'

'True,' says Ava. 'Everyone was unsettled, but *she* was—'

'Troubled,' offers Wick.

'Doesn't seem a big enough word.'

For the next minute or two, Ava and Wick remain silent, weighing up the sense of her account.

'Who,' Wick eventually asks, 'do you think "dunnit"?'

'That,' Ava answers, 'is the question. Two victims and, for the sake of argument, one killer.'

'"For the sake of argument"? Not very scientific!'

'The chances of two unrelated murders occurring in a backwater like this, both poisonings, less than ten days apart, are, I hazard, vanishingly low. It's also *reasonable* to assume, Wick, that someone connected with The Hall is responsible and, since Baumgarten died first, *he* was the primary target.'

'Then Maggie died because she knew too much.'

Ava nods. 'Baumgarten got here less than a fortnight before he was murdered; limited time for a stranger to turn killer from a standing start. That's why any *prior* associations he had with Dorcha, or the people in it, are significant.'

'Prior?' queries Wick. 'He'd been here before?'

Ava hesitates, and makes a quick decision. She will *not* tell Wick about Baumgarten's presence at the Muirheads' car crash – too upsetting for him – but she will say: 'Yes. Bed-and-breakfasted in Drumapple, with Ollach, I believe.'

'When? I don't recall you mentioning it.'

'Need-to-know basis. Suffice to say, it was back in the day. Before The Hall was The Hall. Anyway, if we can establish whose paths crossed with his in the past, examine possible motives, the field of suspects will narrow; not just for his murder, but Maggie's too.'

'How many runners do you have? And "guess" isn't an acceptable answer.'

'A dozen, give or take.'

Wick gasps. 'That's as many heads as the police have corralled up in this place!'

'More, since I include Ollach and Jack Hooley. How many would you have?'

Wick looks thoughtful as he slowly counts on his fingers. 'Three,' he answers eventually, 'and that's pushing it.'

'Crikey! Who've you excluded?'

'All the women, both the children, and our godson. Surely you've ruled him out!'

'I don't believe Alastair's capable of squashing an ant, let alone homicide, and I see no logical reason why he would dish up such tragedy at Dorcha – his home as well as his business – when it represents everything he needs to protect. Same as applies for Fiona. But I won't eliminate him, or his wife, or anyone else, whatever their sex or age, without proof of innocence.'

'Harsh, Ava.'

'Unbiased, Wick.'

'It's very difficult to picture Ollach killing her own sister.'

'Siblicide is much more common than people imagine, especially among Nazca boobies. Nevertheless, Ollach is joint bottom of my list; a position shared with Carl and Martin. But, still, they're all on it.'

'Ollach wasn't even here the night Baumgarten died. Neither was Peigi Hooley. Surely that puts them completely out of the frame.'

'Nope. Either of them could've met him outside for that mystery rendezvous—'

'If you believe that happened.'

'Which I do.'

'*And* you'd have to believe that rendezvous had something to do with the murder.'

'Can't prove it didn't. And I know Baumgarten visited Peigi's studio, and she no doubt came across him when he holidayed with the Kettlenesses. Drumapple is a tiny place. That's "prior association", right there.'

'But why would Peigi want to kill anyone, Ava?'

'Let's say "out of spite". Alastair dumped her for Fiona. She wants to ruin his livelihood and his marriage. Why not kill a guest and a staff member, then stand back and watch what happens next?'

'"Hell hath no fury". That old chestnut, eh? Too much of a stretch.'

'Agreed. Peigi's not an odds-on favourite. Her brother, however, is a different matter. So shifty!'

'You're sounding unscientific again.'

'I'll put it another way then: In the absence of strabismus and all signs of convergence insufficiency, Jack Hooley's oculesics suggest he has something to hide. He avoids eye contact, and that's a red flag. His kinesics are revealing, too. Very twitchy.'

Wick strokes his moustache. 'He's a local person, like his sister. I accept he could've known Baumgarten, and could've spoken with him after dinner. Regarding whatever incomprehensible thing it was you just said, I'll take your word for it. But I can't fathom a motive, especially not for Maggie's murder. Wasn't she his girlfriend?'

'Which would've made it the easiest thing in the world to slip her those chocolates.'

'If you're just working off "body language", though, I see little difference between Hooley's conduct and that of Murdoch. Murdoch's "eye contact" is as limited as his repartee. *He*'s forever sloping off, fists clenched! The man's a law unto himself. If Hooley's in your lineup, then you have to suspect Murdoch too, which would be—'

'Open minded!' says Ava, ignoring his derisory tone. 'Well done! You're getting the hang of it.'

'Not the point I was making.'

'*No one's* discounted, Wick, unless you've something tangible to put them in the clear.'

'Murdoch's loyalty to the Muirheads is indisputable. He wouldn't mete-out such mayhem in Alastair's house unless very sorely provoked.'

'Perhaps Baumgarten very sorely provoked him, then.'

There's a pause. Wick fixes Ava with a discomfiting stare. 'You can't think George did it.'

'Oh, but I can!'

'Seriously!'

'Hypothetically speaking, why not? Seen through an objective lens, her behaviour looks fishy. He died the day she arrived. She minimised the significance of his death – put it down to "a fit of the heebie-jeebies" after "a bucket load of booze" – and promptly swept it under the carpet. She didn't like that the police were called, and wanted nosy parker Maggie off the premises quick sticks, advocating for her sacking. When that failed…'

'Ridiculous!'

'Suppose she came here with the express purpose of settling a score with Baumgarten? All her business meetings were just a cover.'

'Even if that were true, which it isn't, when I invited her to Dorcha, how could she possibly have known he'd be staying here?'

'At her first business meeting, she said *you*'d told her there was a guest, a birdwatcher "from Munich". Did you let slip his name too?'

'I'm embarrassed to confess,' Wick says resignedly, 'I can't remember. But what would be *her* motive?'

'Given time, I reckon I could find one.' Ava moves on. 'Who else, apart from Jack Hooley, is on your roll call?'

'Bernard Addington. By his own account, he's been coming to this part of Scotland since he was a boy, so he could have a history with Loch Dorcha that brought him into contact with Baumgarten. He had the opportunity to kill both Baumgarten and Maggie. The fact he's a chemistry teacher means he knows about poisons…'

'Excellent points, professor! And he openly disliked Baumgarten; found him insufferably dull!'

'Your weakest motive so far. And what about Barbara? In my book, a most improbable suspect.'

'Creatures that seem banal and chitter under stress, Wick, are not necessarily harmless. The slow loris has a gland inside its elbow—'

'If we could just focus on Barbara.'

'She's married to Bernard, who, for aforementioned reasons, is on *both* our registers. If her husband had some beef with Baumgarten, so might she.'

'A suspect through wedlock!'

'Why not?'

Wick doesn't answer.

Ava continues to advance. 'What do you make of Sinclair Stewart? I take it he's your number three.'

'Literally a third party,' says Wick. 'I hardly know him, and that's really the only reason I'd consider him. I can't link him in any way to either murder. I think he's a decent chap, and I'd like to get better acquainted. A mine of information on Rococo furniture—'

'Now who's lost focus?'

'Sorry. Conversation for another time.'

'Stewart is interesting I grant you. Underneath his French-polished veneer of charm lies a man who knows what he wants, and gets it. The approach he's made to Alastair, for The Murder Field, isn't the first time he's tried to get his hands on Dorchan land.'

'Duncan rejected an offer, what…? A year ago?'

'Not long after Stewart moved into Beinn Beithe. Perhaps he's after more than just Duncan's ghillie; he's still hankering after those extra thousands of acres too.'

'When he treated us to lunch, he *did* say he's always looking for his next land acquisition.'

'And therein lies a plot, Wick! Financially speaking, George spelled things out to Alastair in bleak terms. Make changes, or "lose the lot"! If The Hall fails, they'll go bankrupt. Dorcha could be sold out from under him. Has Stewart worked that out too? Disaster for the Muirheads spells good news for a buyer looking for a bargain. As I said earlier, what better way to bring down a hotel business than polluting it with murders.'

'Takes a lot of mental gymnastics to make such subversive, never mind extreme, actions sound credible. And judging by the treasures he showed us at Beithe Towers, Stewart's as rich as Croesus. He could just buy the Muirheads out now – "name your price" – if they were willing to sell…'

Ava continues to mull. 'He and George have been spending a lot of time together. What if they're in cahoots? She could be doing the hands-on.'

'Are you determined to implicate George?' Wick huffs.

'No more than you're determined to defend her. And don't get snappy! Remember, this is all hypothetical.'

'But we're not playing a parlour game, either. We're talking about real people, Ava.'

'I do know that. Now let me see… who haven't we covered?'

'Lauri Levi and Fiona.'

'I'd say the former has a sufficiently brass neck to do anything, only the rest of her anatomy would get in the way. As for the latter…'

'Murder on her own doorstep? Impossible.' Wick sighs. 'Thanks to recent events, Fee's whole life's turned into a nightmare.'

Ava sighs too. 'Look, I don't know who killed Baumgarten and Maggie, and you're right, I *am* keeping some very improbable candidates in my line of sight. But till I've evidence to rule a name out, it stays ruled in.'

'And, *my* name, Ava?'

'Top of the list.'

'Thank you.' Wick's gold tooth catches the light as he laughs. 'I'd expect nothing less.'

27

Mischief of Magpies

On Friday morning, Clowdy and his entourage, including Sergeant Pratt, decamp, leaving behind Cargill as housemaster. The Jaguar is first out of the gates, its bodywork gleaming in the sunshine. Once all are gone, Ava, who watched the exodus from the front steps, follows them a little way down the avenue. It's been three days since her last hole-count. Today she finds twenty, same as last time, and none are fresh. Did he or she find what they were looking for the night Ava failed to stay awake? But since Maggie's murder, police are everywhere, and there is the curfew. Perhaps the digger's gone to ground? Or, Ava wonders, are they 'gone' for good?

Ava's heading back inside when Carl and Martin come into sight, pushing two rickety bicycles. 'Where do you think you're off to?' she calls.

'The policeman said it's okay to ride these, so long as we stick together,' replies Martin.

'And stay in the hotel's grounds,' adds Carl. 'Just need to reinflate the tyres...'

Without further ado, they buckle down. Ava doesn't blame them for wanting to expand their world beyond boardgames and Marvel annuals – they must be going stir crazy – but still... 'You will mind what Constable Cargill said, won't you, lads?'

'We're not stupid y'know,' is Martin's dismissive answer.

Ava clearly hasn't been forgiven for failing to take them to The Murder Field. The fact that The Murder Field has since come to them is, it seems, no consolation.

Wick appears at her elbow. 'So this is where you got to.'

'I'd hardly have gone far. What's everyone else up to?'

'Gathered in the sitting room, for the most part, drowning their sorrows with liquor.'

'Or diluting their fears,' Ava says wryly.

'Whatever the case, seems bourbon tastes better when Stewart pours it. Fiona's with Alastair, in the office. He's been walking around like an automaton. Murdoch's been granted a pass to visit Ollach. Peigi begged Cargill to let her go back to Drumapple too, but he wouldn't allow it. Said he'd have to clear it with his seniors first. Perhaps that's what he's doing now.'

'Talk of the devil!' says Ava as Cargill himself approaches the boys. Having made a brief study of the situation, he promptly flips a bike upside down and removes its chain. Rolling up his sleeves, he rubs together his palms, before taking a turn with the pump. It'll take him a while to get things up and running. Even from yards away, Ava can tell at least one inner tube has a puncture.

'What are you thinking?' asks Wick.

'That now's a good time for our next delve.'

Ava suspects that Maggie's bedroom, as far as it could be called hers, is the smallest, tattiest, and least well-furnished in the guest wing, provided for her use on those occasions when it was too late to cycle home to Drumapple. 'Not exactly the lap of luxury,' she says.

Wick runs a gloved finger along the grubby dado. Like every other surface, it's been dusted for prints. 'What even *is* there for us to go through? Or find? Clowdy's team has already searched here.'

Ava sees his point. Unlike Baumgarten's room, this has neither wardrobe nor chest of drawers; no obvious place to conceal anything, let alone clues to Maggie's fate. The curtains are thin, the rug moth eaten; the walls are bare, apart from a clock and a mirror, no doubt supplied in the hope Maggie would show up for work on time with her headband straight. There's no sign of her uniform; no doubt removed as evidence. Maggie's camp bed is, Ava presumes, as she left it rather than the police: unmade. Ava spots a well-thumbed copy of *Hollywood Secrets* part buried among the twisted blankets. Under the bed, nothing. No suitcase covered with stickers from exotic destinations across the globe, only curls of dust.

'This must be where she undressed, ready to change into her costume. Look!' Hanging on the back of the door, from a satin-covered coat hanger, is a ball gown matching the description of the outfit Maggie was to don for her starring role. When Ava lifts its protective polythene cover, sequins shimmer like hundreds of black fish scales. Apt attire for The Lass of The Loch. 'I'll bet Sheila looked lovely in it,' she mutters.

Wick says nothing.

Ava visualises Sheila at the top of Dorcha Hall's staircase, swathed in spangles, arm in arm with her husband, making an entrance at one of their hunt dos; lingering on the landing while her guests looked up in awe. Judging by the wistful expression on Wick's face, Ava guesses his thoughts are in the same vein. Has his mind's eye edited out Duncan, swaying slightly, reeking of alcohol, leaning on Sheila for support?

'Imagine how much Maggie would have looked forward to putting on that dress,' she sighs. 'Like something out of the movies. In real life, no one would have let her touch it, but for the purposes of some hammy make-believe stunt, she could wear it and sully it freely. That's the nature of generosity. It can be very unkind.' Ava pictures Lauri Levi gifting Maggie a pretty trinket in what turned out to be the final hours of her short life. 'Do you suppose Maggie knew those *stupid* earrings were fake?' she asks. 'Personally, I hope not.'

Still nothing from Wick. He's gazing, abstractedly, out over a muddy courtyard and the dilapidated outbuildings beyond.

'No magical loch view on this side of the corridor,' she says, giving him a nudge...

...which makes him jump. 'I wasn't thinking about the watercolour!'

'Watercolour? I'm referring to the view from the *window*, not Sheila's painting.'

'Ah! Of course. Sorry.'

There's a stilted pause. 'I'm the one who should apologise,' says Ava, aware she's hit a nerve. 'I underestimated the depth of emotion a party frock can stir.' She changes the subject. 'Given Maggie was naked when she died, she must've been taken ill very suddenly, after she stripped but before she got into her costume.' Gesturing at the crumpled bedding she continues. 'Perhaps she lay down for a moment, but as the effects of poison kicked in, she got up again.'

'Why didn't she summon help?'

'I expect she tried, but no one came. Her calls were likely drowned out by the hubbub of us lot downstairs, getting together to watch the performance. I reckon she shouted… staggered around. She may even have fallen. See the way the clock's skew-whiff, and how the chair's backrest is splintered, like it was knocked over? And remember all that banging around overhead while we were waiting? Alastair and Fiona assumed Maggie had got into character ahead of time…'

'We were actually listening to her death throes?'

Ava nods. 'Sickening.' She gives the grotty little room a final scan. 'Seen enough?'

'More than,' says Wick.

They make to leave. As Ava approaches the door, however, the floor beneath her right foot gives, only slightly, but when she treads up and down on the spot, there's definite movement. *Creak, creak, creeeak.* She rolls back the rug and as she anticipated, uncovers a loose board. Using the blade of Maggie's room key, Ava levers it up to reveal… contraband!

'Aha!' she cries. 'I feel like Howard Carter in the bowels of King Tut's tomb!'

Maggie's pick 'n' mix of ill-gotten gains is packed inside a lidless shoe box, nestled between two joists. Ava lifts it out, places it on the camp bed, and takes stock. Top of the heap, the final trophy to be stowed away, is a red velvet ribbon, probably the one used to wrap the box of chocolate cherries. A pathetic keepsake. Beneath this lies an eclectic assortment of items which, as far as Ava can tell, have only two things in common. All are stolen property, and each is small enough to fit in an apron pocket; Ava's own missing comb being a case in point and, joy of joys, her folding field glasses! There's a button matching the one missing from Murdoch's shirtsleeve.

Wick reaches into the box and retrieves the sugar tongs. 'Silver plate. As treasure troves go,' he remarks, turning them over in his hand, 'disappointing. Maggie had ample opportunity to reconnoitre, work out what was worth taking, what to leave behind. A clever thief would've focused on valuables. Besides which, I thought magpies only collected shiny things.'

'That's a myth. They do hoard stuff, but it tends to be edible rather than anything worth pawning. Of course, *exceptio probat regulam*.'

'The exception proves the rule.'

'Quite. So-and-so's missing engagement ring turns up in some maverick *Pica*'s nest, and the bird steals the headlines, if nothing else. What's undeniable, though, is that magpies are highly inquisitive and easily bored. I once watched a pair of them collect twigs, one by one, from the forest floor, then drop them, equally methodically, into the entrance of a badgers' sett, for no apparent purpose other than to provoke a reaction from the badgers.'

'Did it work?'

'Like a charm. I believe Maggie stole for similar reasons. Consumable swag... fruitcake, shortbread... she ate straight away. Probably downed a few miniature whiskies on the sly. Easy come, easy go. Much, *much* more satisfying, however, were the arbitrary bits and pieces she took with the sole aim of being irritating. Her own, private game. She'd whip things whenever people were looking the other way, then stand back and enjoy the fallout. Think of all the ballyhoo about missing earrings!'

'I do recall Maggie giggling away when Lauri and Fiona had their breakfast set-to,' says Wick.

'The times I'd return from a walk, to be asked "seen any bonnie birds, doctor", when she *knew* I hadn't got my field glasses. Butter wouldn't melt!' Ava chuckles. 'Wasn't she wicked? Look, here! Barbara Addington's "lost" jigsaw piece! How rewarding for Maggie, watching Bernard crawling on hands and knees, trying in vain to find it. Barbara even made Maggie herself empty the vacuum bag and had Martin and Carl rake through the contents.'

'Barbara didn't give up for days!'

'And Carl's Monopoly top hat. *That* brotherly tiff came to blows.'

'I'll bet Maggie was sorry to miss the rumpus this little trophy caused,' says Wick, holding up the lid of George's pen.

Ava smiles. 'Before Alastair and Fiona gave her a job, her life must've been pretty uneventful; for a soul such as Maggie, hard to bear. Ollach said her sister lived for the daily dramas she witnessed at work. Imagine the fun she had, creating ripples in the still waters of Loch Dorcha Hall.'

'What shall we do with this stuff?' asks Wick. 'Give it to the police?'

'Given Maggie's gone, I think we should quietly return things to their owners, minimum fuss,' says Ava. 'Besides which, I don't want to explain how we came by them.'

They shuffle through the items, working out who should get what. They decide some bits, like the tongs, carafe stopper, and the knives, forks, and spoons, can be surreptitiously put back into circulation. Other, more-personal pieces, like Bernard Addington's prescription specs, will require a more direct approach. 'Look at this,' says Ava, peeling a strip of yellow and red paper from the bottom of the box. 'It's a docket for a roll of film. George's? She hasn't mentioned losing it.'

'Perhaps she hasn't missed it yet.' Wick slips it into his pocket. 'I'll take the pen lid, too. I should be the one to return that, along with her car keys, if you'd pass those over.'

'I don't see them…'

'Oh well,' says Wick, glancing at the wall clock. 'Cargill can't spend all day doing bike maintenance. Time we made tracks.'

As he replaces the floorboard, Ava has a passing thought. 'It's *odd*, isn't it, that George's car keys aren't here? I mean, if Maggie didn't take them, where are they?'

'Wouldn't lose sleep over it. George probably misplaced them after all.'

28

How Could You?

Pleased to find the kitchen unoccupied, Ava opens the dresser drawer as quietly as she can, and she and Wick hurry to put away Maggie's stockpile of cutlery without being seen. They might have got away with it, had Ava not dropped an entire handful onto the quarry stone floor. 'Bugger!'

In less than a second, Fiona enters through the back door. 'Oh, it's only you,' she mutters, clearly flustered. 'What are you doing?'

'Apologies for the mess,' says Wick. 'We—'

'We fancied a cuppa,' Ava says quickly. 'I was rummaging for a teaspoon.' This fuss-minimising lie is, however, wasted. Fiona isn't listening to Ava, but staring distractedly into the yard from whence she came. Her top lip is sweaty, her pupils, wide. 'Are you okay?'

'Yes.' Fiona sounds very unconvincing.

'You don't look it,' says Wick. 'Where's Alastair?'

Fiona pauses, as if thinking twice before blurting out her answer. 'That's the thing. I'm not sure. He said he was going to go through the books, or try to at least, and he shut himself in the office. But when I looked in on him, he'd gone!'

'He'll have gone to his veg plot to "dig himself happy".'

'His trowel's still here, Wick. First thing I checked. He's been beating himself up about Mr Baumgarten and Maggie. Especially Maggie. I've looked everywhere indoors – no sign. Something feels really wrong. I was about to search the grounds when I heard you two in here, and I thought... *hoped* it was Alastair.

What should I do? I don't want to leave reception unattended, but I need him beside me.'

Fiona's agitation at this moment, the words she's using, remind Ava of a much earlier conversation, just after Baumgarten died; the one in which Fiona first mentioned Alastair's periods of absence. 'Where you can see him?' she offers.

'Precisely!'

'Then he must be found! Now,' Wick continues resolutely, '*you* stay here, get on with whatever else you need to. Ava and I will take over.'

Fiona visibly relaxes. 'You don't mind?'

'There are two of us and one of you,' says Ava. 'We'll be fine, and so will that husband of yours.'

Ava and Wick start in the kitchen garden and its potting-shed laboratory. The former is deserted; the latter, locked, no sign of life within. 'Are you worried?' asks Wick, peering in through a window. 'Because I am, a bit.'

'Not especially. I can see why Alastair would nip out for some fresh air without telling anyone, especially not Fiona, the way she shadows his every move. I'd find that suffocating. Anyway, let's do a quick recce of the outbuildings... exclude them... and then we'll try further afield. The woods. For all we know, he's having a yomp across the moors.'

'Really? It's so bleak up there, not to mention strictly out of bounds.'

'Wild and free, Wick.' Ava looks longingly at the distant purple fells. 'Wild and free.'

And so, in reverse order, they follow the circuit of ruins the Muirheads led them on with George, visiting the kennels, dovecote, pig parlour and stables; each as tumbledown as ever, and devoid of any trace of Alastair. Last stop, the barn. Ava's willing it to be empty too, then Wick'll *have* to sanction a covert field operation, 'for the sake of bringing our godson home.' As they maunder towards its double doors, Ava's unfazed to see these are shut, but when she and Wick get closer she's unsettled to hear noises coming from the other side. A rhythmic *chug, chug, chugging*, and there's a faint smell of burnt oil. Someone must be in there, tinkering about, but the doors seem stuck fast.

'Alastair! Open up!' calls Wick. 'Why isn't he answering?'

'Perhaps he's not in there. Murdoch's always fiddling about with engines, and so's Mr Addington. Bernard!' shouts Ava, leaning in with her whole weight, 'If you push and we pull, maybe these buggers'll—'

All at once, the doors burst apart, and she and Wick are hit by a wave of exhaust fumes so thick it almost knocks them off her feet. Worse is to come. The vapours disperse, to reveal the Land Rover – windows open, motor running – and a body slumped over the steering wheel!

Ava gets to Alastair first. Wrenching the driver's side door, she grabs him by the shoulders and shakes him with all her might. 'Wake up, damn you! Wake up!'

'Tell me he's not dead!' cries Wick, reaching in to turn off the ignition.

Alastair's eyes roll open. 'I'm not asleep,' he says woozily, 'just waiting.'

It takes Ava and Wick a few attempts to extricate their long and lanky godson from his vehicle. With one of his arms over each shoulder, coughing and spluttering, the pair manages to get him outside, where they prop him against a horse trough. He's very flushed, but after some deep breaths, his colour improves, and though confused, he's fully conscious.

'How are you feeling?' asks Ava.

Alastair looks blank. 'Really, *really* tired.'

Wick fumbles to undo Alastair's top buttons. 'What if he's done himself permanent damage! God knows how long he's been in there.'

Ava darts back into the barn and makes a cursory inspection of the floor, and the cars' roof tops and bonnets, before reporting back. 'By the look of things, not long enough to cause serious harm, otherwise there'd be more casualties.'

'Jesus! Other people are inside?'

'A colony of bats, Wick, species undetermined.'

'What have they got to do with anything?'

'Their roost is in the roof. Warm exhaust fumes will rise upwards through the column of air, reaching the bats first. On top of which, bats are tiny mammals with a high metabolic rate, they take an astonishing number of breaths per minute compared to humans. And that means they're more vulnerable to the effects of carbon monoxide than we are. Something of a double whammy, poor buggers. In short,' she continues, sensing Wick would appreciate a more concise answer, 'if the Land Rover had been belting out fumes for any length of time, then the barn's resident chiropterans would've passed out, let go of their rafters, and dropped like... I'm tempted to say "flies", but let's go with "canaries".'

'No little brown corpses?'

'None. I conclude things could have been worse.'

'My head hurts,' groans Alastair. 'Have I been drinking?'

'Come on,' says Wick. 'Home time.'

Once they get Alastair up and on the move, he becomes more coherent, and his coordination rapidly recovers. By the time they reach the back entrance of The Hall he's walking unaided, and they pilot him into the office without any guests noticing. Fiona, however, witnesses all. As Wick rattles off a rundown of what he and Ava encountered, her shock on seeing the condition of her husband is displaced by complete dismay.

'Darling, how *could* you? I should never have let you out of my sight!'

'This is *not* your fault, Fiona,' Wick says firmly, lowering Alastair into a chair.

'Generous of you to say, but I *knew* he was upset... what he might do...'

'We think he's going to be fine,' reassures Ava, 'though Sween should certainly check him over.'

'Peigi? Is that you?' mumbles Alastair. 'I tried to wait...'

Fiona looks horrified. 'Darling, it's *me*. I know things are bad, but—'

'Faithful Fee!' Alastair reaches for his wife's hand. 'I'm sorry I've made such a mess of things.'

Ava's eyes fall upon the scree of documents covering the Muirheads' desk. Bank statements, screwed up receipts... what appears to be a letter to Sinclair Stewart. He must be getting cold feet about the land purchase, judging by Alastair's half-written attempt to renegotiate the sale of Raon Murt. More land for less money. She scoops it up, along with the rest of Alastair's paperwork, empty mugs and chewed pencils, and puts everything to one side. 'Nothing that won't keep.'

'So *depressing*.' Alastair chuckles. 'But important to keep smiling. Why aren't you three smiling?'

'Should we get some coffee inside him?' asks Wick.

'I'm not sure that's the right thing to do. Not till the doctor's examined him.'

Fiona reaches for the telephone, but her hand stops mid-air. 'Oh God! I've had an awful thought. Has anyone else seen Alastair like this?'

'We think not,' says Wick.

'Thank *heaven* for small mercies! The fewer people who know he's harmed himself, the—'

'What's this I'm hearin', missus?' The door swings wide as Cargill tromps inside. 'Yer husband's attempted suicide! Why would he want te do that?'

'Fuck! God! Sorry, constable, for my bad language,' Fiona composes herself with lightning speed, 'but you're putting words in my mouth. I never said "suicide". Alastair's stressed and confused. Even though Mr Baumgarten's death had nothing to do with him, from where he stands, a guest died under his care and he's been having night sweats ever since. The loss of Maggie, a valued employee, that's knocked him absolutely sideways. He's chronically anxious and tired, and it seems he fell asleep at the wheel of his car.'

'Did I, Fee?'

'Did he indeed!' scoffs Cargill, reaching for his notepad. 'Thought he'd take a wee drive when naebiddy's allowed te leave these grounds wi'out permission.'

'Not while he was driving!' Fiona adds hastily. 'He never left the barn. But the engine was running... and the barn doors were closed. A stupidly careless chain of events, without any serious intent.' Fiona throws Ava and Wick a beseeching look. 'Professor Wickremesinghe will tell you exactly what happened, won't you, Uncle Wick?'

'Well, I—'

'And you said he's fine, didn't you, Ava?' Fiona adds ardently, as if willing Ava to agree. 'Though to be on the safe side, I'm calling the doctor right now.'

Cargill's pad stays closed, but it doesn't go back in his pocket. 'Your husband's taken recent events te heart, then?'

'Yes. No. I mean to say, any reaction he's had, *is having*, is entirely understandable, and forgivable.'

'Someone pass me the wastepaper basket,' groans Alastair with a heave. 'I think I'm going to puke.'

Cargill grimaces. 'The state o' him! And ye say Dr Sween'll be givin' him the once over?'

Fiona nods.

There's what feels like a long, long pause before Cargill delivers his verdict. 'In which case, let's hear what he has te say about the matter.'

Once Sween's satisfied that his patient will 'be as right as rain after a good night's sleep', his manner switches from avuncular family physician to that of a deeply disappointed parent. 'I brought ye into this world, young man. I dinnae want te be the one who sees ye out o' it. Do ye understand?'

'Please stop talking to me as if I tried to top myself, Sween, because however this looks, I did *not* plan to die today.'

'Then what were ye thinkin'? Because ye damn well coulda done.'

'I don't know. I don't remember. I was in the office, then I was in the barn, waiting for someone. For Peigi.'

Sween's next question is the same one Ava, and no doubt Fiona too, would have asked next. 'And why would ye be doin that?'

Alastair rubs his eyes with his fists and takes another sip from a glass of cold water. 'Peigi's been wanting to go home to Drumapple. I *think* I agreed to take her.'

It's Cargill's turn to be cross. 'When did she ask ye te do that? *I* gave her nae such licence.'

Alastair shakes his head. 'It's no good. My mind's turned to porridge. I don't know when she asked me, only that she did. I'd like to understand what happened as much as you would, but beyond walking from our office to the barn… climbing into the Land Rover… everything else is a blank.'

'A fine old bùrach, I must say! I should by rights report this te Sergeant Pratt.'

'Alastair made a silly mistake, constable,' Fiona says sourly. 'That's all. Yet you're treating him like a criminal.'

'It wasnae long ago, Mrs Muirhead, that his actions *were* against the law, isn't that right, Dr Sween?'

'Aye, Rory, aye. Though, I've a suggestion that might help ye get te the bottom o' things.' The doctor mutters something into Cargill's very hairy ear.

'Grand idea!' Cargill turns to Wick. 'Professor, find Peigi Hooley and ask her te come here.'

Wick looks taken aback, Alastair, appalled. 'Surely there's no need—'

'Easiest way te clear up who-did-what-when. Off ye go, professor, quick as ye can.'

When Wick returns a short while later, he has Peigi with him, and she looks mystified. 'Alastair! What's happened? You're so pale—'

'Peigi, lass,' interjects Cargill, 'did ye or did ye not request Mr Muirhead te tek ye home in his car?'

Peigi doesn't seem to hear. 'Why are you in bed, Alastair? Has there been an accident?'

'Yes,' says Fiona.

'I'm askin' the questions,' says Cargill stiffly. 'And Peigi'll be answerin' them. Did ye ask him te go te the barn, te wait fer ye?'

'Is that what you said, Alastair?' Peigi looks searchingly into his bloodshot eyes.

'I'm so muddled, Peigi...' Alastair faces away.

'As am I.' For the first time since she entered the room, Peigi turns to address Cargill directly. 'It's been a while since I asked anything of a Muirhead,' she says crisply, 'and that's all I have to say.' She exits as swiftly as she entered, and no one stands in her way. It's obvious to Ava that, despite the young woman's show of composure, she was close to tears.

'Well, now, Alastair,' says Cargill with a disconsolate shake of his head. 'I'm left te conclude ye took yersel te the barn on yer own volition, and ye're bandyin' about Miss Hooley's name now, suggestin' *she* persuaded ye te go there, in an attempt te cover up yer true intention... which was te commit suicide.'

'Silly mistake,' Fiona repeats steadfastly.

Alastair just looks stunned.

'But yer reasons fer so doing,' continues Cargill, 'fer the present, remain unclear. And *that* is what I'll be reportin' te my seniors.'

Sween tuts. 'My, but ye're a lucky fellow, Alastair, in more ways than one. Look at yer wife here. Think o' *her* nerves! How are ye bearin' up, Mrs Muirhead?'

'Don't worry, doctor.' Fiona sticks out her plucky little chin. 'We'll both be fine.'

'Then I'll be on my way. But yer te ring me if ye need anythin',' instructs Sween. 'Understood?'

'Understood. Thank you, doctor. I'll see you out.'

Denuded of its indoor jungle, the orangery feels unwelcoming. Cleared and ready to receive more tables, with no possibility in sight of new guests to sit at them. It's cold inside and, all too soon, it'll be dark out. Then the only signs of human life beyond the walls and windows of Dorcha Hall will be the sparse lights of Drumapple, the other side of the water.

'Scattered clouds in an otherwise clear sky,' muses Wick, leaning back in his chair to stare up through the glass roof.

'A metaphor?'

'I wish. Our reality is far stormier. Could be in for a decent sunset, though.'

'After a shit day.'

'I'll drink to that.' Wick fills Ava's tumbler before pouring himself a double measure.

'What do you think?' asks Wick. '"Silly mistake", or does our godson really want to check out permanently?'

'Haven't the foggiest,' says Ava, 'any more than he seems to. Fiona said he blanks out his "absences" after the event. Turns out she wasn't kidding. We need to talk to him properly, Wick, the sooner the better, and at least try to understand what he can remember, and what he can't.'

'Or doesn't choose to,' broods Wick. 'I believed Peigi when she said she didn't ask for a lift.'

'A passionate denial, certainly,' reflects Ava.

'But why else *was* he in the barn, then, doors shut, engine running? Think back to that stunt in his lab! He said he downed Baumgarten's midge repellent to prove it was safe to drink, but what if he thought it was toxic all along, Ava? Maybe he *did* plan to end it all, in front of you, me... his own wife! When he didn't drop dead on the spot, he laughed it off as an impulsive experiment, then tried a different tack.'

Ava sighs. 'When Fiona warned us about Alastair's fragility, I thought she was exaggerating... catastrophising, even; she's so worried about Alastair, she was letting her imagination run riot. Boy, do I feel differently now.'

Wick sighs too. 'Little wonder she's scared to let him out of her sight. You can understand why Murdoch still calls him "the bairn", and why Sheila asked me to look out for him. It's one thing to be nervy and forgetful...'

'What we saw this afternoon, though, was on a whole other level. Hard to witness.'

'Even harder to know how to help.' Wick swills his drink around despondently. 'In some ways I feel worse for Fiona. She can't have known what she was signing up for when she married him. I'd say their business prospects are in ruins. After what's happened, who'd want a holiday at their hotel? George is no longer interested in helping them. No idea if Stewart's offer is still on the table.'

'Judging by what I saw on the Muirheads' desk, I'm thinking not. Alastair's chasing *him*, tendering the land at a bargain price.'

'And now this!'

'Now this,' echoes Ava.

'When was the last time Alastair was on anything like good form?'

'That morning we shifted the pots out of here. Four days ago. Feels like a *bloody* lifetime.'

'Remember watching that wasp, flying off every which way, always coming back to her offspring. Edifying.'

Ava nods. 'It was.'

'I've no children of my own, Ava. Alastair's the closest I have to flesh and blood. I came here resolved to fix his problems, and I've failed.'

'We had a shared mission, Wick. Current circumstances are preventing either of us from succeeding.'

'Are you a mother?'

This unexpected question hits Ava like a cannon ball. It's not one any man has ever asked her, and she's surprised by how much it hurts. 'No. I have three nephews, whom I rarely see. My brother and his wife – their parents – live in the Home Counties, and being overseas so much, I rarely see them. The older two outgrew me years ago, but I keep in touch with the youngest. Postcards, mostly. He and I have a shared passion for insects. They're the glue to our relationship. I flatter myself he's fond of me. I know I love him.'

'I've made you sad.'

'I was already sad when we sat down.'

'Do you think our godson is still able to find his way back, Ava?'

'Of course!' she says doughtily. 'As long as we keep waving flags to remind him how to find us.'

29

Barking up the Wrong Tree

Ava looks at her watch. 10 o'clock. Still early, but the sun's high in the sky. It's shaping up to be another hot weekend. Hardly surprising, given it's the second week of August. Today the quixotic peaks, shimmering in the heat, have a blithe air about them, as if too high and mighty to fret over any murders that happen to have happened at their feet. They *have* been here for hundreds of millions of years, though. Perhaps they've seen it all before.

When Ava arrived here, she'd expected that, by now, she'd be packing to leave. If not gone already. Standing in the library's bay window contemplating the sparkling loch and the mountains with their beaming crags, she knows that at this moment, a very different scene must be unfolding on Grande Riviere beach, Trinidad. Under the silvery mantle of night, leatherback turtle hatchlings will be stirring beneath moonlit sands. Once free from their eggshells, they'll dig upwards, en masse, to reach the surface; so many of them, each no bigger than a drop scone, all emerging at once, that the beach will seem to boil. A moment to find their bearings, then off they'll go, pulling themselves towards the ocean with their flippers, leaving mini tank tracks in their wakes. Once the vast waters receive them, away they'll swim, as fast as they can. No turning back. One of Ava's favourite sights to see, and she's missing it.

'You look miles away,' says Wick.

'Wishing I was,' sighs Ava.

'Well I bring good news, Alastair's up and about. Just seen him head outside.'

'Alone?' Ava asks eagerly. 'Let's go and talk to him!'

'May not be the time. Murdoch's with him. I thought we might wander out to join them, though.'

'Good idea. Perhaps Murdoch will peel off.'

Ava and Wick don't have to walk far. They find the two men down the avenue, below a beech tree – *the* beech tree – with a show of ripe fungi on its trunk and a small, opencast mine at its feet. Ava does a silent tally. Still the same twenty holes there were four days ago.

'Morning!' calls Wick, a little too brightly. 'What are you up to?'

Alastair may be kitted out for action – trowel tucked into his belt, penknife at the ready – but mentally, he seems abstracted. 'I'm going to make more oyster soup,' he answers flatly. 'Fee says people still have to eat.' One look at Alastair, and Ava's residual hopes of a debrief evaporate. He's clearly shattered.

'She's absolutely right,' says Ava, 'and you've got quite a display here.' Her jovial tone feels as forced as Wick's sounded.

'No better than the last tree I picked from.'

'"Last tree"? This isn't where you collected mushrooms before?' she asks slowly.

Alastair shrugs. 'How could it be? I stripped that site bare. I've been waiting for this lot to mature—'

'Could you to show me exactly where you came picking last time?' Ava's brain cells are firing so fast, it's hard to stay calm.

Alastair saunters across the drive to another huge, but mushroom-free, tree on the other side of the avenue. 'I cut them off this one.'

'Why is this significant?' asks Wick.

'Give me two ticks, and hopefully, I'll show you!' Practically snatching Alastair's trowel from his hand, Ava drops to her knees and starts plunging away. Almost immediately, the blade taps something hard. Eureka! Pressed into the soil, no more than three inches below the surface, is a miniature whisky bottle, like the complimentary ones put in the guest bedrooms, except empty. And minus its lid.

The Beasts of the Black Loch

'Bravo!' chuckles Wick. 'You've struck litter!'

'This may not be gold doubloons but,' she says, holding the grubby bottle up to the light, 'no way is it rubbish, otherwise why go to the trouble of burying it?'

'You think someone put that in the ground on purpose?' asks Alastair.

'Not a doubt in my mind. And that same someone has gone to *more* trouble seeking to unbury it, only they've been looking in entirely the wrong spot.' Ava waves the trowel in the direction of the holes. 'See that lot over there? Ever since they started to appear, I've been scratching my head, asking myself why anybody would want to dig under that tree rather than anywhere else. I think you've been wondering the same, haven't you Murdoch?'

Murdoch grunts.

'And *now*,' continues Ava, 'thanks to a sand wasp, we have an answer.'

'How so?' asks Wick.

'I reckon whoever this bottle belongs to didn't want to be caught with it in their possession. They needed to get rid of it, permanently, but for some reason there wasn't time. So, they decided to do the next best thing. They'd hide it and trust it would stay hidden till they could dispose of it properly. I also reckon this was in broad daylight, which is why they had to act fast. Afraid of being seen, they stopped at the first place they came to out of sight of The Hall... which is right where we're standing. They scraped away at the ground and stuffed the bottle into a shallow grave. They'd salvage it later once the dust settled. But, they asked themselves, how would they know where to find it again? Thinking fast, they looked around – exactly as the mother *Ammophila* did on her orientation flight – and spied a natural landmark staring them in the face. Oyster mushrooms. Loads of them, growing oh-so-conveniently nowhere *except* on the very tree where their loot was concealed. Easy-peasy to spot when it was safe to return. Unbeknownst to them, however, their plan would be thwarted. By you, Alastair.'

'*Me?*'

'Soon after the bottle was buried – in fact, the next day – you decided to make your signature soup. Enough for all your guests to enjoy. So you gathered every oyster mushroom you could lay your hands on until *this* fellow,' says Ava, giving the tree's naked trunk a hearty smack, 'was, as you said a moment ago, "stripped bare".'

'A basketful of ingredients,' says Wick, 'but no more landmark.'

'Precisely!' says Ava. 'Utterly erased! But not for long. Owing to the ever-fecund nature of Nature, on another, nearby beech specimen – the one opposite us – growth was already underway. Over the following warm days, what had been inconspicuous mycoid pinheads quickly burgeoned into a *fresh* crop of fruiting bodies. As chance would have it, just when the mushrooms reached a decent size our bottle-burier decided the coast was clear enough to attempt a nocturnal exhumation.'

'When was that?' asks Wick.

'About a week after Baumgarten died. By then, it was plain the police weren't treating his death as suspicious and guests were no longer on guard or, for that matter, particularly interested. Even *I* had stopped asking questions, to my shame.' Ava sighs. 'Anyway, under the cover of darkness he or she headed down the avenue, to the only beech with fungi on its trunk. Confident they'd come to the right place they must've thought it'd take them a matter of seconds to retrieve their booty. But of course, in the same way that a switch in cues misdirected that little wasp to the wrong patch of flowerbed, the oyster mushrooms flagged up the wrong tree. Imagine the person's confusion, digging and digging.' Ava turns the bottle over and over in her hand. 'When they failed to find this on their first night, they tried again the next, and the next… wondering what happened to it. I'm kicking myself that I never caught them at it.'

'You're talking as if it has something to do with what happened to Baumgarten,' says Wick.

'Aye,' says Murdoch. 'What's yer meanin'?'

'Well, the timing of the first holes points to it, and…' Ava hesitates. She doesn't voice what pops into her head next:

'The fact it has no lid.' Instead, she lifts the bottle to her nose, then inhales, before inviting the others to do the same. 'Smell anything?'

Murdoch snuffles and snores, but offers no opinion.

'Leaf mould,' suggests Alastair.

'I don't know,' says Wick. 'Definitely not whisky, though. What about you?'

'Bicyclic terpenes,' replies Ava. 'But one would expect those when there's a decent population of *Streptomyces* in the soil.'

'Of course.'

Ava gives the bottle a harder sniff. 'Hmm… I'm picking up a trace of something else too. It reminds me of the defensive discharges of a polydesmid millipede. Nasty stuff. *So* important to wash your hands after touching one, never mind trying to lick it.' Memories of close encounters with unfriendly myriapods do not, however, linger long in Ava's mind. Her thoughts fly to what she found in Baumgarten's wastepaper basket, and something Wick said about the quirks of The Hall's plumbing. 'Yup,' she says decisively, 'no doubt about it. The police must have this.'

Murdoch's two eyebrows knit into one.

'Why the police?' Alastair asks thickly. 'I'm so sick of them I—'

'Because, if my olfactory senses serve me correctly, this bottle contained cyanide. Millipedes secrete it to keep the ants off. People have other uses for it, though; some cruder than others.'

30

What's Your Poison?

To Ava's satisfaction, and great relief, Cargill receives her dirty little discovery with suitable alacrity. And so does Pratt. He can smell what she smelled, and understands what that implies. 'Now *this*,' he says gravely, 'is what I meant by evidence.' He puts it in a large brown envelope and two more constables come to take it away. Both beech trees are hastily cordoned off, and a tarpaulin is placed over the holes. Cargill moves out of Baumgarten's room, padlocking it behind him, and is rehoused on the other side of the corridor. Ava manages not to say anything about bolting horses and stable doors, but only just.

DI Clowdy arrives in his shiny black car, and Ava's summoned to the office where he and she sit opposite each other, the bottle – now tagged and bagged in polythene – in the centre of the tabletop between them. Pratt stands, ever ready with his note pad, while Cargill mounts guard at the door.

'Doctor,' says Clowdy, poking the bag with the stem of his pipe, 'you will not be surprised to learn that initial tests confirm residues of cyanide in this container. Remind me who was with you when you found it.'

'Professor Wickremesinghe, Angus Murdoch, and my godson, Alastair Muirhead.'

Clowdy packs his pipe with a generous pinch of Golden Virginia. 'None of them claimed any prior knowledge of it?'

'No.'

'And you say these holes started to appear after Baumgarten died. Do you have a notion as to who dug them?'

'The person who poisoned him, or, at the very least, someone who knows who did. And I do believe Baumgarten was deliberately killed, inspector. Have done since day one, though it wasn't till today, when I found the bottle and realised what it once held, that I worked out how.'

The inspector holds a match over the pipe's bowl and *suck*, *suck*, *sucks* three times in quick succession. 'I assume you have your suspicions about the identity of the perpetrator.'

'My roll call includes staff, visitors, guests at The Hall. Practically everyone connected with this place. Whoever they are, it's not much of a leap to believe they also murdered Maggie, though I'm less sure about their MO.'

'You said "practically"?' queries Clowdy with a look of mild surprise.

'I exclude myself, and Baumgarten. There are plenty of others I'd *like* to rule out, but I'm not abreast of sufficient facts to do so. The scientist in me won't allow it.' Ava's quick to dispel the plethora of mental snapshots she has of Alastair holding his trowel, from the album in her head. One of Murdoch, in particularly sharp focus, standing at the foot of a beech tree, talking twaddle about squirrels and badgers, proves harder to shift. 'There've been no fresh holes since Maggie died. That in itself could suggest she was the digger. But the sudden police presence at The Hall, not to mention curfew, could equally explain why excavations were abandoned. And it's hard to see Maggie as a killer; practically impossible, now she herself has been murdered. Frankly, I don't want to point fingers at anyone. I'd only be expressing my opinions, and those could be wrong.'

'Sergeant Pratt says you raised concerns about a note which subsequently turned out to be innocuous.'

'True, and it did, so you'll understand my reticence now. Though there *is* something else I feel I should mention. Shortly after Herr Baumgarten's death, I happened to look in his wastepaper basket, and found the screw-cap from a miniature of whisky. At the time, it didn't strike me as important. But since this morning—'

'What were you doing in his room?' The inspector throws a side glance at Pratt.

'Searching, trying to get a handle on how he came to be dead. Bearing in mind that, until a few hours ago, it wasn't a crime scene or, as I recall, even locked—'

Pratt drops his notepad. 'Apologies, sir. Butter fingers!'

'So,' continues Ava, 'there was nothing to stop us.'

'Us?'

'Professor Wickremesinghe and me. Anyway, it strikes me as beyond coincidence that you now have this bottle that once contained cyanide, minus its cap, and I found a cap, minus its bottle, in the accommodations of a man who'd just died.'

'Where's the cap now?'

'Murdoch burns the hotel's waste, so I expect your chances of any "the-slipper-fits" moment have long since passed. But reason dictates the bottle and cap belonged together.'

The inspector leans back in his swivel chair, and he swivels. 'Talk me through the murderer's actions, from your perspective.'

Ava takes a deep breath. 'In my view, he or she had to take four, logical steps. First, on the night Baumgarten was to die, they sneaked into his room, opened a miniature whisky bottle that was already there, threw its cap into the bin, then discarded part of its contents before topping it up with cyanide.'

'When was this?'

'Around the time guests were retiring to bed. Professor Wickremesinghe, in the room next to Baumgarten's, heard plumbing noises; sounds, he assumed, of a drunken man doing his ablutions, but now I believe it was the perpetrator pouring whisky down the sink, running the tap to rinse it away. Equally, they could have been disposing of midge repellent…'

'And where, in your opinion, was Baumgarten when all this was happening?'

'Outside, with someone.' As Ava presents her midge-bite-based hypothesis, Pratt writes furiously. Clowdy nods, and scratches. 'How sure are you that this companion exists?' he asks, when she's done.

'As I can be,' says Ava, realising how very lame this sounds. She's glad Wick's not in the room now.

'And their identity?'

'No idea.'

'But not the same person who adulterated the Scotch?'

'Can't have been, since the "adultery" was achieved while they were outdoors, with Baumgarten. Somehow knowing that Baumgarten was distracted elsewhere, the poisoner took advantage of his absence to make the lethal substitution. Must've worked fast. In and out in a matter of moments.'

'Do you think the poisoner and the person who "distracted" Mr Baumgarten were in cahoots?'

'At this point, I've no way of knowing.'

'Quite.'

Ava scrutinises Clowdy's face, trying to fathom what he's thinking, but his expression remains as hazy as his name implies.

'Tell me about the second step, doctor.'

'The murderer had to get the spiked whisky into Baumgarten. There's nothing to suggest they hung around and forced him to drink it, so I'm supposing they put it somewhere he was bound to spot it: on top of his chest of drawers, or his bedside cabinet. Perhaps they *knew* he was in the habit of downing a night cap before going to bed, maybe that was a lucky guess, but one way or another, he drank it.'

Clowdy turns to Pratt. 'On a day-to-day basis, who's responsible for stocking guest's rooms with complimentary whisky?'

'At the time in question, it *was* Maggie Kettleness, sir.'

'Please continue, doctor.'

'Once Baumgarten was dead, the murderer needed to place the empty *repellent* bottle into his hand to make it look like he accidentally swallowed Alastair's concoction. That done, the final, and in many ways, most crucial step, was the removal of the contaminated bottle. It had to be whisked away from the scene before anyone saw it and figured out the bigger picture.'

'When do you think that happened?'

'Potentially, any time between the moment he died, and

the moment his body was found. Although Murdoch says the room was locked when he came to wake him, the keys hang in reception, so with very little stealth anyone could have borrowed one. Nonetheless, I'm inclined to believe the bottle was hidden after sun-up.'

'Why?'

'The shallow grave, its proximity to the house: signs of haste which in turn suggest the burier felt dangerously exposed, and *that* tells me there was no cloak of darkness to protect them. Few burrowing mammals will risk much digging during daylight hours. It's a conspicuous process. At any event, as I explained to Sergeant Pratt and Constable Cargill, when the person in question returned – very sensibly, at night – to unearth the bottle, they looked in the wrong place, over and over again.'

'On account o' the toadstools,' says Cargill.

'Mushrooms,' corrects Ava. 'Though whether that's a meaningful distinction is a moot point. My godson's the person to ask.'

'Your godson,' Clowdy repeats in a tone Ava doesn't quite like.

'Regarding any list of suspects, inspector,' she says hastily, 'it's important to point out that Alastair freely identified which tree he'd cut that first crop of mushrooms from. Moreover, if Alastair was the bottle-burier, then he, of *all* people, would've known where to look for it after the event, and retrieved it. That would seem to put him in the clear, digging-wise.'

'"Digging-wise", perhaps, though who's to say the bottle-burier and the poisoner are one and the same person. Me? *You*...?'

'No, but—'

'Despite claiming to be dispassionate in your reasoning, Dr Dickens, when it comes to Alastair Muirhead, you deflect. My job would be so much easier if I could rely on assumptions, but to paraphrase *your* words, the *policeman* in me won't allow it.'

Privately conceding the point, Ava keeps quiet as Clowdy, apparently lost in thought, swivels his chair some more. 'Well,' he says eventually, 'your methods of deduction are certainly unorthodox, but they're not without merit. Thank you for that canny summary of events as you, Dr Dickens, see them. You did, however, overlook one step. The murderer had to get hold of some cyanide. Are you aware of any poisons kept on the premises?'

This is the question Ava's been expecting and dreading since this 'informal chat' began, but for a moment the answer stays stuck in her gullet. She clears her throat. 'There's a cabinet in Alastair's laboratory, which has some dodgy... that's to say, toxic, chemicals inside it. Kept under lock and key. Usually. I'm sure he'll show you, or better ask Fiona.'

'Laboratory?'

'My godson's potting shed.'

'Is your godson busy just now?'

'I don't think so.'

'Yet you recommend his wife show us his chemical collection, rather than the man himself. I understand there was a medical incident yesterday, when Mr Muirhead seemed somewhat "overwhelmed"?'

'He's fine now.' Ava hopes her inner squirming is not manifest externally.

'Who knows about this cabinet, apart from yourself, your godson, and his wife?'

'Professor Wickremesinghe, Georgina Beckett, Angus Murdoch; I'd say Maggie almost certainly did, given how familiar she was with the workings of The Hall, which means her sister Ollach Kettleness should be on the list as well. Peigi Hooley was a regular visitor here for many years. If she knows about it, so may her brother the butcher. Sinclair Stewart's been staying here for a while, Alastair could have shown him too. There may well be others. In fact, now I think of it, Alastair led a behind-the-scenes tour of his lab. I believe *all* his guests took part.'

Pratt nods in tacit agreement as he jots everything down.

The inspector rises to his feet. 'I now ask that you accompany me to this "laboratory" and show us those "dodgy" substances. PC Cargill, please ask Mr and Mrs Muirhead to meet us there, and make sure they bring the key.'

*

Ten minutes later, Ava, the three police officers, and Alastair and Fiona, find themselves in the potting shed, peering into a void. The cabinet is completely empty; not one bottle, packet, nor vial, remains to be seen.

Alastair and Fiona look gobsmacked. DI Clowdy looks annoyed. 'I take it neither of you two removed the contents?'

They shake their heads in dumbstruck accord.

'When did you last look in here, Mr Muirhead?'

'Yesterday, or the day before—'

'As recently as that?' Clowdy raises an eyebrow, as does Ava, though she says nothing. 'What were you looking for?'

'I needed ingredients for soap-making. Fiona was with me, and nothing was missing then, was it Fee?'

'On the contrary. I commented it was high time we had a spring clean. Some stuff in there was well past its shelf life. I don't understand.' Fiona sounds flummoxed. 'Why would someone do this?'

'Your husband's cabinet likely contained a poison used by a murderer, and person or persons unknown have sought to dispose of the evidence. This much seems obvious. Mr Muirhead, did you keep a supply of cyanide?'

'No!'

Fiona takes his hand. 'Darling,' she whispers, 'what about my old geology reagents?'

'Speak up, Mrs Muirhead!'

'Oh dear, inspector! This is going to sound so scatterbrained, but I fear there *was* a small amount of cyanide, just a sample, left over from my uni days. Not that I ever used it, but it works as a solvent to leach precious metal out of rock samples. I think there was some mercury in there too… and nitric acid. If only we'd had that clear-out.'

'I need you and your husband to provide a list of everything that's missing.'

Alastair scratches his head. 'I'm not sure we can say *what* was in there.'

'Try,' Clowdy says succinctly. 'Constable Cargill will act as scribe.' Leaving Alastair and Fiona to follow through on his orders, he and Pratt depart, though the nasty whiff of suspicion lingers in their wake.

When Ava tracks Wick down, he's alone in the library. Judging by the number of butts in the ashtray at his elbow, he's been there a while. 'So this is where you're hiding! Have you been here all afternoon?'

'Almost, but not hiding. Reading and thinking. How did things go with the DI?'

'It was *completely* empty?' he muses when she's told all.

'Not so much as a grain of Epsom salt.'

'Perhaps the police'll find fingerprints.'

'Not if the culprit wore gloves. May I have one of your cigars?'

Wick takes a case from his pocket and Ava helps herself, as does he. He uses his monogrammed gold Ronson to light up both, and for a little while, they smoke in pensive silence.

'Do you realise,' Ava asks at last, 'it's been almost two whole weeks since Baumgarten died? Yet according to the Muirheads, until yesterday, the cabinet was full. That's a long time for a murderer to wait before disposing of incriminating evidence.'

'I suppose it is,' agrees Wick.

'And it can't be a coincidence that they decided to act on the very day the bottle resurfaced. I could tell that Clowdy's thinking the same.'

'Who else, apart from us… and Alastair and Murdoch, obviously, knew it had been found?'

'Just take a look at the avenue, Wick! A hundred yards of blue and white tape flapping in the breeze must've been something of a giveaway to the person who buried it. They saw that…'

'…and went straight to the lab. Pretty audacious, given the police presence!'

'You almost sound impressed!'

'Perhaps I meant "reckless",' Wick says with a smile. 'But one thing's sure, they'd have had to work fast.'

'That may explain why *everything* was cleared out. Not just Fiona's Pandora's box of chemicals, but harmless nonsense too, like garlic spray and bone-meal pellets.'

'As I said, lots of policemen around,' Wick offers. 'No time to read labels.'

'No time to read labels...' ruminates Ava.

'What did Clowdy make of your theory about how the cyanide got into Baumgarten?'

'Strictly speaking,' says Ava, 'I have no theory, only a hypothesis. Hypotheses graduate into theories once they're supported by evidence. I lack substantiating data. And in light of the expedient clearing of the cabinet, so do the police, which, as it turns out, may be no bad thing after all.'

'Why do you say that?'

'Because I'm fairly sure they think *Alastair* is the murderer.'

'God!' Wick's voice catches. 'I hope you're wrong! I know *they* are. If Alastair had hidden the bottle, he'd also have found it, so—'

'Trouble is, Wick, as Clowdy pointed out, that only rules Alastair out "digging-wise". Indeed, on reflection, given the murderer and the burier could be different people, knowing who dug those holes won't get me, or the police, as close to solving things as I'd hoped.'

'You're suggesting the poisoner had an accomplice?'

'Not necessarily an accomplice, as such, but somebody on their side; an otherwise innocent person who wanted to protect the murderer, and so took actions to conceal the poison bottle on their behalf. They may have had no vested interested in Baumgarten being dead, only a desire to prevent their friend or loved one from being caught out as a killer.'

Wick screws his eyes shut, leans back in his chair, and, for a moment or two, remains silent.

'What's going through you mind?' Ava decides to ask.

'I'm pondering my own whodunnit candidates, considering where allegiances lie, and wondering who'd help who, no questions asked. Frankly,' he says, pinching the bridge of his nose, 'it's giving me a headache.'

'Me too,' says Ava, 'because, when it comes to Alastair, I can see where Clowdy's coming from. Alastair had access to cyanide, not to mention a ready supply of whatever else besides, and he's had every opportunity to abuse it. Plus, his general unsteadiness, it's making him look guilty. How many times has he said to you, me, and anyone else who'll listen, "This is all my fault…" or "I blame myself…" or a raft of other similarly damning words to that effect? *We* know he's talking about *emotional* culpability. To the more elementary lugs of the Law, however, such claims could sound literal.'

'But what about motive, Ava? And the name of his abettor? Bet Clowdy hasn't come up with either of those!' Wick says angrily.

'Not that he told me. Certainly, there was no suggestion of a motive, but the police wouldn't have to look far to find people who care deeply for our godson and might go to extremes to keep him safe: Murdoch, Laurie Levi, his wife… on paper, us.'

'Still,' scoffs Wick, 'I'd no more suspect Alastair of murder than I'd suspect you.'

'Likewise. Of course.'

'When are you and I going to sit him down for that talk, Ava, like we said we would?'

'Can't do it now. He's with Cargill.' Ava continues to brood. 'If *you* wanted to poison someone, Wick, what would you use?'

'Arsenic,' Wick answers without hesitation. 'Old school, traditional, popular since before the Romans. How about yourself?'

'The animal kingdom offers such a smörgåsbord of options, I'd need to give that some thought. *Dendrobatidae*, the dart frogs, are legendary for their batrachotoxin. As little as one hundredth of a milligram is lethal to a monkey. It's so exquisitely lethal, it seems a lazy choice. Black mamba snake venom, that's fast acting too. Mind you, a box jellyfish sting can cause cardiac arrest in two minutes. Is it cheating if the wounded party drowns before the poison actually kills them?'

'No, but you're only allowed to pick one.'

'Tough decision,' says Ava, 'but I'll plump for tetrodotoxin. A bite from a blue-ringed octopus no bigger than the palm of my hand packs enough of the stuff to kill twenty men. Wham! Total paralysis. Victims remain conscious and alert, totally unable to move, speak, even blink. Imagine lying in a rockpool in nothing but a bathing costume, with everyone around you saying useless things like, "Is she dead?" or, worse, "She's *definitely* dead", and being utterly powerless to shut them up. Still, that stage wouldn't last long. There's no antidote. Lights can be out in under an hour. Puffer fish have the same toxin. Equally lethal. Who's to say who looks more dangerous, though? A pretty little cephalopod, or a fish that inflates like a football?'

Wick chuckles. 'Lovely as all that sounds, Ava, I imagine it'd be tricky to find either creature at short notice, and a key feature of *any* murder weapon isn't only how it works, it's whether or not you can get your hands on it in the first place. Which brings us back to Alastair's cabinet of compounds, and the accessibility thereof.'

'In point of fact,' says Ava, after another pensive interlude, 'it makes perfect sense that cyanide killed Baumgarten rather than anything else. Really, I should've caught on sooner, given how much time I've spent with long-tailed macaques.'

Wick laughs. 'It being *their* murder weapon of choice!'

'Actually, this is a sad story. I'd been following a troupe of them – a phenomenal medley of vocalisations, once one gets one's ear in – and became unwisely attached to an orphaned baby. Forced to fend for himself, he survived, for a little while at least, on fruit left as offerings at a local temple, as did his peers. Lowest of the low, he ate last, making do with others' leftovers. One day, half starved, he gorged on a pile of discarded apricot stones and due to the cyanogenic glycosides in their kernels, was extinct in minutes. As his vascular system failed, his blood became over saturated with oxygen… turning his cheeks bright red.'

'What's this got to do with Baumgarten?'

'When he died, his knees *and* his face were, to coin his own phrase "the colour of overripe tomatoes". At the time, I put that extreme blush down to midge bites, and midge bites alone.

Now, I realise more than one physiological reaction was in play. In an ironic twist of fate, his allergy literally "masked" a classic symptom of acute cyanide poisoning.'

'I don't recall Maggie's face being red. At least what I saw of it.'

'Why would it be? I'm certain she was killed by something else entirely. Cyanide's effects are almost immediate. Baumgarten likely lay down and took a swig, threw up, and died of cardio-respiratory arrest. If Maggie was poisoned with a contaminant in those cherries, then its effects were delayed. She ate them no later than lunchtime. She didn't become ill until evening, four to six hours later. And her symptoms were something else too.'

'You can say that again.' Wick shudders.

'The police... and the pathologist... they've a challenge on their hands. *Especially* the pathologist. It's easy enough to say, "Margaret Kettleness was poisoned". When it comes to establishing what with, he'll have his work cut out.'

'Can't he use some kind of machine? What about litmus paper, or injecting a rabbit?'

'Testing for toxins isn't as cut and dried as people think. It's straightforward enough when you've got an educated idea which substance to look for. You test to confirm its presence. Positive result. Bingo! Murder weapon identified. But if you've no clue what you're testing for, then you're playing a long and complicated guessing game. Perhaps it was substance A? Test for it. Result negative. Try again. Substance B? Another blank. Substance C, maybe...'

'Like looking for a needle in a haystack.'

'Right away the pathologist will be able to rule out the usual culprits: arsenic, strychnine, cyanide and so forth. As far as I'm aware, none of these cause hematochezia... the passage of fresh blood from the anus. Maggie's body *clearly* experienced catastrophic gastrointestinal haemorrhaging, and I reckon she was hallucinating as well. But what to rule in. Hmmm... Funny thing is, Wick, I'm sure I *have* seen symptoms like Maggie's before, but I'm buggered if I can remember where. If I could, then I'd be able to point the pathologist in the right direction.

Perhaps the nature of the poison could even point to the identity of the murderer.'

'Want my advice, doctor?'

'Naturally, professor.'

'Sleep on it. It'll come to you.'

The ground in Ava's dreamscape is the colour of rust and the texture of baked earth. The day is stifling hot, and the air filled with the sounds and smells of Africa. Although she's walking down a dead-straight road, she's lost. She should find a local... ask them if they know where's she's going... but this isn't Thailand. No macaques here. There *is* a dog, though, or some sort of canid, anyhow, trotting along beside her, eyes fixed on its own destination. With a fox-like face and large, upright ears, it looks clever. It's bound to have the answers if she can get it to talk. Sadly, when she taps it on the shoulder, the startled animal lets out a shrill yelp and, tail between its hind legs, leaps off into the brush. Ava turns over her pillow, gives it a punch, and allows her addled mind to carry her to cooler continents.

31

Period of Absence

Wick's invitation comes as a surprise.
'Another *outing*?' queries Ava.
'Why not? The forecast's fine.'
'What about Alastair?'
'I was thinking just the two of us.'
'I meant we should be spending time with him. Supporting him. *Talking*. Besides, outings are strictly off limits, and I had you down as a law-abiding citizen.'
'Since serving breakfast, Alastair's gone back to bed. Saw him go. I for one don't want to disturb him. And if I'm watching you, you're watching me, and The Hall remains in sight, we won't be breaking Clowdy's rules of detention.'
Ava's unsure. 'Well...'
'Come on! A couple of hours can't make any difference. Not if Alastair's asleep.'
'What do you have in mind?'
'A short voyage on the waters of Loch Dorcha.'
'All right. But only if *I* can row.'
'It would feel wrong to allow a woman to do the grunt work.'
'Then I'll try not to grunt!'
'It can be much rougher out there than it looks,' says Ava, noting Wick's canvas deck shoes and sharp, navy reefer jacket.
'Hence the outfit,' Wick says breezily, touching the beak of his yachting cap.
Ava dons scarf, macintosh and boots before she and Wick make their way to the boathouse, where an antiquated wooden

dinghy awaits at the jetty. It rocks violently as Ava clumsily steps aboard.

'Someone's yet to find their sea legs!' Wick laughs as he lowers a wicker hamper into her lap. 'If you wouldn't mind stowing this.' With that, he too embarks, lays a crisply ironed handkerchief on the stern seat, and sits down upon it, all without turning a hair.

They shove off and Ava takes up both oars. She soon finds her rhythm – Catch, *pull*, repeat... Catch, *pull*, repeat – Wick jerking backwards with each of her brisk strokes. The current's strong. She has to work hard. The sea breeze whips her hair across her face, and spray from the blades stings her cheeks. It tastes deliciously salty as she licks it away. 'What a wonderful idea this was!' she cries. 'So bracing. Carl and Martin would love it. Much better than a walk to The Murder Field. Which way are we headed?'

'Straight across.'

For the next ten minutes, Wick says nothing more. Peering over his shoulder, his attention seems fixed on the retreating shore. Ava can't tell if he's enjoying himself, but *she's* having a ball. 'Doesn't this feel wicked! Way... Hay... And *up* she rises... Er... Lie... In... The... Moor... *Ning*!'

'Stop!' Wick says suddenly.

'I've other shanties in my repertoire, if—'

'I mean, stop rowing!'

'Had enough? Should we go back?'

'No! This is where we drop anchor.'

Ava manoeuvres so they're pointing into the wind, draws in the oars, and slides across in her seat so that Wick can climb past into the bow.

'Just need to lower the grapnel over the gunwale,' says Wick, and with a degree of adroitness that only comes with practice, he ties off its nylon line with a neat cleat knot. 'We're in! Hitched and fastened till it's time to weigh up.'

'You've done this before.'

'Have indeed! I love boats... being on the water. Rowed for St John's College, back in my day.'

'An Oxonian, eh? As was Duncan.'

'As was Duncan,' repeats Wick. 'Though he was a blue, back in his day. Anyhow, let's see what Fiona's hidden in that hamper.'

'I'm amazed she put together a picnic for us,' says Ava, 'with everything that's gone on.'

'I didn't ask her to, but when she heard where we were going, she insisted. "Take food", "Make a day of it". Incredibly kind.'

Ava extracts a thermos. 'Ready for a hot drink?'

Wick produces a silver hip flask. 'Or a hair of the dog?'

'Why not both.' Ava pours steaming black coffee into two tin mugs, and Wick tops up each with a slug of whisky. 'We should make a toast. Something nautical.'

'Mistresses and wives, may they never meet!'

'Bottoms up!' says Ava.

As they blow and sip, and rock and yaw, they're joined by an inquisitive young seal. Its shiny, black, bowling-ball head is only feet away.

'How charming,' Wick remarks. 'There's something almost human in the way it's looking at me.'

'That's down to his huge, forward-facing eyes. He gazes at us, we gaze back at him, and feel we can relate. He appears child-like and appealing, so we assume he's harmless… vulnerable, even. Have you ever held a tiger cub?'

Wick shakes his head.

'Enough to make a *man* lactate! But an adult *Panthera tigris*'ll crunch through an elephant's femur like it's a stick of celery. Bite force of a thousand pounds per square inch.' Ava sighs thoughtfully. 'It's ironic the facial characteristics we find "cute" are pointers that the adorable bundle of fluff staring up at us is either an apex predator, or will be when it comes of age. It's all about convergent orbits and degrees of ocular vision. Carnivores who kill to eat rely on good depth perception… the ability to focus on what's directly ahead of them as they chase it down. By contrast, prey species – who tend to be herbivores – need to notice approaching danger from all directions without having to turn their heads. Doesn't matter what's right in front of them…

probably just grass any way... as long as they spot trouble in time to scarper. If you're ever unsure whether a wild animal is likely to be a biter, Wick, there's a useful rule of thumb: "Eyes in front, I hunt. Eyes to the side, I hide."'

'What about killer whales?'

'"Rule of thumb", I said, not holy commandment. D'you know rabbits have almost panoramic vision? Practically the whole three-sixty degrees.'

'Practically?'

'We all have our blind spots, Wick. They differ only in their relative widths.'

'Tell me *what*, Dr Dickens, is that seal thinking?'

'"I wish those google-eyed land-lovers would leave me in peace!"'

Wick laughs, and with a sharp expulsion of air the seal slips back into the depths, apparently taking Wick's high spirits with it. Ava makes a more-thorough exploration of the hamper. Parsnip patties. Hawthorn chutney. She reflects that the last time she scratched together a snack for the field, it was Alastair's dried fruit, cherries and all. She tucks in, but Wick holds back. Ava wonders if he's feeling seasick. As she masticates, both take in the scenery. She judges they're parked in the middle of the loch's headwaters, equidistant between opposite banks. The Hall, windows twinkling in the distance, looks so benign, it's difficult to comprehend that two people just died there. Drumapple appears as it ever does – whitewashed and picturesque, though today there are no lines of washing to be seen, flapping and ballooning like ships' mainsails. Unhappy Ollach. It occurs to Ava that Drumapple's first habitants must've looked across the water and seen only mountains and forests, whereas the Muirhead dynasty has always had their ancient settlement in its sights. Another thing occurs to her too. 'Why are we here, Wick?'

'Being confined to The Hall, steeping in one's own juices, is getting to me.'

'And me, but why choose this particular outing, to this particular spot.'

'I like the vista.'

'I can tell. You seem mesmerised, as you were when admiring the watercolour in Baumgarten's room.'

'You recognise the view!'

'I do.'

'Lovely, isn't it. The artist must have painted it from more or less this exact spot, afloat on the loch. It has those qualities of immediacy that make it so... enduring. Sheila and I used to row out here together. It was a favourite place of ours, or *mine*, anyway. Being, as it were, adrift, would somehow put things in perspective. Dorcha Hall looked so small, so remote from us... it seemed unreal... the people in it reduced to tiny figures on a miniature stage set. Practically insignificant.' Drowning in his memories, Wick talks as though Ava's not there. 'For the precious time we were out at sea, no one could steal my happiness in the way they did when up close. It used to hurt my heart when we had to row back.' He drains his hipflask.

Not knowing what to say, Ava continues to squint in the same direction. She can make out someone... a tall man... wandering into the boathouse. There's something aimless about his walk. She raises her field glasses and zooms-in as best she can. 'That looked like Alastair,' she says uneasily, wishing she'd brought Baumgarten's better binoculars.

'Who did?' Wick asks distractedly, tossing crusts at the small flock of gulls that wheels and swoops above the dinghy's stern.

'Should he be by himself?'

Wick passes no comment. Minutes roll by. Ava doesn't see anyone come out of the boathouse, but another person's heading towards it. She's not sure where they came from or who it is, but guesses it's darling Fee keeping up her monitoring programme afterall. But... hang on... it's *not* her! Judging by the multicoloured garbs, it's Lauri Levi. Goodness. She's a long way from base camp! Poor Alastair. Forever hunted down. Ava's about to turn her attention elsewhere, when a *third* figure materialises. It's small, fast-moving... Ava's as sure as she can be that this *is* Fiona, and... uh oh... she follows Lauri straight inside. More minutes pass. No further arrivals. No departures, either. All in all, queer.

The wind picks up. 'Seen enough?' asks Wick.

'Oh… Yes…' Ava stammers. 'It's getting choppier. Let's head home.'

For the return voyage, Ava's happy for him to take the oars. That way, she can keep her eyes on the shore. As they near land, someone does, at last, reappear: Lauri, exiting the boathouse so explosively, she trips over. Hauling herself to her feet, she rips off her shoes, flings them aside and starts to run. What, wonders Ava, spooked *her*? And why aren't Fiona and Alastair beating it out of there too? Though the dinghy's still a hundred yards away, the woman's sense of panic is tangible.

'Wick!' shouts Ava. 'There's something happening up ahead! Row faster!'

Lauri must have heard her. She swings round and starts jumping up and down, waving her extravagant sleeves like semaphore flags. 'Get your goddam asses over here!' she yells. 'Before it's too goddam late!'

Wick sculls with such fury, Ava has to grip tight to avoid spilling overboard. The second the bow hits the jetty, they dash for the boathouse, primed for something bad. The dimly lit space is filled with nautical clutter, it smells like decaying seaweed, and though Ava's never been in here before, she has a sickening sense of déjà vu. In a scene reminiscent of that she and Wick encountered in the potting shed lab, they find Fiona grappling to control her husband. He's propped up against the back wall, arms flailing, looking vacant and jaundiced. Fiona's fighting to keep him from falling flat on his face. Seeing Fiona's on the brink of buckling, Ava and Wick step forward to take Alastair's weight. Together, they lower him to the floor where, like a ragdoll, he slumps into a drivelling heap.

'Please darling!' cries Fiona, dropping to her husband's side. 'Look at me!'

'What the *hell's* going on?'

'Oh, Uncle Wick! He's taken tranquilisers. A whole packet!'

'*Shit*!'

'I can't get him to stay awake, Ava! I've tried slapping him. I've tried—'

'Keep your wigs on, ladies!' drawls Lauri. Ava had forgotten she was there. 'Look what *I've* found!' She waves a foil blister pack in the air. 'Four missin'. That ain't enough to hurt a fella his size. *I've* popped more at parties. You'd need ten times as many to—'

'Where did those come from?' asks Fiona.

'Over there.' Lauri says coolly, her panic apparently having evaporated. She nods at a row of pegs from which hang mouldy life jackets, barnacle-encrusted fenders, and Alastair's corduroy jacket... lining-side out.

'Thank heavens!' says Wick. 'Sounds like he should be okay, though he needs to come round before we try to get him back to the house.'

'Reckon *I'll* sling my hook,' says Lauri, 'once I've gotten my goddam shoes.'

'Tek 'em, woman!'

Alastair lifts his head. 'Murdoch?'

Sure enough, though Ava never heard him arrive, the man is standing in the doorway, as solid and square as a bull musk ox, Lauri's silver-strapped sandals dangling incongruously from his right forefinger.

'You sure know how to make a gal feel like Cinderella,' cackles Lauri, unhooking them and slipping them on. She bends over Alastair and blows him a kiss. 'Here's lookin' at you, kid!' She presses the strip of tablets into Fiona's hand, winks at her, then sways away.

'Thank you, Lauri,' Ava calls after her, 'for raising the alarm!'

Lauri doesn't look back, but like a jockey who knows his horse just crossed the finish line first, she punches her fist in the air. Though *she* may have reined in her wits, Fiona's face is as florid as a baboon's backside. Suddenly self-conscious, she quickly covers her cheeks with her hands.

'Why don't you go on ahead too?' suggests Ava. 'Splash some water over your face and take a breath.'

'Good idea,' says Wick. 'Catch up with Lauri, then neither of you need walk back alone. Ava and I will follow with Alastair, soon as he's ready.'

'It feels wrong to leave him,' deliberates Fiona, 'but it *is* a struggle sometimes... you know... saving my husband from himself. Perhaps I should straighten up a bit. It's bad enough Lauri witnessing as much as she has, without other people catching on. The Hall needs a business-as-usual front.'

It strikes Ava that any hope of achieving that sailed when Baumgarten left in a body bag, but Fiona's fortitude is, she supposes, commendable.

The two women have scarcely left when Alastair opens his eyes. 'Where am I?'

'In the boathouse,' says Ava.

'That's right... The *boathouse*,' he garbles. 'What was it I came here for?' Alastair examines each face in turn: Ava's, Wick's, then Murdoch's. 'It's no good. I've forgotten.'

Wick takes charge. 'Come on! Let's get him to his feet and see if he can walk it off. Murdoch, if you and I take an arm each—'

'Nae,' says Murdoch. 'I'll bide here.'

'But—'

'Somebiddy needs te cut doon the rope.'

Ava and Wick slowly swivel, tracking his melancholy gaze. Only now do they see something that Ava sincerely hopes Fiona did not: a boat's painter line, one end wrapped round a rafter; the other, formed into a loop... or a lasso?... or a *noose*! It must have been hanging there in the shadows the whole time.

'Dear God!' breathes Wick.

'Holy cow!' concurs Ava.

Murdoch draws his sgian-dubh.

32

Slap in the Face

For the second time in forty-eight hours, Ava and Wick find themselves sneaking their worse-for-wear godson in through the back entrance to his own hotel, hoping that Cargill's half-shut eyes are looking the other way. Ava leaves Wick to put him to bed. As she stirs milk into two mugs of freshly brewed Earl Grey, she realises her hands are shaking. 'Get this down you,' she says, passing one to Fiona, who's seated the other side of the kitchen table. 'It'll make you feel better.' She's grateful that her mental picture of a rope swinging from a beam is not one Fiona shares.

Fiona blows on her drink, takes a tentative sip, and grimaces. 'Eww, that's sweet!'

'Strong, sugary tea. Classic remedy for shock. The glucose'll mitigate the depletion of your liver's glycogen stores *and* suppress your brain's hypothalamic-pituitary-adrenal axis, putting the brakes on glucocorticoid secretion. I'm not sure what the tea leaves bring to the party, though red costate tiger moth caterpillars feed on—'

'*Camellia sinensis* is a great source of antioxidant polyphenols and caffeine. Grows best in laterite soil, rich in iron and aluminium.'

Ava nearly drops her mug.

Fiona spasms too, as if stunned by her own words. 'Jesus! Apologies for interrupting, Ava, I forgot myself. The jitters made me speak out of turn.'

'No problem. It's nice to be reminded what a scholar you are.'

'Alastair's the botanist, not me.'

'You're too modest.'

Fiona looks even more uncomfortable.

'Are you all right?' Ava asks. 'Your face is still red.'

There's an awkward pause. 'I take it you intend to report Alastair to the police, even though he didn't know what he was doing.'

'I'd no plans to,' answers Ava, 'though you should speak to Sween.'

'Oh, it's not serious,' says Fiona. 'It barely stings now. Alastair was lashing out and I got in the way. Actually,' she says, taking another sip of tea, 'this is helping.'

Ava's confused. 'Sorry, Fiona, what exactly are you saying?'

Fiona puts down her mug. 'You mean you *didn't* notice? When you sent me back to splash myself with cold water, I thought you'd seen!' Once more, her hand reaches up to cover her face, but she's too slow, and Ava spots something she missed before. The unmistakeable trace of a handprint across Fiona's left cheek. Though faint, and partial, its implication is brazen.

Ava feels sick. 'Did someone *hit* you?' she asks slowly.

'Ava, you *know* Alastair would never, *ever* hurt me intentionally! He's not himself...' Suddenly Fiona's talking ten to the dozen. 'You know he loses himself sometimes, too, and this afternoon he lost it again, like he had when you and Wick found him in the barn. The smack wasn't his fault. I was trying to bring him to his senses, and I went too far.'

Ava's aghast. 'Just to be clear, Fiona... you're telling me that *Alastair* "smacked" you? That just seems... *unbelievable.*'

'Why would I lie?' whispers Fiona, looking away.

'Has he ever "smacked" you before?'

'Never. I swear. And he wouldn't have done today if I'd only kept calm. *I* slapped him first! Involving Inspector Clowdy will achieve nothing.'

'Fiona, *I* won't tell the police about this, but Sween may, and you *must* speak to him. And I fully intend to speak to Wick. He takes his responsibility for his godson's welfare, and for you, very seriously. He needs to know.'

'If you say so.' Though Fiona's answer is curt, she seems to breathe a sigh of relief. Perhaps, whilst she won't admit it, the burden of 'supporting' Alastair *is* becoming too much.

'What happened before Alastair went to the boathouse?'

'We had a row. Sort of. Stupid really. You see, today's our first wedding anniversary—'

'Oh Fiona! I'd forgotten.'

'So had he. I wanted to make it special, or as special as possible under the circumstances, but he didn't. Alastair just wanted to talk about money, and Baumgarten, and Maggie, but I wouldn't listen, because I *can't*... not anymore. He just kept going over and over the same things, again and again. Nothing he was saying was making any difference, or any sense, so I asked him to stop and go for a lie down.' Fiona pauses. 'I find it difficult to repeat his reply.'

'I'd like to hear it,' Ava says gently.

Fiona takes a deep breath. 'He said, "You're right. I think I do need to check out." Then he kissed me... on the lips... and off he went to our bedroom.'

Ava adds another spoonful of sugar to her own tea. 'Is that where he got hold of your pills?'

Fiona gasps. 'How did you know they were mine?'

'Don't look so mortified! Alastair told me... only out of concern for you. I'm sure it isn't common knowledge.'

'Even so, I'm embarrassed. I may seem on top of things, but the truth is, I feel as if I'm on constant high alert. "Where's Alastair?" "What's he doing?" Dr Sween offered me something... NarcoVal tablets... to help me switch off. I *hate* that I need them, but occasionally...'

'When did you discover they were missing?'

'After that "sort of" row, I decided to take one, or just half of one, myself. Alastair had been gone for over an hour, reception was quiet, I thought I'd join him, have a lie down too. I looked in my handbag, saw they'd disappeared, and I just knew Alastair had taken them! I've never felt panic like that in my life. It was like being punched in the chest. He wasn't in the bedroom, obviously, and at first, I couldn't think where he'd be. Then I remembered. Earlier, he'd been talking about you and Wick, out on the loch, asking me when you'd be back – obsessing, same as he was about everything else – and it struck me he might have gone to the water's edge to wait for you. So that's where I went, looked in the boatshed... and there he was.'

'Or *they* were,' corrects Ava. 'Lauri Levi got to him first.'

'That woman,' spits Fiona, 'is what Mother would call, a "slut".'

'What were they doing when you found them?' asks Ava.

'He was on the floor, and she was standing over him, helping him up,' Fiona answers, still vitriolic, 'or at least trying to. But once I showed up, she made a run for it.'

'Why?'

Fiona's voice reduces to a whisper. 'Because she saw Alastair hit me.'

'So she realised the two of you alone couldn't deal with him?'

'I suppose that's one way of putting it, yes.'

While Ava waits for Wick to find words, she looks up at the huge portrait of Sheila and Duncan, their painted expressions unchanged since she was last in the dining room, and wonders what the hell they'd make of everything that's occurred since the crash. What advice would Duncan have for his near-derelict son? 'Have another whisky, lad, then shoot something. You'll be grand.' And Sheila? 'You're married to a good woman, Alastair. Please don't let her down.'

'He *hit* her? *He* hit her? *He* hit *her*?' Wick repeats, over and over. 'No matter where you put the inflexion, it doesn't sound right. You're *positive* it was a slap mark?'

'I'm no expert in dermatoglyphics,' Ava sighs, 'but I know a human handprint when I see one. And it was fresh.'

'And that's what Fiona says happened?'

Ava nods pensively.

'As for the noose, and all that implies...'

'Pills as well,' mutters Ava. 'Talk about "belt and braces"!'

'Quite,' Wick says heavily. 'It's a long time since anything's saddened me as much as the events of today. Alastair's behaviour is starting to frighten me. Sounds like this time, he really meant to go through with it.'

'Did he say anything to you when you put him to bed?'

'Out like a light,' says Wick with a headshake.

'You realise why he kept pestering Fiona about our outing, trying to pin down how long we'd be on the water? He planned to get to the boathouse ahead of our return, so we'd be the ones to find his body, not her.'

'Wanted to spare her that.' Wick mulls some more. 'We only have Fiona's take on what's going on inside Alastair's head, Ava, what made him lash out. Not that I disbelieve her. God knows, I wish I could.'

'*She* wasn't the only person in that boathouse, though.'

'Given how fuzzy Alastair was about what he did in the barn, chances are he won't remember much of this either. Though you and I never did get his full take on things. Perhaps if we *had* done…'

'I'm not intending to quiz Alastair, Wick. I'm thinking of someone else entirely.'

Ava bides her time, waiting for the right moment to tackle Lauri Levi. It presents itself much later that day, when she finds the woman in the sitting room. She's lying on her pew of choice – the time-worn, satin-upholstered chaise longue – one languid arm draped across her forehead, the other trailing on the floor, like a parody of a Victorian lady, mid 'vapours', making use of her fainting couch.

'Evening,' says Ava. 'Mind if I join you? I fancy a bit of company and everyone else has turned in.'

Lauri slowly lifts the arm from her face. 'Pull the other one. You want to kick around that shitshow in the boatshed, woman-to-woman… so to speak.'

'If that's okay,' concedes Ava.

Lauri sits up and slides over, making space for Ava; a tacit sign she's prepared to talk. As Ava perches next to her, she's enveloped by a fug of perfume so thick, she has to clear her throat. 'Quite a day you've had, eh?'

'You can say that again. Lucky me and Ali's screw-bit missus bust in when we did, or it might've been curtains for him.'

'From where I was sitting, out on the water, luck played no part. You were following Alastair, quite deliberately, and went into the boathouse after him. More than that, you and he were alone in there for three, maybe even four minutes, before Fiona arrived.'

'As little as that?' shrugs Lauri.

'As *long* as that. In sixty seconds, a bumble bee can pollinate ten flowers, and a female sunfish can lay twenty-four eggs. So I'm wondering what you and he got up to, with so much time to kill.'

'As it happens, nothin', or,' Lauri qualifies with a smirk, 'nothin' to get excited about. Turned out he was stoned. Must've already popped those pills. When I got to him, they'd kicked in big time. Higher than The Empire State he was, sittin' on the floor, eyes rollin', mumblin' baloney about the German birder and Maggie the maid... how bad he felt. I asked him why he'd come down to the boatshed.'

'His answer?'

Lauri pauses. 'He was goin' to... "hang around" and wait for you guys... you and your Prof... to find him. Pretty much his exact words.'

Ava hears herself swallow. Lauri's hesitance suggests a lot. Does she know about the noose?

'What do you think Alastair was doing before you got to him? Had he moved anything?'

'Ropes, for example?' Lauri scrutinises Ava through half-shut eyes. 'Cain't say. Never been in that shed before, so how would I know what was supposed—'

'Let's be frank, Lauri,' Ava cuts in, 'did it occur to you that you'd walked in on a suicide attempt?'

'It's what *you* thought, ain't it. Anyways,' Lauri carries on. 'I tried to get him to his feet, but he didn't make it easy. Like jivin' with a drunken scarecrow, and *boy* that man is *tall*! And that's when the wife burst in, put two dimes together and made a whole buck. Funny, really.' Lauri laughs wryly. 'Accused me and him of doin' all kinds of things, when I doubt Ali was capable of realisin' I was even there. Then she wants *me* to help *her*.' Lauri adds angrily. 'The goddam cheek!'

'Help how?'

'I dunno! Work together to get him out of there, I guess. We managed to lean him against a wall, but he was so goofy that she started gettin' mad. And then…'

'*Then?*'

'She lost it! Yellin' at him, shakin' him, firin' off the kinds of curse words I didn't think she'd know. I barrelled outta there to fetch old Murdoch, so fast I darned near broke both ankles. But you'd have seen that part.' Lauri raises her fists to her eyes to mimic binoculars, which she trains on Ava. 'Who *are* you anyhow?' she asks. 'Always watchin'.'

'I'm Ava. Ava Dickens.'

'I know your *name*, lady. I mean, what is your purpose? Here, in this place? Jane Goodall, but without no monkeys; bad hair, men's shoes, merrily stickin' your big fat beak in whenever the hell it suits.'

Ava laughs. 'An honest appraisal if a bit harsh. I get my nose from my father's side.'

'Don't get me wrong. I ain't bein' impertinent, I just want to understand.'

'I'm here on holiday, Lauri, at the invitation of Alastair Muirhead. He's my godson.'

'You don't say. And the dumb questions?'

'Natural curiosity, no disrespect intended either.'

'Bull crap!' Lauri chuckles. 'Every time you look at me, I can tell you're judgin' what I got, just like all the other females in this joint. From the size of these puppies,' she says, puffing up her chest, 'to the shape of my rear end. Same thing when I talk. You listen and you judge. And whatever you're seein' and hearin', it makes you look like you sucked on a lemon. I'd say that's pretty disrespectful, as things go. So, how's about you return the favour, and spill your "honest appraisal" of *me*.' The glint in Lauri's eyes suggests defiance… and mischief.

'Fair play,' laughs Ava. 'First, I'd have to say you're far cleverer than you look—'

'Ain't that the truth!'

'And you're diffident about your natural appearance, given you work so hard to conceal it.'

'Trust me,' Lauri gives Ava a conspiratorial nudge, 'if I took off this lot, you would *not* like what you saw! What else?'

'I think you're more vulnerable than you admit, and I'm not talking about poisoned chocolate. You need to take care of your*self*.'

'How d'you figure that?' Suddenly Lauri's not smiling.

Ava forges on. 'You're highly attracted to someone who will never reciprocate your advances, no matter how hard you try, so you're in danger of getting hurt. Alastair is a happily married man.'

Lauri looks like she's been hit by a round from a Gatling gun. 'Jeez, lady. Pull your punches, why don't you. All bullshit!' she mutters hotly. 'Except the part about my brain.'

Ava feels bad. She thought Lauri Levi would take her remarks in the spirit intended: return fire of appropriate magnitude, given the comments Lauri lobbed at *her*. But Ava misread the situation. While Lauri can dish out the truth, it seems hearing it's another story.

'Gimme a cigarette.'

'I've only got rollups.'

'Forget it,' chides Lauri, 'rollups are for bums. Let's talk about you and *your* fancy fella, a *professor*, no less.'

'He is not my "fellow"!' Much to her indignation, Ava feels herself horripilate.

'More bullcrap! You got him takin' you on little trips, and all those quiet evenin's in, just the two of you, chewin' the fat. You must think everyone around you's blind. But take a look at him, take a look at yourself, and then ask yourself what you asked me.

Reckon he's turned on by your ugly-bug stories? Course he ain't. And he cain't be interested in what you've got on show, that's for sure. Acting the detective and expectin' him to play sidekick ain't exactly feminine either. Take a word from the wise,' continues Lauri, inflicting another, sharp nudge, 'as soon as that slicker gets a clear shot at an exit, he'll skedaddle outta here, pants on fire, leavin' you spittin' dust. He's only played along so far because he's bored outta his… tiny… little… mind!' Lauri pokes Ava three times in the chest. 'Stuck here, hopin' he don't die…' Her spite apparently spent, her voice trails away.

Ava regroups. 'Are you scared, Lauri?' she asks softly.

'Of what?'

'Being murdered. Because, if it helps, I don't think those chocolates were meant for you. I believe Maggie was deliberately targeted.'

'Oh, I'm done with scared, Dr Dickens,' Lauri scoffs. 'It don't suit me. If anyone should be watchin' their backs around here, shouldn't it be you? Stompin' around in your size nines, treadin' on people's toes… includin' a killer's. To put it in your language, "Kick the hornet's nest, you'll wind up stung."' As she stands up, she laughs. 'Now, *honey*, I am off to my bed.'

'Just one last question, Lauri,' Ava says hastily. 'In the boathouse, did you see Alastair Muirhead hit his wife?'

The delay before Lauri speaks is so long, Ava wonders if she intends to answer, but answer she eventually does. 'Yes. Now leave me be. Us gals need their beauty sleep… some more than others.'

33

So Long Sister!

Once again, Ava dreams she's in Africa, wandering down the same straight road, still lost, leaving a trail of huge footprints in the dust. Mirages shimmer on the ever-retreating horizon, like puddles of mercury, or distant bodies of water. Like sea lochs. The illusory dog is back too; two paces ahead of her, eyes front, just out of reach. He's lost weight since they last met. She can count his ribs. She realises he's a jackal. Just a puppy. Jackal pups'll eat anything when they're hungry. She offers him a chocolate-coated cherry. He sniffs her fingers, he sniffs the cherry, he licks his lips, and... that's when he starts to howl.

'He's gone!' The yell that severs Ava's sleep is so visceral, her blood runs cold. Another murder! Or has Alastair succeeded in doing what he's tried and failed to do twice before? Heart laden with dread, she pushes her bare feet into her slippers and heads for the source of the commotion. Running along the moonlit corridor, she's aware that others are stirring, and as she passes Wick's bedroom door, he too exits. Without exchanging a word, both race down to the lobby, to find they're not the first on scene.

Constable Cargill is standing hands on hips while Fiona, apparently mid meltdown, is waving a lipstick in his face. The officer is wearing paisley-patterned pyjamas. His clothes are dry. Fiona's wearing wellington boots and a long nightdress that's so wet, it's clinging to her shivering body. Cargill, frowning, eyes wound to the heavens, has the demeanour of a stoic parent waiting for an over-tired toddler to calm down. Fiona has the demeanour of a self-possessed woman who is finally, and completely, blowing her top.

'Just look at *this*!' she shouts, thrusting the lipstick perilously close to the tip of Cargill's bulbous nose.

'If ye'd hold still and pass it te me, Mrs Muirhead,' he answers steadily, 'I'll gladly oblige.'

Fiona ignores him. 'And *you* look at *that*, Ava!' she cries, jabbing at the reception desk, across which are scrawled, in large, oleaginous letters, three words: *SO LONG SISTER!* Ava's not good on makeup shades, but she'd put its hot pink tone at somewhere between 'Livid American' and 'Running Scared'. She's so grateful not be staring at the body of her godson, the triviality of this situation almost makes her laugh.

'I don't know why you're smiling, Ava. Lauri Levi has flounced off into the night, and persuaded Alastair to go with her!'

While the first part of this statement makes some sense to Ava, the second part seems incredible. Surely Fiona can't seriously believe Alastair would choose to be alone in Lauri's company for more than five minutes, never mind flee Dorcha Hall with her. Ava senses, however, that now is not the time to point this out.

'How did she do it?' asks Fiona. 'What did she say to him to make him run away? I've been an idiot! I should have seen this coming a mile off. But no! *Stupid* me, I let it happen. I thought I had things under control!' As she rages on, it's clear Fiona's no longer addressing the three people standing next to her. She's remonstrating with herself. 'He must be found!'

'As I said, madam, Sergeant Pratt is cummin' from Knockinch—'

'Tell him to hurry up!'

'Is there anything I can help with, Mrs Muirhead?' Bernard Addington calls from the upstairs landing. Flanked by his wife and children, he tightens the cord of his quilted satin dressing gown, readying himself for action.

'Have you seen Alastair?' Fiona answers feverishly. 'Do *any* of you know where he is?'

Barbara shakes her head, causing her crown of rollers to quake. 'Sorry dear, no. Have you lost him?'

'What about Miss Levi?'

'Afraid not, constable,' answers Bernard. 'None of us has,' he adds, as recent-arrivals George and Stewart also shake their heads.

'In which case, everyone, return te yer rooms. This is a domestic matter.'

'A *domestic* matter,' Barbara repeats to George, loudly, as the little group shambles off. 'Half two in the morning, and they can't find *either* of them! Not that Lauri'll get far on her own, in the shoes *she* wears...'

Cargill's about to refocus his attention on Fiona, when he's interrupted by the sound of a vehicle pulling up outside. The front door creaks open and in strides Pratt, metaphorical guns drawn and blazing. 'What's this I hear, Mrs Muirhead?' he asks crossly. 'Yer husband's done a runner, tekkin' yer American guest along too!'

'I've already explained to your constable! *Twice*! He's just not listening. I woke up, turned over in bed, and Alastair wasn't beside me. Naturally I went to look for him at once.'

'"Naturally"? When I awake te find Mrs Pratt has arisen in the wee small hours, I dinnae immediately assume she's missin'. I remain in bed and calmly consider her whereabouts. Is she in the lavatory, fer example, or makin' a brew? Has a fox got in wi' the chickens?'

'My husband's very stressed. I was worried...' she stammers, '*petrified* he'd—'

'Made another "silly mistake"?'

'All right, sergeant! Yes!' Fiona throws a scorching look at Cargill. 'That's *exactly* what I thought. So I fetched Murdoch. I went to look in the barn, he headed for the boathouse.'

'Boathouse?'

Fiona looks nervously at Ava. 'There was an incident, yesterday.'

'Was there, indeed?' says Pratt with a censorious click of the tongue. He waits for Fiona to elaborate, but she remains tight lipped, and it seems that, for now, he'll choose to stick to more immediate matters. 'So ye and Murdoch left the premises, under curfew, and went yer separate ways, in the dark, and in the rain? Ye didnae think o' rousin' Constable Cargill?'

'The only thing on our minds was Alastair.'

'And when ye got te the barn?'

'The Land Rover wasn't there, and straightaway I knew he'd left the estate. I rushed back to tell the constable, and then I saw this... *message*... meant for me, and I realised *she's* gone too.'

'"She", bein' Miss Levi?'

'Who else! Daubing her vitriol where everyone will see it. Look how she's ground the stub of her slutty lipstick into the pages of the visitors' book like a filthy fag end. Mocking *me*. She said she wanted to leave. Couldn't have been plainer. Why didn't I listen! And why are you still standing here, sergeant? You as well, constable? Go and fetch Alastair back. Please!' Fiona sounds truly panic stricken. 'I don't care what happens to that... *woman*. I just need him *here*.'

At this moment, the reception phone rings. Fiona snatches up the receiver. 'Alastair!' she breathes. 'Where are you?' But in the next instant her elation switches to confusion. 'Hello? *Hello...?*' After a few seconds, she hangs up. 'How odd.'

'Nae yer husband, I tek it?'

'No. It wasn't anyone. I mean, whoever it was, they didn't speak, or the connection didn't work. If it was something important, I guess they'll try again.'

'Rum time te be makin' a call,' reflects Pratt, before returning to business. 'Where's Angus Murdoch now?'

'Still outside, I suppose. Searching.'

'Ye'll have had a wee gander round Miss Levi's room?'

'Of course!' snaps Fiona.

'Are her belongin's still there?'

'Yes, but—'

'Then yer gettin' ahead o' yersel te assume she's nae cummin' back, or that Alastair's with her, though neither o' them shoulda gone anywhere.' Pratt's about to continue his lecture when the front door creaks open for the second time, and in comes Alastair. The lipstick case shatters as it hits the floor.

'What did I tell ye, Mrs Muirhead!' says Cargill. 'Here's the man himsel, safe and sound. And...?' He, and everyone else too, peers expectantly over Alastair's shoulder. 'Miss Levi's nae with ye?'

'Just me!' Alastair replies with a weak smile. He looks tired and dishevelled. His clothes are even wetter than his wife's.

'You're back,' whispers Fiona, her tortured expression much like the one she wore when he drank his repellent. Though her relief is palpable, when Alastair takes her in his arms, she tenses.

'It's very early,' he says. 'I thought you'd be asleep—'

'Ne'er mind sleepin'!' shouts Pratt. 'Where've ye been? Yer wife was beside hersel. And where's yer American lady?'

'We went for a drive. What's that smeared all over the front desk?'

'A parting message from Lauri,' says Ava.

'God, she's a handful!' Alastair grumbles. 'She must've done that while I was fetching the car. How ungrateful.'

'Drive *where*?' asks Wick.

'Drumapple.' Alastair shrugs. 'Why all the fuss?'

'Because,' Pratt roars, 'between the hours of 6 p.m. and 6 a.m. ye're under police instruction te stay indoors, and at *nae* time are ye te leave the grounds o' The Hall, unless DI Clowdy says so. He's on his way from Inverness now, and he's nae best pleased! So tell me, at what hour did ye and she decide te leave?'

'After midnight. One in the morning, maybe. I couldn't sleep, so I got up to make myself a chamomile tea, and Lauri was here, in the lobby, sitting in the dark. Frightened the life out of me! I asked her if I could get her anything, and she launched into another of her rants. It was about wanting to get away from here, how The Hall's a dangerous place. On and on... she would *not* keep her voice down and I didn't know how to shut her up. I've always been polite to her, tried to be nice, but this time, she got to me. It seemed simpler to do what she asked than argue with her any more than we'd already argued, so I took her to

Drumapple and left her at the phone box, where she could call a taxi.'

'Did she say where she intended the taxi te take her?' asks Pratt.

'"A million miles from this clusterfuck", were our parting words, though I reckon she meant Inverness railway station.'

'Why didn't she simply ring from here?' asks Wick.

'Didn't think to suggest it,' Alastair says flatly.

'Had she packed a bag?'

'Nope. Christ, I'm absolutely knackered. I need to lie down.'

'Ye're goin' naewhere, Sonny Jim,' barks Pratt. 'Why did ye nae wait with her till her taxi came?'

'I wanted to get back to The Hall ASAP, before Fee realised I was gone.'

'Sergeant,' says Fiona, throwing Alastair an almost-pitying look, 'ever since Lauri Levi got here, she's taken advantage—' But whatever apologies and excuses she's about to broker on her husband's behalf are interrupted by the entrance of Murdoch. Given Pratt's mood, Ava thinks it's as well if they remain unsaid. Clad in a dripping oilskin cloak, Murdoch lingers in the open doorway, stamping up and down on the spot, knocking mud from his stout leather boots.

'Ah, Angus!' says Pratt. 'Ye'll see we have Mr Muirhead back in our midst.'

Murdoch harrumphs something to the effect that this is, all things considered, good news, though he's far from happy about being sent 'te hunt the gowk' when he'd as soon have been in his bed. He turns to Alastair. 'Yer car's out front. I'll put her awa' fer ye.'

'No need. I'll do it.'

'You've done more than enough driving for one day!' Fiona's voice is ice cold.

'Quite right, missus,' says Pratt. 'Alastair, give Murdoch yer keys.'

And off Murdoch plods.

'Thank you for your help,' Ava calls after him.

'Yes,' reiterates Alastair. 'Thank you.'

Pratt's brow creases. Something's occurred to him. The same something that occurred to Ava a whole two minutes earlier. 'Mrs Muirhead, I'm wonderin' if yer caller just now coulda been Miss Levi.'

'Impossible. It was a man.'

'You said they didn't speak, Fiona,' says Ava.

Fiona's brow creases too. 'They didn't, Ava. I could tell from their breathing... deep and coarse... *definitely* a man.'

'No clicks and whirs, or *beep, beep, beeps* te suggest the call came from a phone box?'

'None.'

'Och, well,' the policeman huffs. 'Just a thought. Constable Cargill, get dressed and go te Drumapple. See if the lady's where Mr Muirhead says he left her. If she is, bring her back.'

'You're talking as though you don't believe what Alastair's told us, sergeant,' says Fiona. 'He has no reason to lie. Darling, did anyone see you and Lauri together? Witnesses who can vouch for you?'

'I passed someone; Jack Hooley, walking in the woods.'

'How can ye be certain?' queries Pratt. 'It being so dark?'

'I suppose I can't.'

'How about in the village itself, though?' Fiona asks keenly. 'No lights on? Curtains twitching when you dropped her off?'

Alastair shakes his head. 'I'm not sure.'

'What was Miss Levi wearin'?' asks Pratt.

'Same as she always wears. Elastic and zips.'

Fiona emits a derogatory snort.

'Well, Alastair,' Pratt says sternly, 'prepare yersel! The inspector'll be wantin' words! The rest o' you, back te yer beds.'

'I'd like Dr Dickens and Professor Wickremesinghe to stay with me, sergeant,' says Alastair, 'if that's allowed. I feel I need someone in my corner.'

Pratt considers before conceding, cagily. 'I cannae stop 'em.'

Fiona's agape. 'But what about me!' She grasps Alastair's hand. 'You can't send *me* away?'

'Get dried off, Fee,' Alastair says quietly, 'and go to bed like the sergeant's asked. Please.'

'That's what you really want?'

Alastair nods.

'Okay then,' Fiona mutters coolly as she extricates her fingers from his. 'But this is madness! Pure, utter and *complete*!'

34

The Missing M

Ava, Wick and Alastair wait in the office. Ava and Wick's attempts at conversation fall flat. Alastair sits, mumbling to himself, eyes closed, apparently oblivious to his own soggy attire. However much preparation time he may have wished for, it's in short supply. Cargill is back within the hour, and Clowdy arrives all too soon after. The DI doesn't mince his words. 'Mr Muirhead! I was roused by a call from Sergeant Pratt, informing me you took one of your guests on an excursion without permission, in the middle of the night, and that only one of you has returned. Explain yourself!'

'Lauri Levi asked me to drop her off in Drumapple,' says Alastair, 'so I did.' His words are clear, but his voice wavers.

'Is that a fact? You'd no concerns for her safety, or your own?'

'Not at the time, no.'

'In which case,' gibes Clowdy, 'you have appalling judgement! There's a killer at large, and you'd have us believe you took a vulnerable lady away from the protection of the police, before sun-up, and left her alone, yards from the loch shore, in the rain, simply because she nagged you into it?'

'It can be hard to say no to some women—'

'Moreover, this was Miss Levi, the very person who narrowly escaped being fatally poisoned with some substance, likely from *your* depository, concealed in a box of *your* homemade confections. And here you are, home safe without her, while she is now missing.'

'She's not missing. I left Lauri at the phone box. She wanted to call a cab.'

Clowdy turns to Cargill. 'Constable, tell Mr Muirhead who you found at the phone box.'

'I found naebiddy, sir.'

Clowdy addresses Pratt. 'You've contacted all the local taxi companies?'

'In Knockinch and thirty miles round. Neither o' them answered a call this mornin'.'

'So Mr Muirhead,' Clowdy says cuttingly, 'it's fair to say Miss Levi is unaccounted for.'

Alastair looks confused. 'If she's not in Drumapple, and no cab came, somebody else must've collected her. Can *no* one in the village vouch for me? What about Jack Hooley? He must have at least seen me en route.'

'While you've been sitting cosy in the warm, Constable Cargill here undertook a door-to-door of every house in the village, didn't you, Cargill?'

'I've spoken te all yer friends and neighbours o'er the water, Mr Muirhead,' he answers stoutly, 'includin' Mr Hooley, and ye cannae have seen him in the woods. At the early hour in question, he was at home. Says he'll swear te it.'

'He's lying!' Alastair says hotly.

Clowdy sighs the weighty sigh of a man who's about to lose his patience. '*Someone* is, Mr Muirhead. No doubt about that. As I see it, we have two scenarios. Either you dropped Miss Levi off as you say, then, by her own volition, she decided to take off into the wilds, dressed in "elastic and zips", or you never took her to Drumapple at all. Right now, the second of these options is the clear favourite. Can you see why this is concerning? For *you*?'

Alastair moves his head up, down, then side to side, in tacit bewilderment.

'So, I ask you, where is she?'

'On a train,' Alastair offers weakly.

'Rubbish! What state did you leave her in?'

'When I last saw her, she was… fine…'

More notes of insecurity ricochet off the walls and ring in Ava's ears.

'And I'd never harm a woman, inspector. Never.'

Ava doesn't know how Wick reacts to this statement, since she cannot bring herself to look at him.

'Besides,' Alastair continues, 'why would I hurt her? I liked her.'

'"*Liked*", Mr Muirhead?' queries Clowdy. 'You've reason to refer to Miss Levi in the past tense?'

'A slip of the tongue! I only meant that I used to like her more than I do now—'

'Mr Muirhead!' Pratt interjects sharply, but then his voice tempers. 'Alastair, I've known ye since ye were knee high te a grasshopper. Ye were ne'er one for hoodwinkin', and now's nae the time te start. There's somethin' ye're hidin', and I'm askin' what that somethin' is.'

Alastair deliberates, peering at Ava and Wick through his floppy blond fringe. To Ava, he looks as he did when he was six years old. Like a very lonely only child. 'Okay,' he sighs. '*Okay.* What I said about coming across Lauri in the lobby, her wanting to get away, is one hundred per cent true. She was really worked up and upset and I don't blame her. After what happened with Maggie and the chocolates, she's every reason to be frightened. I said to wait till morning. Don't do anything… rash. "Everything looks better in the light of day." Supposedly,' he adds with another forced laugh. 'But she was desperate. So, I gave in. I said I'd help her, and I did take her to Drumapple, but when I spoke to you earlier, I missed something out.'

'Why?'

'Because I didn't want to upset Fee. *God*, this is tough to talk about.'

'You've got this far. May as well rip off the whole sticking plaster,' encourages Wick.

'The thing is,' Alastair says with a sigh of defeat, 'I actually agreed to take her all the way to Inverness in time for her to catch the first train south. I fetched the Land Rover, and off we went, but we'd no sooner reached the end of the avenue when she...' He wavers.

'For goodness sake, Alastair, what happened?' mutters Ava. 'You've turned the colour of a frigate bird's throat.'

'She made a pass at me! At first, I laughed it off. I thought Lauri was just being, you know, *Lauri*. But no. She was absolutely serious. She said she loves me, that Fee doesn't, and we – Lauri and I – should leave The Hall together, as a couple! Would you believe it?'

'Never saw *that* coming in a million years,' mutters Ava. The told-you-so look she throws Wick makes him flinch.

'Nor I,' says Alastair, without a hint of sarcasm. 'I declined the offer, obviously. I tried to turn back, but she begged me not to. She literally had her hands clasped together like she was praying. I tried to be kind, but she was completely *terrifying*. How she got it into her head that I'd ever abandon Fiona for anyone, never mind her? As soon as we got to the phone box at Drumapple, I pretty much kicked her out of the car. She got the message then and turned nasty... made a snide remark about "running back to my wife". I gave her 2p to call a cab, and that was that. When I drove off, I think she was crying.' Wick passes Alastair a handkerchief and he wipes his nose. 'I wish her luck, but I'm glad she won't be coming back. Let's hope she catches the earliest fast-diesel service to Edinburgh and chugs her way to a better place...' Alastair's words trail away.

Clowdy stays put. 'Did you like Mr Baumgarten?'

'Why wouldn't I?' Alastair blinks quizzically, as if thrown by the change in tack.

There's a pause before the inspector responds. 'That I don't know, but I *can* tell you that toxicology results have confirmed that Mr Baumgarten died by cyanide poisoning...'

'...and yer own wife admits ye kept cyanide in yer cabinet,' adds Pratt. 'Where's that inventory we asked fer? The inspector's been waitin' on it long enough.'

'Fiona and I are doing our best, sergeant. I've been... distracted.'

'If ye'd like me to find a quiet corner in the police station, Mr Muirhead, that can be easily arranged.'

Alastair sits, shoulders drooping, chest sunken, while all three policemen look him up and down. Ava's never seen her godson look so fragile or as stupidly guilty as he does now. Judging by the expression on Wick's face, he's wrestling with similarly uncomfortable thoughts. Clowdy starts patting at his coat pockets. Ava fears he's groping for handcuffs, but he fishes out nothing more than his pipe. 'Well,' he says crisply. 'For now, we'll leave it at that. Cargill, Pratt! See me out!' And as fast as he entered, he leaves.

As Alastair rises shakily to his feet, Fiona reappears in a dressing gown, a towel wrapped like a turban around her wet hair. 'Oh *darling*!' Her face twists with emotion. 'You're still here! Thank *God*!'

Alastair takes her in his arms, and unlike earlier, Fiona clings to him with all her might. 'I was so afraid they'd take you away from me. And what would I do then?'

Ava and Wick watch as their godson allows himself to be led away. Wick sighs. 'Who knows *what* goes on in that young man's head.'

'Perhaps not even Alastair,' says Ava.

'Should we turn in too?'

'What's the point, it's dawn. May as well let in the new day.'

And so, they move into the lobby. Wick fetches two chairs, and he and Ava sit inside the open front doorway, bathed in the milky first light of morning. It's still raining; a persistent drizzle, so soft it barely makes a sound. Low clouds obscure the mountains. There is no breeze. Everything, inside and out, seems weirdly calm. And grey. Especially Wick. Ava looks down at her shoes, and thinks of Lauri, making a run for it. 'Do you think I have disproportionately large feet?' she asks.

'As tangential questions go, *that* is out of the ballpark!'

'I need your answer.'

He smiles. 'It would take a strong wind to blow you over, Dr Dickens, and that's a good thing.'

'Is it six o'clock yet?'

'Why?'

'Because you just looked at your watch. I presumed you were checking to see if curfew's ended.'

'Quarter past, actually,' he says distractedly, 'though it feels like afternoon already.'

'Doesn't it just,' breathes Ava. 'Talk about rude awakenings! One minute, the police aren't interested in what happened to Baumgarten, the next, they think Alastair's murdered him *and* had a hand in the disappearance of Lauri Levi. They may have been slow to get up to speed, Wick, but they're moving at a hundred miles an hour now. I thought Clowdy was going to arrest him.'

'I wonder why he didn't,' Wick says quietly.

'Because of the missing "em", as in "MMO". Apropos Baumgarten's murder, the police believe Alastair had the means... that being his cyanide... and the opportunity, since Baumgarten was staying under his roof, but they've no evidence of any motive.'

'And nor will they find one,' scoffs Wick. 'Alastair hardly knew the man. Why ever would he want to kill him?'

'Oh, Wick!' Before she continues, Ava draws a lungful of air. 'Because of Baumgarten's involvement in Sheila and Duncan's deaths. Before Herr Baumgarten came to The Hall, he used to stay with Ollach Kettleness. He told her that he witnessed their crash. He may even have caused the car to leave the road.'

If Ava had released an entire surfeit of skunks into the room and announced they had rabies, Wick could not have looked more horrified. He covers his face with his hands. 'Jesus!' he groans. 'I don't know what to say. Let me think... let me think... let me *think*...!'

Ava falls silent, allowing him the time he needs for her revelation to sink in. Only after a full five minutes does he speak again.

'That's one hell of a thing to have kept to yourself, Ava!'

'I was afraid of upsetting you.'

'With reason,' Wick mutters angrily. 'Question is, does *Alastair* know?'

'Quite.' Ava ponders. 'Given that Ollach knows, we'd be kidding ourselves to think Maggie wasn't in the picture too. Neither sister is, or *was*, good at keeping secrets, especially not from each other.' Ava ponders some more. 'A while ago, when I tried to talk to Maggie about Baumgarten, she was uncharacteristically circumspect. At the time, I put that down to Fiona's gagging order: "Don't discuss dead guests!" Today, I see her unnatural diffidence in a new light. I'm *sure* she was fully aware of his history. In which case, it's not beyond the bounds of possibility that Maggie decided to enlighten Alastair.'

'Alastair is incapable of sitting on a toxic piece of information like that without saying anything.'

'Perhaps he only found out recently, and when he did, he acted. And then Maggie had to be removed next, because she worked out why Baumgarten died and couldn't be trusted to keep her thoughts to herself. I've always thought those cherries were meant for her.'

'Stop it!' snaps Wick. 'You're letting your imagination run wild. It's the police's job to get to the bottom of this, not yours! Talk like this will put our godson in gaol. Surely you don't want that?'

'Of course I don't!' Ava snaps back. 'If I'd wanted to drop Alastair in it, I'd have told the police what I've just told you but, for better or worse, I've chosen not to. My guts tell me Alastair's innocent, Wick, just as yours tell you. But I cannot close my eyes to the evidence I have in front of me. That's not how scientists operate. I'm simply sharing my thoughts with you because...' She hesitates. '... it's a habit I've got into.'

'Always good to know what you're thinking, Ava,' Wick says with a dry cough. 'I appreciate being kept in the loop.' The tension in the air eases, but not by much. 'What do you think he's done with Lauri Levi, then?'

'Nothing... and there's zero *evidence* to prove otherwise.'

There's a prickly recess.

'One thing's for sure,' Wick reflects eventually, 'the Muirheads' money worries pale into insignificance compared to the troubles they're facing now. We've solved nothing.'

'Coming here was the right thing to do at the time, Wick.'

'If you say so, Ava. But it can be equally important to know when to move on.'

35

Not a Child!

That night, and the next night too, Ava witnesses sunsets spectacular as any of the skies above Dorcha have offered; shifting oceans of torrid red and molten gold so vibrant, the mountain tops look like they're on fire. She doesn't watch them with Wick, in the orangery, but alone, from her bedroom window. In fact, over the forty-eight hours since their touchy conversation in The Hall's doorway, it feels like their paths have barely crossed. Ava doesn't believe Wick's avoiding her – she's not avoiding him – so much as retreating from her company; a feat in itself, given the sanctions they live under. Maybe he's still angry she didn't tell him about Baumgarten and the crash. Or is he disappointed with her for saying what she did about Alastair? Whether he is or isn't, though, she stands by her words. She never suggested Alastair *is* the murderer, only that enough stuff's happened to put him in the spotlight. Ava won't seek Wick out, given he's not looking for her, but she's sure his fears for their godson weigh heavily on his mind. Ava knows she's burdened by hers. She wishes she and Wick could have another 'outing', take the dinghy onto the water, just to clear the air. There are *so* many things she wants to discuss with Alastair: cyanide and poison cabinets, NarcoVal and the boathouse, never mind Lauri Levi and midnight drives. But so far, she's held back. Not because she's afraid of what he'll say... exactly; more that they're loaded subjects, and she'd prefer to tackle them when Wick's back on board.

In the meantime, as always, Ava finds solace in walking, albeit inside the confines of the grounds. Having woken early, her pre-breakfast circuit takes her past the barn, and this morning its heavy doors are open wide. Murdoch's inside, standing next to George's MG. Its bonnet's up and both front wheels have been removed. In one hand he's holding a wrench, in the other, a piece of greasy rubber piping, and his ever-articulate eyebrows suggest he's perplexed.

'Morning, Murdoch.'

He huffs in acknowledgement.

'Fixing Georgina Beckett's brakes, eh? I'd forgotten all about them. Glad *you*'ve found something useful to do, unlike the rest of us. She'll be pleased, though she hasn't found her keys yet as far as I know. Not that she can go anywhere.'

No comment. He holds the piping up to the light. As he bends and flexes it, fluid dribbles out of an obvious crack halfway along its length.

'Last time you and I met in here, Murdoch, Ollach was with you. Do you know how she's doing?'

'Loneliest lass on the planet.' Murdoch pauses. 'I shouldnae wonder.'

'Anyway,' Ava says staunchly, 'I don't suppose you've seen any bats?'

Murdoch huffs again, to the effect he has not, and that he doesn't intend to invest valuable time looking for any.

'If I hang around for a bit, have a little look, will I be in your way?'

'Help yersel.'

'They must be about,' says Ava, dragging a fingertip through the thick layer of droppings that's accumulated on the MG's roof. She's tempted to write a childish message in the dirt, like 'CLEAN ME', or 'POO', but Carl and Martin would almost certainly get the blame. There isn't space for 'PIPISTRELLUS WOZ ERE'. 'If you really want to get into Georgina Beckett's good books, Murdoch, you could give her car a wash.'

No response. Ava walks idly along the row of vehicles… Cargill's panda car, Stewart's Aston Martin, Wick's Bentley,

Bernard's Cortina, Fiona's Hillman, each of which has a similar crumble-topping of faeces... but then she notices something odd. 'Murdoch, have you been out and about in the Land Rover?'

'That's nae allowed.'

'I know, but have you? Not during the day when Cargill would catch you, but after dark.'

'Why d'ye ask?'

'Bats defecate as they come and go from the roost; in other words, when they're active. Compared to the other cars in here, the Land Rover's got relatively few droppings on its roof and bonnet. I'd say it's down a couple of night's worth of excremental build up.'

'Is that a fact?'

'Yes.'

'Where would I go?' he asks warily. As he wipes the sweat from his brow, he leaves a smear of black engine oil in its furrows.

Ava finds she has an easy answer. 'To see Ollach, check she's doing okay. I can quite understand why you'd spend some nights at Drumapple.'

'Ha' ye nae decency, woman? The lass is young enough te be ma daughter!'

'I didn't mean sleeping with her, Murdoch, merely that you've been keeping her company in her grief! I know you two are old friends. Allies, so to speak. And if *you* haven't been slipping out after dark, who has?'

Murdoch looks at the Land Rover. He too runs an oily forefinger across its relatively clean bodywork, and then he looks at the broken piping. 'Aye, well, doctor, reckon ye've caught me red handed.' The expression on his, smudged, care-worn face conveys a mixture of shame and sorrow, and Ava feels horrid for bringing such a proud man down.

'Tell me,' she asks lightly, in an effort to change the subject, 'what happened to the MG's brakes? Doesn't look like pothole damage.'

'Chewed by mice.'

'Must have had huge teeth.'

'Rats, then.'

Ava can't be bothered to challenge him. She's in no mood to repeat the nonsensical back and forth they had over those holes under the beech tree. Besides, she's hungry. She'd like to join Wick at their table in the window, as she first did three weeks ago, when she still believed George to be a balding male accountant, and Baumgarten and Maggie weren't dead.

'Are you coming in, Murdoch?' she asks. 'Porridge awaits.'

'Nae appetite.' He picks up a larger wrench, and continues with his project.

To Ava's chagrin, there's no sign of Wick. Indeed, today's tetchy drove of diners is thin on the ground. No German birdwatcher, no larger-than-life American singer, and no new blood to refresh the atmosphere unless one counts resident-gaoler Cargill. Dressed in full uniform, he methodically works his way through a tower of bacon so inelastic, Ava can hear the dispatch of every stringy mouthful from twenty feet away. George sips black coffee whilst winding and unwinding a strand of her hair around the ring finger of her left hand. She stares at Sinclair Stewart, while he stares out of the window, contemplating the rain clouds... or daydreaming about helicopters? Either way, both look miserable. Peigi sits alone, playing with the food on her plate until, eventually, Murdoch joins her. Unwashed, and smelling of brake fluid, he says nothing. Neither does Peigi. The Muirheads raise the total head count to eight souls, but do nothing to lift the mood. They go through the motions of serving their patrons – Alastair pale and lackadaisical, Fiona, an irritable bag of nerves.

Last to arrive, the Addingtons arrange themselves in a huddle around their circular table, heads down, backs to the room, and they eat fast, like wary dingoes at a kill. Even the boys seem on tenterhooks. In the first days after Maggie's death, they'd perhaps been a bit quiet, but they still rode bikes, fossicked on the foreshore, and skimmed stones, *joie de vivre* undimmed. Ava attributed their enviable resilience to immaturity. On the fateful evening, grown-ups told them to settle down, behave, and enjoy 'the performance', so, on one level they did. The girl's gruesome demise was just a show. But now that a week's passed, it seems grim reality has found Carl and Martin too. The fun's over. The older boy looks particularly haunted, and he hardly touches his food.

Ava picks out the sprigs of mint garnishing her tinned-fruit salad and lines them up on the side of her bowl. She never thought she'd miss Lauri Levi, but she does. She wonders where the woman is. If someone picked her up from that phone box and took her to the station, then she could be back in Baton Rouge by now, swatting away 'Johnnys' and swigging bourbon from the bottle. Lucky cow. Ava *yearns* to be away from this place, back in the jungle, surrounded by dangers she properly understands. What was the phrase Wick used? Something about being sealed in a pressure cooker, steeping in one's own juices. Ava's never felt so thoroughly basted in her life.

As Ava continues to stew, the clinks and scrapes of cutlery on tableware grind to a sudden halt; silenced by a hefty *crunch*, this being the sound of Martin Addington's forehead landing smack in his plate of toast. For a fleeting second, Ava, and others too, assume he's playing the fool. Carl Addington certainly finds it funny. Perhaps he dared his older sibling to take a pratfall, to lighten the atmosphere. But when Martin fails to sit up again, general bemusement switches to panic. Stock still, he remains face down, arms limp by his sides.

His parents leap to their feet and Cargill races over to assist. 'Stand back everybiddy!' he orders, pushing Barbara and Bernard aside. 'Someone, summon Sween!' As he tips Martin back in his chair, the boy's mouth lolls open. The toast stays stuck to his temple.

'Let me hold him!' wails Barbara. Bernard struggles to restrain her as she fights to reach their son. 'What have they done to you? My *baby*!'

'I don't understand what's happening,' Fiona stammers. 'How is this possible?'

'Mrs Muirhead!' shouts Cargill. 'Telephone the doctor! Now!'

As if slapped back to her senses, Fiona dashes off towards reception. Alastair remains welded to the spot. Just in time, Ava catches the heavy porridge pot he's holding before he lets the handles slip from his grasp. 'Not a *child*!' he mouths. 'Please, not a child!'

Cargill starts firing off all-too-familiar questions. 'What's he eaten? What's he drunk?'

'Same as we all did,' is Bernard's all-too-familiar answer.

'Mum!' Carl tugs at Barbara's sleeve. 'Mum!'

'Leave your mother be!' says Bernard, himself shocked and pale. 'You can see she's upset.'

Carl tugs harder. '*Mum*! He's all right.'

'You can't know that!' sobs Barbara. 'Look at the state of him!'

'Watch and I'll prove it.' Without further ado, Carl leans across and pinches the end of his sibling's nose.

The effect of this intervention is as swift as it is steely. Martin splutters, snorts, and opens his eyes. 'Ow!' he whimpers, peeling his breakfast from his brow. 'What was *that* for?'

As Barbara lunges forwards and gathers her bewildered-looking boy in her arms, the sense of relief in the room is tangible. Nervous laughter fills the air.

'Thank *Christ*!' breathes Alastair. 'He's alive!' He looks shaken to the core.

'My, my, my,' Cargill tuts. 'Ye had us worried there, laddie. Did ye come over faint?'

'I don't know what happened,' Martin answers, rubbing his eyes with his knuckles.

'You fell asleep,' says Carl. 'You've got marmalade in your hair.'

'Why would your brother fall asleep into his breakfast?' Barbara splutters.

'Because he's been awake for two whole days and two whole nights. Too scared to close his eyes. He told me.'

Martin stares around the room. Taking in his onlookers' faces, his cheeks flush and his chin starts to wobble. 'Are we in trouble?'

Ava sees Carl's lips part as if about speak but his older sibling throws him a loaded look. Carl throws an equally loaded look back. He does not, however, say anything. What a bristly little exchange, and how *interesting*! It's clear Martin was afraid some secret was about to be aired, a secret that could drop him... and Carl... in hot water. Whatever that secret may be, Ava's pretty sure it's at the root of his insomnia.

The tears that had been welling in Martin's eyes breach their banks and stream unchecked down his flushed cheeks.

Cargill removes his police cap. 'Mr and Mrs Addington, best wipe yer boy down and tuck him up in bed—'

'I don't want to go to bed! Mum! Don't make me go to bed!' Martin sounds half crazed. 'I need to stay awake!'

Cargill ignores this outburst. 'And it'd be as well te let the doctor give him the once over, seein' as he'll already be on his way.'

'You won't leave me on my own, will you Mum? Dad? You'll stay with me...?'

'Of course we will.' Barbara dabs his face with a napkin.

'Come on you two,' Bernard says crossly, the anxiety he showed two minutes earlier supplanted by very evident embarrassment. 'Let's do as the constable says. Carl, stay here and finish eating. Quietly. There's been enough of a scene as it is.'

As they exit the room, Fiona re-enters. 'Oh, he's back on his feet! Wonderful. I do hope he's okay. Carson Sween says he'll be here in ten minutes.'

'Thank ye, Mrs Muirhead. I'll wait fer him outside. Mr Muirhead, will ye wait with me?'

Alastair doesn't seem to hear him. '"I *need* to stay awake",' he repeats softly, 'That's what he said. Like he's afraid of his dreams. Poor tyke. When *I* was a boy, I thought nightmares were something I'd outgrow. Turns out they still find me... asleep or not.'

Fiona leads him away.

Murdoch follows.

Then Peigi.

When Stewart, too, joins the exodus, George tosses aside her napkin like a boxer throwing in the towel. 'For God's sake! If I didn't have indigestion after my first mouthful, God knows I do now. What an appalling start to what will no doubt be another appalling day. Coming apart like that, in front of everybody! It's enough to put anyone off their food.'

'Martin couldn't help it, George,' says Ava.

'Not the kid,' she scoffs. '*Your* godson. How Fiona Muirhead puts up with such a featherweight for a husband is beyond me. Then again, for all we know he's some psycho killer, poisoning people for kicks. And this coffee's cold.'

Ava contemplates grabbing George by the throat and yanking out her pluck. Instead, she turns her attention to Carl. Martin's queer turn doesn't appear to have dented *his* appetite. Alone among the wreckage of his family's breakfasts, he crams half a round of bread and jam into his mouth, then flushes it down with a tall glass of milk. He repeats the process with the other half round and more milk, before wiping away his wet, white moustache with the back of his hand. His departure is so abrupt, his chair almost topples in his wake.

Five minutes later, Ava spots him out of the window, slithering around on the loch shore, repeatedly losing his footing as he whacks at the rocks with a long stick. He cuts an exasperated figure. Gauging that a gentle third degree could prove cathartic, and informative, Ava whips a rasher of Cargill's leftover bacon rind, wraps it in her handkerchief, and heads out to join him.

36

Out of His Shell

'Never rockpool in anger!' Ava calls to Carl as she approaches. 'It frightens the sea anemones.'

He swings round, stick mid-air. 'Oh, it's *you*.' His churlish expression slackens into a lop-sided grin.

Ava smiles back. 'You seem fed up. I wondered if you fancy a chat.'

'Not really,' Carl says politely. 'D'you know there's a mint leaf stuck in your teeth?'

'Thanks for noticing.' Ava's first attempt to dislodge the thing using her tongue fails, as does her second. Finally, a thumb nail gets the job done. 'You put away *your* breakfast like a man with places to go, if you don't mind me saying.'

'I had plans,' he sighs, 'but Martin's wrecked them. We were going to collect crabs.'

'Shore crabs? Was that Mr Muirhead's suggestion? Because I can tell you now, *Carcinus maenas* doesn't make good eating unless you're a seagull. By the time you've boiled them long enough to kill any lung flukes, the meat's so chewy, their chelipeds aren't worth sucking.'

'They were for racing, not cooking. I made a speedway yesterday, cleared off the pebbles and stuff so we were set to go... all we needed was the crabs, then Martin throws a wobbly and has to be put to bed. He's *thirteen*! Big *baby*.' He gives the rocks another whack. 'What's the point in bothering now, if I'm the only punter.'

Ava feels sorry for the lad. She'd like to lift his spirits, besides which, getting him to share secrets when he's this despondent could be a hiding to nothing. She comes up with a tentative suggestion. 'If you stop beating the life out of every barnacle in sight, maybe *I* could keep you company. I'm not entirely on board with the racing idea, since that's something crabs are unlikely to enjoy, but I *am* practiced in another intertidal sport which I'll gladly demonstrate, if you're interested.'

Carl weighs up her proposition. 'What sport, exactly?'

'Sizing-Up!' Without waiting for his decision, Ava begins to retrace her slip-slidy way to the top of the beach. A gratifying popping of bladder wracks from astern tells her Carl's following. Only when they reach the hightide line – comprised of crusty black kelp stipes, cork floats and other scraps of fishing debris – does she stop to draw breath. 'Right. What we want is dried-out shells, empty ones. Big ones, small ones, the more variation in size, the merrier. But gastropods only, no bivalves.'

Carl's nonplussed.

Ava sighs. 'Bivalves have two parts connected at a hinge: think mussels and clams. Gastropods are the other kind. A single concha, with the fleshy foot positioned below the guts: think whelks. Don't schools teach Latin these days?'

'They do. I got a B-plus.'

'In future, aim for an A.' Not wishing to sound too bruising, she continues. 'If you can translate Latin names, animal classification becomes straightforward, and when you know your classification, then—'

'The world's your oyster!'

'Exactly!' Ava laughs.

And so the pair walk, stooping this way and that to pick up suitable specimens. 'Excellent hunting spot,' says Ava. 'Nice selection of *Steromphala* and *Nucella*, as well as plenty of good old *Littorina littorea*. I think we already have enough. You double checked no one was inside before pocketing anything?'

Carl nods emphatically.

'In which case, time to select our arena! What we're looking for,' says Ava, as they head back to the wetter part of the shore, 'is a shallow-ish pool with an open, flat bottom, so we'll get a clear view of the action.'

'How about this one?'

'Solid choice.' Ava extracts Cargill's bacon rind from the folds of her hankie. 'Now, drop this into the centre, and we'll see who comes to investigate.'

Carl obliges. *Plop.* Slowly, the bait sinks, releasing a pearlescent twirl of oil behind it. At first, nothing happens. But then, out from under the pool's frilly margins tumble hermit crabs. One, then another... then another... toppling and rolling over each other to reach the meat. Ava's so excited, her heart skips a beat, but Carl heaves a weighty sigh of disappointment. 'I've seen these before, Dr Dickens. I actually think mine and Martin's racing idea was better.'

Ava smiles. 'Give them a chance, and look closely. Is everybody's house a good fit?'

Carl rolls up his sleeve and plucks one of the little creatures out of the water. Instantly, it withdraws into its shell... or tries to. While its hind legs disappear from view, its front claws, antennae, and beady compound eyes remain sticking out on full show. 'This guy doesn't look that comfy.'

'I'd agree with you.' Ava passes Carl her hand lens. She studies the boy's features as, with furrowed brow, he squints through it, solemnly chewing his top lip; a sign that, in spite of himself, he's becoming engaged. 'Have you ever seen the back end of a hermit crab?' she asks. 'It's the texture of school blancmange and the shape of a pig's tail. One of *the* most naked things on planet Earth, is a homeless pagurid.'

Carl grimaces.

'Unlike those appendages you can see – pereiopods, chelae, and so on, which all have tough exoskeletons – the abdomen hasn't any built-in protection. That's why it's got to be packed away inside a shell. When that crab you're holding was tiny, he – with those claws, definitely a male – *he* only needed to rent a tiny shell, but as he grew, his house became too tight, so he sized-up by moving into a new one. Then, he grew a bit more, so he moved again. That's what he's done his whole life, and now—'

'He's ready for another upsize.'

'Precisely! Trouble is, at this end of the strand, real estate's in short supply. And *that* is where you come in! Put him back before his gill filaments stick together, and then we'll go through our pockets. In the world of hermit crabs, Carl Addington, you've a property portfolio to rival the Duke of Westminster's, and the time's come to list it.'

The boy doesn't waste a second, eagerly selecting a slightly bigger shell and placing it next to his protégé. With eyes, quite literally, on stalks, the little crustacean is equally quick to take note. Grabbing the empty periwinkle with his pincers, he starts probing it with his forelegs and antennae. After a brief survey, in a single blink-and-you'll-miss-it movement, he withdraws his mysterious rear end from its existing shelter and, with a key-in-the-lock twist, tucks it inside the new offer. At the same time, he shifts his grip. Taking hold of his old home, he proceeds to stagger around with it, as if dancing an unwieldy waltz.

'Why doesn't he just dump that?' Carl asks.

'When your mum takes you shopping and you try on a new pair of shoes, I'll bet she makes you walk up and down a few times before buying them. He's doing the same thing. He won't chuck anything away till he's sure he's made the right choice. If he's not happy, he can always move back where he came from. As long as he doesn't let go...'

As Ava speaks, there's a development. A second hermit crab muscles in on the action and a wrestling match for possession of the vacated shell begins. While Carl's contender clings on valiantly, other house-hunters join the fight, would-be gazumpers attempting to scoop the occupier, and each other, from their respective accommodations. The ensuing brawl is a clumsy affair, with more-or-less spherical competitors often capsizing and having to struggle to right themselves as battle rages all around. To diffuse the situation, Carl scatters more shells into the water, but this results in a house-swapping frenzy. As spectator sports go, it's exhilarating viewing! Some crabs move once, some twice, some *three* times only to return to their first choice. Others simply sit in quiet contemplation, grooming their eyes with their maxillipeds, as the tide continues to rise.

After a happy half hour, Ava and Carl make for dry land, and settle on The Hall's west lawn to watch the sea roll in. 'Thank you, Carl,' says Ava, lighting a roll up, 'I had a nice time.'

'So did I,' says Carl.

'I'm pleased. You do seem brighter than earlier. I got the impression Martin upset you.'

'I explained about the crab racing.'

'True, but I reckon you were angry about something else. At breakfast time, after you woke him up – which you did very skilfully, by the way – there was something you wanted to say, but he stopped you. I think you two have a secret and he's worried that, if you let it out, you'll get "in trouble". He used those exact words, didn't he, to warn you against speaking out? And because you're a loyal brother, you held your tongue. Under normal circumstances, I'd applaud that too. However, what's bothering *me* is that this secret's frightening, so much so that you're in two minds about keeping it. What, Carl, is Martin afraid will happen if he closes his eyes?'

Carl sidesteps. 'Can *I* have a cigarette?'

'No.'

'Would you of let Martin?'

'No. They wreck the lungs' alveolar linings. I'm only having one now to keep the midges off.'

'Gangsters in films smoke when they're being interrogated.'

'This isn't an interrogation. Remember the day you and Martin were tossing mallets, and I asked for your help? You promised if you discovered anything unusual, you'd let me know. Now's your chance.'

'Do hermit crabs have lungs?'

'Gills.'

Carl takes the last of his shell collection from his pocket and presents it to Ava. 'Was the only reason you showed me Sizing-Up to get me to snitch on my brother?'

'Absolutely not! It's practically my favourite pastime... second only to stalking newts. But you've got to *talk* to me, Carl. You'll be helping Martin and yourself. If he feels in danger, someone needs to know. Plus, whatever this scary thing is, getting it off your chest'll make you feel better than you do now. I guarantee it.'

There's a pause while Carl picks his nose, and then his tale begins. 'Two days ago, when all the grownups were busy gossiping about where Lauri Levi went and how Mr Muirhead took her and she's not his wife or even a nice person, Martin and I escaped! We were riding our bikes, but instead of staying round here like Constable Cargill told us, we cycled to the village on the other side of the loch, where Maggie used to live. It was both of our ideas. We've been wanting to see where The Lass of The Loch died for ages.' He casts a reproachful look at Ava. 'But *no one* would take us.'

'I thought you didn't know how to get to The Murder Field.'

'Used Dad's map to work it out. Easy, when you know the OS symbols. We stopped at the phone box marked with a "T", and hid the bikes in some bushes before walking the rest. Past the houses – they're marked with little rectangles – and the "MS"...'

'Milestone?'

Carl nods. 'To Beinn Beithe. Then we followed the dashed line – that's "unmade-up track" – for eight thousand five hundred yards; pretty much "bracken, heath and rough grassland" all the way. It was fun being away from the hotel. Or fun at first.' Carl tosses an empty whelk shell at the loch, but it falls short.

'What happened next?'

'We came to a field with a load of pink flowers with a falling down dump of a hut in the middle of it—'

'The bothy?'

'That's it... the bothy, and we reckoned we'd found the right spot, but it was a complete letdown. I s'pose we'd expected it to feel a bit... I dunno... *haunted*, or something, and this place was as boring as anywhere else. So we started making up ghost stories of our own, about murders and drownings and stuff... spooking each other... making each other jump. We'd been messing around for a while, when Martin said he could see someone watching us from inside the bothy. I didn't really believe him. I thought he was winding me up, trying to be creepy.'

'Who did he think it was?' Ava asks carefully.

'Mr Murdoch, maybe. It's the sort of place he'd hang out. Or maybe no one. Like I say, I wasn't sure if he was faking. And that's when Martin came up with his stupid game. He dared me to go and knock on the door, and ask if The Lass of The Loch could "come out and play", but I wouldn't. What if it *was* Murdoch? Ever since the mess-up with the cairn, I've been avoiding him. So Martin said I was a wuss and a poofter, and he'd knock on the door instead.' Carl lobs another shell towards the water. This one pierces the surface like a bullet. 'He marched right up and banged on it, really hard. Straight away, it opened, and he kind of fell inside.'

'How do you mean?'

'As though someone grabbed him and pulled him in. I thought it was him being dramatic, acting up to give me the willies. Then came some shouting, which didn't sound like Martin, and some scuffling noises, and I realised he wasn't pretending. Before I could do anything, he came bursting out again, and his face looked proper weird... like he actually had seen a ghost... and he yelled at me to start running. And that's what we both did. Martin kept looking over his shoulder, to see if we were being followed, but I only looked straight ahead. We didn't stop till we were back in Drumapple, and from there we pedalled straight back to The Hall. I think Maggie's sister might have seen us cycling off, but she didn't speak to us or anything.'

'Since you got back, has Martin said much about the person in the bothy? What they looked like? Had he seen them before?'

Carl shakes his head. 'They had on a floppy hat and gardening clothes... a sort of boiler suit, and a scarf covering their face. He thinks it was man. If it was a woman, she was really skinny and weird. Whoever it was, they scared the shit out of Marty. He's *still* shit scared and that's why he's been forcing himself to stay awake. Hasn't slept for a solid fifty-and-three-quarter hours. Not because of Maggie dying. It's down to what the bothy-person told him.'

'Which was?'

'"Piss off, and hold your tongue or my sister'll cut it out while you're sleeping,"' Carl says nonchalantly. 'Which *is* the sort of thing The Lass of The Loch ghost *would* say.'

'If she were real,' Ava mutters under her breath.

'*I* don't think they meant it, but Martin does. You know what, Dr Dickens,' he continues matter of factly, 'I do feel better now I've told you. Can I tell you something else?'

'Go for it.'

'I know who emptied the cupboard in the potting shed.'

'Good grief!' Ava almost drops her lit cigarette into her lap. 'That's a surprise! When was this?'

'The morning you and the professor dug up a bottle and extra police came to take it away.'

'What were you doing in Mr Muirhead's potting shed?'

'Playing hide and seek. It was my turn to hide, Martin's to seek, but as usual he stopped counting and didn't even bother to look. I was about to give up waiting and unhide myself when Mr Murdoch turned up. He didn't see me – I was behind a workbench – and he went straight to that cabinet thing, scooped everything out into a sack then off he went.'

'Where to?'

Carl shrugs. 'Didn't see. I stayed hiding till I was sure he wasn't coming back, then I went to punch Martin.'

'Have you told anyone else this?'

'No. Like I said, Mr Murdoch makes me nervous. Nothing I'd pee my sheets over, but I don't like the idea of upsetting him by telling tales. Martin's so terrified of the person in the hut, though, *he's* wetting himself! *Thirteen.*' He shakes his head. 'Seriously!'

'Well, Carl,' Ava says stoutly, rising to her feet, 'you've given me a lot to think about. One thing's for sure, that hut needs investigating.'

'I think it would be a bit stupid to do that on your own.'

'So do I, which is why I'll invite my friend the professor to come with me.'

'Won't that be hard, now he's left?'

'Left?' laughs Ava. 'He can't have. His car's in the garage.'

'Not anymore. Our room overlooks The Hall's back door, and he drove round there, just before we came down for breakfast. Martin and I watched him load it up with parcels. Most went in the boot, but he put one onto the front passenger seat. Must've been something special because it was wrapped in a blanket. He sort of stroked it with his hand before he sneaked off.'

'Why do you think he was "sneaking"?'

'Because he spotted us spying from our window, and when he did, he signalled for us to keep quiet. You know that thing when you pull your fingers across your lips, like a zipper...'

Ava swallows. 'Yup.'

'And then he winked.'

Ava stares out over the water, to the spot where Wick and she had their floating picnic – the spot where he and Sheila used to drop anchor and gawk at their beloved view – and then she looks up at The Hall. With its blank, all-seeing windows upon her, she feels as reduced and insignificant as it's possible to humanly feel, and her heart hurts.

37

A Clever Thief

The painting's gone. Ava knew it would be, even before she and Fiona set foot in Baumgarten's room. Together they stand, gazing forlornly at the bare patch of wall where, until a few hours ago, it had hung.

'You say Uncle Wick liked it,' sighs Fiona.

'"Adored" would be a better word. Neither you nor Alastair gave it to him? He never mentioned anything about taking it away with him?'

'No. This is as much a shock to me as it is to you, Ava.'

'I'm sure,' says Ava, though she's absolutely certain that's not the case. 'Is anything else missing?'

'I'll have to look.'

'I'd check on the sitting-room vases and work your way out from there.'

'Oh, Ava! How will I tell Alastair?'

'That's for you to decide,' Ava answers thickly.

'Will you come with me? He's going to be devastated.'

'Where's Murdoch?'

'I don't know, but I'd rather have *you* with me when—'

'Can't happen,' Ava says sharply. 'I've other fish to fry.'

It's years since Ava last rode a bike. She's requisitioned one the Addington lads have been using. Its chain's loose, and the saddle's stuck too low. Still, as modes of transport go, it was her most immediate option. She wants to reach The Murder Field fast, and now there's no one she trusts to take her the first leg. Shit, shit, *shit*! When it comes to judging character, she was a bloody idiot to trust *herself*! The harder she pedals, the more her knees ache, but no amount of patellofemoral discomfort will distract Ava from her rampant thoughts.

So Wick's a thief. Though in his words, not any old thief – not some 'shifty dealer' looking for a 'quick steal' – that would be stupid, and crass. Wick is a *clever* thief, who quietly took stock, chose his moment, then made his getaway. Talk about the importance of knowing when to 'move on'! How *could* he? She pictures him carefully removing Sheila's watercolour from its hook, caressing it lovingly in his immaculate, devious, gloved hands. It's an all-too-easy image to conjure, given it's more or less as she found him, 'delving', on the day he and she went through Baumgarten's things. Seems Wick wasn't searching for clues, though. *He* was sniffing out valuables.

She replays the drivel he gave her about 'the good stuff' and how 'the most precious things can be hidden in most modest of guises'... and the way he looked at *her* when he said it. Professor Jayaweera Wickremesinghe, man of the world, knew exactly how that came across. Slowly, slowly, her dowdy, neglected heart convinced itself he admired her, as a *woman* – to this he cannot have been blind – yet he carried on. It must have suited his purposes, letting her believe he was talking in metaphors, when all the time he was telling it like it is. Weighing up what was worth taking... what to leave behind spitting dust.

Such effortless deceit. Ava thinks of their breakfast conversations, chats on the garden bench, and long, contemplative evenings in the orangery, and she winces. She shared every thought she had about the murders: the hows, whys... and the whos. For the most part, *he* simply listened, smiling, waving, and blowing smoke rings up her arse. Another example of feigned interest or, perhaps, a far more sinister conceit? After all, a killer might act the same way; play the part of helpful sounding board, while getting the inside scoop. 'Always good to know what you're thinking, Ava. I appreciate being kept in the loop.' No wonder he'd laughed when she said his name was top of her suspect list. The joke was on her!

She remembers how angry he was when she talked about Baumgarten's role in Sheila and Duncan's accident. Umbrage that she hadn't told him sooner, or rage that she'd worked out why the man died… and the reason why Maggie had to be silenced too? Did Wick know all along that Baumgarten caused his beloved Sheila's death? He was at Dorcha Hall on the day of the crash. He, more easily than most, could've found out what really happened and sought to mete out revenge. Now he's realised that Ava's found the missing 'M', he's buggered off, pilfering the picture for good measure.

Ava's eyes water and her cheeks burn. 'Enough!' she reproaches herself aloud, wrestling her white-hot indignation elsewhere. In less than a second, it buries its teeth in a fresh casualty: Murdoch. Ever since Ava arrived at Loch Dorcha, he's been shifty as shite. Slipping out in the Land Rover in the dead of night. She'd had to worm that truth out of him. Bat droppings don't lie! And now it turns out *he* emptied the chemical cabinet. He knew the police would find an incriminating bottle of cyanide, and perhaps whatever killed Maggie too. How? Because he'd already made good use of them? Has solid, faithful Angus Murdoch, seasoned oak galleon in oceans of chaos, sunk as low as it's possible to sink? Surely not!

On ditching the bike at Drumapple's phone box, Ava marches through the village. The fishing boats are at sea. Hooley's van is parked outside Peigi's closed-up studio, though there's no sign of Jack. The only soul in sight is Ollach, or at least a version of her, standing on her doorstep; hollow-eyed and vacant, it's unclear whether she's aware of Ava's presence. But then she speaks, and Ava's left in no further doubt.

'What brings ye te these parts, Dr Dickens?' she asks sharply. 'The Hall's dirty linen?'

'Good morning, Ollach, I—'

'Och, it's far later than that,' she snaps. 'It's afternoon, and there's nae one good thing about it. Have ye come te pass on condolences fer my Maggie?'

Ava shakes her head, ashamed the thought never occurred to her.

'Hamish Pratt's been, Rory Cargill… Carson Sween… he's been… even that skinny-bit-o'-a piece, Fiona Muirhead, she's been. And there was me thinkin' that on Dorchan soil the milk o' human kindness, what's left o' it, only runs through men's veins.'

'No one's supposed to leave The Hall.'

'*Ye're* here!'

'I trust Murdoch's been a comfort.'

'Murdoch? He cannae face me! But that's nae surprise either. When push came te shove, he was bound te throw his lot in wi' his precious Muirheads.'

'You've every right to be angry, Ollach. What happened to your sister is truly dreadful. Please accept my deepest sympathies.'

Ollach glowers at her. Ava's relieved when Jack Hooley appears as if from nowhere, hopefully to steer Ollach inside. A vain notion. His tone turns out to be even more acrimonious than hers. 'How *are* things at The Hall, wi' Peigi? And the Muirheads? Will they be wantin' more meat, or have they enough blood on their hands?'

Ava sidesteps. 'I should keep going, or else the midges'll find me. I'm on my way to The Murder Field.'

'Ye and the rest,' mutters Ollach. 'Ye and the rest.'

'Shall we come wi' ye, doctor? Fer the company.' Hooley chuckles, leaning in so close, Ava can smell his breath. 'Wouldn't want another woman te go missin' in these parts, would we?'

'I can look after myself, thank you.'

'Mind ye're nae bitten te death, then.' Ollach's laugh is lifeless. 'And holler if ye change yer mind.'

'Not that anybiddy'll hear. Maybe I should follow her, Ollach. What d'ye say te that?'

'Really. No need,' says Ava as she backs away.

Hooley waves a rust-stained palm in mock salute, before he and Ollach disappear into the cottage, slamming the door in Ava's face.

The Beasts of the Black Loch

Ava ploughs on. She follows the route she took the day she met Baumgarten, along the rough cart track; to her left, the loch, her right, the mountains, above, a vast, cerulean sky. Last time she walked this path confident steps carried her over the rough terrain. She held her head high, happy with her own company. This time, heather scratches at her legs, and the mighty stacks seem overbearing and oppressive. When she set off for The Murder Field, anger, and the surge of adrenaline that came with it, fuelled her flight. Now that's spent, she's questioning the wisdom of going there alone. Not that she believes in malevolent ghosts. Those are the stuff of good stories and bad dreams. Unfortunately, however, recent experience tells her that in the surrounds of Dorcha, malevolent *people* are all too real. Who did Ollach mean by 'the rest'? The bothy's occupant? Does Ollach *know* who that is? Ava contemplates returning to Drumapple and simply asking her, but envisaging a less than warm reception, decides against. Besides, it's a long way back to the village now.

When Ava spots the bothy, she stops, hanging back some thirty yards. In the centre of its incongruous garden of pink wildflowers, the building's as humble as she remembered it, and as exposed. If anyone were to enter or leave, she'd see them, but it's equally impossible for her to approach undetected. There's no obvious sign of life within. No woodsmoke exits its chimney, and the door is open, flapping wide on its hinges. But from this distance, she can't be certain it's empty. What the *hell*, she asks herself, is her plan?

'Halloo!' she calls. No answer. Just the faraway *pop* of a shotgun, which does nothing to soothe her nerves. A passing breeze makes the flower heads dance and the door creak. Throwing caution to the wind, heart pumping, Ava marches straight up to it, and it's the work of five seconds to establish that no one's inside. Certainly no malignant spirit ready to sever her tongue. Nevertheless, it's clear somebody's been there recently, and by the look of it, made themselves at home.

There are ashes in the hearth. Still warm. Biscuit wrappers litter the floor, as do cigarette butts, and there's an empty bean tin. The detritus of a selfish traveller who's disrespected the ethos of bothy use: leave it as you'd hope to find it. How disappointing. But then she spots something else. The wooden bunk is draped with a woollen blanket; green and red, with tasselled fringes, like the ones she and Wick put over their knees in the draughty orangery! How did *that* get *here*? Whoever's been using this place clearly has some connection with The Hall. She wonders if the occupant was passing through, or whether they intend to return. If he or she is still around, they could be back any minute! Should she wait to confront them, or beat a retreat? Ava decides to hedge her bets. She'll take cover, and watch to see if anyone comes.

Treading her way back to the long grass, once again a breeze stirs, turning the field around her into a shifting carpet of magenta. They put on a bonnie show, the legendary 'useless pink flowers' of Dorchan lore, growing in resolute profusion on this accursed, blood-stained spot where nothing else will. Wick-the-fork-tongued-bastard would doubtless argue that, for their aesthetic value alone, such lovely things have worth. Ava would argue they're important, because somehow or another, they'll be a useful cog in the circle of life. They'll be here for a biological *reason*. She wonders what that is. Double checking to make sure no one's around, she risks a closer look.

Each plant comprises a rosette of flat, blade-like leaves, from which grows a single, erect stem crowned with little bunches of inflorescences. Spotting something small and six-legged struggling to climb to the top of one, Ava uses her hand lens to home in. An ant is fighting to free itself from a sticky exudate that coats the stem, and it's not the first to come a cropper. Judging by the number of trapped beetles, moths, and midges… all dead… the goo's proved the comeuppance of plenty more herbivorous insects and other would-be nectar thieves. From the plant's point of view, an effective defence mechanism; from the ant's, an absolute bummer. As Ava contemplates whether or not to attempt a rescue, she's plunged into shade. She turns, expecting to see a passing cloud, to be confronted by an altogether stormier sight. Standing over her, blotting out the sun, is Murdoch.

Ava practically jumps out of her skin. 'Jesus *Christ*!' she gasps. 'Where did you spring from!'

Murdoch the poison-cabinet-emptier and twister of truths doesn't immediately answer. The rifle slung over his shoulder has a long barrel. Its stock is well worn.

Ava's heart thuds so hard in her chest, she wonders if he can hear it. On the off chance that Murdoch's less likely to blow her head off mid-sentence, she keeps talking. 'You're surprisingly light on your feet, I must say, for such an enormous person... I mean... for someone so tall. I suppose, being a stalker, you're good at creeping up on—'

'Catchflies,' says Murdoch.

'Pardon?'

'Catchflies,' he repeats. 'That's what ye're lookin' at.' The man's raised eyebrows, huge and bushy as they are, do not suggest murderous intent so much as bewilderment.

'Well knock me down with a turquoise-browed motmot feather!' breathes Ava, aware her eyebrows must be expressing much the same as Murdoch's. 'When Baumgarten said I'd find "flycatchers", he didn't mean birds. He wanted me to see *these*! A simple misunderstanding, and I quite see how catchflies get their name. One look at their stalks is enough to explain every—'

'What brings ye here, wi' a murderer wanderin' free?'

'Thank you for your concern, but I'm not easily intimidated.' Ava hopes she sounds a deal more nonchalant than she feels. 'Besides, I could ask you the same question.'

Murdoch pats his gun. 'Poachers. Maybe bidin' in the bothy. I cannae be doin' wi' poachers.'

'You're looking for *poachers*!' Ava's so relieved she goes weak at the knees. 'If it's a poacher, Murdoch, then they've come from The Hall. I recognise their bedding. Come and see—'

'Steady yersel, doctor!' Murdoch grabs Ava's arm so tightly, she fears she relaxed too soon.

'Let go of me at once, or I'll—'

'Steady yersel and *listen*, damn ye!' Murdoch's grip tightens, and Ava decides that now might be a good time to shut up. She stands, breath bated, waiting for his next instruction.

He lets go, screws shut his eyes, and cocks his head to one side. 'Would'ye hark at that!'

Ava closes an eye too. Keeping the other firmly fixed on Murdoch, she strains to hear whatever it is he's hearing. The cry of an eagle? A wigeon? Then she catches it. A distinct buzzing *thrummm*. 'Swarming flies!'

'Fuaim a' bhàis!' he growls. 'The sound o' death! They've downed *another* Muirhead stag.' Cursing savagely, he galumphs off towards the buzzing, which is coming from the direction of the loch. Ava hastens after him. Determined to keep up, for every one of his immense, angry strides, she takes two, and when he comes to a stop close to the water's edge, it's so abrupt she almost collides with him. As she does so, with an eerie *swoosh*, a black veil of ten thousand startled flies lifts to reveal… not the entrails of a slaughtered deer, but…

'Holy crap!' The display confronting Ava and Murdoch really isn't pretty, and for a moment, neither has more to add.

38

No Flies on Her

The body is lying on its back, legs together, arms wide. Though dressed in men's clothes – baggy gardening overalls and over-sized tweed jacket – it's that of a thin, pale-skinned young woman. Her feet, which are bare, are covered in blisters and cuts. It's impossible to see whether she's blond or brunette: her hair's tucked inside a knitted woolly hat; nor can Ava tell the colour or her half-open eyes, because these are filled with what look like tiny, creamy-white grains of sticky rice. Blowfly eggs. Thousands and thousands of them. They're in the holes of her pierced earlobes, they're up her nose, they're between her weeping, raw toes, and many, many more fill the deep, bloody gash in the side of her neck. The tool that caused it is still embedded in the wound: a rock pick. Ava recognises it as the one Alastair kept in his potting-shed cabinet, along with his now-missing collection of chemicals. The collection which Murdoch took away. Nevertheless, if Murdoch used it to skewer someone in the jugular, he's doing an Oscar-winning job of acting clueless. At this moment, the fact his levels of shock and horror match hers is very reassuring.

'Who is she?' he breathes.

'Martin Addington's Lass from The Loch, I'm guessing. Beyond that, I've no idea,' mutters Ava. 'But there's something in her side pockets. We should see if she's carrying any ID.'

Murdoch recoils in horror. 'I'm nae touchin' her!' Gutting wild animals is one thing, but it appears that handling a dead woman's clothing is, as far as he's concerned, beyond the pale.

'Okay, I'll do it.' Gingerly, Ava reaches inside the folds of fabric and fishes out not one, but two rolled-up pairs of socks. Unhelpful. As she and Murdoch continue to scrutinise the woman's face, however, an unsettling sense of familiarity washes over Ava. There's something about the tilt of the dead woman's nose, the arc of her plucked eyebrows… her hands. 'Murdoch! It's Lauri Levi!'

'Nothin' like her.'

'Look at those fingernails! They may be chipped and broken, but I'd know that crimson varnish anywhere.'

Murdoch stares, and stares some more, then nods in agreement. 'Aye, I see it clearly now.' Given how much he'd openly disliked Lauri, he sounds surprisingly sorry.

Ava's sad too. Stripped, as Lauri is, of her stuck-on lashes and painted sulky pout, she's a different person. It's as if the flashy woman Ava knew has metamorphosed into a watered-down, less-alive variant of herself. 'I wonder if she moulted unaided, or did her killer kit her out?'

'Who e'er he is, the man's a *monster*! He's done awa wi'er bosoms!'

Ava passes him the balled-up socks.

He quickly passes them back.

'Her poor feet! Do you think her attacker chased her through the heather… ran her down? There's been no attempt to hide her body.'

Murdoch doesn't seem to be listening. Once again, he's fixed on the body or, more specifically, the vicious little rock pick protruding from the severed vein that will never pulsate again. His eyebrows knit and unknit themselves as he ruminates. 'Dr Dickens, have ye told Hamish Pratt that the German fellow killed Sheila?'

'If you're referring to Herr Baumgarten's role in the car accident, then the answer's no, not yet. And neither have I told him or Clowdy who cleared out Alastair's cabinet, though I know it was you. Carl Addington saw you. But I don't like keeping secrets, Murdoch. If the police ask me a direct question, I'll give them a direct answer.'

'Will ye. Will ye. Aye, well, thank ye fer that.' Murdoch doesn't sound sarcastic, merely resigned, as he often does. His next actions though, take Ava's breath away. Slowly and purposefully, he lifts his rifle from his shoulder; its loading lever makes a business-like *clunk, click* as he pulls it back.

Ava hears herself gulp. 'Murdoch!' she cries, staggering backwards. 'Please—'

He takes a step forwards. 'Here!' he says flatly, placing the weapon in her arms. 'In case ye need her. I'll be tekkin' my leave.' There's a resonance of finality in his tone.

'Why? Where are you going?' stammers Ava.

'Te fetch the police. Watch out fer poachers,' he says as he trudges off. 'They're lawless.'

'Hurry back!' Ava shouts after him.

'Goodbye, doctor!' he calls. But he doesn't look round.

Alone with Lauri Levi, Ava takes off her jacket and swings it around in the air; a vain attempt to stop the blowflies re-alighting. Midges are biting too, but they're only interested in Ava. Unlike her, they use *their* innate skills to avoid dead bodies; a gift which, at this moment, she envies. Ava considers outpacing them by running up and down, then decides against. It would be disrespectful to attempt anything so vigorous when she's supposed to be mounting guard. So she sits, swatting and scratching, contemplating Lauri's fate.

It was two days ago that she flounced out of The Hall, but it's clear she hasn't been dead anything like that long. Aside from those signs she was camping in the bothy, the flies tell Ava this is very a recent death. Like all necrophagous Diptera, *Calliphora* are superbly proficient at what they do. Within fifteen minutes of an animal taking its last breath, adult blowflies will find the carcass and start stuffing its warm, damp orifices with their eggs, hundreds at a time. These eggs don't wait around either. Depending on conditions, maggots hatch within hours, and today it's warm; over twenty degrees, judging by the stridulating grasshoppers. Since Lauri is *not* a crawling heap of feeding grubs – Ava can't spot even one – she's probably lain here less than twenty hours; perhaps as few as twelve. Ava checks the time. It's coming up to three o'clock. That means Lauri died sometime between yesterday afternoon and the early hours of this morning. A recent addition to the food chain. How many eggs is it a single fly can lay? Three hundred, is it? If Wick were here, she'd make him guess. Ava sighs. 'Hat's off to you, Lauri, you were goddam right about *that* slicker.'

There's nothing to suggest more than one person's been sleeping in the bothy, so it's likely it was a makeup free Lauri who scared the pants off Martin. But how on earth did *she* get *here*? Did Alastair bring her on the morning they left – a Land Rover could navigate the rough track – and ask her to wait for him? Were he and she lovers after all? Or did somebody else help her, for reasons unknown? As Ava meditates, she takes another look at the woman's stained, unshod feet, and the truth dawns. Lauri made her *own* way, barefoot, stumbling through the mud and heather! Quite a walk, especially in the rain with only the light of the moon to guide her. It's strange that Lauri headed off into the night at all. She never called that cab. The police established that much. But she could've sheltered in the phone box, or knocked on doors in Drumapple. Someone would've taken her in. Ava's surprised Lauri even knew the bothy existed, though Murdoch *did* mention it in his party piece. Lauri must have been paying more attention than Ava thought.

Be that as it may, since Lauri got here, she's had help. Must have. She left The Hall without taking a bag, so someone's brought her food, fags, a change of clothes… not to mention blankets. Ava reckons the Land Rover's been used to ferry supplies on at least one surreptitious nocturnal trip; that would account for its deficit of bat droppings. But who was behind the wheel? Alastair? Murdoch? Not necessarily. Given the Muirheads' casual attitude to where they keep keys, it might've been anyone. And how did they pass through the village without being seen? Or perhaps they didn't! Perhaps Ollach saw them, 'and the rest' being the Land Rover's driver. None of this, however, explains how Lauri Levi from Baton Rouge wound up murdered on the banks of Loch Dorcha, or what her death has to do with those of Heinrich Baumgarten aus Deutschland and Maggie Kettleness from ancient Drumapple.

Again, Ava studies Lauri's features. The harder she looks at them, the more familiar they seem. Not just that upturned nose... but also the chin, the slant of the cheek bones. Ava gets the strangest feeling she's seen Lauri Levi without makeup before! But she cannot for the life of her think when. A determined fly emerges from the depths of Lauri's right ear canal and heads for her left nostril, and the paradox in the meaning of '*Calliphora*' – 'bearer of beauty' – makes Ava cringe. 'Oh Lauri! I wish I knew whether the friend that fed you and the fiend that stole your last breath are one and the same person.'

As if in reply, there's a sudden gust of wind, stronger and colder than those that came before. For a brief moment, the flies ascend, the midges disappear, and the merry pink flowers tremble and sway. 'If only catchflies could talk, then all these mysteries would be solved.'

After what feels like a very long wait, Ava spots approaching vehicles pitching and rocking as they labour their way towards her. All are Land Rovers, but not green ones like The Hall's, but blue and white. An assortment of officers quickly decants. Some, she's met all too many times of late: DI Clowdy, Pratt, Cargill... Dr Sween is with them too... and Ewan and Robbie. The fact she's got to know the two stretcher bearers by name, not to mention Paul the police photographer, makes her queasy. Others, like the three men in white overclothes, armed with rolls of tape and long steel poles, are fresh faces.

'Stand back!' orders Pratt, relieving her of Murdoch's gun. 'Let the dog see the rabbit!'

Clowdy peers at the cadaver, tilting his head and tapping his chin. 'And Mr Murdoch says the deceased is Lauri Levi. What do you think, Sergeant? Sween...?'

'Aye, well,' says the doctor, 'I see that it is.'

'Mind, she's nae lookin' herself,' adds Pratt.

'Agreed,' says Clowdy.

The photographer *click, click, clicks* away, contorting himself into every kind of pose as he attempts to capture Lauri Levi from every kind of angle; under other circumstances, attention the woman might have enjoyed. Doctor Sween prods and pokes at her body. Using forceps, he removes her hat, to reveal a nest of matted peroxide hair, dark roots showing along her parting. Meanwhile, the trio in white works around everyone else, putting up a tent. This explains the poles.

'Have you touched anything, Dr Dickens?'

Ava hands over the socks.

'So much for respecting the crime scene.' Clowdy tuts as he taps out his pipe.

'Where's Murdoch?' Ava asks. 'I thought he'd bring you here.'

'Nae need,' Pratt answers curtly. 'Mr Murdoch was able te give us very precise directions.'

'But still, I imagined he'd come back with you.'

'The only place Angus Murdoch is headed is behind bars,' Clowdy says brusquely. 'As I speak, he's in the back of a police van, on his way to a nice warm cell. Under arrest for murder.'

'Confessed te the lot o' them!' adds Pratt.

Ava's so stunned she laughs. 'He can't have.'

'Handed himself in,' says Clowdy. 'Seems the first killing was an act of revenge after he learned Mr Baumgarten played a part in the deaths of his former employers, the senior Muirheads. He killed Miss Kettleness because she knew what he'd done, then he killed Miss Levi because he believed she'd guessed his role in the aforementioned murders. It was when she made a too-close-for-comfort remark about him wishing *she'd* eaten the poisoned chocolates, that he decided she "had to go". Sergeant Pratt confirms several guests overheard her comment...'

'...including yersel, doctor,' Pratt says with a sigh. 'If you recall.'

'That was nothing more than an exchange of words, surely. Besides, he was as surprised as I was when we found Lauri's body. He would never have harmed Maggie... and... and he didn't find out about Baumgarten and the car crash until after Baumgarten was dead! Has he said when this latest murder is supposed to have happened?'

'Grabbed his chance the morning Miss Levi persuaded Alastair to help her leave The Hall,' says Clowdy. 'Turns out his account of how he left her at the village phone box was true. When he returned, without her, Angus said he'd put the Land Rover away in the barn. In fact, the man drove it to Drumapple where he found Miss Levi alone in the dark. She hadn't called a cab for the simple reason that she didn't know the number for one. He brought her here where he did the deed. In the interests of full disclosure, he has also owned up to a fourth attempt on a life. That of Miss Georgina Beckett.'

'What? *How?*'

'He cut her brakes.'

'No! He's the one who spotted they were leaking. I was there! And *he* repaired them. Why would he want to kill her anyway?'

'Never liked her, apparently. He was especially angered by her actions regarding the Muirhead memorial cairn. "Good riddance te bad rubbish", were his few well-chosen words.'

Ava's incredulous. 'Where's the proof, inspector?'

'Mr Murdoch says Ollach Kettleness can confirm his motive for the first killing. He's admitted using cyanide from Mr Muirhead's shed to dispatch Baumgarten and Maggie Kettleness. He's admitted to emptying the chemical cabinet after the event – retaining the rock pick for later use – and named a witness, the younger Addington boy, who can corroborate this.'

'But it was *I* who told *Murdoch*—'

'It's only a matter of time till we gather enough evidence to prosecute. Mr Murdoch is cooperating fully.'

'Rubbish. He's lying through his teeth!' cries Ava.

'These are nae things a man would usually lie about,' Pratt says gravely.

'I couldn't agree more,' says Ava, 'but it doesn't add up. For a start, how did Lauri Levi end up dressed like this? And—'

'We will talk more to Mr Murdoch in due course. No doubt he has answers.'

'Ask him about maggots! This woman's been dead for hours, not days. And you *cannot* say that cyanide killed Maggie!'

'And *ye* cannae say it didnae!' snaps Sween.

'For what it's worth, Dr Dickens,' interjects Clowdy. 'Mr Murdoch is deeply ashamed of his actions, especially that he allowed Mr Muirhead to become the focus of police attention when he himself was our villain all along.'

As Ava battles to round up her thoughts, her tongue runs away with her. 'If you must arrest someone, why not Professor Wickremesinghe? He's waltzed off with the last of the Muirheads' family silver, right under your constable's nose!'

Clowdy looks enquiringly at Pratt.

Pratt looks enquiringly at Cargill.

'First I heard o' it, sir.'

'Well... he has...' huffs Ava, hating herself.

'The sergeant will, of course, look into what you say,' Clowdy says irritably. 'As you can see, Dr Dickens, at this point in time he has more pressing matters to deal with. Sween,' he continues, turning his back to Ava, 'are you happy for us to remove the body? We want to get moving before we start losing the light.'

'I am, Donald, aye.'

'Ewan!' barks Pratt. 'Robbie! On the count o' one... two... three... and... What the...?'

Out from a back pocket of Lauri Levi's overalls drops a passport, and judging by the UK royal coat of arms embossed into its navy front cover, it belongs to a British citizen. Clowdy picks it up and opens it. He scours the corpse's face, then looks again at the passport, checking the mugshot. 'Well, well,' he breathes. 'Seems The Hall's American visitor wasn't such a true-blue Yankee after all. "Miss Jane Finnock" of Crannock Crescent, Peebles. Ring any bells, Pratt? How about with you, Sween?'

The pair shrugs.

'*I*'ve heard the word "Finnock" before,' offers Ava. 'It's an alternative common name for *Salmo trutta trutta*, the anadromous, that's to say "sea-running", form of brown trout; specifically younger specimens returning to fresh water after their first taste of marine living. Are you not fishing men?'

Clowdy eyes Ava up and down as though she's lost her marbles. Pratt ignores her. His focus is on something he's spotted among the flattened catchflies where the body had lain. 'Car keys, sir. The lady must have a vehicle.'

'I'm not so sure,' says Ava. 'Look at that enamelled logo on the fob! "MG". Georgina Beckett drives an MG, and she lost her keys last week.'

'So we're looking at an imposter, and a light-fingered imposter at that,' says Clowdy. 'I look forward to hearing what else Angus Murdoch can tell us about her.'

The trip back to The Hall is, in every sense, bumpy. While Lauri gets a chauffeur-driven wagon to herself, Ava rides with Pratt, Cargill, and her bike which they collect from Drumapple. Her dogged attempts to air the subjects of fake confessions, flamboyant American singers, alter egos, and plain Janes from Peebles are all wasted. Neither man will be drawn. Both do, however, talk between themselves... about Wick, 'wolves in sheep's clothing', and 'turn-ups for the books'.

On arrival at the hotel, the policemen accompany Ava inside, where Pratt briefs Fiona and Alastair.

'A body has been found which we have reason te believe is that o' yer missin' guest.' He makes no reference to Miss Levi not being Miss Levi, but goes on to say, 'We understand she was murdered by the same man who took the lives o' Mr Baumgarten and young Maggie.'

'Good heavens!'

'You've found her?' stammers Alastair. '*Dead?*'

'Aye, dead. On a pocket o' open land close te yer border with Beinn Beithe, at the... er' – Pratt hesitates – 'bothy.'

'You mean The Murder Field?' asks Fiona.

'As legend would have us call it, madam,' coughs Pratt.

Alastair turns pale.

Fiona shudders. 'She's been gone for two days. To think of the times I've looked out of our windows, stared at that view, and she was lying out there in it *all* that time. The hairs on the back of my neck are standing on end.'

'Time o' death isnae confirmed, Mrs Muirhead, but rest assured, Clowdy has his man. Angus Murdoch has confessed.'

Alastair crumples into the nearest chair. Fiona stays standing, though she looks equally stunned.

'Confessed?' Alastair mouths. 'Murdoch says *he* killed all those people?'

Pratt pats him on the shoulder. 'Mr Murdoch says he's sorry, lad, fer lettin' ye down. As fer the professor, we'll be lookin' into *his* crimes in the mornin'.'

'The *professor*? *Uncle Wick*! I don't understand.'

'Seems he's left Dorcha Hall, tekkin' some o' yer valuables wi'im,' says Cargill.

'One of your mother's paintings,' whispers Ava.

'Ava... Fee...? This can't be happening! Is this another bad dream? When I wake up, I'll have forgotten everything.'

'I'm sorry darling, I didn't know how to tell you. But the news about Angus Murdoch, that's *fantastic*! Apologies again... wrong word,' she corrects herself, before continuing excitedly, 'I mean, no one's coming to arrest you. No one's coming to take *you* away!' The depth of her relief is blatant, but when she reaches for Alastair's hand, he brushes her off.

He rises unsteadily to his feet. 'Fee, this is more than I can process. I'm done.' Off he walks, and Ava's instincts tell her to leave him be.

'Will he be all right, Mrs Muirhead?'

'Don't worry, constable, I'll look after him. Honestly,' gushes Fiona, 'I can't believe it. Thank you so much for letting us know, sergeant. Please thank the inspector too, from Alastair and me.'

'Will do. We'll be on our ways too. Mrs Cargill's been on her own a fair while now. The constable here'll be hankerin' fer his own bed.'

'Of course. Does this mean our guests are free to leave?'

'Not quite. Inspector Clowdy wants te speak te the Addington lads, put young Martin's mind at rest.' Ava expects Pratt to bring up Jane Finnock's name, but he stops short. 'Suffice te say, we've loose ends that need tyin', best brought up when yersel and yer husband are both runnin' on full steam. Nothin' that won't keep till light o' day... though ye can let Miss Beckett know we've good news about her car keys. Rest easy, Mrs Muirhead, and yersel, Dr Dickens,' says Pratt, replacing his cap, 'ye're all safe now.'

39

The Stuff of Nightmares

It's really late, Ava's bushed, yet sleep's nowhere to be found. She screws her eyes shut and contemplates the spectrum of swirling colours moving across the insides of her lids, like the aurora borealis. 'Phosphenes'. Everyone gets them, but a lightshow as hectic as this one signals just how tired she is. Still, she'd rather be seeing stars than explore the sequence of disturbing scenes parading through her head: that gap on the wall where Sheila's landscape hung, Murdoch coming at her with a loaded gun, human carrion swarming with flies. By far the worst, though... the image Ava can't shake... is that of Alastair as he'd wandered away. For all his height, with Murdoch and Wick – the bedrocks of his life – kicked out from under him, he'd looked like a lost child. She'd desperately wanted to go after him, tell him that she *knows* Murdoch is talking cobblers, but as she'd watched 'the bairn' amble off, the reason behind all Murdoch's wretched untruths strode into sharp focus, and she'd been glued to the spot.

Murdoch thinks Alastair, Sheila's child, is the murderer! Murdoch's taking the blame to protect him, just as he's protected him his whole life. Just as he promised Sheila he would. Murdoch's supposed motives, the ones he explained to the police, likely tally with those he reckons drove Alastair to kill: revenge over the death of his parents, followed by the need to eliminate people who could incriminate him; the cutting of George's brakes being a side-order of rage. Ava replays Murdoch's behaviour when Ollach disclosed Baumgarten's role in the car crash. Like Ava, he guessed that Maggie could have let slip as much to Alastair, giving Alastair grounds to kill. As for the holes on the beech avenue, he always thought Alastair dug them, hence the nonsense about squirrels. Murdoch was there when the buried bottle finally turned up, and that's when he stripped Alastair's cabinet, to remove any other damning evidence before the police could get to it. The fact that the cabinet was emptied of everything, and not just one or two bottles, is telling. Since Murdoch wasn't the real killer, he didn't know what chemicals had actually been used... or might be used in the future... and that's why he took the lot. At that point, the rock pick must've already gone. When Murdoch saw it again today, sticking out of a corpse's neck, it cemented his belief that Alastair is a murderer.

Fiona's reaction when she received the news of Murdoch's confession – a candid mix of unbridled surprise and unashamed relief – suggests that until then, she too had been convinced of Alastair's guilt. God knows, she's had cause to be frightened by Alastair's behaviour. He's shown himself to be capable of spectacular levels of dissociation, of hitting his wife, capable of forgetting what day it is and, perhaps, the difference between right and very, very wrong as well.

Ava feels sick. Terrifying as the notion is, Ava has to entertain the possibility that Murdoch and Fiona are on the mark. They know Alastair better than she does. So what if her gut still says Alastair's innocent, that he really is the gentle man he's always appeared to be? Good scientists don't rely on their guts and, as she once cautioned Wick, her understanding of hominids sometimes falls wide. Just look at how she misread *him*!

Ava sighs a deep, inward, sigh. No matter how much Fiona wants Murdoch's admissions to be true, his selfless efforts to divert attention away from Alastair won't work forever. His account is riddled with holes, and the police'll find them. His claim to have poisoned Maggie with cyanide, *that* simply doesn't wash. For all man-of-medicine Dr Sween's puffing and blowing, he *must* know Maggie's symptoms point to an altogether different substance. No doubt the coroner's pathologist knows too, and pathologists are no strangers to the lifecycle of blowflies, either. Ava hopes Lauri Levi's body is stowed somewhere cold, otherwise those eggs'll be hatching. Except it's not Lauri's body, it's Jane's. And who the *hell* is she?

There always was something caricature-like about Lauri Levi, as though the showgirl was literally putting on a show. Still, it's hard to imagine what could have made an unremarkable-looking woman from the Scottish Borders, posing as a singer from the sultry Deep South, book a 'vacation' in a remote hotel. All that deception, for whose benefit? Maybe her own. Jane Finnock was enjoying the ultimate Highland escape. She'd come to a place where no one knew her and assumed a larger-than-life ego, likely the polar opposite to Jane's persona at home. Being Lauri allowed her to be centre stage, loud, rude – behaviours she perhaps couldn't get away with in Peebles – while safely clad in the body armour of improvised breasts and bedazzling layers of glitz.

Such reasoning, however, seems flawed. 'Lauri' stayed at The Hall for *six* weeks with no departure date mentioned; a very long time to devote to a little harmless role-play. And what on earth was she doing with George's car keys? The keys to the car which had its brakes cut, so that George never got to drive it away… crash… and die in a fireball. There's something else Ava's hypothesis doesn't cover… the *only* thing about 'Lauri' that was authentic: her feelings for Alastair. Ava's certain these went deeper than passing attraction. She loved him so much she couldn't hide it.

All very confusing and, frankly, bizarre. Ava yawns and rubs her aching eyes. By hook or by crook, *someone* stabbed Jane in the neck, someone dosed Baumgarten with cyanide, and someone fed Maggie… what? If only Ava knew… could *prove* it's got nothing to do with Alastair… or anyone else she cares about… then everything might be all right after all…

When, at last, the dream comes, its meaning is transparent. The jackal puppy is back, and he leads Ava to the end of his hot, dusty road: his final destination, a village in Botswana, where he's the half-tame pet of the locals. A group of women sits together under the shade of an acacia tree. The puppy joins them, and Ava goes with him, grateful to escape the heat of the sun. Everyone's busy, threading beads into necklaces, and they're happy in their work. Everyone's smiling. The jackal's mischievous eyes sparkle, and he wags his naughty tail. The smooth, shiny beads are pretty... marbled shades of maroon and brown and black... only they're not beads, they're seeds! As Ava holds up a finished necklace to take a closer look, the puppy licks his lips... prepares to spring. Although Ava knows what's going to happen next, all the horrors to come, she's powerless to intervene, so she simply has to watch.

Ava wakes. It's still dark. She doesn't bother to dress. Leaden steps carry her along the unlit corridor, past the spot where Maggie took her last breath, and down the creaky stairs. The phone call she makes to DI Clowdy is brief. She doesn't need many words to make herself heard, and despite the hour, he thanks her for ringing him so promptly. He'll come. He'll send men. They'll be with her soon.

Ava hangs up the receiver. For a while, she sits in the lobby. Alone in the shadows. Miserable. It's a surprise when Fiona appears, also in a nightgown.

'Ava! You made me jump! Let me put on a light.'

'Sorry. Hope I didn't wake you?'

'Not at all. I can't sleep either. Alastair's still dead to the world, though. What are you doing downstairs? You look terrible.'

'Do I?' Ava answers vaguely. 'I expect I do. You see, I know what killed Maggie. Something about her symptoms, they were so extreme, so *distinctive*... they struck a chord. Ever since the day she died, I've been trying to work out what that something was. Now it's come to me.'

'But you don't have to work out anything, Ava,' says Fiona. 'That's the police's job. Murdoch's going to help them fill in the gaps—'

'Oh Fiona! He can't do that, can he? Because he's not the killer. I think we both know that.'

Fiona draws her dressing gown around her bird-like body. 'I don't know anything,' she says tightly. 'Whatever you're thinking, Ava, it's wrong.'

'Maggie didn't die from cyanide; she swallowed a highly potent biological toxin called ricin. I've seen its effects before, in Africa, in a young canid that ate *Ricinus* seeds. Six hours later, he suffered an excruciating death right before my eyes. Pulmonary oedema... haemorrhage... I now realise Maggie's nervous system, her organs, were damaged in the same way. Do you remember the blood?'

Fiona nods dumbly.

'And how disorientated she was, the way she talked about drowning, as though she was reliving the death throes of The Lass of The Loch? That was down to the toxin too, making her hallucinate, filling her lungs with fluid till she couldn't breathe.'

'But where would Murdoch get hold of this "ricin"?'

'The thing is, Fiona... there's no easy way of saying this, there are several specimens of *Ricinus* here at The Hall. The castor oil plants which Alastair was nurturing in the orangery.'

'Are you saying my husband is a murderer, Ava?'

'I am.' Ava looks long and hard at Fiona, Alastair's wife, and Fiona stares back at her with equal intensity, and such defiance that Ava's blood runs slightly cold. If ever Clowdy sought a soul who'd act to shield Alastair from the consequences of his own behaviour, there's one standing right in front of Ava now. Ava wonders how long Fiona's been aware of her husband's murderous intent. Why did it never occur to Ava before that Fee's obsession with keeping eyes on Alastair wasn't just to protect him from himself? It was about keeping others safe from the harm he planned to inflict as soon as her back was turned!

'Fiona, the night Baumgarten died, did you meet him outside?'

Fiona's laugh is brittle. 'Why would I do that?'

'To warn him his life might be in danger.'

Fiona offers no response.

'And the bottle that contained the cyanide used to kill Baumgarten, did *you* bury it?'

This question, too, is left hanging. 'Clowdy's established that Murdoch—'

'Murdoch has many skills, Fiona,' Ava says steadily, 'but he's not a botanist. Alastair is. He'll be more than aware of the scientific properties of *Ricinus* seeds. That's what I've just told the police, and they're on their way here.'

'They're coming to get Alastair!' Fiona sounds completely panic stricken. 'But they mustn't… they *can't*! Not today!' she cries, wringing her hands, pulling at her cheeks.

'Fiona!' Ava says firmly. 'For Alastair's sake, get a grip! I'll make you some sugary tea.'

'Tea?' Fiona's laugh borders on the hysterical.

'Like I did after Alastair slapped you. You said it helped.'

There's a pause. 'Yes,' says Fiona. Her voice is calm. She looks half mad. 'Yes. That's actually not a bad idea. In fact, Ava, *I'll* put the kettle on… take Alastair a cup too.'

40

The Full Picture

Ava continues to wait in the lobby, beneath the stuffed stags' heads with their dust-caked leather noses and unseeing glass eyes. She thinks Fiona's doing the right thing, taking Alastair a drink. Once again, the young woman has surprised her, being stronger and more pragmatic than she looks. Fiona can wake him with it, explain what's happened; try to prepare him for what's to come. Better her husband's dressed himself, had a shave, before the police arrive.

Ava eyes the still-steaming brew Fiona brought her. That was kind. She'll drink it when it cools down. She could do with a sweet tea to reset her own hypothalamic-pituitary-adrenal axis... quell her raging remorse. She's thrown her godson under the bus! Beautiful, ethereal Alastair, who trusts her absolutely. Some part of her still can't accept what he's done. There's a jagged shard of doubt she can't quite shake; as though she, like a far-sighted rabbit, is missing something important right under her nose. But wishful thinking won't save him. Thanks to her, the pathologist knows what to test for and proof that Maggie died by ricin poisoning will follow soon enough. Alastair's fate will be sealed. She wonders if he knew Lauri Levi's true identity. All those trips to Inverness, the two of them, did she give herself away? If so, how much did that have to do with her death? Perhaps nothing. He'd already killed twice. Whoever this woman was, if he thought she'd rumbled what he's done, her number was up. Maybe he thought she was a threat to his marriage, too. Funny he kept her alive at the bothy for those two days. God knows *what's* been going on in his head. What'll his defence be? Insanity? How awful that, at this moment, she truly hopes he's mad.

Ava hears footsteps outside. The police are here much sooner than she expected. Rather than bother Fiona until she absolutely has to, she opens the front door, braced to greet... 'Wick!'

'Ava! Lovely to see you too, but shout any louder and you'll wake the whole house. I wasn't expecting anyone to be up yet.'

'You're back!'

'Of course I'm back!' It's Wick's turn to sound incredulous. 'Like I said I'd be.'

'What are you talking about?'

'You must've found my message. I left it under your pillow yesterday morning.'

'No, I did *not* find it! What a bloody stupid place to put something,' Ava mutters. 'Why didn't you just give it to me?'

'I tried, but when I knocked on your door, you weren't in. I'd no time to look for you, because I wanted to make a clean escape before Cargill finished breakfast. Then I remembered a remark you made about checking under your pillow for scorpions – I think you wanted me to guess how long one can hold its breath – and I had a brainwave. A brainwave I was rather pleased with.'

'Really!' Ava says acerbically.

Wick looks aggrieved. 'I'm sorry you didn't know where I'd gone, Ava, but I'm here now, so what does it matter? In fact, I bring good tidings! I departed The Hall with a plan, and that plan's worked out far better than I dared hope. I've a *lot* to tell you.'

'Likewise.'

'Well, let me in and we can swap stories!'

They head for the orangery. 'Isn't it nice to be back in our "office",' comments Wick as he passes Ava a blanket for her knees, 'especially since we've both got news to share. So...' He looks at her expectantly. 'Ladies first!'

'I'd much prefer you to start.'

Wick needs no further persuasion. 'I, Dr Dickens, have been in Inverness, where I went to meet a certain Mr Cavendish-

Bowles, a contact recommended to me by Sinclair Stewart. He's a London-based antiquarian specialising in British landscapes. We rendezvoused at my invitation, as I wanted to show him Sheila's view of Dorcha Hall. For a long time, I've suspected it to be the work of Oakley Williams, a much-sought-after Victorian watercolourist, but I couldn't be sure. I was keen to get an expert second opinion, because I knew if my hunch was right, it would be a valuable piece. My plan was, if Alastair was happy to part with it, to offer it for auction... but only if it would make a decent amount. Perhaps a few thousand pounds towards The Hall's costs. Long story short,' Wick says excitedly, 'I was correct about the identity of the artist, but totally unprepared for what the picture's worth. When Cavendish-Bowles told me what *he* thought it would go for, I practically fell off my chair. Not four figures, Ava, not five. *Six*! Cavendish-Bowles will stake his reputation on it.'

'Why the secrecy, Wick? Why sneak off?'

'I didn't want to raise Alastair and Fiona's hopes.'

'That makes sense I suppose,' Ava says morosely.

'But it's astounding, isn't it? With money like that, Alastair could sort this place out properly, even build that stupid yoga studio... get Fiona a white peacock! Just imagine! And I've another surprise for you... or *us*, really... an intriguing find, which I've yet to properly unpack. Nothing as significant as the painting, but I think it's only right that we look at it together. What do you say?'

'I'm lost for words.'

'Frankly,' Wick says tetchily, 'I'm disappointed. I wasn't expecting you to jump for joy exactly, but I flattered myself you'd crack a smile when I told you about the valuation.'

'I *am* pleased, and impressed, and *really* glad to see you. Twenty-four hours ago, I might even have turned a cartwheel. This morning, though...' Ava pauses. 'You said you'd come up with a rescue plan, Wick, and you have, unexpectedly and brilliantly... but it's come too late.'

Wick's X-ray eyes lock onto Ava's and, blink as she might,

she cannot look away. 'Dr Dickens, it's *your* turn to tell tales now.'

And so Ava does. She describes discovering Lauri's body on The Murder Field, spread-eagled on a carpet of pink catchflies, with a rock pick sticking out of its neck. She recounts Murdoch's confession, why she thinks he's confessed: to save Alastair. And she explains her dream. 'You said to "sleep on it", and look where that's got us!'

'Ricin eh?' Wick says slowly, stroking his moustache. 'Interesting.'

'From the *Ricinus communis* plants which Alastair kept in this very room. When he and I shifted them outside, he went on and on about protecting "tender specimens" from frost... Obviously, they were far more special to him than I realised.'

'But, Ava,' Wick says evenly, 'what makes you certain it was *Alastair* who used ricin to kill Maggie?'

His question surprises her, as does the insouciance with which he's taking her revelations. 'Who else round here could be expert about the dangers of *Ricinus* seeds? I mean, do *you* know how much ricin you'd need to kill somebody? I'll tell you—'

'Five hundred micrograms.'

'Yes!' Ava's astonished. 'Good guess. It's six thousand times more poisonous than cyanide—'

'And twelve thousand times more poisonous than rattlesnake venom. All to do with the glycoprotein's "enzymatic" and "lectin" chains.'

'You're scaring me, professor. For a man whose technical interests are generally limited to the ideal temperature to serve Bordeaux, you're very well informed. To understand the workings of ricin takes skills in botany, toxicology, at a push—'

'Phytoremediation?'

'Pardon?'

'Phytoremediation,' repeats Wick. 'The use of green crops to mop up pollutants from contaminated land, thus restoring soil fertility. Recent research suggests *Ricinus communis*, by virtue of its deep-penetrating roots, is particularly good at accumulating the kind of nasties left behind in mining spoils… so, aside from any nefarious applications, it's got the potential to be really helpful. As it happens, I've picked up one or two facts about catchflies, too, if you'd like me to share?'

Bereft of speech, Ava nods.

'The catchfly, or "clammy campion", *Viscaria alpina*,' he recites as if addressing a class of students, 'is a "metallophyte", able to thrive on metal-rich soils most other plants can't tolerate. When catchflies are seen in abundance, where nothing much else is growing, they flag the presence of valuable deposits in the ground beneath. In other words, they're natural indicators. Prospectors have known as much for decades.'

'Those useless pink flowers aren't so useless after all,' breathes Ava.

'No indeed,' says Wick. 'You've seen them at The Murder Field?'

'Solid with them. Seems it's not a worthless pocket of blood-soaked land, but an untapped acreage of… what?'

'Copper ore, most likely,' says Wick. 'It would be a criminal waste to sell it off as a helipad. The "Viscaria mine"… guess how it got its name…' He chuckles. '*That*'s brought in millions of Krona, apparently.'

Ava's pulse starts racing. 'Does Sinclair Stewart know this?'

'I doubt it.'

'And why would *you*, Wick? Who, told *you* all this?'

'I read it,' he answers matter-of-factly, 'in Dr Finnock's thesis.'

Ava's aghast. 'You know Jane Finnock!'

Wick's expression shifts from slightly smug to clearly confused. 'Not Jane, *Fiona*. "Finnock" is her maiden name. Though I shouldn't call her "doctor", should I, since her dissertation is only a Master's: *Applications of Dicotyledonous Flora in Geoscience – A Review*. Fiona may be an earth scientist, but "technically speaking" she knows all about castor oil plants, the significance of catchflies in the landscape, and a slag heap of other interesting stuff too. As for Jane Finnock, I've not met any of Fiona's siblings—'

'But Jane Finnock is the woman Murdoch and I found dead!'

'I thought that was Lauri Levi!'

'No! "Lauri", *she* was all an act. What you've just said... what it *means*... is the person who's been staying at The Hall these last weeks, sparring with Fiona, fawning over Alastair, is, or was, Fiona's *sister*!'

'They weren't the least bit alike.'

'That's because they were deliberately trying to appear different. Mousy Mrs Muirhead, who literally matches the furniture, versus larger-than-life, look-at-me Lauri, who stood out like a sore thumb. Neither was presenting her true self. Without makeup, though, there was a family resemblance. *That's* why Jane Finnock's face looked familiar to me. On a subconscious level, it reminded me of Fiona's.' Thunderstruck, Ava battles to join up the maelstrom of disconnected thoughts storming her brain. 'Finnock and Finnock. *Two* slippery fish, muddying Dorcha's waters.'

'This is all—'

'Where is the Viscaria mine, Wick?'

'Sweden.'

'Yes, yes... I gathered as much from the "Krona" comment... but whereabouts *in* Sweden?'

'Kiruna, I believe.'

'Where Baumgarten saw a three-toed woodpecker!'

'Ava, I—'

'Quiet!' cries Ava, throwing aside her blanket and jumping to her feet. '*Please*! I must *think*.' Pacing up and down, she revisits her first meeting with Baumgarten, the candlelit dinner where guests presented their party pieces, things he said, Maggie said, and Wick... and Fiona. Her heart's beating so fast, she feels it might burst out of her thorax, and when realisation finally strikes, the pain is actually physical.

'If you're not going to drink this,' says Wick, lifting Ava's tea cup to his lips...

She knocks it out of his hand. 'Stop! I've made a terrible, terrible mistake. We have to move, *now*, and pray we're not too late!'

Ava is the first to reach the Muirheads' locked bedroom door. No one answers her frantic banging... not that she dreamt they would, so she and Wick break it open. Together, they kick at the hinges and slam their shoulders against the wooden panelling. It gives suddenly, and with a splintering crash the pair burst inside. A dramatic entrance, but it's as if neither occupant heard them come in. Alastair's on his back, motionless on the bed. Fiona's kneeling astride his chest, pushing a pillow onto his face. Wick shouts her name, and Ava clutches her round the waist, using all her might to try to pull her away, but Fiona continues to push down. Her face is scarlet, her teeth bared, and she's snarling like a starved dog guarding a bone. Despite the bedlam all around him, Alastair does nothing to help himself. He lies perfectly still, arms at his side... like a corpse.

At last, Ava and Wick manhandle Fiona off the bed, but neither dares let go of her. With the strength of a woman possessed, Fiona fights back, spitting and thrashing to get to her husband, knocking over a nightstand and smashing a table lamp. An empty teacup breaks into smithereens as it hits the floor. So do Fiona's tortoiseshell-rimmed specs. In the end, they pin her down, face first. Wick has her by the shoulders. Ava sits on her calves.

'I only need another minute with him!' she screams. 'Then I'll be done.'

'Stop it!' pants Ava, breathless from her exertions. 'You've done more than enough already.'

'And *you*,' cries Fiona, 'need to mind your own bloody business!' With that, she twists round and gouges her fingernails into Ava's cheek.

Ava stays put, but Wick releases his grip. Fiona elbows Ava in the ribs, she manages to grab the pillow, and...

'Fee?' Alastair says dreamily, picking a feather from his mouth. 'What's going on?'

Everyone freezes except Alastair, who lifts his head and surveys the scene. 'Why are you on the floor?'

The Beasts of the Black Loch

In an instant, Fiona relaxes. She tucks her light-brown hair behind her red, throbbing ears and, with a steady hand, rebuttons the lace collar of her flesh-toned winceyette nightie. As if a switch has been flicked, dismissed is the seething Valkyrie, back is the loving wife. 'Everything's *fine*, darling,' she says sweetly, reaching for his hand. 'You've just had another one of your turns. Have a little sleep, and when you wake up, you'll have forgotten all about it.'

The entrance of Clowdy and his men could not have been more theatrically timed. Fiona does not go quietly. 'Get your filthy hands off me! I've done *nothing* wrong and I'll never say otherwise!'

It takes Pratt, Cargill, Ewan *and* Robbie to get her handcuffed and into the back of their waiting van, but her protestations of innocence and pleas to her husband and the police fail to wake Alastair. Sween, and Peigi, stay with him, waiting for the effects of the NarcoVal his wife gave him to wear off. Meanwhile, arranged in the library's bay window, the rest of the residents watch the spectacle unfold, much as if this were another of the Muirheads' surprise entertainments. Fiona doesn't disappoint, kicking and screaming all the way. Even Clowdy seems impressed.

Show over, the Addingtons are the next to leave. Bernard and Barbara have the Cortina loaded within the hour. Ava's truly sorry to see the boys go. Martin shakes Ava's hand, Carl hugs her, and both lower their car windows to wave as their laden vehicle rocks-and-rolls its way down the craterous driveway.

George is advised that her car keys are now police evidence, and will be returned in due course. She seems unconcerned when 'due course' might be, though. Her goodbyes to Wick and Ava are perfunctory. She climbs into the front passenger seat of Sinclair Stewart's Aston Martin, and is still buckling her seat belt as it pulls away. Soon after, a helicopter rises above Beithe Towers and swoops down the glen. The echoing *chop-chop-chop-chop* of its blades remains audible for a long time after the aircraft itself is out of sight.

Wick turns to Ava. 'Dr Dickens,' he says. 'It may be obvious to *you* why Fiona became a murderess, but if you wouldn't mind humouring me, I'd appreciate the full picture.'

'In which case, Professor Wickremesinghe, we should adjourn to the kitchen garden where we can sit in peace, and,' she says, scanning the bookshelves carefully, 'let's bring that copy of *The Illustrated World Atlas* with us.'

'Whyever—?'

'All in good time, Wick. All in good time.'

Thus equipped, they wander outside, to the bench. Ava rolls a cigarette, while Wick unwraps a cigar. He pops open his portable ashtray and places it between them. Both light up. Ava leans back, closes her eyes, and lets the sun warm her throbbing cheek. She hears Wick take a drag, then exhale.

'Are you sitting comfortably,' she asks without opening her eyes.

'Comfortably enough.'

'Then I shall begin.'

41

You Cain't Help Who You Love

'This, Professor Wickremesinghe, is a saga of greed, deception, and unrequited love. Its opening chapters are set in Scotland, when Duncan and Sheila were alive and well, and their son was away studying. One ordinary day, somewhere in the corridors of Edinburgh University, earth science scholar Fiona Finnock encountered aspiring botanist Alastair Muirhead, and they became friends. *Just* friends. Their early acquaintance was, as you framed it, casual. Alastair had a sweetheart at home. Fiona was focused on her Master's. That said, two years ago, Alastair invited a group of pals, postgrad students like himself, to spend the summer on his father's estate. Fiona happened to be among them. They'd all explore its plants and outcrops, soak up the scenery, have fun. No more than that. Then Fiona went overseas for a research trip, and while she was away, something changed. Back she came to see off Peigi Hooley and nab Alastair for herself.'

'What made her do that?'

'A sabbatical spent at the Viscaria mine, in Sweden, where she learned the significance of catchflies. She'd already seen them growing on Dorchan land, and she knew how valuable an untapped deposit of copper could be. She also knew the Muirheads were oblivious to the fortune hidden under their feet. The latter nuggets of information, of course, she chose not to capture in her dissertation. She did, however, share them with her sister, Jane. Together, this twisted pair came up with a murderous plot to get rich, the first step being—'

'Become a member of the Muirhead clan,' Wick breathes. 'Hence the whirlwind romance...'

'All whipped up by her,' concurs Ava. 'Getting Alastair to fall for her as hard and fast as he did was, in my opinion, Fiona's seminal feat. She chose the moment when Peigi left for Glasgow to pounce, offering him company at a time when he no doubt felt abandoned, playing on their shared interest in natural sciences.'

'Sounds like a euphemism, Ava.'

'Doesn't it! But Fiona's sharpest move wasn't bedding Alastair, it was winning over his mother. She wooed Sheila as assiduously as she wooed Sheila's son. Always at Dorcha Hall, being "a shoulder to cry on". Fiona presented herself as a steady, head-screwed-on-right person, who'd stick by Alastair's side, and *not* squander what was left of the Muirheads' money then drink herself stupid, leaving a spouse to cope alone.'

'The antithesis of Duncan.'

'Precisely. With Sheila supporting, even *promoting* the match, half Fiona's work was done. In her last letter, Sheila wrote that Fiona was like a daughter to her. You know it was Fiona who proposed to Alastair, at The Murder Field?'

'Cynical choice of location,' reflects Wick.

'Her desire for a quick wedding had nothing to do with passion, it was all about who owned those bloody pink flowers.'

'And the "shotgun" element?'

'Fiona, doubling down. She told Alastair she was pregnant, safe in the knowledge that, decent man he is, he'd marry her without delay with everyone's blessing. Needless to say, it turned out to be a "false alarm" – Fiona had no intention of producing *any* Muirhead heirs – but Alastair didn't mind...'

Wick sighs. 'Because he really loved her, baby or not.'

'Little did he know that once that knot was tied, Fiona and Jane's first two marks were on borrowed time.'

'Baumgarten and Maggie?'

'Yet to come into range. I'm talking about Duncan and Sheila, who stood between Alastair and his inheritance. Somehow or another, almost certainly by tampering with the car's brakes, Fiona orchestrated their accident. Baumgarten, who witnessed it, said the car never slowed down before swerving full speed into the trees.'

Wick's jaw clenches. 'But Fiona was supposed to travel with Duncan that day, not Sheila.'

'But she didn't, did she? Because Fiona, the ever-thoughtful daughter-in-law gave up her chance for a day in town so Sheila could visit the hairdressers and spend her birthday voucher; a treat, also a gift from Fiona.'

'The scheming little—'

'Precisely! And with them gone, Fiona aligned her sights on her new husband. The removal of his parents must've felt straightforward: a treacherous road, a reckless driver known for his drinking, still one over the eight after the night before. Mix in the general assumption that an animal jumped out in front of them. An accident, nothing more to say.'

'You and I bought it,' mutters Wick.

'But the dispatch of Alastair would be more complicated. No sooner had The Hall become his, he opened it as a hotel. Alastair's idea, *not* Fiona's, and she can't have been too pleased. Instead of it being a private home, strangers were coming and going, sleeping under the Muirheads' roof, potentially seeing things Fiona would prefer to go unseen. And Alastair is a young fit man, not a risk-taker like his dad. If he were to suddenly drop dead, questions *would* be asked. To murder him under the noses of a resident audience required an accomplice.'

'In swaggers Lauri Levi!'

'Or rather, Jane Finnock in disguise, plastered in makeup, draped in a rainbow of fandangle and polyester. No way would anyone imagine Fiona and "Lauri" shared fifty per cent of their genes.'

'A risky form of disguise, Ava.'

'Counter intuitive, I grant you, to wear bright colours and bling when one's trying to hide. But "disruptive camouflage" is more common that you'd think. All that razzle-dazzle breaks up a body's outline, making it hard for predators to recognise it as a whole. Works for jewel beetles and butterflyfish.'

'Jane was right in front of us, and we couldn't see her for what she was.'

'And we didn't spot what Fiona was up to either, though *she* deployed classic Peckhamian mimicry to stay under the radar… where a predator presents itself as harmless to deceive potential prey. Think bird-dropping spider.'

'Or devious bitch,' mutters Wick. 'What was their plan for Alastair?'

'For him, Fiona… and I'm sure Fiona was the mastermind in all this… came up with an altogether-stealthier MO. She and her sister would make it look like Alastair took his own life. Afterall, the man already seemed broken. Thanks to his failing business and recent bereavement, his exhaustion and sorrow weren't only genuine, they were obvious. Still, Fiona took no chances, taking every opportunity to highlight how low he was. She implied he was confused, forgetful, and mentally fragile, and made loaded asides about needing to keep an eye on him; casually lobbing that "periods of absence" grenade into her ever-thickening duplicitous soup. After Alastair drank the homemade repellent, he dismissed his own foolhardiness with a shrug. Fiona, by contrast, made his actions play to her script, sobbing all over him, publicly questioning his true intentions.'

'You're right! Alastair may have looked tired and stressed, even to the point of distraction, but until he supposedly tried to kill himself, I never *actually* heard or saw him do anything unreasonable. His instability was always second-hand news…'

'Reported by Fiona. And when she had you, me, Sween, even Alastair himself doubting his own sanity, she escalated things.'

'The debacle in the barn!'

'The timing of which was significant. Sinclair Stewart wanted to buy The Murder Field and, worse, Alastair was prepared to sell it! From Fiona's point of view, catastrophic. It must have been music to Fiona's ears when, after Maggie's death, Stewart backtracked. Disaster averted. But then Alastair tried to renegotiate! I saw a draft letter on his desk, offering more land for less money. It's no coincidence that his first "suicide attempt" happened before that letter ever got sent.'

'How the devil did she do it?'

'Brewed him a cuppa loaded with NarcoVal – the pills she persuaded Sween to prescribe for *her* but never took – then sent him to "wait in the Land Rover"; her justification being something to the effect that Peigi Hooley had been allowed to go home, but only if he drove her to Drumapple. With a killer on the loose, it would hardly be safe for poor Peigi to walk, would it! Ever dutiful, Alastair followed his wife's orders. The drug took its inevitable effect. Presumably, having gone to check on him later, Fiona found him asleep at the wheel. She had only to switch on the engine, shut the barn door, and stand back till someone else discovered the tragic scene.'

'Which we did, Ava, just in time.'

'Or, from Fiona's point of view, much too soon. Remember her dismay when we brought him to her. Such *frustration*! Not because her husband had harmed himself; she was spitting tacks her scheme had failed! Still, she turned it to her advantage. Under the guise of "I'm too guileless to keep secrets", Fiona made sure to let Constable Cargill know what her husband had supposedly done...'

'Introducing the police to the notion that Alastair was a man with a death wish. I take it events in the boathouse were her next escalation?'

'Yup. More or less the same MO. She'd drugged Alastair with the intention of staging his suicide, this time by hanging, when we intervened. Fiona's decision to use the boathouse rather than anywhere else was especially manipulative. When you mentioned we'd be having an excursion on the loch, she was *so* kind. Even supplied that picnic hamper, so we could "make a day of it". All part of her calculations. She wanted us out on the water long enough for her and Jane to get the deed done, then *we'd* come back and find his body while she was innocently going about her business in The Hall. I wouldn't be surprised if she sent Alastair, compliant as always and nicely doped up, down to the boathouse to wait for us.'

Wick shudders. So does Ava. Both sit in silence to reflect on what might have been.

Wick strokes his moustache. 'Why did *Baumgarten* have to die?'

'Because he clocked who Fiona and Jane were.'

'When?'

'Nineteen days ago, at Alastair and Fiona's special dinner, where us guests had to show off our party pieces.'

'And what a lark *that* was!' Wick says wryly.

'Top of the bill was Jane, or "Lauri" as we knew her then. All tits and tinsel, she delighted us with a racy rendition of "Big Spender". For added effect, at the end of her performance – which, in spite of appearances, was for our godson's benefit – she plonked herself in Herr Baumgarten's lap. While she was busy making come-hither eyes at Alastair, she failed to notice who was taking a good look at *her*: Baumgarten, and he was disconcerted by what he saw. At the time, I thought he was merely unsettled by her suggestive behaviour, but now I know better. In those up-close-and-personal few seconds, he spotted something that got him thinking. And so he sat quietly, drinking, trying to fathom what that something was. Meanwhile, it was time for the next act. Me.'

'With your charming account of a shark's banquet. I recall it featured an anteater and a chihuahua.'

'A porcupine and a Pomeranian, but close enough. Can you also recall that the shark had swallowed a US licence plate?'

Wick shakes his head.

'Well, if Baumgarten were still here, he would have done, because the plate had a pelican on it, and that seemed to really strike a chord with him. Which American state has *Pelecanus occidentalis* as its emblem symbol, Wick?'

'Oh God!' he answers apprehensively. 'Have I to guess?'

'No, you'd take forever. Hence this,' says Ava, handing Wick the atlas. 'See what it has to say about state flags.'

'Well, would you look at that!' exclaims Wick, after a quick flick through its pages. 'Louisiana! "The pelican in her piety", with a nest of chicks, too! Did you know that?'

'Nope. Worked it out an hour ago. Baumgarten, though, I'll wager *he* knew exactly where the plate came from. Think of his suitcase, covered in travel stickers, each a memento of some place he'd been, practically all of them depicting birds.'

'So why didn't he pipe up with the answer?'

'He was waiting for someone else in the room, a particular person by the name of Lauri Levi, to speak out. When she didn't, that silence said a *lot*. Baton Rouge, her supposed hometown, is the capital of Louisiana, yet she was as clueless about the pelican as everyone else, bar him. Within seconds of her lower buttocks hitting his upper thighs, Baumgarten suspected she was an imposter. Now he was sure! At this juncture, he almost said something, but inflexible Fee was having none of it. Guests had to stick to the order of play.'

'So Murdoch gave his colourful account of two warring women…'

'One a plain shrew, the other, a wanton exhibitionist, and Baumgarten's brain made a compounding connection which, for him, proved fatal. Fiona and Lauri might be polar opposites but, like the protagonists in The Lass of The Loch, they were sisters, nonetheless. And he'd encountered them before. Thanks to Murdoch's references to the field of pink flowers, Baumgarten remembered where and when that was: he met Fiona and *Jane* in Sweden, on his previous birdwatching expedition to Kiruna, the site of Viscaria copper mine. He may not have known what they were up to here at Dorcha Hall, or understood the deeper significance of the catchflies, but given the duo's elaborate efforts to conceal their relationship, he reckoned it wasn't anything good.'

'The cogs in Baumgarten's head must've been whirring at a thousand revs a minute.'

'Mustn't they! So much so, he issued a booze-fuelled threat to blackmail them, and he issued it right in front of us.'

Wick looks flabbergasted. 'If he did, I missed it!'

'Remember Baumgarten's description of a hunting osprey?'

'Only that I was supposed to do my turn next, and he pushed in.'

'*I* recollect it clearly. Often the case when people get things wrong. Their inconsistencies stick with me long after I've forgotten the rest of what they had to say. He was so *specific* about the bird's choice of prey: "young sea trout" – repeated it two or three times – but went on to imply that the migratory form of *Salmo trutta* morpha *trutta* would be found in land-locked lakes. Clearly incorrect. Being anadromous, they hatch in fresh water, but they must have access to the ocean because that's where they grow to maturity. I did wonder why he bothered to name the exact form of fish, only to slip up on the biology of where it lives. But he was drunk, so I put it down to blurred thinking. With hindsight, though, I realise how incredibly focused he was. To him, whether the fish were in a Scottish loch or an inflatable paddling pool was irrelevant. He did, however, want to make damn sure that two, chosen listeners were tuning in to his words. The "young sea trout", aka Fiona and Jane "Finnock", were in the room, and it was them alone he was addressing!

'Once Baumgarten had their attention… and I think Fiona, if not "Lauri" too, cottoned-on fast… he added more detail. By setting his party piece in a fanciful, frozen, "Nordic" landscape – incidentally, not a place you'd find osprey in winter – he was making a cryptic reference to Sweden. The sharp-eyed osprey, who spots its prey, even when they're hiding, was, of course, him. In saying that its cry can travel for miles, Baumgarten warned the Finnocks he could expose them. His finishing flourish, that he'd photographed what he saw, meant he'd got evidence to back up any claims he made. Sure enough, the sisters heard him. On the pretext of another one of their rows about Lauri's missing earrings, they convened into a huddle, and hatched a needs-must scheme to silence him, permanently.'

Wick scratches his head. 'I'm trying to piece together the order that guests left the room.'

'Lauri flounced off first, acting the drama queen, ahead of Baumgarten. She waited for him to totter out after her, and invited him outside for a chat; an offer he'd have taken as welcome affirmation she'd "got the message" and was willing to talk. Strapped for cash, struggling to pay his bills, it would be worth being ravaged by midges, if she was going to pay up.'

'So he *wasn't* alone outside. He was with Lauri! I'm sorry for my early scepticism, Ava.'

'All forgotten, Wick.' Ava smiles before continuing. 'While Lauri had Baumgarten distracted, using the need to prepare his packed lunch as a ploy, Fiona dashed to Alastair's lab and grabbed the cyanide. She returned to The Hall, went to Baumgarten's room, and doctored his bedside whisky accordingly.'

'The sounds I heard through my bedroom wall, the ones I attributed to Baumgarten's ablutions, they were Fiona washing whisky down the sink!'

'Next morning, after Murdoch discovered Baumgarten's body as Fiona hoped he would, Fiona sent him out of the room. While Murdoch was fetching me, she made a crucial substitution, pocketing the contaminated whisky bottle and placing the empty repellent bottle on the body. "Lauri" then arrived on scene, wearing a face pack to conceal any midge bites she'd incurred the night before, and promptly "fainted", providing Fiona with an excuse to remove her sister and the whisky bottle from the room. As Fiona summoned a doctor and the police, Lauri was tasked with disposing of the evidence, which she did hastily and, as it turned out, badly.'

'Fiona drew our attention to the repellent bottle clenched in Baumgarten's hand.'

'True, and she was frank about all the nasties "silly" Alastair kept in his cabinet; even drew Clowdy's attention to the fact there'd been cyanide in there.' Ava laughs dryly. 'She's danced a fine line, engaging with the police as much as she has. On the one hand she wanted to come across as cooperative. Nudging Alastair into Clowdy's line of sight sat well with her narrative "my husband's so bonkers, perhaps he's a murderer." On the other, she's never wanted them to arrest him. To inherit Dorcha estate, she had to be Alastair's widow, and she could hardly get shot of him if he was behind bars. All those times she's said, "I need him with me", she was deadly serious.'

'Murdoch's confession must've seemed like a gift from the Gods.'

'Fiona barely contained her joy! Called it "fantastic". Things were back in check, and she had Alastair where she wanted him. But this respite was brief. Only hours later, *I* got it into my head he used ricin to poison Maggie. When Fiona found out I'd called Clowdy, and he was coming to take Alastair away, she lost the plot. In a now-or-never moment, she threw caution to the wind. She brewed him a cup of hot sugary NarcoVal, one for me too, and waited till he was incapacitated. If she was quick, if she was lucky, her husband would "kill himself" before the police got here, and I'd sleep through the whole thing.'

Wick's temple furrows. 'What about Maggie? Never any doubt that *she* was murdered.'

'Poor Maggie. Always poking her nose in, she knew too much. Signed her own death warrant. She'd seen Lauri without makeup; said as much to Fiona. Worse, she made the passing observation that if Fee "made a bit of effort", she and Lauri might even look alike. It was just a question of time till Maggie joined the dots and started doing what she did best.'

'Talking!'

'To get Maggie out of her hair, Fiona gave Maggie the sack, but almost at once, Alastair reinstated her; a magnanimous act that sealed Maggie's fate. Even Jane was disgusted by the cruelty of the girl's last breaths. I believe this death-too-far triggered Jane's decision to wash her hands of further killings. She'd leave, and take Alastair with her.'

'Is that why Fiona killed her?'

'Ultimately, yes. Furious to discover "Lauri" had absconded with their principal quarry, Fiona's rage must've amplified tenfold when she read that taunting graffiti, "So Long *Sister*". But Fiona was no doubt furious with herself, too. She should have seen this coming! Jane had long since ceased to be an ally; she'd become a saboteur. You see, Wick, for all her cold-blooded scheming, there was something Fiona forgot to factor-in.'

'Love?'

'The more time Jane spent with Alastair at The Hall, on those just-the-two-of-them drives to Inverness, the more she was drawn to him and, yes, grew to love him. Couldn't help it. She no longer wanted to kill him, but rescue him. It's why she stole George's car keys. When George offered to drive Alastair to Inverness, Fiona was over the moon! "You go to the bank, darling. I'll hold the fort here." Blah, blah, *blah*! And no wonder! She wanted rid of Miss Beckett, the annoying accountant who was trying to sell off Dorcha's copper deposits, *and* she wanted rid of her husband. So, Fiona cut George's brakes, same as she cut Duncan's; fingers crossed, she'd take out two birds with one stone. Jane, however, who knew the workings of her sister's mind, made sure that MG wouldn't make it out of the barn. She still had the keys on her when her body was found.' Ava sighs. 'Murdoch spotted the brakes were cut straight away, but he guessed the wrong culprit.'

'The day we took the boat out, it was Lauri... sorry, *Jane* who waved us back to shore. She wasn't there to help Fiona hang Alastair, but to stop her. Fiona must've been incensed!'

'Incandescent, I imagine. It would've needed the two of them to manhandle him, drugged-up-sack-of-potatoes that he was, into position, but Jane refused to play ball. There was a scuffle...'

'Jane slapped Fiona in the face!'

Ava nods. 'Jane's distress that day was bona fide. She fought for Alastair's life, and when she urged Alastair to flee with her, her motives were sincere. "Come with me and save yourself." Ardent pleas that were, ultimately, in vain. Alastair summarily dumped her at the phone box with enough loose change to call a cab. But she didn't dial a ride, she phoned her sister. All by herself in the dark and the rain, she needed help. Who else could the wretched woman ask?'

'The call Fiona took, right in front of us, that was from Jane!

When she said it was a man, it crossed my mind it was Jack Hooley on the other end of the line.'

Ava nods again. 'Especially after Alastair said he'd seen him out and about on the road to Drumapple. But Jack was too busy poaching to be making any calls. No wonder he told Constable Cargill he was at home in bed and never saw a thing.'

'Poacher, eh?'

'Bagging more of the Muirheads' own game for Alastair's pot. The rogue! I reckon Murdoch's suspected as much for a while. Anyway, Jane, alone and afraid in that phone box, told Fiona she'd go to The Murder Field and hide out in the bothy. She managed to drag herself up there, ripping her feet to pieces in the process, and later, Fiona took her a change of clothes, food etcetera. Having to pass through Drumapple on the way, Fiona, Maggie's murderess, popped in on Ollach to pay her respects.'

'As audacious acts go, mind blowing!' breathes Wick.

'Also very clever. Fiona knew she was highly likely to be seen. If challenged, she'd say she broke Clowdy's rules of confinement just to see Ollach. So decent of her.'

'Sounds like Jane was stymieing Fiona at every turn.'

'And, thanks to "Lauri's" disappearance, the police were sniffing around more than ever, making the logistics of Alastair's suicide even more problematic! Still, Fiona would see to it. All Jane had to do was stay out of sight. But Jane didn't. She allowed Martin Addington to see her.'

'How did Fiona find out?'

'Jane herself must've told her when Fiona revisited the bothy, which she did, at night. It'd be easy enough to creep out without Alastair noticing; just had to slip him another pill. Anyway, once they got talking, perhaps Jane goaded Fiona further, repeating the veiled warning she'd given the boy about a homicidal sister waiting to come and get him. One way or another, Jane was a liability, so Fiona killed her. Given Fiona went to the bothy pre-armed with the rock pick, it seems she'd already planned as much anyway. Must've had it a while. Judging by the way Murdoch gawped at it when he saw it sticking out of Jane's neck, it wasn't among the things he emptied from the cabinet. At that moment, though, he believed Alastair was the one who'd taken it.'

'Why,' Wick ruminates, tapping his chin, 'didn't Fiona hide the body?'

'Perhaps she intended to roll it into the loch as per the legend, but ran out of time. Or, more likely, she simply didn't care. No sane person would associate meek Mrs Muirhead with murder, let alone such a maniacal one as this. If they were going to suspect anyone, it'd be Alastair.'

'Until they realised how the two women were connected.'

'Good thing you read Fiona's thesis, Wick.'

'Good thing you know your sea trout from your salmon, Ava. But unless Fiona confesses, how can anyone prove Baumgarten met the Finnocks at the Viscaria mine?'

'The police only have to look at the stamps in their passports to know all three were in Sweden at the same time. We know Fiona went to Kiruna, as she herself recorded, and I know Baumgarten went to Kiruna because he'd been there birdwatching. But you're right,' sighs Ava. 'I can't prove their paths crossed.'

The pair fall into a companionable silence. A blackbird pogoes across the grass, and Ava wonders if it's found a new mate. 'Ready to head back?' Wick asks eventually.

'Not till you've shown me your other surprise; something we should "look at together"?'

'Goodness! Completely slipped my mind! When I was in Inverness, I came across the chitty from Maggie's cache tucked inside my wallet. Realising it was a receipt from Boots photographics, I nipped in to collect George's snaps—'

Ava gasps. 'Did you say "Boots"!'

'As I think you've guessed...' Wick pauses to extract a packet from his breast pocket, 'these are *not* George's.'

'They're Baumgarten's! When he went to the chemists, it wasn't for any medications, it was to drop off a roll of film!'

'I took a quick peek, and it sure looks like it.' Wick smiles as he gives her the packet.

Ava's hands shake as she shuffles through the colour prints of snowy owls, a Siberian jay, common goldeneyes... more common goldeneyes...

'It would be too ironic if there's one of a flycatcher!'

'There won't be. These were taken in winter. *Ficedula hypoleuca*, like the osprey, is migratory. Here's a lovely one of a waxwing.'

'Not a very rural scene.'

Wick's right. Although there are mountains in the background, like everything else, blanketed in snow, this shot was taken outside a building. A shop? Perhaps a museum? Some sort of public place... plenty of people around. The plump little bird, its reddish crest proud and erect, is perched on top of a sign which is, in turn, fixed above the building's open doors. It's difficult to decipher what the sign says, so Ava takes out her hand lens: *VÄLKOMMEN TILL BESÖKSCENTRUM I VISCARIA-GRUVAN – WELCOME TO THE VISCARIA MINE VISITOR CENTRE.* She makes out something else, too: Two young women, trussed up in winter woollens – unmistakeably Fiona and Jane – standing in the foreground. Arm in arm, squinting at the sun, breath visible in the air, they seem oblivious to the camera, and utterly carefree. Speechless, Ava passes Wick her hand lens, and waits for him to see all.

'Blimey!'

'Couldn't have put it better myself. This,' says Ava, 'explains the state of Baumgarten's room. When we searched it, I arrived after you, and the place was upside down; a mess I blamed on you. But it'll have been Fiona and Jane who ransacked the place. Baumgarten threatened them with photographic evidence of their identities. They needed to destroy it. When they found none, they must've heaved a sigh of relief... thought the dead man was bluffing after all. They didn't know about the docket, or the fact that Maggie Kettleness, in an act of simple mischief, had swiped it.'

'Good for The Magpie,' says Wick.

'In some ways, she had the last laugh.'

Wick extinguishes his cigar and shuts his ashtray. 'What'll our godson do now? He's facing the realisation that his wife is a murderess, and she tried to kill him too. She never loved him, and only ever wanted him dead. So, Alastair gets the money to mend the bricks and mortar of his birthright, while his heart's broken into smithereens. How's he supposed to rebuild that?'

'Perhaps he won't,' Ava says stoutly, 'but he *will* survive.' She knows all too well that a person can continue breathing in and out pretty effectively, even when they're shattered inside. In fact, they can keep it up for decades without anyone noticing a thing. She's mindful, too, that fifty-something childless females who live in the jungle are supposed to be ignorant of what it's like to love, never mind keep on loving, however long-lost their cause. Aware of Wick's searching gaze upon her, Ava's afraid her eyes have started to water. Did she speak with too much conviction, and reveal a glimpse of her private ghosts?

If she did, Wick passes no comment. He simply says, very quietly, 'Yes, quite right.' Ava can guess who's ghost just visited *him*. The passing pain he felt was palpable. He is, however, quick to rally. 'Though I choose to root for a happy ending. I've never believed Peigi Hooley returned to these parts because of the quality of the light. Alastair has a true friend in her, and friendship can blossom into something more.'

'One way or another, he has a bumpy road ahead,' says Ava.

'Time we checked on him then,' says Wick.

As they wander back to The Hall, Ava studies his features. His clever face, those dark, dark eyes. He looks pensive. 'Penny for them!' she asks with a smile.

'A rum thing, really. Earlier, right before the police drove off, Pratt was acting very odd. He said I wasn't to "think I'd got away with it" and he'd "deal" with me later. Any thoughts…?'

Epilogue
As it Ever Was

The weather's fine, and there's just enough breeze to blow the midges away. As Ava inhales, drawing in the smells of the Highlands, she catches a whiff of change among the pitchy scents of forest pine. Soon, the bracken will bow down, the heather will fade, and Dorcha's mercurial mountains will assume the tapestries of autumn. Red and orange, rich, bright, and glorious, they'll be a riot of colour, but Ava won't be here to see it. When the scene that's unfolding before her is over, she must leave.

The work force is subdued, but the mood is purposeful rather than sad. Nobody's in charge, nobody's barking orders, but instructions are not required. There's a tacit understanding of what has to be done, and so the five companions, Alastair and Murdoch, Ava and Wick, and Peigi, move about the clearing, gathering scattered stones. One by one, with great care, they stack them. Large flat rocks to form a base, medium-sized rocks to build height; layer by layer, each building block positioned then repositioned to ensure all facets meet. As the stack grows, Ava feels a satisfying sense of restoration. She's helping put back what should never have been brought down. It occurs to her that, even if every displaced piece were found, there must be a near-infinite combination of ways they could fit together. The cairn cannot, ever, be exactly as it was. It also occurs to her how unimportant this is. This memorial, reassembled with undying love and respect, means so much more than the sum of its parts.

The Beasts of the Black Loch

When Murdoch places the final stone on top, he recites something... a poem... in Gaelic. Although he alone knows what he is saying, the meaning of his words is perfectly clear.

'He worshipped Sheila, didn't he?' Ava whispers to Wick. 'A one-woman man.'

'And she was a one-man woman.'

'I'm sorry, Wick. I know you hoped—'

'Don't be sorry for me. She gave her heart to someone far worthier.'

'You, Professor Wickremesinghe, are a better person than Duncan Muirhead ever was.'

'True enough, but neither he nor I was the father of her bairn.'

Acknowledgements

It was not without the support, expertise, and encouragement of many clever people that Dr Ava Dickens tromped her way onto the shores of Loch Dorcha. First thanks go to my agent, Eugenie Furniss, who thought this book was a good idea long before I got around to writing it. Her belief in me and in Ava has never wavered, and for that I am truly grateful. I am, once again, hugely indebted to everyone at Bedford Square Publishers for their professionalism, creativity, and care at every stage of publication. The editorial input I received from the brilliantly insightful Caroyn Mays helped shape this story into something far, far better than I could ever have achieved alone. It's been a privilege. Sincere thanks, too, to the designers, copy editors, and proofreaders who made sure the finished tome looks and reads just right. An esteemed list of contributors, to which I must add one more: the ecologist who influenced me most in my life – my mother.

Elisabeth Marris was the woman who, when I was a child, bought watercress from the market – not just for salad, but for the living treasures it contained. She'd run each bunch under the cold tap, catching water lice, snails, and leeches in her kitchen sieve for my brother, sister and me to examine – 'Count their legs... feel their shells... be *gentle*' – before releasing them into our garden pond. She was the woman who, by hand, painstakingly pulled fifty bloated ticks off a sickly hedgehog before that, too, was set free. The ticks, however, she retained on a china saucer, so that we could observe their mouthparts through Dad's magnifying glass. My earliest memories are of digging in our compost heap with Mum, looking for worms. Our final conversations were about slugs, the spider she could see from her bed, and what animals her now-adult grandchildren might encounter on their travels. She was a natural 'natural historian', but also enquiring, knowledgeable, and razor-sharp. She respected the order of wildernesses, the mysteries of metamorphosis, and the importance of even the lowliest forms of life in what she called 'The Grand Scheme'. More than anything, she believed deeply that, 'All Creatures Great and Small', whether or not they are made by a divine hand, are miraculous. This last truth remains a precious legacy, and I thank her from the bottom of my heart for sharing it with me.

About the Author

Photo courtesy of Gay Marris ©

Dr **Gay Marris** is a retired research scientist. Her career focused on insect ecology, parasites and honey bee health. Her first novel was *A Curtain Twitcher's Book of Murder*, set in the deceptively dangerous suburbs of 1960s London, where she grew up. Gay now lives in York with her husband, a cat and a tortoise.

Bedford Square Publishers is an independent publisher of fiction and non-fiction, founded in 2022 in the historic streets of Bedford Square London and the sea mist shrouded green of Bedford Square Brighton.

Our goal is to discover irresistible stories and voices that illuminate our world.

We are passionate about connecting our authors to readers across the globe and our independence allows us to do this in original and nimble ways.

The team at Bedford Square Publishers has years of experience and we aim to use that knowledge and creative insight, alongside evolving technology, to reach the right readers for our books. From the ones who read a lot, to the ones who don't consider themselves readers, we aim to find those who will love our books and talk about them as much as we do.

We are hunting for vital new voices from all backgrounds – with books that take the reader to new places and transform perceptions of the world we live in.

Follow us on social media for the latest Bedford Square Publishers news.

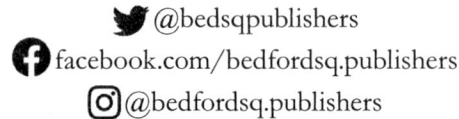

bedfordsquarepublishers.co.uk